THE DEMON'S DEAL

THE
DEMON'S DEAL

THE DEMON PRINCES
BOOK ONE

L. ALEXANDER

The Demon's Deal
The Demon Princes Book One

ISBN: 978-1-958933-02-2 (Ebook)
ISBN: 978-1-958933-03-9 (Paperback)

Cover Design: Jessica, Enchanting Covers
Interior Design: Stephanie Anderson, Alt 19 Creative
Edited by: Krista Dapkey

For anyone who learned something about themselves
when Howl said, "That's my girl," to Sophie.
This one's for you.

And for me too, because same.

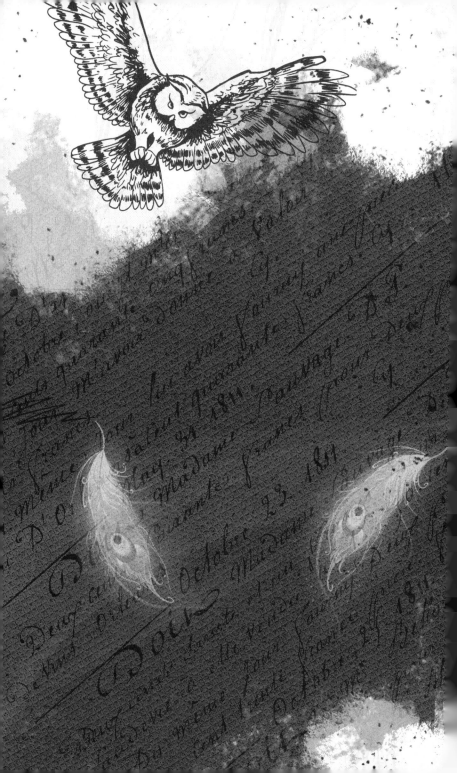

He was her

DARK FAIRYTALE

and she was his

TWISTED FANTASY

and together

THEY MADE MAGIC.

— F. SCOTT FITZGERALD

AUTHOR'S NOTE

This is not a dark romance, but there are some potentially triggering themes that come up throughout the book. You can find a list of tropes, content warnings below.

Please reach out to me directly for specifics if needed, I'm more than happy to give details, page numbers—whatever helps you best decide if your mental wellbeing and this story are compatible.

Tropes: fated mates, who hurt you, one bed, hidden powers, training sequence, amnesia, magic, familiars, gargoyles and demons, pseudo-medieval European setting, praise, affection through care-giving

Content: kidnapping, instances of abuse & sexual abuse, explicit violence, death, explicit sexual content, brief gore, use of magic

CHAPTER 1
CALLA

"STOP! NO!" Thunder cracked angrily, swallowing my protests as a storm raged all around me. "Let me go!"

Rough hands pulled at my arms, dragging me out the door of my grandparents' home into the cold rain. I dug my heels into the dirt, but it was useless. The heavy rain had already turned everything to mud. I slid along behind my captors as lightning brightened the night sky with lethal beauty. The horses thrashed in the barn; their high-pitched whinnies screeched across the yard as the heavy clatter of hooves struck the walls.

"Please, take whatever you want! There's nothing of much value, but I have tools and bags of rye grain ready for market. There's no reason to—" A meaty hand cracked across my cheek, leaving behind a hot sting and stunning me into silence.

Taking the brief opportunity my shock provided, they picked me up and tossed me into the back of their wagon. My ribs protested as I landed hard on the wood floor. Hope flared as four young women reached forward to grab onto me as I tried to regain my breath. Their hold was decidedly unfriendly instead of welcoming, and my thoughts of gaining allies evaporated. These were not women in my same predicament. They were accomplices.

The man and woman who had knocked on my door requesting shelter from the storm just a few short moments ago climbed into the wagon after me, blocking the exit. With all of our bodies crammed into the space, there was hardly room to breathe.

"Silence!" The woman was well dressed, though bedraggled thanks to the heavy rainfall.

"Why are you doing this? I don't understa—"

The man's fist clipped me above the ear, making my head ring. "Quiet!" he admonished, the scowl on his face stealing every bit of what might have once made him handsome. "Girls, hold her tight. No matter what happens, don't let go."

My stomach twisted, and a deep ache took root in my hip and shoulder where I'd struck the unforgiving wagon floor.

"Yes, Father." The chorus of their voices was weak, as though they were empathetic to me but grateful someone else was on the receiving end of his wrath.

"Drink." The woman shoved a small vial between my clamped lips. I thrashed, which only resulted in another cuff from the man. She muttered something low while pinching my chin, and the bitter contents of the tube ran down my throat as I sputtered and coughed. "You are a simple girl with no living family. You ran away from a farm you could no longer maintain on your own. You have nothing and no one."

"What? No! That's my home, I..." My tongue grew thick and unable to form coherent words as I processed what she said. Whatever she'd given me to drink made me dizzy and stole my strength. The taste reminded me of how the tiny green berries my grandmother warned I was never to eat smelled as they shriveled on the vine. Acidic, sweet. Poisonous.

Panic made my heart pound in my chest as the paralysis took hold.

"I can't believe it's true," one of the girls whispered anxiously, her grip easing away from my wrist as I struggled to keep my eyes open. "There's been rumor of a girl being born to that family, for years and years, but nobody's ever actually seen one. Mother, are you sure this is her? She's older than Stella! At least twenty-five. How would they have kept her hidden for so long?"

"Hush!" the woman ordered. "She said the old man died two winters ago, and the old woman recently. Then suddenly this girl was spotted in the fields. It seems like a reasonable assumption, but it doesn't matter either way. We've done as promised whether she's the Noctua girl or not." She then muttered some words under her breath, holding a small clay seal in her fingers.

I opened my mouth to protest, recognizing what she was about to do. It was no use, however; nothing in my body worked properly any longer. The heavy sensation rendered my limbs as useless as my tongue.

"This better work," the woman muttered, shaking her head.

"What choice have we now? Just hurry up. We need to go before the rain washes out the road completely." The man flicked the cloth closed behind him irritably as he dashed back out into the rain.

Resolve steeled, the woman pressed the raised pattern of the seal into my forehead, where it burned, but not on the skin. It hurt inside my skull, a deep ache in my mind. Then she broke the clay seal in half, declaring, "You are an orphan with no home. We picked you up on the road. You remember nothing of your life before today. Not your family, where you live... not even your name. Once we leave your sight, you'll forget us as well. You'll never speak of what happened this night, not to anyone. It is a secret, and you will take it with you to the grave."

The words chased around my head, taunting my inability to utter them out loud.

Kidnapped.

Cursed.

I tried to shake my head, but only managed to turn it enough to see the girls' faces. I found a mix of pity and malice in their features as tears leaked from the corners of my eyes. Something heavy was tossed into the wagon behind me as I continued to stare at them, each blink slower and heavier than the last.

Everything in me screamed to argue, to fight. Instead, I lay there unable to even twitch a finger as the darkness swelled up and swallowed me whole.

I WOKE IN the back of a wagon, propped up against sacks of grain. My head throbbed viciously, like I'd drunk too much honey wine. Perhaps I had. I couldn't recall any part of how I'd gotten to be in a wagon.

Desperate for some water, I used my joined hands to dig around in some crates.

"Leave it," hissed a whispered voice just outside. A girl poked her head through the curtain that served as a door. "He'll be angry if he thinks you're trying to steal something."

"Oh! Hello. I'm not trying to steal anything, I was only looking for something to drink." Nothing about my situation made sense, and trying to remember what happened was similar to gazing into a lake on a moonless night. There were vague outlines and shapes but nothing I could grasp onto.

She pursed her lips, and the tight expression she wore faded into something bordering on sympathy. "Here." She pulled a skin from one of the top crates and handed it to me.

"Thank you." My voice was gruff and crackly with a bitter taste I couldn't name clinging to my throat. I drank down my fill and offered it back.

"Keep it." She squatted down to take a closer look at me. She was pretty enough, her eyes a bright blue and her features soft. I was fascinated by the way she had her long dark-brown hair tied back in braided loops. Her dress was faded but made of fine cloth, and her shoes were nearly new. If I were to guess, we were around the same age. "Do you recall what happened last night?" Her eyes raked me top to bottom as she awaited my reply.

I opened my mouth, but nothing would come. My thoughts were a tangled mess. Anything I tried to say seemed to get stuck in my throat.

"I don't ... I don't know. Can you tell me? I have the strangest feeling ..." I closed my eyes tightly against the fierce pounding in my head. It was as though trying to access the memory had caused the flare of irritation. "I ... I don't think I belong here, but I don't even know where here is."

Her eyes went wide, and her mouth dropped open. "It worked."

"Worked? What did?"

She shook her head and got to her feet. "Never mind. You won't know what I'm talking about, but your animals are safe. Everything at the farm will be taken care of. It's better if you don't try to remember anything. You won't be able to tell anyone about it anyway."

"What do you mean?" Horror settled icily into my bones. I couldn't put my finger on what the wrongness was, yet I felt it all around me. Inside me. Understanding hovered just out of reach.

"It really doesn't matter. Soon enough it will be like we never existed anyway." She brushed aside the cloth and reached out. After sliding me a plate of food across the floor, she jumped out of the wagon, leaving me alone.

I ate and drank greedily, my stomach painfully empty. I stood, stretching my muscles once I was finished. I wanted to sleep, but my body begged for some comfort after all the time spent on the wooden floor, especially in the places where I was bruised. I wished I could recall anything at all, but it was like a curtain had dropped over my memories.

A girl popped her head in as I slowly paced the tiny space and offered to take me to the woods for some relief.

"Oh, that would be lovely, thank you." When I climbed out of the wagon, I was greeted by three other girls, all of similar features. "Hello."

They glanced at each other, sharing a wordless conversation that made me feel strange.

"Let's go," the oldest one said, guiding us into the trees to use the latrine.

They all joined me in the back of the wagon after that, and it started to move down the road. Time was oddly elastic as we traveled. Nothing made sense, and my mind was endlessly foggy. I ate at least once more, but I couldn't seem to grasp the passage of hours. It could have been days for all I knew.

My only solace was being somewhat familiar with the road we were headed down. The sharp edge of panic was a near-constant companion as the mystery around what was going on hounded me. I felt where the knowledge once had been, and the emptiness frustrated me.

Then the rains came. Lightning struck the ground close enough to cause the hair on my arms to stand on end. As we neared a large manor house, thunder clapped so loud we all squawked in surprise. Then, the horses spooked, the wagon nearly toppled, and everything changed.

CHAPTER 2
CALLA

"YOU'LL DO NICELY." A portly man with a walking stick leered at me, running his tongue over yellowed teeth. His fingertips brushed the ends of my hair, making me twitch. "Get her cleaned up, would you, Serena? It's fortunate timing that we found someone new to serve as laundress, don't you think? His Lordship will be pleased." He prodded at the corner of his brittle mouth with a wormlike tongue in a way that made my skin crawl.

"Yes, of course, Baron Cross." The housekeeper pulled me by the arm. I wasn't sure which question of his she was answering, but the response seemed to cover all bases. "Let's go."

I was relieved to be away from him but found myself grasping at memories of what had happened, frustrated that time and the order of events slipped through my grasp like grains of sand. I remembered the thunder. The horses had reared up, and the wagon had broken a wheel. Fixing it would take time and daylight, but thankfully the manor was right off the road. It didn't make sense that I'd been alone, because why would I have a whole wagon and horses for myself? But I couldn't recall anyone traveling with me.

I'd been welcomed into the house to take shelter during the storm, but now the wagon was gone ... and I was still here.

"Excuse me, I think there's been a mistake—"

"You'll speak when spoken to." The housekeeper's tone was exasperated but held an edge of authority. She turned a glare on me as we walked up some stairs and down a cool stone hallway. "The people you arrived with warned us about the unfortunate situation with your memory. Just so we're clear—I'm sympathetic but lies and delinquency will not be tolerated here, I know how your kind can be. I am a patient woman but do not have time to explain things to you over and over again. They said you're capable and used to work. You're under my charge while you're employed here. You may call me ma'am or Mistress Serena. Understand?"

My 'kind'? And what people? I was sure she was mistaking me for someone else. As far as being employed ... I was able to gather context clues I suppose. My lack of memory about anything at all continued to be quite disturbing.

"Yes ma'am. But—"

"You do know how to bathe properly at least?"

"Yes, of course—"

She opened the door we'd stopped at, revealing a bathing room. "Clean yourself up. I'll leave a fresh gown outside the door. Do not leave this hallway, I'll come fetch you." Her stern tone brokered no argument, and she clearly had no problem interrupting anything I might try to say anyway.

"Alright."

"What is your name, girl? What are you called?"

"I ..." My brow furrowed. I couldn't summon my name, no matter how hard I tried. "I don't know."

She clicked her tongue in a disappointed tut. "Well. Think on it, yes? Until you recall, *girl* will do." She stomped off, muttering under her breath.

I stood there a moment, still stumped that I couldn't come up with my own name. Bothered but thrilled at the prospect of getting clean and soaking out some of my aches, I went into the bathroom and closed the door.

The manor was equipped with modern fixtures, including some kind of boiler system that allowed for the tub tap to run hot water directly into the basin. It was a marvel that captivated me for far longer than it should have. I washed the lingering dirt from traveling off my skin, taking stock of every bump, bruise, and scrape. The hot water soothed away some of my tension as I scrubbed, rinsed, and scrubbed some more. When the water cooled, I rose from the tub and toweled off. I found the promised clothing outside the door after a concerted struggle of combing the knots out of my hair.

Once dressed in the rough-cloth gown, I opened the bathing room door to find the stern housekeeper waiting for me, hands joined at her waist. She was perhaps thirty-five, but she carried herself with the air of someone much older. Her face had some deep crags from how she frowned, but her light-brown eyes were keen.

"Come." She flicked her hand at me, not waiting for a response.

I followed at her heels as she led me back down the stone-walled hall. I peered at the lavish tapestries hung along the corridor as we went. I'd never been in a home quite so opulent ... that I knew of. She strode with purpose down the stairs and through the main part of the house into the kitchen. We didn't encounter a single other person on our journey, which seemed strange for a house so large. Wordlessly, she gestured to one of the long dark wooden tables where a bowl of soup and a hearty piece of bread waited. My stomach rumbled at the sight.

"Eat. I need to prepare your room. Can you find your way back to where we just came from?"

"Yes, I think so." I nodded, wishing I was brave enough to consider running away even if I had no idea where to run to. My forehead pinched as my thoughts turned to the strange emptiness in my mind around where home was located.

"If I haven't come back by the time you're finished, meet me there."

"Yes ma'am."

I ate with enthusiasm, reminding myself about halfway through the bowl that I could afford to breathe and enjoy the soup. The bread was rich with seeds, though a bit dried out. I found, however, that made it perfect to scrape every last drop of broth from the bowl. Once my meal was gone, I stood, glancing around the large room, looking for somewhere to wash the dishes.

Hoping I wasn't about to get scolded, I located the sink and a drying towel and made quick work of my dirty dishes before getting a better feel for the layout of the room. Three large hearths stood at the ready for kettles, and two brick ovens lined one side of the room. There were two long tables beside one another near the fireplaces and a large bank of countertop over near the ovens.

Feeling anxious being in the room alone, I worked my way back to the corridor with the bath. I took in the stately decor, realizing that the lord of this place was wealthy beyond anything I could imagine. Heavy carved furniture, plush rugs, and tapestries were elegantly arranged in every space. Books were stacked on mantels and shelves, ready for anyone to pick up and read while they lounged on one of the soft tufted sofas.

Someone in the house had an affinity for owls. There was a bronze one the size of my hand stationed on a side table, carvings in the lintels of the fireplaces, and even some on the door arches. It seemed the more of them I noticed, the more appeared.

I mounted the stairs with my heartbeat thumping in my ears. I didn't know how I'd come to be in such a place.

"Good, good," Mistress Serena muttered as she spotted me. "We're limited on space just now. This'll have to do."

She set two thin blankets in my hands and gestured to an open door. I looked inside, then back at her. The questions I had must have been written on my face.

The room she'd prepared for me was a closet.

As in, there were still a couple of brooms standing sentry in the corner, and there wasn't space for much of anything other than the thin straw mattress slumped sadly on the floor. I couldn't help but wonder how much more comfortable I might have been on the lush blue sofa I'd seen downstairs.

"We'll get it sorted properly later. I'll be up to wake you in the morning. You're free to use the toilet, but don't be wandering the halls. The other staff keeps to themselves, as should you. If you have a question, ask, but don't interrupt their work. Understand?"

I nodded, and she seemed satisfied. She dusted her hands on her skirts before handing me the small candle from one of the tables lining the hall and simply walked away, leaving me standing there.

The flame threw disconcerting shadows over the walls in the pitch-dark room as I spread one of the thin blankets over the top of myself and tried to relax. There was no window. No way to get outside air or tell if the moon was out or the sun. I had to remind myself that I wasn't trapped—I could open the door to the hall at any time if I needed.

Exhaustion pulled at my limbs, so I blew out the flame and settled in, adjusting this way and that as the straw prickled my skin. Closing my eyes, I tried to find any memory before being in the wagon in the darkness. The emptiness around who I was, where I'd come from, and how I'd ended up employed as the new laundress at a manor house was dense and unforgiving. I couldn't shake the feeling that there was something unnatural about the giant gap in my recollection, but there was also nothing I could do about it.

A sharp ache stabbed between my eyes as I searched for anything from before. I rubbed at the spot with my fingertips, frowning as I tried to find a comfortable way to sleep.

I could only hope that tomorrow I would remember today and build from there.

CHAPTER 3
CALLA

"DO YOU HEAR ME, GIRL? Time to get to work! Get up!"
A banging noise grew more insistent, louder as I swam
toward consciousness. I realized slowly it came from
the door to my small closet and overlapped the confusing dream
about shadowy endless rooms I was trapped in.

"Yes, I'm awake," I managed to say loud enough to quell the
knocking. I dragged my eyelids open, blinking heavily against
the darkness of my small room. I scanned the shadows for the
figure I'd been trying to find in my dream, but there was nothing
there except the old brooms. I felt silly then, that I'd been restlessly
searching for nothing more than cornstalk and wood.

Without a window, it was impossible to tell what time it was,
but I assumed it was sunrise, if not before. My body complained
loudly that it hadn't gotten quite enough rest, as did my head. The
ache inside my skull was so fierce blinking my eyes hurt.

The door opened, revealing Mistress Serena, her disapproving
face tight as she looked down at me. "Toilet quickly, then meet
me in the kitchen. Keep to yourself."

"Yes ma'am."

Wiping at my bleary eyes with icy fingertips, I still felt disoriented and like I needed another few hours' worth of sleep to feel right. Unfortunately for me, I didn't have that kind of time. On the bright side, I had memory of the day before, which felt like a fortuitous start.

I scurried down to the kitchen after a quick freshening up, passing three women on my way in. One of them gave a gentle smile and inclined her head at me in greeting, but the other two acted as though I were invisible.

"Nice to see you can follow instructions," Mistress Serena said as I approached one of the dining tables. She pointed at a small bowl and spoon on the table. "Eat quickly, then I'll show you your chores. I have some things to take care of in the meantime."

"Yes ma'am." I tucked into the runny porridge, the grains settling my sour stomach. The cool water I'd been given to drink helped the slightest bit with my headache. My food was gone regrettably fast. I scraped the bottom of the bowl clean, frowning as I rose to go wash it out.

"Grab that bucket and come this way, girl."

Mistress Serena didn't know a leisurely pace. She trotted wherever she went, leaving me to quickstep in her shadow or be left behind.

She gestured widely to the pens. "Chickens and pigs. Feed is kept in the small shed over there, except for the kitchen scraps." She pointed to the bucket in my hands, which contained an array of peels, ends, and other vegetable waste. "You are to feed and water these animals first thing every morning. Chickens get one handful of scraps, the rest goes to the pigs." She took the bucket from me to demonstrate, chucking the contents into the pens.

"Yes ma'am." I helped her draw water from the nearby well for them both, then we collected all the eggs in the empty bucket.

"You can do the washing, yes?"

"Yes, I believe so."

My lukewarm confidence did not impress her. "Let's find out then." She strode off ahead of me, towards a sturdy wooden outbuilding.

Smoke billowed from the chimney, a fire already lit under the kettle. The closer we got, the more I could smell the sharp tang of lye and vinegar. Mistress Serena threw the door open, and the odor embraced me so fiercely I lost my breath for a moment. The space was perhaps the size of the kitchen, hosting a wide hearth with two massive iron kettles on a tilting mechanism.

"All household linens come through here. Sheets, towels, clothing. You're responsible for figuring out what is highest priority. It should go without saying that anything I bring to you directly and anything that belongs to the lord of the manor takes precedence."

"Yes ma'am." I felt as though I were walking around in a fog, the information logical and manageable but still foreign. I knew how a household ran, despite not being able to access the memories around why. All the tasks were absolutely within my capabilities, but my thoughts felt heavy, muddled. I could only hope that the feeling wouldn't hang around too long.

"Good. Come inside midday. If there's anything for you to eat, it will be left for you on the porridge pot. You may get as much water as you need. Someone will retrieve you for the evening meal. Understood?"

"Yes."

She looked me up and down; judgment and what felt like disapproval dripped from her gaze. Without another word, she left me in the laundry to stir waterlogged sheets and wonder how in the world I'd ended up there.

THE SAME MAID who had nodded at me that morning as I entered the kitchen came to fetch me for dinner.

"No need to bank the fire, one of the field hands will do it on his way in for the night." She gave me a kind smile as she escorted my weary body back to the house. "They'll light it again for you in the morning on their way out, as well."

"That's kind of them," I said, my arms feeling like soggy noodles. Stirring the kettle was no easy task.

"I'm Elizabeth."

"Pleased to meet you, Elizabeth." She waited for me to return the introduction but, after a few steps, seemed to understand one would not be forthcoming. I wasn't trying to be rude; I simply had no name to give her.

Thanks to Elizabeth, I learned that the estate I found myself at was the country home of a wealthy archmage who spent much of his time in the city. The baron ran things in his absence, with Serena's help.

"After dinner, Serena likes us to bathe and go straight to our rooms. There's not much time for socializing." Her hand reached for the back door. "It was nice to meet you."

"Thank you, it was nice to meet you too."

Elizabeth went straight to a table to collect her dishes. I felt out of place as I stood by the door, unsure of what to do. Everyone turned to look at me as they rose from their tables. Maids, farm hands, and kitchen staff watched the new girl like the curiosity I was.

Remembering what Serena had said about the pot in the kitchen, I walked that direction, hoping for something substantial. My stomach had been loudly growling since shortly after midday. Lunch had been a single slice of bread, burned around the edges, and some hard cheese. After the slim portion of porridge, the light lunch, and the hard labor I'd done in the laundry, I was famished.

I brightened, finding my bowl on the lid. It was mostly full of thin soup; with another chunk of the overbaked bread I'd had for lunch. It was not quite what I'd hoped for, but better than nothing. I ate at one of the empty tables as the kitchen quickly emptied.

The door creaked open, and the baron smirked as he crossed the room toward me. My heart thumped behind my ribs, and I hurried to soak up the remnants of my soup with the bread. Nothing good that would come from being in a room alone with that man, I could feel it.

"Ah, there you are. How wonderful." He sauntered over, the heavy stick he carried around to help him walk clanking against the stones on the floor. "Did Serena find the laundry suitable for your skills, then?"

"Yes sir."

He made a noise in his throat that set my nerves on edge, his tongue swiping along his lips in a decidedly disgusting way.

"Good, good." He brushed too close to me as he peered over my shoulder to see what was in my bowl. His breath was hot on my cheek, potent with the smell of alcohol. "Already all done, I see. That's a shame. Perhaps you'll join me for a meal tomorrow?"

Taking the opening, I stuffed the remaining piece of soggy bread into my mouth and hastily got to my feet. I went over to the sink, hoping to keep some distance between us, but he followed at my heels.

"Perhaps," I said finally, wishing for anyone at all to join us in the quiet room. "I should go, Mistress Serena—"

His mouth flattened. "Yes, of course." He waved his hand in dismissal, but left it extended toward me, his fingers dangling near my face. "I'm sure you're grateful for your position here at Stolas Manor? Considering your origins, I don't see how you wouldn't be."

Ice dripped down my spine. Panic rooted, screaming through my body. I couldn't confirm or deny anything about where I came from, but it didn't matter. "I suppose."

"Good." He leered at me, that brittle smile back as his eyes roved up and down, making me want to run to the baths as quickly as I could to rinse off the residue of his stare. He twitched his hand at me, and I understood what he was after. Repulsed but terrified, I took his fingers into mine and pressed a chaste kiss to his knuckles. Everything about it felt wrong, and the soup crept back up my throat as I performed the action.

As he was about to say something further, the outside door opened as one of the field hands came in late for his meal. He looked from me to the baron, saying nothing but clearly noticing the tension between us.

"Excuse me," I said, taking the opportunity to dash off through the house and up the stairs.

Hands shaking, I gathered clean clothing from my meager accommodations, grateful for the hot water and soap available in the bathroom.

Not to mention the locking door.

CHAPTER 4
CALLA

"Up, girl! Time to get to work! If you know what's good for you, you'll get gone and stay that way until you are called back today, do you understand?"

"Yes ma'am." I was woolly-headed as I fought to grasp her words.

Trying to shake the never-ending tiredness that lingered in the cramped, windowless room was a challenge that hadn't gotten any easier during the weeks I'd been at the manor.

"Up!" She rapped on the door one final time, her urgency pushing me from my bed.

My meager breakfast of watered-down porridge awaited me in on the lid of the pot hanging in the hearth. Meals, sadly, hadn't improved in either quality or quantity. Sometimes, I would get lucky and find part of a boiled egg in my dish or perhaps some bread that had burned. I was up and moving so early the cooks were still forming the loaves to bake, so the few bites of bland oats I was allotted Mistress Serena had likely scraped from the bottom of the pot from the day before. If I got lucky, I'd find something edible while taking care of my chores outside.

I dreamed of fruit and roast meat most nights ... and most days. I rarely ate with the other staff, as my assignment had me on odd hours off by myself, but I assumed they were provided more than I was, as they were all quite hale. The scraps kept me alive, but my body had thinned considerably since I'd arrived.

Serena didn't care for me. I couldn't prove it, but I believed she was keeping me hungry and tired intentionally. The oldest cook appeared sympathetic, but after offering me something once, she'd turned up with a broken wrist. She'd kept her nose down after that, which I could understand.

By the light of the bright moon and the illuminated windows of the house, I drew buckets of water from the well for the pigs and chickens. Over my weeks of employment, there had been a handful of times I'd been hungry enough to steal from the pigs. Today was one of those days. I never took more than enough vegetable scraps to fill my stomach, but I knew by acting on my desperation I risked punishment.

It had only taken a couple of days for me to learn that something dark had happened to the previous laundress, though nobody would speak plainly of it to me. I got the distinct impression that she'd died, and the baron had everything to do with it.

He and Serena managed the staff of the household with iron fists. There were only a handful of rooms I was even permitted to enter, which left much of the house, its contents, and the occupants a mystery to me.

The staff avoided the baron whenever possible, which told me plenty all by itself. He had a way about him that was completely unsettling. His habit of leering at the women on the staff from around corners and with his hands in suspicious places seemed the mildest of his offenses.

I made sure to lock the door of the laundry whenever I entered, because he often popped by when least expected. That first evening in the kitchen was only an introduction to his awful proclivities.

Twice early on, he'd caught me unaware and had spent the better part of an afternoon leaning into my body lewdly while fondling my hair and breathing his foul breath into my face. He'd brought extra bread and fruit with him both times. I recognized the bribe for what it was, but ate it nonetheless.

I was too hungry not to.

I knew I was fortunate to have escaped those incidents with no further injury than paranoia over where he might be at any given moment. Stirring wet cloth in a large kettle was lonely, sweaty work that had left my muscles wiry but not strong enough to displace his dense, large body.

It was to my great misfortune that the baron happened to come around the edge of the hedgerow just as I shoved a carrot end I'd salvaged from the pigs' vegetable scrap bucket into my mouth.

"Thief!"

My heart stopped, then began racing. I stiffened my back and proceeded to dump the bucket into the trough.

"Don't think I didn't see that. Serena warned me about you. Turns out she was right!"

Confused by his statement but more startled that he'd caught me, I stuttered, "What? Sir, I—"

He raised his walking stick and soundly rapped my hands twice with the length of the stout, heavy wood. I cried out, dropped the empty bucket, and after a breath of feeling nothing, my hands gave off a fierce burn. I was worried they might be broken, but a cautious test showed my fingers still moved at least. "Saints! That hurts! Why on earth did you do that?"

I could guess a motivation of his was that he held a grudge against me for not falling for his schemes and locking him out of the laundry. He was a mercurial man at the best of times, so it could have been any number of things.

"I'm sure Serena would love to know she's got a greedy thief on her hands. I'm more than happy to carry out the punishment for such an offense. In fact, it would be my pleasure." He gave a vicious smile as he wrapped his pudgy fingers around my upper arm and yanked, pulling me through the yard.

He called out to Serena as he dragged me into the kitchen and flung me into one of the tables. My ribs screamed as the tabletop jammed into them. The other staff scattered like startled mice at the sight of us, and I didn't blame them. Elizabeth's eyes went round as she pinched her mouth in sympathy before scuttling off.

Mistress Serena came rushing into the kitchen from the hall, skirt fisted in her hands. "What is all this racket?" She looked at the baron, who had pressed his side into my body, his round gut perilously close to my face. I cradled my bruised hands to my chest while he held me down roughly by the shoulder as though I might float away.

"I caught this girl eating from the pigs' slop," he sneered. "She's a thief and should be punished." He took far too much glee in announcing this, and I could see the careful way Mistress Serena weighed his words.

"I'm not a thief!" I argued, rubbing at my side.

With a glance at me, she said, "Have you forgotten yourself, Cross? His Lordship has returned home and has requested a full head count." She flapped her hand at him in frustration. "And here you've brought her damaged for inspection. Over what? Some potato shavings and cabbage core?"

He blustered. "It was a carrot, if you must know—"

"She was outside, and she was *working*. We might have bought some time to explain the situation, but now she's in my kitchen instead of busy elsewhere. He will have heard you shouting, besides. Do you not ever think things through?" She turned her heated gaze to me. I was in awe of the way she'd managed to put the man in his place so efficiently. "Get to the main hall near the lounge. Be invisible. We'll discuss the other issue later."

I squirmed out from under the baron's bruising grasp and rushed out of the kitchen. The whole house was already gathered in the hallway when I arrived. I slipped into the middle of the group between two maids, flattening myself against the stones of the wall in an attempt to blend in.

As the baron and Mistress Serena strode up together, a regal man in fine attire came around the corner near the main door, straightening the cuff of his black shirt.

He was a study in monochrome from his boots to the ornate embroidery on his vest. An owl was stitched over his heart among ornate scrolls and vines. The only relief to the layers of black was a splash of red in the side lacing of his vest. It was as intimidating as it was attractive.

My breath caught in my throat as I took in his sharp features, my heart stuttering against my ribs. He was tall and broad, with eyes the color of dark honey. His hair was glossy like raven feathers, and his skin a warm bronze. He was more beautiful than a person had any right to be.

I kept my eyes on the floor as he slowly paced up the row of bodies, quietly greeting everyone by name. He paused in front of me, and my pulse pounded in my throat as his gaze raked over me. When he didn't move, I raised my head. As I met his eye, the corner of his lush mouth gave the barest twitch downward. My heart sank as he stepped further down the line—he was displeased.

When he spoke, his voice vibrated down my spine, something familiar about the sound sending a spark through my veins. "Thank you, all. It's so lovely to be home. Mistress Serena and Baron Cross, a moment please?"

Once he'd moved down the hall with the two stewards on his heels and vanished behind the office doors, the staff gave a collective sigh, chattered briefly, then scattered back to their work.

I moved slowly toward the kitchen behind two maids who had their heads bent together in gossip, unsure what I should be doing but in need of some wrappings for my hands.

As I passed the closed office door, Mistress Serena opened it.

"You, girl. In here."

"Me?" I hated the quake in my voice.

"Yes." She heaved a breath, frustration pulling her mouth into a frown. "I should have known better than to think he wouldn't notice you. Another fine mess to clean up," she muttered. "Come on then!"

I swallowed, throat dry and heart pounding, as she yanked me through the heavy wood doors.

CHAPTER 5
CALLA

THE EXPANSIVE DEN was the most formal, masculine room I'd been allowed into. The tapestries and rugs were all done in deep jewel tones, the furniture stout dark wood and leather. It echoed the living room with the plush blue sofa, but everything in here was somehow *more*. Perfectly organized bookshelves lined the stone walls, and a massive desk dominated one end of the room. A bank of windows along the outside wall boasted colorful stained-glass scenes in the center. They looked like they were telling a story, but I wasn't close enough to see them clearly enough to identify which one.

The handsome archmage stood behind the oversized desk, his back to an unlit fireplace. The wall above it hosted six blades, each a varying size and style. They had clearly been carefully crafted and well used prior to their retirement.

My eyes landed on a stunningly realistic statue of a massive black owl perched to the side of the wide wood mantel. I squawked an embarrassing teakettle noise when it moved, intelligent gold eyes blinking as they stared right at me.

"Apologies. Seeing him for the first time can be quite a surprise. Archimedes," the lord said, glancing over his shoulder at the bird, "say hello."

The owl fluffed his feathers proudly before extending one foot and dipping his head, eyes closed. It was the most unusual, incredibly polite bow I'd ever witnessed. "Hello." I gave an awkward curtsy in return, and Archimedes gave me another long look then turned his head into his wing, clearly done with socializing.

The lord of the house leaned forward, one hand flat on the desktop, his face frozen in a stern expression as he regarded first the baron, then the head housekeeper. I straightened as he dropped his heavy gaze on me.

"I don't believe we've been introduced." His voice was deep and resonant but much softer than I'd expected considering Serena's urgency.

I stood in front of a tufted bench before his desk, both Cross and Serena slightly behind me on either side. I could see them in my periphery, which was disconcerting. He walked around to the front of his desk and headed straight for me. I swallowed, my throat impossibly dry.

"What's your name?"

"Girl," I replied with a rasp.

His dark eyebrows dipped, coming together in a vee. "That's not a name. What are you called?"

My name had not yet come back to me, much to my frustration. "I am called girl." Irritation flashed across his dark features. "I'm not trying to be clever, my lord," I rushed to explain. "I do not know my given name. I cannot recall it."

I felt tension radiating from all around me. The mistress and baron were afraid of him. Or perhaps ... afraid of what I might tell him.

"That's unfortunate, indeed. How long have you been under our employ?" He leaned back against his desk with his arms and legs crossed. The way his eyes captured mine left me standing straighter, every muscle drawn taut. It wasn't fear, exactly. More a desire not to be found wanting in his assessment.

"Several weeks, sir. I came during the rains."

His eyes drifted to the baron, over my right shoulder. This was enough to prompt a hasty explanation of how I'd become part of the household staff.

"My lord, she was traveling through with a family on their way to Revalia. They picked her up on the road near one of the farms and were desperate for funds to complete their journey. They bartered with us for fresh horses, help repairing their wagon, and some silver. It was a blessed time for them to be passing through, as we'd recently lost our laundress. Bringing the girl on felt quite opportune despite her ... deficiencies."

The lord's eyebrow went up in question. "Mistress Serena? I wasn't aware we'd lost a member of the staff. What happened to Wilhelmina?"

"It was a sudden loss, my lord. Very unexpected." She said nothing further, which made the archmage frown.

"I should have been informed. There are many ways to get a message to me at d'Arcan, as I'm sure you know. I'd like to offer her family my condolences, of course."

"Yes, my lord. Apologies. It won't happen again." She bent at the waist in deference to him.

He turned, slid a brown leather-bound ledger across the desktop, and readied a quill and inkpot. "Tell me, what skills do you have, *girl*?" His mouth twisted as he said the word, his distaste for my temporary name undisguised.

"I have performed adequately in the laundry. I can cook some, clean. I'm familiar with animal care, though I haven't had an opportunity to be introduced to the horses here. Basic healing."

"Mm." He presumably noted my skills next to a new entry in the ledger. "Anything else?"

"I can read, my lord. And write."

His eyes snapped up to mine. "Indeed? That's unexpected but very welcome. Can you also do sums?"

I hesitated, but something in me responded positively to the idea. "I think so, my lord. I can't recall the specifics of having done it before, but I feel like the answer is yes."

"That's wonderful news." He smiled gently. "I've been in need of a secretary for quite some time. Cross doesn't have either the disposition or the patience, and Serena has no head for numbers." They both scowled at his assessment. I looked at the floor as I bit the inside of my lip to keep from smiling. My heart soared at the compliment he'd given me, even if he hadn't intended to do it. "We'll explore that further, shall we?" He swapped ledgers. "Serena, where is she roomed?"

"The third-floor corridor," she said carefully.

"Those chambers are all occupied, are they not?" he asked, consulting his pages.

Mistress Serena at least had the courtesy to look embarrassed when she replied, "She is housed in what was formerly the brooms and simples, my lord. Wilhelmina kept her quarters in the laundry, and we thought it best ... considering the circumstances ... we not repeat that. Besides, there was no way to know how she'd behave. This was only a temporary measure, of course."

He blinked slowly. I didn't know this man, but I was reasonably adept at reading people, and he was absolutely furious under his cool exterior. Heat radiated off of him, even from a distance, and something like static electricity prickled along my skin.

"What behavior, exactly, would earn a member of staff a *closet*, Serena? Why has she been housed in such a space when we have ample accommodations and no other guests? We have plenty of resources to cover any shortcomings. She could have been roomed with one of the other maids at the very least."

I could have sworn his eyes flashed red for a moment, but as I stared, all I saw was the honey color.

"We've made it as comfortable as we can, my lord. She's voiced no complaints."

I was surprised by the suggestion that I could do any such thing. No matter the size of my challenge in the early days, I'd been rebuked and silenced. I'd requested another sheet to keep the straw from poking me all night; for my meals to be larger since I was starving nearly all the time; gloves so the lye didn't burn me quite so much. All requests had similarly been scoffed at. Denied. Instead, I'd made do with scraps of foods and bits of fabric I'd scrounged up. And I hadn't bothered asking for anything in weeks.

The noise he made in his throat very clearly communicated his displeasure with that statement. His eyes pierced mine, holding the gaze as he searched for the truth.

"Any complaint I made was not well received, sir."

"I see. And your pay?" he asked me directly, and I gaped at him like a landed fish.

Pay? I hadn't even considered that I'd be paid. I was just glad to have a roof and food, meager as it might be, until I could remember who I was and return where I belonged.

"That's not been settled, sir," Serena rushed to answer. "We were waiting on your authority."

His fist tightened around the quill, flattening the delicate feather.

"I see. I heard shouting earlier," he said, the casual tone belying the frustration evident in the tightness of his mouth. Baron Cross shifted his weight, the heavy fabric of his clothing rustling as he moved. "What was that about?"

"Nothing, my lord—" Mistress Serena started, but the baron interrupted her.

"I saw the girl sneaking food. Stealing."

"Stealing?" His tone was more curious than anything as he assessed me with his sharp amber eyes. I began to sweat in earnest under his full attention over the accusation.

"Indeed," Cross affirmed.

I spun. "It was a carrot end, barely a single bite. It is not my fault I'm sometimes driven to supplement my meals in such a way."

"Now listen here—" The baron's face turned red as he took a step toward me, a threatening finger raised.

"Silence!" the archmage boomed, energy crackling through the room at his proclamation. The air was heavy, nobody dared to so much as breathe in response to his command. "Tell me what happened. You will not be punished for telling the truth." His voice was low, somehow focused exclusively on me, as though nobody else existed at all. It echoed warmly through my bones. I found it difficult to imagine refusing him anything when he asked like that.

I glanced at Mistress Serena, and her mouth was drawn into a line so tight her lips had disappeared. "I was not left much for breakfast this morning—a few bites of porridge—so I ate a carrot end from the pig bucket. Baron Cross saw me and struck my hands with his walking stick."

"I assure you, my lord, this one is willful and likes to cause trouble. The people who sold her to me warned that she was addled and prone to telling tales," the older man blustered.

"As I said before, I have no reason to lie. And I'm not *addled*," I groused, despising the very word never mind his insinuation.

The beautiful archmage's features darkened in displeasure. His attention slowly turned from the baron's face to mine. "Thank you." He crossed his arms, focusing on the pair behind me again. "I've issue with plenty of things, none of them this woman."

"Sir, I—" Serena attempted to interject.

"Do not. Interrupt me."

I flushed hot, my body recognizing the danger in his quiet rage.

"To start, I take issue with the fact that you believe you've *bought* this girl, Cross. You hired her for the house. By rights, the money you offered on her behalf should have been paid *to her*, not the people she traveled with." The baron scowled but said nothing. "You've been here nearly two months if you arrived during the rains, girl. Would you be able to identify the other staff by name?"

"Some, my lord."

"Only some?"

"I don't see many of the other staff, sir."

"Tell me more about your meals." The shift in his demeanor was unsettling. He'd become wholly interested in what I was saying, and his sharp golden eyes bled genuine concern. I felt safe for the first time since my arrival.

"I don't know what others eat to give a fair comparison."

"That's alright." He glanced at Serena, his words clipped. "I'm fully aware of what you *should* be getting." He flung his quill down, a tiny splash of ink staining my dress. "So this woman—who has ample skills nobody bothered to even inquire about—has been isolated from the other staff, is sleeping in a closet, and is being woefully underfed all while going *unpaid*. In addition, she may have broken bones in her very capable hands thanks to your over-reaction about a *carrot*? Have I missed anything?" Heat dripped from his words, causing the hair on the back of my neck to rise in reaction to his mounting rage. I sucked in a breath, thankful his mood had darkened on my behalf and not because of me.

"Sir, I—"

"You are hereby *forbidden* to act on anything without my approval, Cross, let alone mete out punishments. Am I understood? You are excused."

Cross grumbled as he left the office, slamming the door on his way out.

My hands had begun to swell. I alternated slowly rubbing my fingers over the puffy skin, a deep ache throbbing in my bones. The archmage's eyes fell to where I was fidgeting. Nervously, I dropped my hands to my sides.

"Are you injured badly?"

"No, my lord," I said, unsure how true that might be.

"May I see? Please?" His tone was kind, deceptively gentle. Anger still rushed through him, but it was not directed at me. He took a step in my direction, his palm up, fingers outstretched. I raised my hands, a tremble running through them until he stilled it with his warm grasp. Electricity traveled up my arms as his skin met mine. "I'm afraid the care you've received since your arrival has been inexcusable, at best. I'll be fixing that, immediately."

He released my hands, his serious expression impressed upon me. Oddly, my hands didn't hurt nearly as much as they had before he'd touched them. "You will outfit one of the empty chambers here on the main floor—"

"One of the guest suites, sir? But—"

"Does interrupting me again seem wise, Serena?" The words sliced through the air, her eyes widening as she realized her error. She snapped her mouth closed and shook her head. "As I was saying, prepare a room for this woman. We'll sort out a more permanent arrangement in short order, but we've no guests, and I'll not have any of my household sleeping in a literal closet. I dare not guess what bedding she's been using." His jaw clenched, the muscle rolling as he ground his teeth together. It was unreasonably attractive, like everything else about him.

"Of course."

"It appears I need to interview my whole household to be sure we all understand one another. Lying is not tolerated, as I'm sure you're aware. Get the room prepared. She will be dining with me this evening."

"Sir?" Mistress Serena dropped her arms to her sides in shock.

"I did not stutter, nor did I mumble. We'll eat in my suite."

Her mouth opened and closed a few times, but she was eventually able to answer an affirmative before scuttling out of the room.

I shifted on my feet as he made some final scribbles and slammed the ledger shut. Any special treatment from him would earn me further disdain from the other members of the household, guaranteed. I didn't need another target on my back.

"I appreciate your generosity, my lord, but it's not necessary to do those things."

"It *is* necessary. It is." He heaved a low breath as though regretful about what had happened. There was no arguing with the sincerity of his words. "May I?" He pulled a metal tub of salve from his desk drawer. "It should help with the swelling. Does it feel like anything is broken?"

"I don't think so."

"He should not have done that." A muscle ticked in his jaw as he scooped out a healthy dollop of opaque ointment. A minty smell wafted to my nose as he gently rubbed it into the backs of my hands. The pads of his thumbs probed at the fragile bones and joints, checking for any breaks as his fingertips pressed into my palms. My heart raced at his careful ministrations, my breaths shallow as he leaned into my body. He smelled like citrus and iron, and the combination lingered in my throat, making my mouth water.

The way he touched me was terrifyingly intimate while also completely innocent. A pulse throbbed between my legs, embarrassing as much as it was intriguing. When he let go of my hands and returned to his chair on the other side of the massive desk, I felt unreasonably bereft. None my reactions to him made any sense.

"Thank you."

"It's the least I can do." He cracked the smallest of smiles, and it nearly undid my composure. I was already shaky on my feet, unsure what it was about this man made of shadow and electricity that made me positively giddy.

But his smile? That would certainly end me.

CHAPTER 6
RYLAN

"COME IN."

The rap upon the door had been gentle, hesitant. I knew it was her on the other side of the wood. She smelled like the floral bath oils, though the scent of lye lingered faintly on her skin, even from a distance.

The woman called *girl* stepped in cautiously, waiting at the edge of the room. Her lovely dark hair was braided back away from her face, still damp from her bath. I couldn't distinguish whether the plain beige gown was the same she'd worn earlier but noted to inquire with Serena as to why she had no other wardrobe. It was another item in an ever-lengthening list where she was concerned. I had a lot of catching up to do with the whole of my staff, it seemed.

Her thoughtful dark-brown eyes were wide as she took in the room.

"Please, come join me." I closed the journals I had open on the table amongst the plates Serena had brought in.

She slid carefully into the chair across from me, where the other plate and cutlery were stationed. I heard her stomach whine and regretted that the lavish meal might feel like an insult after what she'd reported to me earlier.

"Are you looking for something in particular?"

Her lush mouth parted, embarrassment plain in her rounded eyes. "I was ... Archimedes, my lord. I just wanted to have an idea where he was so I didn't get startled again."

Of all the answers she could have given, that wasn't what I'd expected. "No need to worry, he's out hunting for the evening. He doesn't frequent my rooms at all, honestly. He prefers my office."

"I see." She settled back into her chair. I wasn't sure if it was out of relief or disappointment. I had no reason to be jealous of my owl, but the idea that she'd anticipated seeing him even half as much as she did me sent an irritating itch coursing through my chest. "Please, help yourself." I took my fork in hand. In truth, I was much more interested in watching her than I was in eating, no matter how delicious the meal Mrs. Brisbane had provided.

In fact, I'd been captivated by the new addition from my first glimpse of her standing in the hall, trying to stare a hole through the floor and melt into the wall. An impossible feat, that, as she was taller than everyone around her by nearly a head. There was something about her that called to me, something wholly apart from the earthy magic I'd brushed against in her veins when I touched her hands. It was a familiarity I didn't altogether trust. I'd also bet she had no idea she was a witch.

She used restraint at first, selecting dainty bites from the serving platters with her fork. Her hands were clearly stiff and quite bruised, though the salve appeared to have worked nicely on the swelling. The appreciative noises she made in her throat as she tasted things heated my blood. I clamped down on the unwelcome sensation immediately.

Her appetite stoked, she became more confident and piled fruit and meat on her plate, along with bread and some of the candied carrots I'd requested be made especially for her.

I couldn't wait for the curves hidden under that shapeless gown were nourished back to good health. It was criminal how poorly she'd been fed in my absence.

She looked up from her plate, frozen as she met my eye. It was almost as if she'd just remembered I was there. I understood, though. The pork was worthy of devoted attention.

She blotted her rosy mouth on a napkin, pausing to take a sip of water. "This is wonderful, thank you."

"I'm so glad you're enjoying it. Would you mind looking at some ledgers with me after our meal? I thought it might be a good way to gauge if you'd like to take on the secretary position. It is your choice, in case that wasn't clear. If you're content in the laundry, that's fine, you're welcome to stay as you are."

"I'd be happy to look at the ledgers." She ducked her head and set her fork down, embarrassment bringing a hot flush to her cheeks.

"Please don't stop on my account. Eat your fill. There's plenty of time to review the books later."

She gingerly reached for an apple slice; she favored the red over the green. "I'm afraid I may have already been overly enthusiastic, my lord." She leaned back in her chair, one hand on her stomach.

I gestured to the pot of tea on the side table. "Perhaps some tea then? It's good for digestion, among other things."

She opened the lid and peered inside, asking, "Is it choke weed?"

"Choke weed?"

"The vine that likes to climb up the fence near the chicken coop. I don't know what it's really called. It grows wherever it likes, choking out other plants. The leaves are triangular with edges like a saw blade. It smells like lemon but tastes like mint."

She was full of surprises. My heart thumped warmly behind my ribs, giving off a sensation I hadn't been aware I could still feel. Unease crept in at the realization, denial right behind it.

"Lemon balm. But yes, that description is all accurate. Good for digestion, reducing tension, and promoting sleep. It was one of the ingredients in the salve I used on your hands."

"I've eaten some of the leaves ..." She trailed off as she poured us both a cup, the smile slipping from her mouth. "They're not as good plain as when made into tea."

My brief smile fell, knowing exactly what had driven her to eat a literal weed growing in the yard. A thousand apologies backed up in my throat, but none took shape on my lips. "Thank you." I accepted the tea she offered. "Is your new room suitable?"

She met my eye over the top of her cup, her lips a perfect o as she tried to cool it enough to drink.

"It's decadent, my lord. Thank you." She turned a tantalizing shade of pink. "Having a bath in my own room is truly an indulgence. I very much look forward to sleeping in the bed. It looks like a cloud."

I barked a rusty laugh, and her skin darkened to red. Mine tingled in response, her happiness sending a thrill chasing through my blood. "I'm sorry, I truly don't mean to make fun. I'm happy you're excited about it. I'm very sorry about how you've been treated since you came to us." Her head dipped, her gaze lost in the cup. "Perhaps you'd humor me and read a bit while I finish?"

Her expression gave way to wonder as she scanned my shelves.

"What would you have me read?"

I pointed to a volume bound in green leather with gold foil lettering on the table next to the sofa. "That one, if you please."

"Of course."

She rose and selected the book, opening it to where the ribbon had my place marked.

"When the formula is mixed with the proper balance of herbs, one will create a tincture good for relieving aches, cough, and pleurisy ..."

I watched her pace a few steps, the book balanced carefully in her stiff hands. Her long dark braid fell over her shoulder, teasing along the gentle curve of her neck. Her dark-brown eyes scanned the letters on the page, her voice clear and resonant as she read. This woman was captivating in a way I had long thought I would never find again. Something deep in my chest ached when I looked at her. I didn't like it.

I realized I didn't have a good grip on my tumultuous emotions when she stopped reading and glanced around, looking for the source of the disturbance. Pulling the edges of my power back in, the crackle of electricity stopped and the low hum went quiet.

"That's enough, thank you. I'm well versed on tinctures, and he's got a number of things wrong already." She closed the book and set it down, looking at it as though she regretted her time with the pages was done. "How are your hands?"

"They're better, I think. The salve is very helpful."

"I have some in here also, I can apply some more before you go back to your room if you'd like?" The desire to touch her was potent, which was equal parts terrifying and fascinating.

"That would be nice." She tucked a loose strand of hair that had fallen from her braid behind one ear, nervousness evident.

"Shall we move to the sofa?" I rose from my seat and gestured for her to walk in front of me. Once we were seated, I retrieved one of the ledgers used to track our grain harvests and opened it. "Would you take a look for me? Tell me what you see."

She took the large volume into her lap, studying the contents.

Her finger traced along the columns as she reported, "This one is the raw weight of harvest by person. These are the price at market per bushel. This is the price per pound of flour." She flipped the page. "And this is the rate for whiskey, but you appear to have lost your distiller midwinter."

My smile was immediate and generous. She was bright, well spoken, and much more than she seemed, judging by how my body responded to something as simple as her voice. "You've been terribly wasted in the laundry," I said, accepting the book back from her as she blushed that lovely pink color again. "Would you like to remain there, or would you like to take on the task of being my secretary?"

She folded her hands in her lap, breaking eye contact after a long moment of silence. My heart pounded in anticipation. I liked the idea of having her near me, no matter how irrational that might be.

"I'm afraid I don't know what becoming your secretary entails, my lord—"

"Rylan," I corrected. "You may call me Rylan." She pursed her lips as though tasting the sounds of my name, and heat bloomed in my chest. "You'd travel with me to Revalia when I go, of course. Maintain the ongoing account of my personal treasury and that of the household." She blanched at my mention of the large responsibility, but her attention was rapt. "You would of course be paid for your services and welcome to explore further education if you so desire, as well. Honestly, we may have to figure some things out along the way. I've never had a secretary before." Truly, having an assistant was a novelty, but my wish list was long when I thought about the instances where I could have used a capable set of hands to help me out.

I took that opportunity to reach for the pot of salve. I gently probed with my power as I rubbed the ointment into her skin, finding the same odd block inside her that I'd encountered before. The earthy magic she held felt odd but familiar. Even shuttered behind the wall, it was obviously intense. It would take effort, but I suspected I could break through the block given time.

I wondered who she might be when she remembered herself.

"Education?" she asked.

I paused, loving that she'd chosen such a detail to grab onto. "Yes. I encourage all my staff to study any subject that interests them."

"I ...yes. I think I would like that very much."

Salve thoroughly applied, I regretfully let go of her hands. She smiled appreciatively, making me wish I'd held on a bit longer. I cleared my throat, re-centering my thoughts. "Let this week be a test then, of whether or not you can stand to be in my presence for long periods of time."

"My lord?"

"Being my secretary means you'd be with me nearly always. If you can't stand me ... that might be a problem." I'd tried for a joke, but my tone hadn't quite landed the way I'd hoped. Seriousness threw a shroud over our previous levity. To my surprise, she cracked a smile in response. "I'd like you to speak freely with me. I'm not my title. I'm just Rylan."

"Alright." She swallowed hard, the column of her throat working.

"So, you'll join me again tomorrow?"

"I would be honored, my—" She stopped as I raised a finger in correction. "Rylan." She flushed that gorgeous pink color again, and my pulse throbbed in my ears.

Her blood called to mine in a way that terrified me. She was special. I'd known it from the moment I saw her in the hallway. She was surely not meant for me, however. Such a thing was impossible. I'd had a mate before ... and I'd lost her. Fate didn't reward such crimes with second chances.

It had been a very long time since I'd been so interested in a woman, however, so there had to be a reason for it. Keeping her too close would be a dangerous test of my will, but I hated the idea of her elsewhere. It was all fiercely confusing.

She felt like she was mine. And I had to figure out why.

CHAPTER 7
CALLA

"I'M SORRY?" Rylan glanced up, surprise written in his features. His amber eyes were wide but warm as they peered back at mine.

"You asked what I was called before. What I would like to be called."

"Is that ... have you remembered your name?" The excitement on his face made me sag.

"I ... no. I truly don't recall my given name. Perhaps it's close? But I think that is what I'd like to be called, my lord. There are some lovely purple ones growing out near the pigs." A blush heated my cheeks, something that had a habit of happening when I was around him.

I was drawn to the simple flowers, the way they spread out as far as they could with their greenery before slowly opening their elegant blossoms. The name had repeated in my head a thousand times over the last few weeks, and it seemed a fitting choice.

"As you wish. Calla it is." His smile was broad, the sharp planes of his features softened by the joy as he looked back at the ledger.

If the test was about whether or not I could stand to be near him, I'd say we were passing with flying colors. I looked forward to my time with him more than any other part of my day, and had joined him in his rooms for the evening meal the last six nights. He was easy to speak with and treated me as an equal always. Even when he was teaching me something, he was never condescending.

He felt comfortable. *Safe.* I knew I should be wary of a man so beautiful, especially one as powerful as he was, but my heart pounded when he looked at me. Under his potent gaze, I felt like the most beautiful creature to ever exist. Intelligent, capable, desired. He was impossible to resist, especially when he smiled.

"Have you been taking the tincture I made you?"

"Yes. It's quite foul by itself, so I've been mixing it with lemon balm tea."

The corner of his mouth tipped up as he scribbled something into a ledger. "Good. And your hands?"

"They're much improved. Only a bit of bruising left. Stirring the laundry kettle only makes them ache a little, now."

"Wonderful. Is Elizabeth doing well then?"

"Yes, she's a very quick study. She and I traded recipes for healing poultices today."

"Dare I assume you were sharing something you've learned from me?" he teased.

"I was, actually. She thought your addition of oats for itchy rashes was odd but inspired. She nearly fell on the floor she thought it so humorous that someone might mistake their treatment for breakfast and get a terrible surprise."

He laughed, the sound resonant in my bones. I was not a particularly amorous person, but the things he made me feel led me to believe that I could be, given the right motivation and outlet.

"The charcoal element would make that particularly awful, I'm afraid. But good for the gut should there be toxins present." He turned his full attention to me. "Now that we have a name for you,

there's the business of your employment contract to organize."
He pulled one of the new books from the shelf behind his desk,
one with the oxblood leather covering. "Look this over closely,
make sure I've not taken any liberties." His seriousness gave me
tingles along my ribs as he pulled a folded piece of heavy paper
from between some pages near the back.

I gazed at the document, the wording complex but nothing I
couldn't decipher. It stated that I would be employed at Stolas
Manor until such time as I chose to leave. My pay was listed, some
description of my duties. I was no lawyer, but even the fine print
seemed in order.

"I don't see anything out of line."

"Wonderful." He produced a quill and ink. "Would you sign for
me please?" Rylan's amber eyes glowed as I took the pen in hand.

"I ..."

"It's just a formality. What you print there isn't terribly important. We can always make an amendment later, once you recall
your given name," he said, understanding my hesitation. "Calla
is fine for now."

I appreciated that he believed my remembering was an inevi-
tability. My hand hovered over the paper. Taking a breath, I wrote
my chosen name with a flourish.

"Perfect. The deal is done. I'll put this away—" I sucked in a
breath, yanking my stinging fingers away from the paper he'd
started to pull out from under my hand. "Are you alright?"

"Yes, only a paper cut."

"Apologies. I should have waited for you to set the quill down."
We both looked at the contract, finding a tiny droplet of blood
near where I'd signed. He folded the paper up, then returned it to
the journal before putting it back in its spot on the shelf.

"May I see?" He reached for my hand. His clever eyes examined
the slender cut, which still stung but had quit bleeding. I inhaled
through my nose as he brought the pad of my finger to his mouth,

pressing his lips to the wound. "No real harm done, I suppose. These hands are very talented, I'd hate to see them damaged." A riot of butterflies erupted in my stomach. He'd kissed my finger and still held my hand, his thumb gently tracing along my knuckles.

We stood locked there, in that moment. His amber eyes searched mine, the tension so thick between us I could hardly breathe. It wasn't until he released my hand like it had burned him that time started to move again.

Rylan cleared his throat. "Sorry. Where were we?"

"Ah, payroll," I swallowed over the heaviness in the air. "Five percent increase for all staff after fall harvest is complete. Additional bonus to be paid before winter celebrations." I paused, a thought striking me. "Does the staff travel home for solstice or the new year holiday?"

Rylan's serious expression softened. The more time we spent together, the less I saw his rough edges at all. There was something about him that pulled at the center of my chest. It felt endless. Dangerous.

"Yes, many do. Some staff stay here year-round, but I try to be sure they have a chance to travel to see friends or family. At the very least to get into the city. Everyone needs some time away. Even if it's just for a change of scenery."

"That's very kind," I said, returning my gaze to the pages, my cheeks warmed by a blush. The way his attentions focused so directly on me made me nervous. It was as though he looked directly into my soul at times, and while I reveled in having gained the eye of such a man, I was also self-conscious about it. There were no danger bells with Rylan—which was a nice change from the baron, who set them all off.

I wasn't a fool; I knew wealth when I saw it. I couldn't recall what kind of life I'd come from other than I'd been on a farm, but this place was positively sumptuous. For all his fancy embroidered vests and the air of authority he carried himself with,

Rylan seemed far more concerned with his book and herbs than money or power. The way he spoke to and cared for his staff was unusual in the best way.

"What would you do during your holiday?" he asked, genuine curiosity crinkling the corners of his eyes.

"I ..." My eyes drifted to the many shelves lining the walls. "I would read, I think. I have nowhere to go, obviously, but I could travel endlessly through the books in this library." The room offered so many books I thought I could have started reading and not come close to finishing before my time on earth expired.

The corners of his mouth twitched. "That sounds like a lovely way to spend leisure time. I don't spend nearly as much time as I should reading for pleasure." He got to his feet, huffing a breath out his nostrils as he did so. "You're of course welcome to borrow any volumes you like."

Excitement built as I watched him travel the room. A tingle chased down my back as he ran his fingertip lovingly over some of the spines on the shelves. He was a picture of civility as he stood straight and regal, one arm tucked across his middle. His back was to me, but I noted the very put-together way his long hair was pinned back with a strip of leather, his clothing miraculously unrumpled despite the hours he'd spent sitting in his office chair. His black vest corseted up the back and along his sides with red laces, his pants a suede leather that hugged along the curves and dips of his body. I wondered if he knew how striking he was, if he worked at it. He seemed unconcerned about such things but was always so carefully assembled it was hard to work out if it was effortless due to years of putting on the clothing to play the part of lord or simple vanity.

"Have you ever been to a proper library?" He turned with a mischievous grin on his mouth, like he knew I'd been looking.

Vanity, then.

"I don't think so, my lord." I set the journal I'd been recording in off to the side of the bench and stood, joining him at the shelves closest to the door.

"There's one in Revalia. It's a lovely building. The architecture is much like that of the cathedral, which I've always thought fitting. The monks have gifted many volumes. Perhaps you'd like to visit one day?"

"I'd like that very much."

He nodded, pleased.

We worked quietly for a few minutes, then I gave voice to a worry that had been bothering me more and more. "Is it odd to not remember anything at all before being in that wagon? Not even my parents? Or the people who brought me here? Especially when all my skills are intact?"

He raised his head slowly, setting his quill and book aside. "Do you want the whole truth or just the part that will make you feel better?"

"What's the difference?"

"Quite a lot. I don't want to upset you." His brows pinched.

"Why would I be upset?"

"Because ... I'm afraid I haven't been entirely truthful with you, Calla."

I blinked, enjoying the sound of my chosen name on his lips but not the news that he might have been lying to me. "All of it then."

"Your bravery is impressive," he evaded. "Have I told you that before?"

"Once or twice." He had done so several times, and he knew it. The idea that someone like me was brave seemed silly, but he made sure to tell me every time I didn't hesitate to try something new, like testing out one of his disgusting herbal compounds.

"Yes, well, it's true. You shy away from nothing, and your natural proclivity for medicine tells me you have some sorcery in your bloodline."

"What?" The shock of that statement nearly made me drop my ledger. I set it aside as he had done, giving him my full attention.

"I can feel something else, too. I'm not quite sure what yet. But it doesn't matter."

"Doesn't matter? I'm part witch and something else, and that's not important?"

He laughed, the dark grating noise scraping along my spine. "No, little owl. It's not. The number of people you know who have magic in their family tree is much larger than you can imagine, even if the council reserves practitioner licenses to a select few like myself."

"I'll have to take your word for it." I tipped my head to the side. "Little owl?" I inquired.

His amber eyes were warm as he explained the nickname. "When you're surprised or intrigued, your eyes go wide and your mouth forms a perfect little *o*. You look like a little owlet. When you're getting cross with me, your gaze slants the same way a screech owl glares. I should know, Archimedes has given me the same look at least a thousand times." I couldn't help but smile. His companion was incredibly expressive for an animal, and I'd seen them have that kind of interaction a handful of times already. He continued, "I noticed the resemblance early on and couldn't ignore it." The way he pressed his gaze into me made my heartbeat pound in my throat. He clearly had an affinity for the creatures, though I wasn't sure what it would mean for me to be included in his collection.

I swallowed, trying to remember what we had been talking about. "What of you not being honest?"

He exhaled. "The tincture and the lemon balm tea are indeed helpful for your injuries, but they can also be useful for removing hexes."

My breath stalled in my throat. "You think I've been cursed?" As I said the word aloud, the truth of it echoed in my heart. It was startling, but the notion didn't feel wrong.

Rylan nodded, stood, and came around to the front of his desk to take my hands in his. "It makes sense given your memory loss. That's also what it feels like when I probe at the edges of your mind."

I snatched my hands back. "You've been trying to get into my head?" Threads of betrayal wrapped around my heart, strangling out the warmth. "You can do that?" I sat there with my mouth open, stunned.

"I can. I've done it only in order to help." He ducked his head, and there was something about this massive, powerful man capitulating over something so small in the grand scheme of things. "I'm sorry, I should have asked permission. Please forgive my thoughtlessness."

His eyes were truly remorseful, the amber color softened by his pleading look. I believed him, even if I shouldn't. Especially because it felt like there was still something he wasn't telling me. "Please don't do it again," I said, my voice low but firm. I was proud it didn't quake. "Not unless you ask. I'm not able to access much of my mind myself, it's terrifying to think that you—or someone else—could. Especially without me knowing."

"Of course," he promised, regret and sincerity evident in the downward pull of his mouth. He opened his hand, palm up. "May I see your hand? I'll show you what I do, what it feels like."

I placed one of my hands in his, leaving the other in my lap. That low, electric hum traveled up from where he was touching me to my shoulder. The slight ache I'd been feeling from the injury disappeared under the infusion of energy.

"I can feel the blackness. A cloud or a curtain, like you've described before. I believe the herbs, among other things, will chip away at it over time." He let go after giving a gentle squeeze.

"That's it?"

Rylan chuckled, the sound a low rumble. "That's it. I have a little bit of healing power, but not much. My strengths lie elsewhere. It will take time for me to unravel the magic, but getting your memories back is a top priority, of course." His head tilted, expression contrite as he sought answers in my face. "Forgive me, Calla?"

I exhaled, realizing I was in serious trouble where this man was concerned.

"You'll help me?"

"Of course. With your memories and your magic, if you'd like."

My heart stuttered. He said it so casually, like I should have expected no less.

"Yes, I'd appreciate that very much. But please don't do anything without my permission. I'd rather know what's going on. There's enough mystery around my life, I don't want to add any more."

"Absolutely, Little Owl. No more deception, if it can be avoided. We'll have much to discuss on our travels, I think. If I haven't said yet, I'm happy you're here, Calla. I've been waiting a long time for you."

The potency of the affection in his voice was dizzying. "Waiting? For me?"

"In a manner of speaking. I've been without a companion for ... I suppose it doesn't matter. What's important is that you're here now. As long as you still find the arrangement suitable?"

"Yes, my lord." I was breathless. I needed space but didn't want to move even a hair away from him.

That citrus and iron scent filled my nostrils again as he reached up to tuck some hair that had escaped my braid behind my ear. After he'd done so, he frowned as though disappointed in himself for doing it. His mouth brushed my cheek as he turned away from me, provoking a shiver. "Wonderful. We leave for the city soon. I'll make sure to prepare everything you need."

CHAPTER 8
CALLA

"IT MUST BE my lucky day."

Terror made me freeze. I could have sworn I'd locked the door behind myself. I spun from the wardrobe where I'd been hanging my clean gowns, hearing the rasp of the latch slip into place. Baron Cross had locked us in my room together.

"You have no business in my room." I tempered my voice as well as I could. He seemed to enjoy it when we showed fear. "Leave."

The grin on his face put ice in my veins. He paced slowly toward me, knocking the pretty, delicate things decorating the tall dresser onto the floor with his detestable walking stick.

He'd avoided me since Rylan had scolded him and started inviting me to dinner. He'd been notably absent from his usual leering spots and the house altogether—which had, until now, been a relief.

"Baron Cross, if you don't go, I—"

"You've bewitched him somehow. I can see it plain as day." He advanced on me with a speed that was shocking for a man of his size and age, cowing me into a corner near the fireplace.

"What? I'm not sure what you mean—"

His foul breath was hot on my cheek as he leaned in as close as he could. Unless I was mistaken, he'd had quite a lot to drink already, and it wasn't even midday.

"Wheedling your way into a guest suite? Meals with him every night since he returned? Making him secure you a position as his *secretary*? You think you're something special, no doubt, but I'm not fooled. You need to be reminded of your place. Reminded who you belong to. *I* was the one who brought you into this house, and I'll not have that forgotten."

My blood ran cold; my heart pounded frantically behind my ribs. "The exchange you made with those people is none of my business. I don't belong to anyone, let alone you. There's no trickery here. Now, if you don't mind, I need to get back to work." I was mentally begging him to leave, or at least turn around so I could grab something to throw at his head. The bronze owl on the table near my bed would do nicely.

He barked a chuckle and backed off a step. I straightened and took a full breath, scanning for a weapon. "You girls are all the same, you know. Predictable. Wooed by his good looks and strong body. You're not actually different, you understand? His fascination with you will come to an end soon enough. Have you let him touch you yet? Has he fucked you?" He sniffed the air between us, as though able to tell from that. "I'll bet he has. I'm sure you're a whore for him, like all the others."

His words burrowed under my skin, but I did my best to ignore them. It wasn't fair of me to judge anything Rylan had done. I was nobody, and his life belonged to him alone, just like mine belonged to me. Besides, I had bigger issues at present. I'd managed to get myself out of the corner, but the best weapon nearby—the fireplace poker—was still out of reach.

"I don't know what you're talking about, nor do I care. You need to leave. Now." My voice was loud, but I could no longer keep the tremor out. There was murder in his eyes, and it struck terror into my gut.

For a man who smelled like he'd drunk an entire distillery for breakfast, Baron Cross could still whip his walking stick around with precision. The first lash took me across the shins, making me crash gracelessly into the floor with a scream, the front of my legs on fire.

"There you go. That's more like it."

I dropped to the side and scrambled across the floor, clawing to get as far from him as possible. I was begging for him to stop, to think about what he was doing, but I wasn't sure he could even hear me. I managed to grab the iron fireplace tool and swung wildly, landing a few blows I thought would have at least slowed him down. He was like a mad animal, focused only on his goal. Unfortunately for me, that goal was punishment.

"Baron Cross! Stop!"

His walking stick cracked against the arm I held the poker with, causing me to drop it. The pain was swift and all-consuming. He followed that quickly with a stripe on my back, stealing my breath and putting me once again on my knees. I managed to twist and get behind him, kicking out with my feet so he lurched forward into the fireplace. His head cracked off the mantel while I made as much noise as I could, struggling loudly in hopes someone would hear my cries.

"You bitch!" Blood ran down into his eyes as the stick swung toward my face. I curled in on myself, the blow landing across my kidneys as I screamed. "It's your fault I've lost his favor. You made me and Serena look bad, and he believes you because he enjoys what's under your skirt." He pressed the blunt end of the stick to my throat, pinning me in place. Fighting with the fastening of his breeches with his free hand, sweat poured off his face as he furiously tried to free his cock. "I'm sure I have no disagreement there, if I'm being honest. Though your attitude could use some work, you were a wonderful replacement for Wilhelmina. If only he hadn't come home, everything would have been fine."

I realized his intentions then. Causing pain aroused him. This was his way to get a thrill. I was his prey. "Stop! No! I beg you!"

"That's right, beg. I love it when they beg." He laughed hollowly. It was the sound of madness. His pants undone and his hand momentarily freed, he grabbed the neck of my dress and pulled, dragging me to the tight corner between the fireplace and the wardrobe. "Move and I'll push you in."

My skin immediately flushed from the heat. He yanked again, and the fabric gave way. I huddled into myself, holding the tatters to my chest, trying not to allow the fringes to catch fire. He called out his grievances with me as he smacked the walking stick against the bare skin of my back. I gritted my teeth against the pain, tears flowing down my face. I screamed and begged, but he was unmoved. I wondered if I could manage grabbing one of the burning logs, and whether I'd hurt him more than I'd hurt myself if I did so. The pain became so intense I couldn't even think past it.

The sounds of him fisting his cock became furious, and as he moaned out, a warm splash hit my back, stinging as it ran into the marks he'd left. He grunted, then I heard fabric rustle again before he stumbled out the door, letting it slam behind him.

I tried to get to my feet a number of times, but simply couldn't manage it. I tipped myself toward the floor and crawled away from the fire.

Then everything went blessedly black.

I AWOKE SOMETIME later to Mistress Serena calling out for me.

"Girl? Are you in here? You've left your apprentice to do all the work by herself, have you? It didn't take long for you to become spoiled. His Lordship has been asking where you are—" The housekeeper's bluster disappeared as she neared where I lay on the floor. "Oh, hellfire and damnation. Not again."

It hurt to raise my head, but I gave it my best effort. I understood now what had happened to Wilhelmina. "He ..." I closed my eyes as warm tears slid down my face.

"No, no." She shook her hands at me, gathering her skirts in her hands before dropping low to examine me. "Don't move. I'll get help, okay? Just stay there." It was the most empathy I'd ever experienced from her, and I hated that I didn't trust it. She dashed out of my room again, the sound of her footsteps echoing down the hall.

I DIDN'T RECALL closing my eyes but opened them to find Rylan kneeling before me, hot, wild energy making my skin prickle as he leaned close.

"Who's done this to you?" The words were quiet and dark, dripping with violence. His nostrils flared as he took in a deep breath, and his mouth twisted into a cruel line. His eyes flashed red, and I was sure I wasn't imagining it this time. I shivered as he scooped me into his arms, both from the sensation of cool air on my wounds as he carried me out of the room and the deep growl of his voice as it echoed though me. Every flame in the room seemed to flare and dim erratically, and I was so disoriented I wasn't sure if that was actually happening or not.

"Baron Cross is to be taken to the cellar *immediately*. Get the field hands to help you. Lock him in."

"If it's that serious, my lord, perhaps you should do it yourself?" Serena wrang her hands.

He snarled, "It is for his protection that I am asking you to find someone else to handle it, Serena. Is there a reason you insist on questioning me rather than following my instructions?"

Serena's mouth was drawn tight as she trotted along beside us, trying to keep up. Surprise and embarrassment flitted across her face. "No, sir. Right away. Sorry. Sorry, my lord." She blustered through half a dozen apologies as she went toward the kitchen.

The energy pouring off Rylan took the edge off my pain despite the fact that it was rooted in rage. I stared up at his sharp features, unafraid of his anger while also being certain it could cause an infinite amount of destruction.

Rylan turned toward his suite, his long strides managing not to jostle me as he walked.

"Hurts," I muttered as my body took that moment to make me well aware of everything Cross had done to it.

"I know. I'm so sorry, Little Owl. He won't touch you again, I swear it." Under his breath, he swore, "Nobody will." He maneuvered me like I weighed nothing in his arms, turning on the bath and adding handfuls of healing herbs with one hand as he held me with the other. My arms were still pulled tight to my chest, covering what they could with the tatters of the dress.

"Shall I call one of the maids in to help? Elizabeth, perhaps?" he suggested.

I shook my head, the muscles in my neck and back screaming in protest. "No."

"The dress has to come off, Calla." I choked back a sob at the thought of shifting enough to make that happen. His expression turned frantic for a moment at my distress. "It's alright, we'll figure this out. Here. I've got an idea." He leaned forward, setting me in his oversized tub with the dress still on. He didn't let go until

I was fully submerged in the milky water, wetting his sleeves up to the shoulders. Even his vest had become saturated.

He grabbed a towel and placed it on top of me. My perplexed face communicated what I needed it to.

"Use it to cover yourself. We'll get the dress off and out of the tub, then I can work on your injuries, alright?" His voice was low, his hands humming with quiet energy. He pressed a cup to my lips. "Drink this. It will help with the pain."

I swallowed obediently, grimacing at the flavor. Why could none of his healing potions taste good? When the cup was empty, I leaned up, enabling him to slip the scraps of fabric from my shoulders. With one arm, I held the soaking-wet towel to my front and with the other I worked on pushing the dress down to my hips, where it got stuck.

"I'll pull. Ready? Lift your hips if you can, flower."

Rylan shoved his arms fully into the water again, nimble fingers grabbing the bunched fabric at my hips and giving a tug. I appreciated that he carefully avoided touching my skin even the slightest bit. I shifted each direction, and the lacings finally loosened enough for him to free it from my body. He pulled the garment and my underthings up out of the water, giving the mass a squeeze before tossing it across the room. It landed with a muted splash on the stones.

"There we go. Lie back in the water so the medicine can do some work, okay? I'll be right back."

I did as he asked, leaning back until I was submerged to my chin, the towel still clutched to my chest. I closed my eyes, willing even the edge of the pain to subside. After a few moments, I heard his footsteps return. There was the sound of a stool being placed at the edge of the tub, and he settled down on it.

"Can you lean up?" Rylan asked quietly. I did as he requested, his touch warm and gentle as he moved my hair out of the way to take a closer look. "I'll do my best not to cause any more discomfort." He used a cloth to swipe gently at my back. Though pain flared briefly, it then dissipated via whatever magic he channeled through his hands.

I found a comfortable position with my front leaned up against my knees and closed my eyes again. Without a word, he scooped handfuls of water into my hair, then he scrubbed in some shampoo before rinsing it again. I relaxed under his ministrations and found the pain fading away.

"I'm going to dress you in a robe and put you to bed. Alright?"

Through the fog, I realized that the tub was emptying. Rylan had also wrapped two more towels around my body to dry me off. I was losing time, and couldn't even summon the energy to care. I trusted him.

Reality came fleetingly when he laid me in his bed. As sleep reared up to claim me for good, I wondered what exactly he'd put in my drink and tried to remember to thank him for it.

CHAPTER 9
CALLA

I WAS WARM AND cozy in a nest of blankets, sleep clinging to me like moss on a stone. Through the haze, I heard voices. While trying to open my heavy eyelids, I concentrated on the muffled conversation.

"It belongs to the lady of the house!" Serena's whine pierced through my plugged ears.

The door creaked, and the voices became clearer.

"I'm aware. Move her things from the guest room to that suite. *Today*. She'll not be going back to that room. I'll manage the cleaning myself."

"But, my lord—"

"This is not up for discussion, Serena." His words were icy, and the tone helped shake the last layers of sleep from my mind.

"Rylan, please." He barked a warning laugh at her casual use of his name, and she quickly revised whatever she was about to say. "My lord, I had thought—"

"What? What had you thought?" Rylan's words were clipped, his patience clearly at its limit with her.

"I'd thought ... that perhaps one day those rooms would be mine, my lord. As head housekeeper—"

"Those rooms were *never* going to be yours," he boomed. "Especially not after the stunts you've pulled in regard to the woman lying injured in my bed. Your behavior in my absence proves to have been deplorable and is not much improved with me here, I might add. At worst, you're in league with Cross—"

"Never, my lord, *never*—"

"At best," he interrupted her right back, "you're a scheming coward who can't see past her paltry grasp at power. An innocent woman *died* on your watch, Serena. Another has been brutalized after weeks of horrible mistreatment. You alone carry the burden of responsibility. I'm sure a thousand little things have occurred with other staff too. Make no mistake, I will be finding them all out. You're not fit to be lady of this house. You never were."

I heard her give a meek apology, but he wasn't having any of it.

"Have her things moved. We're done here."

I was so enthralled by the conversation, I forgot myself and tried to sit up. Pain had me gasping, and Rylan's voice barked a final command at her before coming back into the room.

"Hold still, Little Owl." Rylan appeared at my side, his features pinched. "Let me help you." Strong arms curled around me, and I was lifted into a seated position, then propped against what felt like an unreasonable number of pillows. Sleeping on a cloud indeed. "Here, drink this."

He handed me a steaming mug, leaving the tips of his fingers balanced on the bottom until he was sure I had a good grasp on it. I wondered how he wasn't burning himself. "What is it?"

"More disgusting tincture in your favorite tea. I added some honey to help with the taste." He raised his eyebrow, pleased with his offering. I hadn't thought I'd made the commentary about their flavor aloud, but now I wondered.

"Is it the one that made me sleep?"

"No, it's a less potent brew but still good for pain."

Pleased by that response, I sipped carefully, the familiar minty flavor of the lemon balm and the sweetness of the honey masking at least some of the bitterness of the medicine.

"Did you sleep well?"

"I think so. Thank you, for ..." I frowned, unsure where to go with my gratitude. Did I tell him I appreciated the bath? Because in the light of day, there were many reasons for my insides to twist over how he'd so carefully handled me into the water. My cheeks heated, recalling how he'd divested me of my dress. Under different circumstances ...

I stopped that train of thought and turned my attention to my tea.

"You do not owe me thanks for that, Calla." His voice was low and cold, so unusual I couldn't help but stare at him.

"My lord?"

"Please," he sagged, sitting on the edge of the bed near my legs. His voice was breathy, and I didn't know what to do with that. "Please call me by my name."

My insides flipped, everything turning liquid at the desperate plea.

"I'm ... sorry, it's habit."

He dropped his face into his hands. He didn't look tired, but I would bet he'd spent most of his night caring for me. "Are you hungry?"

I frowned at the subject change, but my stomach growled enthusiastically. "Yes. Can you please help me up? I need ... I need to visit the bathroom." My skin flushed hot as I whispered the last. It was mortifying, even if wholly the truth.

Rylan was unbothered. "Of course. Do you want to try to stand?"

I nodded, and he wrapped my arm across his broad shoulders, gently easing me to my feet. A whimper escaped my lips, sweat instantly beading on my forehead.

"It's terrible for a few days. But the more you move, the better."

I took a tentative step on the cold stone floor, followed by another. Muscles screamed, the broken skin on my back protesting the movement. I tried not to dwell on the fact that he'd said those words as though he had firsthand experience.

"Wait." Rylan lowered me carefully to the side of the bed. "Let me use the ointment first. I'll be quick. Would you mind sliding the robe off your shoulders?" My blush returned with a vengeance as I nodded. The fact that he'd already seen most of me was only a partial comfort. I clutched the front together as he pushed the collar down near my waist.

Instead of making me move, he crawled onto the bed, kneeling behind me to gently apply the greasy salve all over my back. His warm touch and the current of his magic stole much of the sting from whatever area his skin roved over. I had half a mind to ask to stay like that for as long as possible.

"Hopefully it won't leave marks if we keep up with treatment," he muttered, peering closely as his fingertips traced the edges of my wounds. "Better?"

"Yes, thank you."

"Alright, let's try again, shall we?"

After pulling the neckline of the robe carefully back up, he scooped my arm over his shoulders again, and while it was slow and plodding, I was proud of having made the journey across his large room on my own two feet. After I took care of my business, he helped me over to the table, where he'd substituted the hard wooden chair I usually sat in for a plush velvet one I recognized from the smaller lounge area in the main hall.

"So you'll be comfortable," he said, seeing my hesitation. My heart thumped at the thoughtful gesture.

Breakfast had been left on the table while I was in the bathroom—eggs and bread along with fruit and more tea. Rylan dished me up a plate as I sat there stunned and beyond humbled that the lord himself was serving me breakfast, carrying me to the bathroom and bringing in special chairs for me to sit in.

Serena must be positively seething.

I ate methodically, noting exactly which muscles moved when I raised my arm or shifted my leg. The way everything in my body was connected to all the places that hurt seemed absolutely ridiculous.

Rylan was distracted as he ate. I could tell he didn't enjoy anything he put in his mouth; he was only servicing a bodily need.

"Rylan."

His amber gaze snapped to mine, urgent, pulling him back from whatever distant thought he'd been lost in. "Sorry, what? Are you alright? Do you need something?" He pushed his chair back, getting to his feet.

"No, no. I'm fine. I just ... I don't mean to belabor the point, but the way you treat me ... us, as a staff ... it's not common. I can't explain how I know that, but I do."

Rylan glanced away as he settled back in his seat. "I feel there's a question in there somewhere," he teased gently, some of his levity returning as he poured us both more tea.

"Yes. My question is why. We're hired help, yet you know everyone well enough to be family. You didn't know me, yet you were highly offended by my treatment when you found out what was going on while you were away. None of that feels ... normal."

"It should be," he said plainly. "It should absolutely be normal to know the names of your employees. And their children. And where to send news if they're injured or sick." He pushed his fingers through his hair. "To treat the members of your household with respect. Give them proper rooms, plenty to eat, and clothing. To pay them their worth. It's the bare minimum."

"You refer to us as your employees, your staff. Not your servants."

"Because you are more than that," he explained gently, stacking up our dirty dishes. "So much more. In a while, I'll take these down to the kitchen, and if Mrs. Brisbane doesn't happen to be around, I'll even wash them. Because they are my dishes and this is my house, and I'm not above a menial chore simply because I'm the lord of this manor. I clean up my own messes. When the harvest is abundant and we need more hands to do the work, mine count too. To slaughter a pig, to cut firewood. It doesn't matter. I am responsible for the house and all of the people in it. It is mine, but I am nothing without these people. Nothing runs without them. Without you."

I was moved to speechlessness momentarily, but then managed, "That's a lovely sentiment. I wish there were more lords like you in the world."

"Me too," he sighed. "But I'll settle for managing my tiny slice of earth with care."

I smiled at him, frozen as something in my chest gave way and glowed just for him.

RYLAN RETURNED TO the room with dinner, my body having demanded rest for most of the day. There was a hearty soup and plenty of bread, plus some of the sweet red apples I found irresistible.

"What will we do in the city?" I asked, trying to focus on my excitement for our upcoming trip instead of the insistent ache that had returned to my body.

Rylan brightened, his smile contagious. "There are a number of little shops I do regular business with. You can find anything you're looking for I'm sure. I believe you'll very much enjoy the food, also." His smile faded. "I've dallied too long, too often there. But I'm not sure how not to linger. It's where I have a ... labor of love."

"What is it? A business?"

"A school." He said nothing further for a moment, and I worried he was back to condemning himself for the actions of another. "I think you'll fit in there quite nicely, Calla. It's the best place I know of to explore your memories. Your magic."

"You think so?" I clung to the promise of such a thing.

"I do. I shouldn't have stayed away from here so long." He began to drum his fingers on his leg, a muscle twitching in his jaw as he ground his teeth.

"Are you talking about Cross?"

He ducked his head. "I am. As a start, anyway. I should have known what he was doing. I trusted him with so much. I can't believe I didn't see it. He should never have been allowed to do those things. I should've seen the signs. Serena too. It seems my trust has been misplaced."

"How long were you gone this last time?"

"Half a year."

I didn't have anything to say to that. It was a long time to be gone from home, but I didn't know how bad Cross's actions had been before I arrived, nor how long Serena had been covering up for him and performing her own misdeeds.

"You can't blame yourself. I have a feeling you will anyway, but their terrible actions are theirs, not yours."

His gaze was fierce as he stared at me for long moments. I expected him to say something, but he never did, though his jaw ticked as he repeatedly clenched it.

"I want to go to the cellar with you."

He froze, knuckles white as they gripped the blankets. "You wish to be with me when I confront Cross for his crimes?" he asked, eyes wide. "You don't know what you're asking, Calla." There was worry there but also a wicked gleam in his eye, as though the idea thrilled him but he didn't want to admit it.

I could happily go the rest of my life without ever seeing Cross, but I found the promise of punishment in Rylan's gaze. A dark part deep inside of me curled lovingly around the idea of exacting vengeance for what he'd done, even though I knew it was wrong. "Yes. I need to see it."

"It's going to be brutal, that much I know for sure. I have no patience left for him, and that's dangerous. I don't know that you should see that."

"Rylan. Please," I begged. "I deserve to see him punished for what he did to me."

He shook his head, one hand rising to cup my face. "There's no going back if you do this. Do you understand? You cannot unsee some things. They change you."

I settled into my need for vengeance, determined to at least see what Rylan did to him if I was not getting an opportunity to strike back at him for myself.

"I don't care. I'd allow everyone he's ever hurt to be there if it would ease their minds."

"That I simply could not allow." His eyes searched my face. I held as neutral an expression as I could. "If you are absolutely certain, Little Owl."

"I am." I should have been afraid, but the sudden fire in my blood was anything but fear.

He sagged, a breath flowing from his lungs. "As you wish." His hesitation melted away after a moment, revealing a smile that was broad and sharp. "He did bring you to me, I'll give him that. But everything else? He'll pay for. I promise."

CHAPTER 10
RYLAN

"How dare you! Putting me in the cellar like a common criminal!" Cross protested, his fear potent on the air. "I've been down here for two days! Fed slop not fit for the pigs—"

"Silence!" The barred door rattled as I grabbed onto one of the rungs. I was grateful for the strength of the metal. My rage with him knew no bounds, and needed an outlet. If I lost focus, it would still end badly for Cross but far too quickly. The more I'd thought about what he'd done to Calla over the last couple of days while she healed in my bed, the more enraged I'd become. It was a wonder I'd held onto the lightning chasing under my skin at all.

As it was, the dishwater had boiled under my hands when I'd taken our dishes to the kitchen after breakfast and Mrs. Brisbane recounted how her wrist was "accidentally" broken when she'd dared supply Calla with more to eat. My control slipped, caused my vision to go red, and all the soap bubbles fizzed as the water roiled under my touch.

My patience with him had officially expired.

Elizabeth and Calla arrived at the bottom of the stairs. I waited for them to gingerly walk to where I stood in front of Cross's cell. I reached out to hold Calla by the waist as Elizabeth retrieved a chair from near the door.

"Thank you, Elizabeth."

"Archmage." She offered a quick curtsy before going back up the stairs.

I lowered Calla into the chair. I respected her strength and determination. She looked as though she were sitting in a throne, she was so elegantly poised. Though it absolutely pained her, she'd insisted on moving around as much as possible over the past few days. She would not be swayed on coming here with me, either. I'd argued against it, but in the end, I couldn't deny her.

I was furious I'd failed her so completely. I should have known better than to trust he'd leave her alone by my say-so. I was not such a fool that I didn't realize her impending promotion put her in a perilous position with the rest of the staff, I just hadn't thought the treachery would come from the man who had once been my most-trusted advisor. Especially not in the short time I'd left the manor to collect supplies for our travels.

"Could you please tell me how you came to be injured?" I asked her. I'd put the pieces together, but I wanted to hear it plainly from her.

"Baron Cross accosted me in my room. He forced me to my knees and struck me with his walking stick. Repeatedly. He seemed to find ... excitement ... in causing pain."

Rage and bile rose swiftly, lashes of energy swirled out of me uncontrolled.

Blustering, the baron began to stutter out an explanation that he was only concerned for my well-being. "She is a scheming servant, my lord. She has bewitched you! Do you not see it?"

"Hold. Your. Tongue." I snapped the words, pointing a threatening finger at him through the bars. The subterranean room became charged, balanced on the edge of tension like the moments just before lightning strikes the ground. "You were forbidden from making decisions of any kind, as I recall. Punishments were certainly outside of your authority. I'm an archmage of Cyntere, do not speak to *me* of bewitching." I gentled my tone before turning to her. "Please, elaborate, Calla."

"He was ... pleasuring himself. While striking me. He ... *finished* on my back."

A feral sound started low in my chest. The reminder that someone had debased her in such a way enraged me. I saw her hand flex against the chair cushion out of the corner of my eye. She was terrified, frozen in the chair. I placed my hand on her shoulder, hoping to soothe her. I was indeed on the edge of losing control, but she was not my target.

"She is *bold*, my lord. Do you not see through her fabrications? She's even invented a false name for herself."

I couldn't believe his audacity. Attempting to lie when her wounds were evidence of what had happened.

"I have no reason to lie," she said firmly, her word an echo of how she'd stood up to him in my office. Pride in her ability to assert herself to his face gentled some of the heat in my blood.

"I have eyes, Cross. And a nose." His eyes widened, understanding my meaning. Smelling his rotten stench on her skin was something I wasn't likely to ever forget.

"You have to understand—"

We were interrupted by one of the field hands bringing Serena down the steps.

"Unhand me, Joseph!" She struggled to free her arm from the broad man's grasp. He did just that, timing the opening of his fingers with her struggle. As she pulled away, he let go, and her knees hit the floor with a fleshy smack.

"Welcome, Serena. You've arrived just in time. If you'll stand over there?" I gestured to the far side of Cross's cell door, so she would be as far from Calla as possible but still within my reach.

"He's lost his mind, Serena! You've seen what he's done, leaving me here for days—"

"Silence!" The air crackled as my anger took physical form, threads of lightning chasing up the walls and between the bars of the cells. I took a deep inhale to steady myself. "As I was saying, she's free to call herself whatever she likes. Anything is better than *girl*. I'm guessing that nickname was intentionally given to be as dehumanizing as possible." Cross shifted uncomfortably, clearly annoyed I wasn't agreeing with his assessment or backing down. "I made an inquiry with the staff about the two of you. Would you be interested in what they had to say?"

I began to recite a long list of offenses, noticing that many of the items made Calla shift in her seat. She seemed particularly uncomfortable when I described Cross's habit of making an offering of a special treat to those he was harassing. While she'd rested, I'd interviewed anyone in the house who had a complaint about the management while I was away. There were very few who'd had nothing to add. Only the hands, who were larger of stature and often only in the house for meals, had no specific complaints to lodge.

Cross at least had the sense to look nervous as I rattled off one after the next.

"You disgust me. I've given you all you've ever asked for, trusted you implicitly, and this is how you repay me? By taking advantage of your position in every way possible? Neglecting your actual duties, serving yourself the best my pantry has to offer, and abusing women?"

"You're going to believe this ... this ... low valley whore over me, my lord?"

With a rough shout, I released some energy toward Cross, who folded in half as it blasted into his midsection. He wheezed for breath as the flesh of his gut sizzled and burned. Serena gasped at Cross's injury, all color draining from her face as my attention fell to her.

"Serena, please tell me the conditions under which Wilhelmina, rest her soul, departed this earth."

Her eyes were wide, shimmering with tears. "As I said, it was sudden, sir."

"Do you really want to play coy? You could just as easily be in the cell with him," I threatened.

Cross was red in the face, sucking small breaths in through his mouth as he fought to stand upright once more.

Serena's lips parted, but it was Calla who spoke. "When she found me, she said, 'Not again.'"

The soft words hit me in the chest. I had to focus on breathing around the sensation that I was strangling. "Serena?"

She looked at Cross, who pleaded at her with his eyes.

"I did, my lord. It was the same condition we found Wilhelmina in. Except she ... she was no longer breathing when I found her."

"How dare you!" Cross cursed, raising a fist in rage at the housekeeper, the other still firmly latched around his middle as though he was afraid something might spill out if he let go. "Rylan, you can't possibly believe these lies! I've been faithful to you all this time—"

"Your *faith* does not excuse what you've done. Neither does your loyalty. You forget yourself, Cross. Worse, you forget *me*." I looked at Calla, and she flinched back from my cold smile. I was sure I looked nothing at all like the man she'd spent the last week in close quarters with. No doubt all the gold had vanished from my eyes. They were almost certainly a terrifying red thanks to my rage. I felt a burn in my scalp above my temples, a warning that my horns had slipped out and were now visible. "Tell me, Little Owl. What do you think his punishment should be?"

She glanced nervously between us as though unsure how to respond.

To ease her hesitation, I continued, "Whatever you suggest will not be judged. I want you to say whatever is your heart's request for this putrid excuse of a man. You wanted to be here, so this is my gift to you for your extraordinary bravery." The column of her throat worked as she considered. She turned her body to look upon him, the pain of doing so etched into her face. "I also need to make clear that anything you thought you knew about me may change the minute you make your decision. But I am the same man I was before. Do you understand?"

Those large brown eyes turned to me, and I couldn't help but soften under their gaze.

"Can you help me stand, please?"

"Are you sure?" I took her hand, gently lifting her to her feet. She locked her knees, sweat beading on her forehead as she forced her body to do something it didn't want to. She was weighing her words carefully. "I have not always been a good man." I put my mouth next to her ear to speak, reveling in the shiver she gave as my lips brushed against the delicate lobe. "I would never claim such a thing. I am not always the man you have dined with and read stories to. But I am him and he is me. We are the same." I hated to think that I might lose her trust over what she saw in the next few minutes, but it was a risk I had to take. This deed had to be done.

Her head swiveled and her round, dark eyes met mine again, her lush mouth close enough to kiss if I leaned the barest bit. Her eyes drifted to my lips, and I lost grip on my control. I closed the distance between us, brushing my mouth against hers for the briefest of moments before shock pulled me back. She tasted of apples and honey wine. Crisp, bright. Blood rushed through my body, the threat of violence mixed with lust sang a siren song to my dark soul. Our forbidden connection shrieked at me despite my adamant denial.

She blinked at me before responding, her tongue darting out to taste her lips. I barely suppressed a groan at the sight, everything inside me at war.

"He likes to look at the girls. It's not friendly," she accused, diffusing the tension lingering between us. Cross grunted, shifting around on his feet as though he could already feel the coals beneath them. "It's lewd. He hides around corners to stare while he touches himself. It makes everyone uncomfortable. I would ..." She stopped, but I felt what she wanted to say. My heart rejoiced in my chest, venom pumping dark inside my veins. "I would like for him to not be able to do that anymore."

I grinned, power thrumming through my body.

"My lord! How can you listen to her about things such as this—"

I pulled a thread of hot power from my center and unleashed the energy through my hand. The smell of char burst into the air as his eyes evaporated out of his skull, leaving behind a sooty black smudge.

Calla inhaled sharply beside me.

Serena passed out cold, bonelessly sliding to the floor.

Cross began to scream, the sound breathy and choked. "I can't see! My eyes! What've you done!"

"That's the least of your worries, I'm afraid." Another bolt traveled from my hand, efficiently removing the appendage he was so fond of stroking, scorching the soiled fabric of his trousers in the process, melting the fabric to his tender skin.

His screams turned guttural as he registered the pain. "You bastard! How could you?" he sobbed, clutching at his crotch as he went to his knees.

"Oh." Calla swallowed, swaying at my side. "I ... What ..."

"It's best not to ask, Little Owl. Not now. Is that all? Is that enough punishment for his offenses? You heard the list. Nearly no one has escaped his behavior. Perhaps I should also be punished for allowing it to go on so long."

Her body trembled against mine, and my cock throbbed. It was not the time to give in to my carnal desires, but I couldn't help it. Her scent was everywhere, and there was no mistaking the bloom of lust in the air between us. Not even if it was mixed with horror.

"He should be repaid every strike he made with his walking stick," she said, voice low and quiet but full of conviction.

"Excellent. It is to be truly righteous justice, then," I said. Twisting my fingers, they blackened up to the first knuckles as I funneled the energy into the wood. Cross shouted as the stick became animated of its own accord.

Before long, he was a sniveling mess huddled up on the floor, begging for mercy while the lump of oak beat him about the body and head. The heavy noises it made as it thudded into his flesh echoed off the walls.

I leaned into Calla, my arm wrapping around her waist both as a way to steady her, and as an excuse to pull her into my side. She was a perfect fit, her head notching right into the hollow of my shoulder. Her whole body trembled with the effort of keeping herself upright, but she refused to sit back down. She seemed more fascinated than disturbed by what was happening, which only heated my blood further.

"Are you ready to end this, Little Owl? Shall we be merciful?" I nuzzled into her neck, brushing her collarbone with my mouth as I breathed her in. Every cell in my body pulsed with need.

"He's bleeding on the floor," she whispered, and the distant look in her eyes warned that I might have pushed too far.

"So he is."

She dropped back into the seat. Once she was steady, I clapped my hands together, dispersing the energy I'd been channeling. The stick fell, splatters of blood flying as it clattered to the stones. Calla jerked, a whimper escaping her lips. Cross was silent, and would remain that way. At least until I returned for him. Serena stirred on the floor, groaning as though she'd been the one to receive the blast.

"It's over?" My brave Little Owl's voice was breathy.

"It is," I confirmed.

She gave a single nod and passed out cold.

CHAPTER 11
CALLA

I WOKE TO A repetitive scratching noise.
Carefully shifting myself, I pulled my body into a seated position against the mountain of pillows. My whole body still hurt, but at least I could move more freely.

"Is that ... blood?" I asked, a waver in my voice as I took in a shirtless Rylan. Standing in front of the washing basin, he scrubbed at one of his black shirts and then his hands with a small brush. The coppery scent of blood was potent, even from across the room. Everything that happened in the cellar came back to me in a rush, and my stomach lurched.

"It is." His voice was oddly emotionless. There were black designs scrawled along the span of his shoulders and trailing down his spine. When he turned, I saw crimson splashed across the ripples of his torso and the rounded muscles in his arms. The same black ink decorated the space along his collarbone and down his breastbone. It looked like writing, but I couldn't see it clearly at such a distance.

"I ..." I swallowed, throat dry for multiple reasons. "Why are you covered in blood?"

"I clean up my own messes, as I told you." He watched me for a moment, gaze cold. Seeing my discomfort at his distant response seemed to snap him back to normal. "Apologies, Calla. I've forgotten myself." He wiped the stains from his skin with a damp rag and hastily pulled on a shirt. "There's a certain ... detachment required to manage some things."

It was natural linen, the only clothing I'd ever seen him wear that wasn't black. It softened him. Rylan approached the bed, warmth back in his eyes as he regarded me with concern.

"Shall we try that again? Are you alright? Do you need anything?"

"I'm fine," I said, scooting back a fraction as he settled on the edge of the bed.

His face dropped, mistaking my trying to make some room for him as me shifting away out of discomfort. "I'm sorry. I should perhaps not have allowed things to go so far. Or maybe tried to prepare you better."

"I don't think there's any real way to prepare for that," I wheezed.

Rylan barked a humorless laugh. "You may be right. Still, I'm sorry. You did wonderfully, all things considered. I hope you don't think too differently of me? Though I will say, I half expected you to run screaming once you woke, so this is going much better than I feared."

"I can't run," I reminded him. "Not quite yet, anyway."

"Yes, there is that." He looked solemn as he pulled one of my hands across the coverlet. I let him take it, and he cradled it between his larger ones. Energy zipped along my skin, warming it and making my fingers tingle. "Are you frightened of me? It would be understandable if you were."

I looked into his warm honey eyes, unexpectedly finding vulnerability. He was worried about how I saw him.

The notion that the powerful archmage who'd just unleashed hell itself on a man in the cellar was concerned about *my* opinion of him made me blink. I took a deep breath and tried to allow myself a moment to feel before I answered.

My instincts may have been damaged or broken altogether, because my gut insisted that there was nothing scary about this man. Knowing he could electrocute me on the spot, poison me with one of his herbal remedies, or simply hurl me into a wall with ease didn't change the fact that there was no part of me that worried for my safety where he was concerned. Quite the opposite, despite what I'd seen happen to Cross. For some reason, I believed this man would move heaven and earth to keep me safe, even if I had no idea why. The truth of it echoed in my bones.

"No."

"No?" Surprise transformed his face.

"I'm not afraid of you. I wasn't in the cellar either. I wasn't the focus of your anger. You wouldn't hurt me. You were angry *for* me."

"I saw the fear in your face, the way you grabbed onto the chair," he said quietly, turning my hand over and tracing the lines of my palm. "Do you trust me, Calla?"

"Yes."

"Just like that? Without hesitation?" He cocked his head to the side.

"Yes. I don't understand why, but I trust you implicitly, my lord." My use of his title was intentional, and he seemed to realize it. His shoulders sagged.

"I'm flattered. There's much to discuss—I'm sure you have many questions. I need some time to get things in order. Do you feel you'll be ready to travel soon?"

I shifted around, gauging the discomfort. Sitting in a carriage that bounced and swayed would be taxing but not impossible, especially with his remedies at hand.

"Yes, I think so."

"Good. If we have to wait a bit longer we can, but I'd like to get back in time for the new students to arrive. I've a few more things to do this afternoon before the wagon arrives to carry Cross's remains to his family."

"Is that why you're covered in blood?" I asked, and even the word on my tongue left a metallic taste in my mouth.

"Yes." He paused long enough I realized he was keeping something from me.

"Was he dead after …"

"No, he was not."

I sucked in a breath. How he'd survived after all that I had no idea. "But he is now?"

"Most assuredly." His expression was unrepentant. The part of me that wanted to know what else he could possibly have done to Cross was outweighed only slightly by the part that did not. Maybe I'd ask another time. "I also had to move him from down below so he could be prepared for travel."

Without stopping to censor myself, I asked, "Why not incinerate?"

Startled, Rylan's mouth opened in shock. "He wasn't wrong about your boldness, Calla, though his intent was to make it an insult when really it's one of the most impressive parts of you." He pulled my hand to his mouth and rubbed his lips over my knuckles. "I could have. I thought about it, if I'm being honest. It's much cleaner, though there is a certain smell that lingers. No matter his end, his family deserves to put him to rest how they see fit. If his shame follows him there, that's his fault. I'll not keep any secrets in the letter that will travel with his remains."

"And Serena?"

"Alive and undamaged. Quite unhappy, however. She's left Stolas Manor permanently, and a similar letter detailing her misdeeds will follow her to future employers. I can only assume she'll return home, disgraced, though with plenty of time on her hands to improve herself."

"Oh." I was surprised by that assertion. I'd assumed she'd be punished in some way, but I was positive banishment was a fate worse than death in her eyes.

I lifted my other hand and touched his hair. His eyes slipped closed as he leaned in to my touch.

"There were horns here. Black ones, with rounded ends. I saw them." I traced where they'd lain against his scalp, nearly camouflaged by his dark hair.

The amber orbs opened. He'd had horns, his eyes had been red, and his fingertips were blackened after he'd shot lightning from his hands. I knew I hadn't imagined any of that.

"Yes," he confirmed with a whisper.

"Can we talk about that?"

He exhaled through his nose. "Yes, Little Owl. We'll talk about that. Shall we also discuss the fact that I kissed you?"

I battled not to gasp when a fierce throb echoed between my thighs. He'd kissed me. He'd held me tightly to his body, and I'd felt the need coursing between us. The overwhelming sense of rightness.

"I should not have," he continued, face falling. "My apologies, Calla. That was uncalled for to say the least."

Ice splashed through my veins. "I ..." My throat clogged with disappointment, confusing me even further. "Heat of the moment ..." I couldn't even finish the thought.

"Well. I have much work to do, and you need to rest so you can heal." He lifted the hand I'd left resting on his shoulder and pressed it between his before giving mine a brief pat. It was awkward and made my stomach roll. "When I return, I'll bring us something to eat." He stood, gathering his soiled clothes on his way out the door.

Guilt crept in that I wasn't pulling my weight, that Elizabeth had been left to do all the laundry in my absence. She'd reassured me on our way into the cellar that she was managing just fine and

I should worry about getting healed up, but I was used to working. Leisure was utterly foreign to me.

I slid off the bed to tidy a few things, but my body quickly protested. He'd left me a pot of tea, so I drank a cup, realizing too late that he'd doctored it with the sleeping tincture. As I got back in bed, I noticed the vase on the bedside table. It held several of the purple calla lilies that grew in the yard.

I softened at the sweet gesture, further confused by his apology and the way he pulled back from me after our attraction had seemed so natural. Mutual. I gazed at the flowers as I melted into the pillows, the medicine working fast. I blinked heavily in the span of a few breaths.

Work would have to wait, and so would everything else.

CHAPTER 12
CALLA

I WOKE WITH A start, my heart fluttering madly behind my ribs as though I'd been chased by one of the lurking shadows from my dreams.

The low fire was still aglow, though it was the only light in the room.

"Rylan?" I called, not finding his form in the bed or on the sofa. I got no response.

I slipped from the bed, pleasantly surprised at how little my back protested the movement. I got a drink of water and even ate a few bites from the tray of fruit and cheese he'd left on the table after our evening meal to settle myself. Unfortunately, the racing in my chest continued, as did a drive to find … something.

Following a pull I could not explain, I felt my way along the wall near the large tapestry depicting a map of Cyntere. There was an owl carved into the wide beam there, and my breath caught when my fingers brushed against it. Pressing my whole palm into the bird's belly, it shifted backward, and something in the wall gave way.

A door opened behind the tapestry, a cool breeze wafting out at my feet. My heartbeat slowed enough that the crushing sensation in my throat lessened, but I still felt an urgent pull behind my ribs to go through the hidden door.

I grabbed a candle lamp from the side table near the sofa. Once I had it lit, I ducked under the heavy tapestry and realized I was in a stairwell. The cold stones stole all the warmth from my bare feet as I started to climb.

The stairs curved upward in a tight spiral. Flickering oil torches in iron sconces were fastened to the wall, illuminating the way once I got around the first bend. I continued on for three full revolutions around the center pillar, my pace slowed by the ache in my back. I tentatively walked forward when the stairs ended in a short landing that led to an archway with no door. Each stone in the arch had a symbol etched into it. Familiarity tickled in the back of my head, but there was nothing more I could get to. My heart throbbed in heavy beats, the sensation almost painful as I pushed myself through the doorway.

Behind a desk as massive as the one in the office on the main floor sat Rylan. His eyes were wide as he took me in over the top of some papers he held. Archimedes gave a cursory feather fluff and chirp in greeting from a tall wooden perch off to the left of where the beautiful archmage sat.

He set the papers down and stood, crossing the room in a handful of long strides, his face unusually stern. "Calla? How did you get up here?"

"I feel like my heart is trying to explode out of my chest," I complained with a pant, the rapid beats beginning to stress me. I was sweating and out of breath, unsure whether to blame the stairs or something more serious for my state.

"Here." He took the candle from me and set it down before pressing his hand into the soft flesh of my breast over my heart.

His eyes slipped closed as he mouthed something under his breath, electricity dancing where our skin met.

My pulse slowed, and Rylan removed his hand once my heart had returned to a normal beat. "Thank you. Where are we?" I gazed around the nearly circular room.

"We're in the tower. This is my ... *other* office." His scowl deepened as he crossed back to his desk and closed the books he'd had open. "Nobody except myself and the dearly departed baron know how to access it. And Archimedes, of course. How did you come to find the entrance?"

The owl chirped again, relaxing into a sleepy state after being acknowledged.

"I don't know. I woke up with my heart pounding, and was driven ... I can't really explain it. I had the feeling I was being pulled? Until I got here."

I looked around the room in awe. Where the office downstairs was jewel tones and masculine order, this one was pure chaos in every way. Books, papers and scrolls were stacked and stuffed into shelving made up of mismatched lumber built into the very walls. Tables of every shape and size took up much of the available floor space, though a single large sofa piled with assorted pillows and blankets sat facing the desk. It looked as though it had seen a great many naps in its time. Next to the desk, pointed out the nearest window, was an ornate telescope—another perch for Archimedes—and a lever system I could only guess allowed the bird to come and go at will.

This office was wholly lived-in, obviously loved. The one downstairs used for household matters was all business, and, I realized, perhaps mostly for show.

It was a lot to take in.

My eyes drifted around the room again, finding stations for displays of crystals, racks of dried herbs, and rows upon rows of glass vials. Charts of the stars hung at odd angles and sat half-unrolled on tables.

I understood then—this was where Rylan worked his mage craft.

"Is your back alright?" he asked with great concern, though his frown never budged. I worried he might be cross with me, though my arrival here was not my fault.

"I'm fine, just a little sore."

I rolled my shoulders and tested lifting my arms, something that had been beyond impossible a couple of days ago. My hands came nearly up to shoulder height.

"Well, it looks like we're going to be able to travel soon for certain then. Come, have a seat." He ushered me over to the plush red sofa, his warm fingertips gently resting on my lower back.

"How did you get all this up here?" I asked, trying to picture the desk and sofa in particular coming up the winding stairs.

Rylan chuckled. "A little bit at a time, mostly. When something breaks, it goes out in pieces or into the fireplace, I'm afraid."

As I settled into the stunningly comfortable cushions, Rylan retrieved some glasses and a bottle of wine from behind the desk.

Time felt oddly suspended in the magical room. Night stars lit up the sky as far as I could see outside the small diamond-paneled windows, but there was no meaning to the hour as we sat there, sipping wine and purely existing. The fire in the hearth behind his desk crackled low as the couch cradled me into complacency.

"I'm sorry to have interrupted. May I ask what you're working on?"

"Just getting a few things in order before we leave. Business, for one. But when we get to Revalia, it will be time for the new students at the school to take their entrance exams. I'm sure the staff has it handled, but I love to be involved. We'll have plenty of time in the carriage for me to write up some questions."

"Mm."

"Ask what it is that's on your mind, Little Owl. I can feel you straining to keep it in."

I let out a heavy breath. "Most archmages don't change form, do they?"

He cleared his throat and set his wine down on the low table in front of the sofa. "No, not usually."

"Then why do you have horns? Why do your fingertips blacken and your eyes glow red? I have tried to explain away how I could have seen those things, but I cannot. I know what I saw in the cellar."

He stared at me, those kind amber orbs pleading as he debated how to respond to me. "This is one of those times where if I answer you with honesty, you may not like the answer, Calla."

"Should I have started with the kissing question, then?"

He barked a laugh, and I reveled in the way his eyes crinkled at the corners when I shocked him into joy. "Perhaps." He took my hand and pressed his mouth to my fingertips. "If I answer your other question first, you may never want to discuss kissing with me again."

"I don't think that's true."

"It might be for the best if it was, Calla." He took a breath, his gaze never leaving mine. He had loosened his hold on my hand, but seemed disinclined to let go.

"Can I … see them again? See you like that, I mean. Without you having to become angry?"

He flinched back, expression shuttering again. "You … want to see my horns?"

"Yes, very much. " He'd confirmed my question without addressing it directly with his response.

He turned to look out the window, and my heart sank into my stomach. I'd clearly pushed an issue I should not have. "I'm sorry, Rylan, I didn't mean to offend—"

"No, no. It's not that. I'm just ... surprised. And I'm struggling here, Little Owl. The kissing issue has arisen with a vengeance with you asking about my horns. You have no idea how you affect me. I don't understand it myself."

I flushed, my cheeks hot as I watched him shift in the seat. If how I made him feel even held a candle to how I felt around him, I understood just fine.

"We could do that, too, if you like. Before you show me. If it helps."

He shook his head, leaving me feeling an odd sense of shame as his hand rose to rest on my cheek. "You are the loveliest gift, Calla. Truly. I'm not sure what brought you to my door. I am thankful." He leaned forward, his eyes caressing my mouth as his fingers traced my cheek. "But I don't deserve you."

"That's not true," I argued, mustering up all my boldness.

"It is. Are you familiar with the term *fated mate*?"

"Fated? That sounds quite serious," I teased, but his words had my heart thumping again.

"It's a rare, powerful bond between two people. We have a connection of some kind, but ..." He trailed off, gesturing with his glass. "Do you feel anything unusual?" He was nervous, which made my heart glow a bit warmer. "I realize that's an odd question, and maybe impossible to answer since you don't recall any of your life before coming here."

"Yes," I said, finding no reason to hesitate or temper my answer. "Your voice, for one. It was like I knew it already when I first heard it in the entry hall that day."

His mouth ticked at the corner. "Perhaps I underestimated you again, Little Owl. I'm learning quickly that I should ask you things directly, or I risk being humbled at the hands of the universe."

"Are we ... fated?" Even asking the words felt strange on my tongue but also sounded right.

"I don't know for certain, but I'm not sure how we could be. I already had a mate. Though the things I feel with you ..." He stopped, exhaling a stilted breath as though a battle raged inside his body.

After several long moments, where all I could hear was my blood rushing in my ears, I finally worked up the courage to press my mouth to his, just as an experiment. The feel of his soft lips against my own immediately sparked a deeper need, making me shift in my seat.

"Calla." He breathed my name, half benediction, half curse.

I tilted my head, drawing his mouth against mine exactly how I wanted, my fingertips on the edge of his jaw. The taste of iron and wine filled my senses as my lips sipped at his, my tongue gently probing against the seam of his mouth. He groaned deep in his throat, his hand also rising to my face, thumb tracing along my jaw as he took control of the kiss and plundered my mouth. Our tongues twined, and my body sang out with desire. It didn't matter if he didn't believe we were fated. Nothing mattered at all except the insistence in my blood that I needed him. I belonged with him. That was the only reality and the truth of that throbbed in time with my pulse.

Abruptly, he pulled away, chest heaving. I, too, gasped for breath, upset that the moment had ended. "Oh, Little Owl, you're divine. But we cannot. I'm sorry."

I wasn't sure what to say, so I remained silent for a time, the tip of my tongue collecting his taste from my lip. "Why not?" I asked finally.

Rylan exhaled firmly through his nose. "You do not want a man like me, Calla. I'll only disappoint you."

I flinched, anger rising in response. "Shouldn't I get to decide that?"

He gritted his teeth. "I can tell you with surety, you deserve better."

"That's unfair." My emotions were high, all of them competing for dominance under my skin.

"You haven't even seen all of me, Calla," he argued, a muscle rolling in his jaw.

"So show me." There was no way for me to explain why I wanted to see it again, but it seemed important. Thrilling, even. "I'm not afraid of you."

"I need you to remember you asked for this," he grumbled.

Rylan stood and walked to an open part of the floor. Then he bowed his head, his golden eyes slipping closed as he focused. Horns slid from his scalp, parting his hair as they emerged. Inky blackness spread down his fingers and sharp claws emerged as I watched. When he opened his eyes, they were the color of rubies, and there was something heavy at his back, though I couldn't quite see what it was. Feathers the color of pitch lined his arms up past his shoulders, and his canine teeth were slightly elongated.

I got to my feet, inexplicably drawn to the version of Rylan standing before me. He was the same but different; the new features leaving him at least as attractive as he was the other way, if not more so. He twitched as I reached up and caressed one of the horns, the smooth black bone warm under my touch.

Rylan extended blackened fingers toward my face, the claws at the tips having retracted at his will. He stopped just before brushing my skin and dropped his hand to his side. "You're truly not afraid?" he asked, his voice slightly more gravelly than it had been, but still clearly communicating his awe.

I raised my eyebrows, realizing what I was seeing over his shoulder. "Why would I be afraid? You're still you. You're not going to hurt me. Are those ... wings?"

My question made him smile, and the slash of his white teeth combined with the red of his eyes proved a shocking combination. I let out a gasp as he extended the appendages. On the underside, they were leathery and bat-like, but facing out, they had the same dark feathers that had sprouted on his arms. They extended twice as wide as his fingertips would reach and explained why he was built so broadly through the shoulder. He needed the strength to hold them up and make them work.

I worried for myself then, because I was fascinated by what I was seeing, amazed, but not surprised. Fear was the furthest thing from my mind. Maybe it was the wine, or maybe I'd known of things like this before and was missing the memory of it like everything else. Either way, it seemed unreasonable that seeing a man with horns and wings would be less than startling, but I simply was not shocked. I was intrigued.

And I wanted to touch every inch of him.

"Have you figured it out yet, clever one? What I truly am? I bet you have."

The answer to his question presented itself as I raked my eyes over his features again and again. I tried to distract myself from the thoughts that insisted I kiss him immediately while he was in this form, to see if he tasted any different than he had the other way.

"Yes," I answered, breathless as the word formed in my mouth. "You're a demon."

CHAPTER 13
RYLAN

THERE SEEMED NO end to the number of ways Calla could find to surprise me.

I'd been wrong at every turn where her limits were concerned so far, and I was depraved enough that it made me want to continue pushing until I found one she didn't want me to test.

She had to be tied to me by fate somehow, I was certain of it, even if I didn't understand how. No other woman would have looked me straight in the eye with wonder the way she was. Fear or discomfort, absolutely, but not the cheerful awe Calla glowed with as she took all of my other form in.

"A demon," she repeated as though tasting the words thoroughly, her eyes lit up with wonder.

It took every ounce of willpower I had to stand there, unmoving, as her fingers gently stroked along the sensitive feathers on my arms. Every cell in my body begged for me to pin her to the wall and make her mine in every way as she traced along the runes inked across my chest with those delicate fingertips. I wanted to trace every dip and curve of her frame with my hands and my tongue. I wanted her breath on my neck and the scent of her hair in my nose while I filled my palms with her softness. I wanted it all.

But she was not mine to have.

As she came forward for another kiss, I hesitated, forcing my demonic features to retreat.

"No," she gasped, nearly begging. My cock throbbed at the sound, her voice my very undoing. "Stay like that."

I growled, releasing back into the shift as I lost restraint and wrapped my arms and wings around her body. I dove into the kiss, pressing my mouth to hers, all gentleness gone. Her breath hitched as I nipped at her lip with my sharp teeth, so I did it again, enjoying the warmth of her body against mine as she sighed into my mouth. Her pleasure was my pleasure, and I would happily pay any penance owed for indulging just this once.

She pulled away, mouth swollen and eyes clouded, as she peered up at me. "You're beautiful." She barely breathed the words, as drunk as I was on lust. It somehow made her more lovely than she already was.

"As are you, Little Owl." I carefully retracted my wings, stilling as shame crept over her features.

She stepped back two paces, fingertips to her lips. Wide-eyed, she flushed a bright red. "You think I shouldn't want this, but it feels right to me."

I inhaled carefully through my nose, trying to settle the rush of energy humming under my skin. "I understand."

"You do?"

I wanted to touch her again, but it wasn't wise. "I do. I feel a pull to you as well, but this cannot progress between us."

She blinked, hurt flashing across her face, which made me feel even worse. "Okay," she whispered, putting on a brave face after a pause and touching one of the star charts that dangled off a table edge. "Why do you have so many of these?"

I cleared my throat, tension slowly leaking out of my body. As the seconds ticked by, my mind struggled to keep up with her abrupt subject change. "They change a bit over time. I do a record every season to track it. Different stars are visible during different parts of the year."

"How many years do you have charts for?" Calla asked, stifling a yawn.

"That's another tricky question, Little Owl."

Calla raised an eyebrow at me as she moved on to peer at the collection of crystals I'd amassed. "I'm not afraid of your answers either, Rylan."

My blood sparked. She challenged me, and I begrudgingly loved it. "One day you might be." She pinned me with a stare, and I relented. She was very rarely deterred by my evasions. "I've been tracking for 237 years."

Her hand stilled over the tip of an amethyst point. "But that's not as many as you've been ... here."

"No, it's not."

She nodded once, accepting my answer but not pressing me further. I wasn't sure what kind of woman heard I'd been practicing astronomy for two and a half centuries and just moved on with her questions, but I liked her all the more for it.

"What does this one do?" She held up an egg-sized knot of obsidian.

"That's a good one for you to put in your pocket, Little Owl. That's obsidian. Good for protection, clearing obstacles, and clarity of mind."

Her eyebrows went up. "Could it help with my curse?"

"Perhaps. Keep it with you and we'll see."

She smiled, and my heart gave a squeeze. "Is this where you make your potions?"

I could tell she chose the word intentionally, making it sound as though my herbal medicines were nothing more than a play at witchcraft.

"Indeed. Is there one you'd like to try? That green book you read to me from had a number of terrible recipes in it I'd bet you could improve upon." I got to my feet and joined her, lighting a flame under the small kettle on the table with a touch, grateful for the distraction and change of subject. The supplies were more scientific than alchemic, but I'm sure they looked like nothing more than a tiny cauldron and eye of newt to most.

"Can we make some more ointment?"

"Of course." I turned to a set of shelves and pulled out ingredients she'd need along with as a clean container to keep it in.

"What do I do?"

"I know you can't see your memories, but perhaps you know more than you think you do? You have full access to my supplies."

Calla's brow knitted, but I saw her gears turning as she examined the tools and ingredients on the table. She touched every item as though seeing if it sparked any kind of memory first, pausing twice to rub at a spot between her eyes.

I went to my desk while she settled in to work. As I packed up the items I wanted to travel with us, her exclamation rang out. Worried she'd burned herself, I stood. She was pouring the finished product into the tin, face pinched.

"Everything alright?"

"Yes," she said, making sure the pan was safely set down and the flame out before speaking further.

When she met my eye, hers were glossy with tears. "Are you—"

"I used to make something like this with my gram. We used goose fat with beeswax. She swore by the blend of mint or lemon balm, bitter orange, and devil's claw." Her breathing became ragged, and her face dropped into her hands. I rushed over to pull her into my arms. "I had a gram. I remembered I had a gram." She dissolved into sobs against my chest.

"Shhh. It's alright, Little Owl. It's excellent you've remembered something. I'm so happy for you." I muttered useless words into her hair, stroking along the silky strands as she cried herself out. My heart thudded softly, my hands stilling against her as I felt it slow to sync with hers. I stiffened, and she pulled away. I regretted the loss, which only added to my frustration.

"I'm sorry," she apologized, wiping her face on her sleeve.

I took the tin of salve she'd made and put the lid on to avoid meeting her eye. "That's perfectly alright, Calla."

"Would you ..." She thrust her hands at me. "Do that thing? Where you check my mind. Please?" She sniffled, but her fierce determination had returned.

"If you'd like." As I took her hands, my cautious probes encountered the same blank space as before, but there was what felt like a crack beginning along one edge. She smiled despite the grimace on her face as I relayed the news. "Hopefully we can find some answers and start getting your memories back. Are you alright?"

"My head is pounding, but that's nothing new."

I frowned. "It's not? How often do you get headaches?"

She shrugged. "Mostly when I try to think about my past or remember things. But I get one most days. They're worse if I don't sleep well, though that doesn't happen much anymore. My dreams are better too."

She'd confided in me about the shadowy figure she was always pursuing in her dreams, but the headaches were a new revelation. "Here." I pressed my fingertips to her temples, pushing energy into her scalp, willing any tension to relax.

"That's better, thank you. Should I pocket another crystal? Which one goes with the obsidian?"

"I've got a selection of those put away also, and where we're going is ... suffice it to say, the building itself is quite prepared for all things magical." She looked at me as though I'd hung the moon for her personally, and my heart squeezed. "You should get some rest."

She looked disappointed as I ushered her toward the stairs but didn't follow her down into the bedroom. I shared the sentiment. But I also knew if we pushed too far, it would end in disaster, and I wasn't sure I would survive such a thing again.

CHAPTER 14
CALLA

"**W**E'LL STOP AT an inn for the night," Rylan said, calmly working on his exam questions. "Then we should arrive shortly after midday tomorrow."

"Oh. I didn't realize we'd be stopping."

All the excitement I'd built up over the previous few days for taking the trip became stifled almost immediately by the lengthy journey. Mrs. Brisbane had prepared everything for us, and between her and Joseph's father, the manor was taken care of in Rylan's absence.

The carriage, though luxurious, was cramped and moved much slower than I'd been prepared for. Rylan sat on one side and I on the other, with Archimedes in a cage against the wall between our knees. Outside the windows, pastoral farmlands passed at a decent pace. Small homesteads, horses, fields. It all seemed familiar enough as I gazed at it. I rubbed my thumb over a smooth divot in the obsidian inside my pocket.

"How many students attend your school?"

"A few dozen."

"Admission is selective?"

He quirked a grin, leveling me with a coy stare. "Very."

I cocked my head. "How so?"

He set down his quill. "We admit only those magically inclined. Our purpose is to train witches, mages, and healers—specifically those who wouldn't otherwise be taught."

"Those with latent abilities?" I asked, not quite understanding.

"More like those who come from ... unsupportive homes." He leveled a look at me that spoke volumes. "As one of few mages licensed to practice and train, I'm very proud of what we're doing for the next generation of magic. Our success rate is nearly one hundred percent thus far. We take on mostly young adults but some children and older students as well."

"How many graduates?"

"One hundred and seventy-seven."

I gasped. "That's a lot. In how much time?"

"Fifteen years."

"Incredible. I can understand why you spend so much time devoted to it."

He smiled and returned to his pages. I opened the book I'd selected to read for the trip, but couldn't manage to get lost in the words.

"Here." Rylan offered me a spare quill and some papers. "See how you do with this. It's our entrance exam from last year."

"A test?"

"Perhaps reading the questions or searching your mind for the answers will reveal how much knowledge you have stored in here." He tapped my forehead with a finger.

The first few questions were basic herbalism, and I answered them with confidence, the information logical and common sense. The next section was all about energy transfer, and while I thought I made some reasonable guesses, they were not my strength. Then there were some about crystals and I gave up completely trying to even guess. By the time I got through the second page, I was rather defeated.

"I don't believe I'd be admitted to your school." I sighed and handed the test back.

Rylan paused what he was doing to scan through my answers. "Nonsense. You did better than most of our students do when they first arrive."

"I did?"

"Absolutely. Talent and power aren't the same as knowledge. It's learning how to link them that's important. I can't wait to see what you can accomplish given the right tools, Little Owl. In fact, while I'm sure your help with my paperwork will be invaluable, discovering your magic and returning your memories to you is far more important, and I plan to dedicate my attention to that while we're there."

"That's ... Thank you."

He smiled at me, and I glowed under the praise, forcing myself to relax and let him work while the carriage swayed down the road.

THE HEARTH AND Cask Inn was the only attraction in an otherwise sleepy little town. The carriage driver accompanied the horses to the stables as we stretched our legs and went inside. Firelight was the main illumination for the handful of tables. Only three had patrons, but they all stopped to watch us walk to the counter at the back of the room where the innkeeper was busy pulling ale.

"Ah! My lord. Always a pleasure to see you. Your room is ready now if you'd like."

"Thank you, Bertold. Is there another available? As you can see, I'm not traveling alone this trip."

My heart thudded against my ribs, torn between relief and fear. The innkeeper scanned me, an apologetic smile on his lips. "I'm afraid we're quite full this evening."

Rylan glanced and me and gave a short nod. "That's alright, we'll figure something out. Clem is in back with the horses, so I'll need him accommodated too."

"Yes, certainly. I'll have him lodged with the stable hands. And the bird? Is he with you?"

Rylan smiled broadly. "He is."

"Ah! It's been a while. I'm glad to hear he's returned. I'll let the game ward know he's not to be bothered. The rodent population is open to him, of course." The aged innkeeper swept me with a look, his smile broadening. "Would you and your companion care to bathe before or after supper?"

"Calla?" Rylan turned to me.

"After would be lovely, thank you."

"I'll have dinner brought out for you then. Unless you'd like it in your room?"

My heart thumped. Despite having slept in his bedroom for multiple days, the idea that we were going to be seen together and known to share a room felt borderline scandalous.

"No, we'll eat here. My favorite table?"

"Of course." The innkeeper collected more mugs than he should have been capable of carrying all at once and winked at Rylan before heading off to deliver them.

"Come, Little Owl. I know we've been sitting all day, but it's worth a little more time in a chair to eat some of Bertold's meat pie while we drink his summer ale."

He guided me with his hand at my lower back to a well-worn table in the far corner of the room. We were no longer the topic of interest for the locals, who had all turned back to their conversations as the innkeeper delivered fresh tankards for them to drink.

"What did you think of your first day in a carriage?" Rylan asked me after our food had been delivered.

I sipped at the ale, which had a pleasant citrus taste under all the hops. "My back is a bit sore, but otherwise it was as anticipated, I think. I feel like perhaps I used to make a journey somewhere. It seemed ... familiar."

He nodded and picked up his fork. "It's likely. Most farm families must ferry their crops to market, so if you lived on one and could ride a horse, you may have been the one in your house to do so."

I hadn't remembered anything further about my family or previous life, but knowing I'd managed to recall once having a woman called Gram in my life gave me hope that I might one day remember who I used to be.

I took a bite of the meat pie, which had a rich sauce and plenty of vegetables. It was delicious. Rylan grinned at the noise I made in response. "I told you. He's only skilled at making this one dish, but it's masterful."

I laughed. I couldn't imagine only being able to cook a single thing, but it worked for Bertold. After we'd eaten our fill, Rylan requested more ale and water be sent up to the room. Nerves took over as I found myself outside of my normal environment. I fidgeted with my skirt as Rylan unpacked clean garments for both of us, then led me into a room across the hall from ours. The ale had my muscles relaxed and my head the slightest bit fuzzy, but I was still very aware of our close proximity.

Rylan ran the water in the large singular tub, his muscular forearms bare as he'd rolled up his sleeves.

"Shall I turn around?" he asked, voice hushed.

"Turn around?" I rasped.

"While you undress." I could only stare blankly at him, so he clarified, "There's no lock on the door. While I trust Bertold, some of the clientele is ... questionable." His mouth drew into a tight line. "As part of that questionable clientele, I can assure you that under no circumstance am I leaving you in here alone."

"Oh." Butterflies swarmed in my stomach, the tension between us thickening. "Okay." He turned to face the door, and I disrobed before settling myself in the tub.

"Let me know when you're ready for your towel." He turned his head to the side, not quite looking over his shoulder. There was nothing for him to see but some collarbone, but it still made me blush.

As I washed my legs and torso with the heavy soap the inn provided, I noticed that the water became opaque. "You can turn around if you'd like."

"What?"

Emboldened by the tension in his voice, I chose to be brave. He'd seen me in the bath before, though he'd taken as many measures as possible to protect my modesty. I'd slept in his bed for nearly a week, though I had no idea where he was getting his rest while I was there. We'd kissed more than once. We were far from strangers, in any case.

"You can turn around. I could use your help both with checking to see how healed my back is and washing my hair." I turned to look at him, and he was craning his head over his shoulder, nostrils flared and jaw clenched. "If you don't mind."

"Of course," he ground out. His tension manifested like an electrical charge; I felt it spark as I sat across the room in the water. Thankfully, he managed to calm himself as he prepared the supplies. I was fairly sure his magical current couldn't electrocute me, but I'd rather not test that theory.

He pulled over a low stool to sit on. As I continued to lather the bar in my hands to use on my arms, he settled himself behind me. I heard him exhale before he dipped a pitcher he'd taken from a stand near the taps into the water.

"Thank you. Raising my arms over my head is still very difficult."

"I'm happy to help, Little Owl." His strong fingers kneaded my scalp and neck as he worked shampoo through the strands.

"Where did you sleep?" I asked, my thoughts running away with my mouth.

"Sleep? When?"

"While I was hurt. You had me in your room. Where did you sleep?"

He huffed a breathy laugh as he filled the pitcher and rinsed my hair. "When I sought rest, which was likely far too little, the sofa in the tower office was usually where I started."

"Started?" I was hot from head to toe, and it had nothing to do with the water temperature.

"Sleep never quite found me unless ... I was lying next to you."

I turned my upper body, sending water splashing and allowing my breasts to rise momentarily above the waterline. "Next to me?"

Eyes wide, he glanced down then forced his gaze to stay on mine. His hands were suspended in the air, one palm toward me as though offering surrender or warding off a strike, the other still holding the pitcher.

"Yes, Little Owl. To be fair, you were in *my* bed at the time, but at your side is the only place I've gotten any rest at all since I arrived back at the manor."

CHAPTER 15
CALLA

I PACED OUR ROOM as Rylan finished bathing. His confession hit me harder than it should have. When I'd turned around, it was all I could do to avoid launching a thousand other questions at him. It was worrisome that I'd slept so deeply I'd never felt the bed move, for one thing, which made me want to know what I'd been given as medicine. For another, him sleeping next to me felt somehow more intimate than the kisses we'd shared or even the gentle way in which he'd helped me bathe. Twice.

The bed in our rented room was much smaller than the one back at the manor, and the only other furniture for comfort was a single wooden chair. The porter had lit the fireplace and left some ale and water on the small table along with a loaf of heavy brown bread.

My sleeping gown felt simultaneously too heavy and entirely unsubstantial as I walked back and forth along the creaky floor. I tried not to think about how I'd scuttled from the bathroom the moment Rylan started to take his shirt off. And how he'd repeatedly pushed me away when everything in me wanted to get closer. Because obviously, he wanted that too, no matter how much he denied or fought against it.

Frustrated, I gave up trying to braid my hair back after the third failed attempt. While my wounds were mostly healed, the inability to use my hands above chest level was problematic to say the least. My hair would have to be left wild for the night.

A knock at the door set my heart racing.

"Who's there?"

"It's me. May I come in?" Rylan asked.

I rushed to pull the heavy wooden door open. "It's your room," I chided, my nerves coming out as anger, which I immediately regretted.

"So it is," Rylan said, eyebrow raised as he came in, locking the bolt behind himself.

I stood off to the side near the table where our extra ale and water had been left, toying with my hair over my shoulder.

Rylan packed away our soiled clothing and sat on the far side of the bed. "Calla," he called, pinning me with an unrelenting gaze.

"Yes?"

"Come here, please." I cautiously approached him, his handsome face betraying amusement. "Have I made you uncomfortable?" He took my hands into his, rubbing the backs in the same soothing way he'd done when he'd been applying the healing ointment.

"I ... No." I hated how out of sorts I felt, like my insides were all tangled up. "Yes."

"How can I make you feel better?"

"That's ... that's working pretty well, actually."

He chuckled. "Go sit in the chair, and I'll fix your hair. It seems a bird of some sort has taken up residence in the short time between washing it and now."

I snorted at his teasing but did as he said. Taking long strokes with a brush, he pulled out all the knots before separating it into sections and making a perfectly smooth braid that ran down my back. He'd clearly had plenty of practice, and certainly did a better job than I ever could have.

"Thank you."

"Are you feeling better then?"

"A little."

"I didn't think my honesty would send you into such a state or I might have tried to soften my words. You usually prefer it straight." He sat on his side of the bed, leaning back against the meager offering of pillows. He patted the mattress next to his body. "This would be a very interesting time for you to decide to fear me." He was being playful, but the look in his eye was hunger.

I recognized it because it was an echo of my own.

Before joining him, I picked up the tankards of ale. I figured the alcohol probably wouldn't hurt my stressed state. "I'm not afraid, exactly, I simply don't know what to ... prepare myself for." I whispered the last, burying my face in the cup afterward. I wished for an ounce of the bravery I'd had in the tower about wanting to touch him. It would seem it had all left me once we were no longer in that room.

"Calla." Seriousness coated my name, making it thunderous despite his low volume. It absorbed the whole of my attention when he said it that way. "There's nothing to prepare for." His eyes were pained as he watched me. "I'll sleep on the floor if needs must. Or the chair. I've certainly been in far worse circumstances."

I couldn't help but blush. Shame and embarrassment made me want to crawl into a hole and hide. I settled for shaking my head and gulped the ale.

"Oh my. It's serious then." He got up, taking the cups to the table and putting out as many of the sources of light as possible before returning with the stiff chair in his hand. He spun it backwards to straddle the seat and rest his chin on his arms. "Let me explain."

Feeling pleasantly fuzzy around the edges, I nodded.

"Those first couple of days when you were healing, I kept as much distance as I could so I wouldn't disturb you. I've spent many a night on the sofa in my tower office, or even dozing on the one in my room. Neither offered any respite, however. I had to have you within my sight for my mind to stop spinning. Within range to touch you to actually fall asleep."

"Do you feel the thing in your chest I do?"

He tilted his head. "Can you elaborate?"

"I don't know how to explain it. It's a burning sensation. Makes me want to be close to you."

"Perhaps."

"Not for certain? Is it the fated thing?"

He exhaled, briefly resting his forehead on his arms. "I don't know. I do know ... I've not felt like this for anyone in centuries, Calla. Not since the only other time the universe generously sent me someone I believe was my fated mate. But you only get one of those. I don't claim to be a saint—quite the opposite, as you've seen personally—but pleasure of the flesh has never been my favorite indulgence. I had far more curiosity about the stars, for one. I had plenty of other things to keep me occupied, I didn't often feel the need to go out looking for momentary carnal pleasure."

The heavy sentiment choked me up as I was reminded of something Cross had said. It would surely splash ice all over our moment, but I couldn't help how badly I wanted to ask.

"Cross asked me if you'd had your way with me yet. That day." Rylan's hand tightened against the back of the chair, the surge of power in him palpable as his body tensed. "He was very crass about it. What he asked was if ... if you'd fucked me yet." I pulled a face, the memory of the old man hurling the phrase at me making me grimace. "He said something about 'all the others.' That I'd be your whore, like them."

Rylan sat up straight, got to his feet, then returned the chair to the table. "I'm sorry he said those things to you." His voice was tight, the rage instantaneous and manifested in the flashes of red in his eyes. "I'd kill him again, more slowly, if I could. But he didn't have a clue what he was talking about. There've been very few others over the years, and never one at the manor."

The remote possibility that he was lying was thoroughly tempered by the fact that I was certain I'd feel it. I didn't know how or why, but I suspected my heart would hurt if he were being untruthful. But Rylan was not a liar. He seemed as surprised about our connection as I was and much more resistant to explore it.

"I believe you."

"You do?" he queried, gazing down at me, perplexed. The rage evaporated from the surprise.

"Yes. You're not a liar. You can ... lie here with me if you'd like."

His nostrils flared as he considered. "I am losing grip on my control where you're concerned, Calla," he grumbled, striding over to the other side of the bed.

"That's okay," I whispered, sensing I was walking a fine line as he positioned himself carefully on his side. I scooted down and rolled onto my back.

"This is how we slept in my bed, Little Owl. Me trying to maintain my distance while you dreamed peacefully an arm's length away." His eyes flashed red as I watched, and a thrill surged through me. "In truth, all I wanted to do was pull you close, like this."

I squeaked as his arm banded around my middle, then he pulled my body flush against his, and I couldn't help but melt into him as he snuggled me closer. My head was pillowed on his bottom arm, his chin tucked into the top of my head. I felt his chest rise with every inhale, and—even though he kept trying to move back so I wouldn't—his cock thickening against my backside. My heartbeat slowed to match the even thump of his once the surprise passed.

He shivered behind me. "I shouldn't want you like this, Calla. It terrifies me."

"I'm not afraid," I breathed, the half-lie falling off my tongue with ease.

"No?"

"No. You don't scare me, Rylan. Not like this. Not with your magic wild while you punish someone who did a terrible thing. Not in your other form."

His chest rumbled as he propped himself up on one arm. I maneuvered so I was on my back again, with his beautiful face hovering above me. His lips hovered close enough to touch mine. Desire pressed heavily on me as he lifted his hand, first gliding it down my cheek, then pressing it across my throat. One intentional clutch, and he could end me, but his touch was gentle as he stroked along the tender skin. He paused with his thumb over my pulse.

"Shall I kiss you then, Little Owl?"

"Yes. Please." I was prepared to beg for it with all the blood lingering at the surface of my skin, primed for his touch.

He did, a soft test at first, then again and again, driving me mad with want before he committed to devouring me. His lips meshed with mine, his tongue licking into my mouth before tangling with my own.

A noise escaped my throat, and he responded by tightening his grip across my neck just once and only enough to make me gasp in surprise that such a thing had caused a flood of arousal.

"Are we finished?" he asked, face going serious. "We should be. I shouldn't have even done that. You deserve better. I've already had my chance." His voice was strained.

"No. Please." I wasn't sure what I was asking for, but stopping seemed like the most painful option in the world. A throb pounded in the hollow between my legs, a beat that matched the gallop of my heart. His warm hands sent a thrill through my skin wherever they touched.

"Tell me what you want, Little Owl," he requested, firelight reflected in his eyes, the flames merging with the honey glow.

"Touch me." I knew his fingers would send an electric current wherever they brushed, only heating me further, but I *needed* it. I was desperate to know what it would feel like to be completely at his mercy while he explored the parts of me he so modestly hid from himself in his bathtub.

Needing no further invitation, his large hand coasted down the planes of my body over the top of my simple sleeping gown. His fingers tightened around the peak of my breast, pinching the aching point for a moment before continuing down across my belly. He grazed the other breast, huffing out a breath as he placed a kiss on my collarbone.

"I'm at your mercy, Little Owl. Ask for what you need."

"You," I panted, reaching up to hold his face. "I need you to kiss me. To touch me."

He curved his body over mine, his arm banding me against him as he dove in for another thorough kiss. The ties on the back of my gown were undone in short order by his nimble fingers, but he didn't pull the fabric down. Instead, after he'd had his fill of my mouth, he crawled down my body. His nose pressed into the fabric as he inhaled deliberately while crossing the apex of my thighs.

I trembled as he looked up at me, eyes swirling ruby and gold as he licked his lips. Need flared hot at the sight. His hands pushed my skirt up clear over my middle, leaving me bare to him. He angled one of my legs so my foot was flat on the bed, then placed the other over his shoulder. Without warning, he pressed his tongue along my cleft, using his thumbs to open me to his liking.

My head tipped back as he licked from bottom to top, pausing only long enough to tease the tight bud at the top with a hard suck. I cried out, and he growled deep in his throat, settling in further to feast. "So sweet, Little Owl. I've dreamed of this. No matter how hard I tried not to, your scent haunted me." He hummed, tensing his tongue and spearing it inside me.

I was a writing mess, held still only by the firm grip he kept on my stomach with one hand. As I gave in to the waves of pleasure coursing through me, he changed tactics. I moaned out as one of his fingers pressed inside me, and he focused on the tight bundle of nerves with his mouth. He sucked, then licked, then sucked again as his finger plunged in and out of me. Wet noises echoed around the room alongside my breathy pants as energy gathered low in my abdomen.

"Come for me, my clever Little Owl. I want to taste you as you come undone."

I gasped as a second finger joined the first, and the thumb of the hand holding me steadily crept to where he was stroking my nub with his tongue. I reached down, grasping for something to hold onto and found that his horns had slid out. I gripped them tightly, and he groaned in response as my climax began to build, threatening to turn me into a pile of useless mush.

The subtle electric current he carried in his touch pushed me over the edge as his thumb brushed my clit. Everything in my body clenched as I cried out. His fingers clamped inside me, and his mouth locked over that sensitive spot. My legs shook, and I let go of his horns as I collapsed into the mattress, sweaty, panting, and in need of another bath.

"Good girl. So beautiful letting go for me," he muttered, placing the fingers he'd had inside me into his mouth.

I made a noise in my throat at the sight, my body clenching at the emptiness he'd left behind. He pulled my light skirt back down, latching wetly onto one nipple then the other through the cloth as he made his way back up the bed.

I stared at him, the pleasure having left me foggy headed as he stood and went over to the terrible wooden chair.

"I could—"

"You'll not."

"But you—"

"Go to sleep, Calla." He yawned, propping his heels up on the table. "We have another day of travel and much to do when we arrive. You need your rest."

"What was that about?" I whispered, much to my own mortification. I knew *exactly* what it was. That's not the question I'd wanted to ask but words were failing me completely.

I heard the smile in his voice, and it made my stomach flip. There was no arguing with his response either. "You did say I should kiss you, Little Owl. You did not specify where."

CHAPTER 16
CALLA

THE CITY OF Revalia loomed into view about an hour before midday.

"Those buildings, they're so large!" I gasped, marveling at the size of the structures and the sheer amount of wall that surrounded the city proper. I sat forward in the carriage seat, my face nearly pressed against the glass of the window.

"Yes, the cathedral alone is very impressive. The architecture is stunning, as is the craftsmanship in even the smallest of details." He smiled mischievously.

"Can you ..."

He laughed. "I had a feeling that would be exactly where your mind would go. Yes, I can walk into houses of faith. They are human structures, not truly the house of God. Besides, I'd like to think He'd welcome those of us now inhabiting Earth, as long as we were repentant for our misdeeds and not dedicated to causing further chaos. That's one of the foundations of faith, is it not?"

I shrugged. "I suppose. I don't know much about religion. I'm mostly impressed by the architecture. The colored glass is so lovely."

"Yes, I'm partial to stained glass myself. The windows in my main office were done by an incredibly gifted artist."

"What is the story in them? I've never gotten a chance to look closely, but it felt familiar."

He grinned again. "It's our genesis story. It focuses on the alleged mother of my kind, Lilith."

"Lilith?"

"Yes. Adam's first wife. The story most often told is that she was banished from the garden for refusal to obey her husband. It's more accurate to say that she believed herself an equal—and by rights she was, created from the same clay as him—but she left because she would not be treated as lower, like Adam wanted her to be. She simply flew away rather than bow to her equal."

A cool shock rushed through my body as he explained. The way he treated me in particular, but all people around him made much more sense with this information.

"Is she your mother?"

He shook his head. I could see the scholarly side of him take over. It was a subtle shift of his shoulders, the way he held his jaw. I'd loved watching it happen since I'd first noticed over a discussion of tinctures in his room.

"No. Higher-level demons, like myself, are fallen angels." He vanished for a moment, turning inward as though recalling the event. I had a whole new rash of questions to ask, but it wasn't the time. "As for Lilith, I've had the pleasure of meeting her a time or two. She's truly quite lovely. She's as baffled as the rest of us how she had wings to fly over the garden walls as a brand-new human, but we don't question such gifts. Once you get past the lot of us that sided with Lucifer and intentionally fell, there's no way to know which origin story they get to claim. It doesn't really matter, in any case. There's truth in every version of the stories." I must have had a pensive expression as I digested that information, because his expression softened, and he asked, "What are you thinking, Little Owl?"

"I'm wondering how, if that was the origin of humans, we ended up where we are. If God started us as true equals, why Adam demanded to have more power than his mate."

"Hmm." He was pleased with my question, a hum rolling through his throat and a warm tingle crossing my skin from a surge of his power. "I can't speak to humans, but Hell is simply another realm, another kingdom, and it's no different there. Those who, by whatever means and for whatever reason, have power—strength, money, land—have a habit of choosing to mistreat anyone less powerful than them. It doesn't matter where or what you are. It's a way to stay in a position of control. To feel more important. Animals do it too. Demons, people … it's all the same. Weakness will always be exploited. There's always some kind of hierarchy.

"As someone who holds a lofty, though mostly useless title in Hell, I still see it for the nonsense it is. It took me a short number of years earth-side to realize how the system fails exponentially more than it rewards. It's why taking good care of my small gathering of humanity is important to me. I spent far too much time taking advantage of the system for my own personal benefit. I'm just trying to balance the scales, even if that's an impossible task."

My heart glowed at the sentiments of this man, this demon, who seemed to have some things much more worked out as far as practicing humanity than most of us.

"You have a lofty title?" I was teasing, having picked out that detail in his words as a point of interest. He smiled, amused by my prodding.

"Indeed. I once was a Great Prince of Hell. Commander of twenty-six legions, one of less than a hundred such high-ranking demons." He threw his arms wide, gesturing to exaggerate the impressiveness of the words, and startled Archimedes, who flapped anxiously inside his small cage. "Sorry, my friend." Archimedes made a chittering noise, a very concerted airing of his annoyance.

"We'll arrive soon enough. Though you're welcome to go now if you'd like?" The owl perked, increasing the throaty chirps he was making. "Alright."

While the carriage was still moving at full speed, Rylan opened the door. Road and greenery rushed by, and a breeze whipped in, mussing my hair.

"Out you go then." He slid the big cage across the floor, then opened its door as close to the open carriage doorway as he could. Archimedes darted out, making me gasp as he failed to extend his wings for a moment. Once he was clear of the carriage, he snapped his feathers out and glided alongside before taking off out of sight. Rylan shut the door with a snap and set the cage on the far side of the floor.

As his hands returned to his lap, his mouth curled into a rueful grin. "Where were we?"

"Your title," I provided helpfully.

"Yes of course. In any case, the pit was not ... a thoroughly fulfilling life for someone like me. I requested to come here so I could further my studies in astronomy, among other things."

"Can you go ... home? If you want to someday?" The idea of being without him crushed into my chest like a boulder, but I wouldn't live even a fraction of his impossibly long lifespan.

Rylan's head tipped to the side, and he graced me with a smile that melted my very bones as he leaned forward and took my hands into his.

"Lovely Calla, what a silly question. I am home."

WHEN RYLAN FIRST told me about the school, I'd pictured a small building, perhaps twice the size of the laundry at the manor, with a collection of desks and maybe a few tables. He'd said it was in "the city," but I'd imagined it somewhere on the edge of town with children running around outside.

The Collegium d'Arcan was far more than a simple school. This was a collegium, complete with dormitories and a dining hall and an entire suite of specialized classrooms. There were indeed a few children, but there were mainly young adults in attendance along with a few students nearing middle age. It was perhaps a third the size as the cathedral I'd marveled at, but nearly as impressive and right in the thick of things.

"We'll stay here?" I asked, trotting to keep pace with Rylan, who led the way across a cobbled courtyard with a running fountain in the center.

"Yes, there are apartments on the upper floors." He held one of the main building's heavy double doors open for me, glancing at the sky. "If we hurry, we'll still be able to catch lunch. Are you hungry?"

My stomach, ever demanding, let out a whine. "Yes. Bertold's breakfast wasn't nearly as satisfying as his supper."

"I'd have gladly taken more meat pie over whatever was in those eggs," he agreed with a grimace. He wasn't wrong either. There had been something suspiciously green and chewy in them. "Go up to the third floor. At the top of the stairs, go left. Last door on the corridor."

Rylan smiled as he guided me toward the staircase at the far end of the hall, clearly glad to be back. His arms were full of our luggage, but he carried the extra weight effortlessly. I couldn't help peering into rooms as we passed them, but there wasn't all that much to see. Many of them had closed doors and those that were open were vacant.

I followed his directions, noting that there were only two other doors in the whole of the hallway.

"Do others live here also?"

"Yes, students and teachers, though some do come and go like I do."

He pulled a key out of his pocket and unlocked the door, unceremoniously dumping the cases of clothing on the floor, then gently setting down the locked boxes.

"What will the carriage driver do?"

Rylan smiled, leading me through the open living space toward the bedroom.

"He has his own entertainment arranged."

"Oh." I blushed, gathering quite well what that might be.

"Would you help me open the windows? It gets stuffy in here when I'm gone for any length of time."

"Of course."

We made the rounds in the room, opening all the glass. A cool breeze swept through, despite the heat of the summer day outside.

The apartment was one large open room. He'd sectioned it off with furniture to have a living area and separate bedroom space. The toilet was the only thing behind a door, as the bathroom facilities were simply off in the far corner with a tub and sink out in the open. The loft was cozy, and very clearly belonged to Rylan. It was nearly a clone of the tower office, though this space was much better organized and there was a proper bed to sleep in. The sitting room had two very worn sofas facing one another across a low table. One of the walls was lined with bookshelves and the other with tacked-up star charts. There was a telescope by the bed, though it was far less elaborate than the one in the tower.

He retrieved the locked boxes he'd brought and put them on the working tables flanking yet another desk.

"How do you keep track of what things you have where? I'd lose my mind constantly trying to find something I left at least one day's travel away."

He unpacked the box of herbs, arranging vials and packets as though looking for something. "I'm fortunate enough to have collected multiple copies of my most useful things. I rarely have a need for something I've left here at the manor as I have one there also. It's a decadent luxury, for sure. Though you see all that I've brought with me, even so." He frowned, looking at me. "Where is your ointment?"

"Oh, sorry. I didn't realize that's what you were searching for. I have it." I pulled it out of my pocket.

"That explains why it's not in my travel case. Do you need some?" he asked, already moving toward me, hands out for mine.

"I'm alright. I'd rather we didn't miss lunch."

He took the ointment and slipped it into his pocket. "Later then."

As we hurried back downstairs and across the courtyard to the building with the dining hall and classrooms, I watched in awe as Rylan somehow became younger. This place made him positively giddy, and the weight of authority—and much of the responsibility he carried around the manor—slipped from his shoulders.

Students filed past us as we approached the doors of the dining hall, and I worried we'd cut it too short. There were a number of food options right outside the entrance, however, I'd seen many vendors and stalls as we'd come through. We certainly wouldn't go hungry even if we couldn't get served here.

The lofty ceilings of the hall were breathtaking. Massive beams suspended iron chandeliers with innumerable candles, and torches were stationed along the wood that held up the stone walls. Each pillar appeared to have a different animal carved into it, which I hoped to take a closer look at very soon.

"Archmage!" one of the staff exclaimed as she ferried a platter with leftover food away from a table. "Welcome back." Her smile for him was warm and friendly. "Who have we here? A new student?"

"Hello, Grace. This is Calla." He held me by the shoulders almost reverently as he introduced me to the pretty woman who I guessed to be about my age.

"Pleasure to meet you, Calla."

"Calla is my personal secretary. Any receipts you have for my ledgers can be delivered directly into her capable hands."

Grace beamed. "Ah! How lovely. I'm glad you've found someone you trust to help you with those things."

"Indeed. She's to be treated as an extension of me," Rylan stated. "Anything she wants, assume she has my authority."

I blushed, smiling back at Grace. She seemed unbothered by his declaration. "Noted. Can I get you anything?"

"Is there still lunch to be had?"

"Of course."

"And we'll need to settle the matter of a room for her, as well."

Grace shifted on her feet, eyes darting between us.

"Regrettably, sir, until the additions and renovations on the south hall are finished, we're at capacity with this new crop of students, I'm afraid. But perhaps we can impress the need for one of the rooms to be completed with urgency?"

"Ah." Rylan stiffened the tiniest bit. "Perhaps."

"Sit anywhere you'd like. The students have all returned to their introductory lectures."

When we were seated across from one another at the nearest table, he muttered, "I'll sleep on the sofa. It would seem there's a serious dearth of rooms at the moment."

"That's alright." My cheeks heated as he stared at me. I was much happier to share his space than be too far away in a new one. "I'm sure we can make it work."

Grace returned with plates and a full teapot moments later. As I was about to take a bite, I noticed a very large, regal man crossing the room, headed straight for us. His face was all hard angles, his mouth a firm, straight line. He stopped just before reaching Rylan, his towering height as impressive as it was intimidating. Everything about him was sharp and oversized.

"Well, if it isn't the mysterious headmaster of the school and archmage of the realm. Face me like the devil you are, Stolas of the rye lands. I'd hate to make a fool of you in front of your lovely companion."

CHAPTER 17
RYLAN

I WATCHED CALLA'S FACE drain of all joy, then pale as the deep voice rang out behind me. She frowned when I winked at her.

"I'm certain you couldn't take me, Magnus, despite your size, but I'm willing to give it a go if you are. I certainly wouldn't want to be embarrassed in front of her, after all." I glanced over my shoulder to find him glaring down at me, his arms crossed tightly over his chest. As I moved to release a bolt of energy into his midsection, he wrapped one of his beefy arms around my neck, lifting me out of my seat.

"Rylan!" Calla squeaked, hands out as she, too, rose from the bench.

I signaled for her to stay put, and Grace rushed to her side, carrying two more plates and a pitcher of ale, plus a stack of papers shoved tidily into the cover of a ledger under her arm.

"Oh, not this again," Grace shook her head. "Don't you go breaking anything, you hear me? My dining room is not a playground," she scolded us, patting Calla on the shoulder before heading back to the kitchen. "Pay no mind to those two overgrown children, my lady. Working out some piss and vinegar, I'd wager. I'm not kidding, you two! You're responsible for any messes you make! I'm certainly not your mother, nor your maid."

Summoning all the energy I could muster, I put my hands on Magnus's forearm and released the frenetic electricity in a concentrated stream straight through his skin. He grunted, his grip loosening but not dropping altogether. In a swift move, he spun me and tried to deliver a sharp elbow to my face. I dipped and released a ball of flame into his middle, which made him stop and grimace.

"Damn. I should have said no fire. This was my favorite shirt, you devil!"

"Tough luck, I guess." I was breathing heavy, but he was unmoved, his eyebrows pulled together in frustration as he examined the singed linen.

"You owe me one. And you know how difficult it is to have them made in my size."

"I'm sure the tailor at Whethersly's over near the bridge will have no trouble. He never has."

We stared each other down for a long moment, but a broad smile broke on his face the same time its twin did on mine. He opened his arms wide and pulled me into a hearty embrace.

His meaty palms thumped my back. "It is good to see you, old friend."

"And you. It's been too long. Are you back in Revalia permanently?"

"For now, still temporary, but I'll be around at least a few months. I managed to convince the council to station me here, as there are a few situations we're keeping tabs on. I can fill you in later, if you'd like. But you know how I love to spend time in your observatory."

"You and Gaius do love to battle over who gets that post." I turned from my friend to find Calla frozen as she watched our greeting. "Apologies, Little Owl. Might I introduce my dear friend Magnus. Magnus, this is Calla."

"Pleased to meet you, my lady. Apologies for any fright I may have caused you." He sank into a deep bow, his arm swept across his waist.

"That's alright," she muttered, slowly sinking down into her seat. Grace left the requested receipt ledger on the table next to her plate, and she eyed it warily.

Magnus pulled over the two plates Grace had brought for him, sitting on the bench a reasonable distance from me so the table would hold and took a deep drink from the ale pitcher as though it were a cup. In his grasp, it appeared small enough to be.

"Where's your fancy robe, little archmage?" Magnus teased.

I shook my head. "I find them quite pretentious and unnecessary. They're very difficult to move around in day to day. They'll have to settle for my sigil if they want me to display my rank."

"Which sigil?" Magnus prodded further. He was trying to both embarrass me in front of Calla and show off my status to impress her, I was sure of it.

"Either will do, will it not?"

"I have no idea about such things, Stolas of the rye lands. That is far beyond my expertise. I'm but a simple soldier."

I glanced at Calla, who was chewing slowly while she watched the two of us with wide brown eyes.

"You're anything but simple, old friend. It's Rylan now."

Magnus stopped chewing, eyes darting between Calla and myself. "Apologies."

"None required. It's been a long time since we saw one another. Things change."

"That is certain." He studied Calla again before sending me an inquisitive glance. "Which house do you claim, Lady Calla?"

Calla looked up from her meal. "House?"

It was my turn to be surprised. "She's stone kin? Are you certain?"

Magnus nodded. "Most definitely. Her blood is a cross of multiple things, but it's there."

"What is stone kin?" Calla asked. "Is that a witch term?"

"No, Little Owl. Something entirely different." I turned to Magnus. "How much time have you got? We've just arrived, but we would benefit greatly from your help."

Magnus lifted his plates one by one, tipping the remains into his mouth before answering.

"I've all the time in the world. I'm not on duty until next week."

"Wonderful. Can we monopolize your evening?"

"Certainly. As long as you feed me, I'll show up wherever you want."

"Nice to know I'm not alone in that," Calla muttered, spearing her last chunk of potato.

Magnus, taken by surprise, barked a laugh that rattled the chandeliers. Calla's head snapped up, her eyes wide as she took him in. There was no end to her awe where he was concerned. I understood, to be honest. He was large, imposing, and could be quite terrifying.

"Perfect. Dinner in the observatory then? Are you going to examine the new students?"

He nodded and stacked his dishes. Grace had a keen sense about people and their eating habits, and reappeared to collect everything as he did so. How she managed on her own was a mystery.

"Yes, I'll come with you to the classes. There've been a couple the last few cycles that needed some guidance. Looks like there's at least one this time." He locked eyes with Calla.

She swallowed hard, but stared right back.

"So it seems," I agreed, curious as ever about the woman the universe had delivered to me. "Let's go see how many more, shall we?"

CALLA WAS OBVIOUSLY and understandably perplexed about everything that had happened since we'd arrived, but we moved from one task to another without much opportunity to say anything at all for most of the afternoon. Even my blood was up an unusual amount, my need to be near enough to touch her amplified to a maddening level.

I'd opened the door for such things by allowing myself to indulge in pleasuring her at the inn, and there was no way to close it again. If fate had linked us together, it was a Pandora's box, and I would have to adjust my expectations and reactions where she was involved.

When we finally headed back up to my apartment, her tension was palpable. "Trial by fire is an understatement," she complained as the door closed behind us.

She had acquired more paperwork as we moved from place to place throughout the day, and she dropped it all on the coffee table in her frustration, a few scraps and receipts fluttering to the floor.

We'd shared looks and brushes throughout the afternoon, my desire for her increasing every time she blushed at the sparse contact or a compliment I gave. By the time the last class was over, we were both flustered, though I'd thought for very different reasons. I'd assumed she was feeling left out, but now with her in my grasp and the crackling of energy between us, I'd assumed quite wrongly.

"I'm sorry, Little Owl. I swear I'm not trying to make you anxious. Magnus will help explain things."

"Who is he?"

"A very old friend. He's a soldier, and a damned good one. I would not be who I am if not for him."

She huffed. "Then I suppose I'll try not to be too cross with him leaving me wondering what other facet of myself is a mystery."

"Is that really what you're upset about?" I leaned a hip against the back of the sofa, arms crossed to prevent myself from reaching for her.

She sagged. "No. Having to watch all those lovely people display their magic, wondering where mine is buried and how to get it back, all while having to remain a silent, ignorant observer left me feeling ... inadequate." The bluster seeped out of her muscles, I could feel it. Her frustration had an underlying scent of arousal, which only fed my own need. "Besides, I feel"—her hands flapped as she gestured to her body—"strange. I don't understand it, but you ..." Heat rose in her cheeks again, making them rosy and increasing the bloom of her scent.

"I?"

"You weren't close enough. I don't know how to explain. I wanted to touch you more, but we were flitting this way and that, and you were always too far away. That sounds so ridiculous, and I know where you stand on that besides." She buried her face in her hands.

"Calla," I prompted, pleased when she dropped her hands to look at me. "You've had quite a lot going on in the past weeks, and we've been together for most of it. The bond, such as it is, may be increasing those kinds of feelings. I ... perhaps know a way to make you feel better."

"You do?"

I grinned, blood already pumping in response to the flush in her cheeks. The part of me crying out to stop, to resist the pull of her was fading quickly, overtaken by desire. "I could kiss you, of course."

Her lips twitched. "You could?"

"Shall I?"

"You might encounter some teeth if you do. I'm still quite frustrated."

Sparks flew from my fingertips as a hot pulse threaded through my blood. I felt my horns slip out along my scalp at the invitation. "Mm. That's a risk I'm more than willing to take, Little Owl. In fact, I'd say you're threatening me with a good time saying things like that."

I'd enjoy every second of her tearing me apart if that's what she needed to do.

She shocked me again as she pushed herself onto her toes and melded her mouth to mine. Her burst of confidence inspired my lust. We'd had a very different introduction to things last night, but now it seemed she had located her bravery as well as her need. I shoved every denial and fear down, diving into the moment with her instead.

I used my hands to grip her bottom and lift her. Her legs locked around my middle as I sipped at her lips, licking in with my tongue and nipping at her full bottom lip with my teeth. I walked us over to one of the sofas and sat down with her still in my lap, inhaling her scent. Her legs shifted so she was straddling me, balanced on her knees.

Panting, she broke our kiss. "I want to feel you." She ground down, her skirts puddled around her thighs. I groaned, the heat of her center close but not close enough. I was hard as stone, the very proximity of her having instantly driven me into frenzied desire.

"Calla, I'm not sure you're—" She silenced me with her mouth, hands pressing between us, searching.

"I need ..." She left the thought hanging there, eyes glossy with desire, her body thrumming hot in my lap. I wasn't strong enough to resist her when she was so motivated, but it was far from time for us to couple. I didn't even know if that was something I should entertain at all.

Undeterred, she undid the laces on my pants and freed my throbbing cock. She took it into her grip, and I groaned into her mouth as she squeezed. Momentarily frozen by the leap our contact had taken, I breathed through a red haze before shifting her underthings to one side. I rubbed my thumb along her slit, finding her already wet and wanting.

She pulled her mouth away from mine and tipped her head back, a deep sigh of relief seeping out of her as she sank down on my waiting fingers. My cock twitched as she did so, her greed the most arousing thing I'd experienced in decades. I used my thumb to draw circles on her clit, her hips rocking as she fisted me in the same rhythm.

"I've never wanted anything the way I want you," she moaned. "I don't even know how ... why ... ohhhhh."

I curled my fingers, and her words failed her. I couldn't contain my groan. "Take what you need, Little Owl. Yes, just like that. I—" I tensed as her grip around my fingers and my cock tightened at the same time. She moaned as she coated my fingers in her release, and I inhaled with surprise as I spilled with her.

I panted, trying to calculate when I'd last done so, especially so quickly, but it didn't matter. It was *her*. I realized that no matter how much I fought against whatever was happening between us, there was nothing she could ask of me I would not do.

I was further pleased to find that the pet name I'd given her was never more appropriate than when she was either blinking at me with surprise or fully given over to her pleasure.

"I truly had no intention of ravishing you when we came up here," I admitted, kissing her lips softly as the daze began to wear off. Her breaths came more evenly, but she hadn't moved from my lap.

"I'm pretty sure this was my idea," she gave a languid smile.

"Perhaps. But I don't want to push you too far. I didn't mean to lose control. Well. Part of me wanted to claim you, or I wouldn't have allowed myself to respond as I did."

"I'm fine. I trust you, Rylan."

"I am honored, Little Owl." I dipped forward and kissed her mouth. When I pulled away, I noticed the mess I'd left on her thighs, and took the opportunity to rub it into her skin.

"Why did you do that?" she asked, still looking down at where I'd touched her.

"I want you to smell like me," I admitted, feeling as though I were standing outside myself as I realized it was true. It was a primal, base reaction to knowing she'd be in the same room as another man, and I knew it made me seem uncivilized. Further, I didn't care. "And me like you. So there's no question who we belong to tonight."

With her lips parted, her mouth still swollen, and her hair mussed, she was the embodiment of beautiful sin. It terrified me, but I knew without question, I'd burn for her.

When she simply smiled in response, I knew I'd underestimated her. Again. And fate? Fate was definitely in control of this strange link between us. I was doomed to follow the thread wherever it led to.

Because she'd burn for me too.

CHAPTER 18
CALLA

"DURING THE SUMMER, the roof of the observatory is left open nearly all the time. We only close it up if there's dangerous weather. Should I come up missing at any point during our stay, it's a reasonable bet this is where you'll find me."

Rylan led me by the hand up what felt like a thousand stairs. At the top was a vast round room with a gigantic telescope, plus many small ones. The roof was indeed open to the evening sky, and though the sun hadn't fully set, I could see how it would be one of the most captivating places to be in all the world.

Archimedes hadn't yet arrived, but there was an elaborate perch made from weathered tree branches and other items clearly belonging to him off to one side of the room. As Rylan pointed out the tools and described how things worked, a red-cheeked and out of breath Grace crossed the room with two overloaded baskets pulling at her arms. Magnus, grinning and unbothered, breezed in right behind her with three more.

"I never remember how much I hate having to serve you trou-blemakers up here until I have to do it again," she said, fondness in her tone despite the scolding she gave out over several depleted breaths. "Though the view is always stunning. Better be, after that many stairs."

"Thank you, Grace." Rylan smiled and took the baskets from her hands, then set them on the lone desk.

"You're welcome, Archmage. Do you require anything else?"

"No, this is perfect."

"We'll bring down all the dishes, as I promised," Magnus gave her an incredibly charming smile, and she ducked her head.

"Fine, fine. Leave them in the kitchen, I'll handle it all in the morning."

Rylan nodded, but I knew from experience he'd do no such thing. I wondered if Grace would appreciate the gesture or give him a hard time after discovering he'd washed all the dishes himself.

Magnus wasted no time opening the baskets and setting out the virtual buffet she'd put together for us. I wasn't very hungry, so I wandered around the marble room, looking at the hanging star charts Rylan had surely made, enjoying the way every sound echoed back at me.

"Calla?" Rylan put a hand out, summoning me to his side. He handed me a plate full of cheese and apples before breaking off a piece of fluffy white bread and adding it to the dish.

"What have you told her," Magnus asked, staring at me but addressing Rylan.

"About?"

Magnus grunted. "You."

"Are you asking if I know he's a demon?" I asked, nibbling on a piece of pungent hard cheese.

Magnus blinked, surprised by my forward response, but recovered quickly. "I ... Yes, I was."

"She figured it out herself," Rylan said proudly. "She's clever."

"But has she seen you?" Magnus asked.

"She is right there. You could ask her," Rylan gestured to me with one hand. Magnus raised an eyebrow and tilted his head. I assumed that meant his question had been redirected to me.

"I have."

"Were you afraid of him?"

"No. I have no reason to fear Rylan. I find him quite handsome, regardless of which form he's in."

Magnus's face went from confusion to blank as he blinked, considering my response. After a heavy moment, his expression changed to pure joy.

"So, you've finally found one, have you?" he asked Rylan.

"Perhaps. There's certainly ... *something* at play."

Magnus nearly dropped his plate. "By the stones. You lucky bastard. Take the gift fate is offering, my friend. I can see you questioning it, but you should not."

I couldn't help but blush under the awed scrutiny of the two men. While appreciated, their staring made me uncomfortable.

"Would one of you kindly explain what stone kin is?" I hoped a subject change would distract them.

Magnus looked at Rylan, who made a gesture of approval. "If I may, my lady." Magnus removed his jacket, then began to loosen the ties on both his pants and his shirt.

"Um, I'm not sure—"

"It's alright. He takes up more space the other way, is all."

"Other way? Wait, *more* space? How much larger could he ge—"

With a horrid scraping sound and a roar that made me want to cover my ears with my hands, Magnus became a larger, stone version of himself. Size and skin aside, the changes included lion's paws for feet, fangs protruding upward from his bottom jaw, and massive wings with vicious spear points at the tips made of dark bone.

I stared, drawn to touch his arm to see what his new rough, gray skin felt like. "Oh my. You're even more massive than you were already," I said, to which he laughed. The sound was even more booming, the way it rolled around the marble observatory amplified. "May I?"

"Of course, my lady."

"I am no lady, but thank you." I stepped forward and put my hand into his, running the pads of my fingers along his palm. He'd grown such that my whole hand barely covered three of his fingers. "It's not as rough as I thought," I muttered. "And it's warm."

I looked up to find both of them beaming at me, bemused.

"You're truly unbothered." Magnus was shocked, his mouth remaining parted as he stared at me. He turned to Rylan, who set his plate down and transformed as well.

He was always beautiful, but there was something special about him with horns, wings, and red eyes that made my heart stutter. "Truly," I confirmed, walking over to Rylan so I could run my hand over a horn and gaze into his ruby eyes.

Magnus cleared his throat, giving us a moment as he shifted. Once he was back to his regular abnormally large size, he tightened up the lacings on his clothing. "*I'm* stone kin," he said, tearing my attention away from Rylan's adoring gaze. "We were created to protect humanity from evil."

"Gargoyles," I muttered, wondering how it could be possible I was in any way even partially like him.

"Yes. We're of two houses—gargoyle and grotesque. Though gargoyle is most commonly used to classify us all."

"What's the difference?"

Magnus made a frustrated noise in his throat. "If you're asking my personal opinion, not a damn thing. If you ask those dedicated to keeping the two factions separate, everything. In the beginning, the gargoyles were water keepers. We literally funneled water away from buildings to prevent damage and were charged with guarding against creatures like your beloved devil here."

"We'll get to how you and I met in due time, old friend." Rylan smiled, having returned to his wholly human self once again.

"Grotesques were not given that ability. They were purely decorative, aside from the whole soldiers-against-evil thing. The purpose is the same. We are of the same original blood. There is no difference, but those who want to hold the power continue to do everything they can to insist there is, and that grotesques are somehow not worthy of rule." He pulled a disgusted face and reached for a pitcher of ale, emptying it in one go.

"How can you tell I'm ... well, like you?"

"I can hear it. There's a resonance, in your blood. A depth that others don't have. It's hard to explain."

"I'm finding lately that many things are," I muttered, ready for some ale myself. "Especially the important ones."

"That's always true, in my experience," Magnus commiserated.

Rylan must have seen my exasperation because he took up the conversation on my behalf.

"Her memories are blocked. I suspect a curse of some kind."

"And she's got magic?"

"Yes. But with no memories, it's hard to know where to focus. She's got innate knowledge of herbs and hedge witchery, but I feel something more there, behind the block. I was hoping that bringing her here would help."

"That's a sound notion."

I felt like I was on display in a museum the way they kept staring at me.

"It's quite an honor to meet you, if I haven't already said so," Magnus said, stunning me with the reverence in his tone. "Stolas—*Rylan*—is long overdue a good match. You seem a perfect complement to him."

I flushed hot under his compliment and implication. "Thank you. What is Stolas?"

"My name," Rylan said. "My old name. Some would say my true name, I suppose, but it isn't who I am anymore."

"I can understand that," I reassured him, blushing deeper as I said the words.

"Of course you can, Little Owl." His mouth ticked up on one side.

"What is a sigil?"

Magnus's eyebrows went up. "Inquisitive."

"You have no idea," Rylan grinned, and I felt his pride under the fake exasperation. He liked my curious nature, fostered it where he could. "It's a symbol. Like a signature or a brand. As Stolas, Great Prince of Hell, I have one, though it's gone unused for more than a century now. As Rylan, Archmage of Cyntere and lord of Stolas Manor, I have another. I use it on my most important binding documents."

"How do I find out what house I'm in?"

Magnus regarded me carefully. "I don't know. As I said, there's no real blood difference. Since you don't have any memories, that makes it harder. At least with a family name there's some direction to look. I'll ask around to see if anyone knows another way. One of our elders may have a technique."

Rylan grinned. "You're going to ask Ophelia?"

Magnus nodded. "I'm overdue a visit."

"Perhaps we'll accompany you, if she's amenable."

"I'll ask." Magnus turned back to me. "The oldest of us gets a little wily. The years can take a toll. But she's skilled in many things the rest of us have forgotten. A sorceress, if you will. But she's not very keen on outsider company."

"I understand. Thank you, Magnus, I appreciate your help." I turned my attention to Rylan. "How do I find out what kind of magic I have? And how much?"

"We practice." He grinned at me. "Come, the sun has set. I'd like to show you both some of my favorite stars."

As Rylan turned knobs and shifted things around, Magnus packed up the baskets, and I looked between them. "Do you have someone, Magnus? A mate?"

His hand stilled as he tucked a plate away.

"I did, my lady. We were blessed with a long, happy life together. She was slain a number of years ago, however."

"I'm so sorry." My heart throbbed seeing the giant so saddened.

"Don't be. She lived a long, incredible life. We were lucky to find one another fairly young. Probably comparable to your age, if we were human, which is quite early for us."

I stilled. It was odd not knowing how old I was.

"Can you tell how old I am?"

"Not precisely, but you appear to be approaching your third decade or so."

"Thirty?"

He laughed at the horror in my tone. "Perhaps a few less. Your bones have settled, so you're beyond the developing years. Your features have lost their childish softness, but your hair has no silver." He shrugged.

"That's a very logical assessment, thank you. What was her name?"

"Ygritte." He smiled softly as he tasted the sound of his mate's name. "We were a good match. She kept me in line better than any commander I've ever had. We were blessed with five children, which is sadly not common among our kind. She was a fierce warrior, and died doing what she loved."

"I'm sure she was incredible." I placed my hand over his, offering what meager comfort I could for his loss.

"She was. It was her fault that one"—he tilted his head toward Rylan—"managed to get in our good graces in the first place. I tried my very hardest to send him straight back to Hell."

"I have many scars to prove it. But now you love me."

"Don't push your luck." He shook a meaty fist at Rylan, but there was a quiet adoration in his eyes. Their friendship clearly ran as deep as it did long. "My apologies, Lady Calla," he said.

"I have no title, Magnus, but I appreciate you trying to be polite."

"Nonsense, if you are matched with a lord, you are a lady."

"As you say, but I'm not sure that makes it so. Apologies for what?"

As I made my way toward the telescope at Rylan's bidding, Magnus continued, "You try to deny what she is to you ... yet you found it necessary to mark her, old friend. Do you not know and trust me better than that?" The smirk on his face was pure glee at having gotten one over on his friend.

Rylan ground his teeth together, his eyes flashing red for a split second. I gasped, understanding what the apology was for. These two had a lifetime worth of brutal playfulness to work out, and I was caught in the middle.

I wasn't sure we were all going to survive the week if Magnus planned to spend much time with us.

CHAPTER 19
RYLAN

"JUST TRY IT," Magnus growled. "You're driving even me mad with your insistence that she cannot possibly belong to you, when by your own account she arrived as if by magic." He stopped and stared at me for impact. "At your very door."

"Coincidence."

He snorted. "And you instantly felt a connection you cannot explain. A draw to possess her. An inability to sleep when at a distance or to resist touching her. The desire to own her body and soul, to consume her—"

"Are you quite finished?"

"Not quite, devil, and it's terribly rude of you to interrupt. In any case, are you really going to claim how that's all some kind of elaborate coincidence?"

I knew he wasn't wrong, but my insides still fought against the notion that I'd been given another chance at something I'd ruined once before. "And if it doesn't work?" Something dark slithered through my stomach at the idea.

"Then you still have more information than you did before. As a scholar, I'm sure you know that."

Frustrated with his sound logic, I gathered the simple ingredients required for the spell and skimmed the grimoire one last time despite having memorized the instructions.

"Are you staying?"

"Absolutely, I want to see your face when the magic proves I'm right."

I grunted as my old friend leaned his body against the wall, patient as I wove the plants together and muttered the ancient incantation.

"It wasn't your fault," he said quietly.

My head snapped up. I found his somber gaze fixed on me.

"I was given a mate and I lost her," I argued. It was the same old conversation we'd had over and over again for decades. "It was my fault."

Magnus sighed, shaking his head. "It doesn't work that way, Stolas." He only invoked my old name when he was cross with me or needed to get my attention. I had a feeling this time it was for both reasons. "How long do we have to wait?"

"I'm not sure. Spells don't usually have time limits that way."

We were in one of the classrooms, and I'd left Calla down the hall in the dining room to go over some receipts with Grace. I'd tried to wait until she'd be mostly finished, so as not to interrupt her work, but had grown impatient once the spell had come to mind as a test of our bond.

The echo of footsteps coming down the stone hall made my back straighten. Magnus's eyes went wide in anticipation as the door opened.

Calla's flushed face sent a pang through my chest. She was clutching at her heart, the same way she'd done that night in the tower.

"I'll be damned," I whispered, shock leaving my energy wild under my skin.

"You certainly will." Magnus chuckled. "'I told you so' doesn't cover it, but I'll settle for having gotten to see your face in this moment. And of course by watching you be consumed by it. You have a *mate*, Rylan."

Those words echoed in my ears, fear and joy mixing in a heady cocktail inside my veins. Denial raced to my lips. "I shouldn't."

"You don't get to decide. Fate does. Do not squander this gift." Magnus stared into me hard, then turned and offered a bow to Calla. "My lady. Have a pleasant evening, both of you." He strode out the door, closing it behind himself.

"I feel strange again." She approached me, breath labored. "My heart is beating too quickly—"

"I'm sorry, Little Owl. Here." I pressed my palm to the space above her breast, forcing magic through her so that her pulse would slow.

"What's happening? This is like that night ..."

"It was a test, a spell. I'm sorry to have done it without your permission."

"What kind of spell?" She frowned at me, suspicion in her eyes, and guilt sank deep.

I gestured to the table where the grimoire sat. "It was a heart-call."

"What does a heart-call do?" Calla scanned the book, then peeked into the small cauldron I'd set the woven herbs in.

"Essentially, you use the spell to draw your mate to you from wherever they are. If you're powerful enough, and the bond is strong, you can call them from across a continent. No obstacle is too great, death aside, of course. It's powerful old magic."

"Mate?" Her eyes were wide and round.

"It seems so." The admission resounded in my chest. "It is far more common for fated pairs to respond to the heart-call. Not impossible for others but not as likely. And it helps that you have some magic of course ..." I was rationalizing.

"Is this how I found your office? Did you do this then too?"

I shook my head. "No. I was quite surprised when you appeared at the top of my well-hidden stairs, Little Owl."

"It was like I knew exactly where to look," she muttered, rubbing a palm across her chest a few times. "Lucky for me I only had to walk up the steps. My heart trying to fly from my chest across a whole continent would have made me lose my mind."

I barked a laugh. "Noted. I'll not be trying it again unless I lose you and get desperate." I drew her into my arms, forcing away the last of my resistance to how she made me feel and allowing the warmth of her to seep in. There was no way to fake this spell, nor the way the bond started to glow in the center of my chest with her pressed against me.

Fear was still there and would always be. But this was my chance to change things, to do better. Calla had been brought to me, the most unexpected, lovely gift. I would not take it for granted.

I would not fail her.

CHAPTER 20
RYLAN

"A GAIN," RYLAN INSTRUCTED, expression closed as I focused on the wick of a candle.

"It's no use," I sighed, feeling hollowed out from the trials I'd been put through the last several days.

"You're so close, Calla. Just one more try. Please?" He set his hands on my shoulders and kissed my neck where it met my shoulder. It was a dirty trick but effective.

Rylan had warmed infinitely to our bond since performing the heart-call spell. That, plus several conversations with Magnus, plus failed trials at sleeping apart seemed to have convinced him to accept our being fated. Close proximity was required for peace, and he'd made his own with the unusual situation we found ourselves in.

"One more try. Then I'm sleeping for at least a day."

"I can't agree to that, but I do promise to take you out into the city to do some shopping. I still owe Magnus a new shirt, and there are a number of places I'd like to take you."

I brightened. We'd been so busy putting me through a battery of tests trying to determine how much and what kind of magic I was capable of, we hadn't even left the collegium grounds.

I went through the steps he'd taught me—focus on the elements around me, mentally state my intention for the flame, concentrate on the energy, then throw it toward the candle. I felt an odd tingling sensation in the tips of my fingers, and inhaled in anticipation.

Then, as every time before ... absolutely nothing happened.

My shoulders slumped in defeat.

"The others were able to do this in a few tries. I've been at it for days. Why can't I do it?"

He gathered me to his side, pressing his lips to my temple as we walked out of the small classroom. "I don't know, but it's nothing to fret over. It's only one of many things we can try. It could be related to your memory block. We don't know the details of the curse, only that it made it so you can't remember things before a certain date. They could have intentionally locked down your magic too, if they knew you had some. I'm not worried, Little Owl, nor should you be."

We walked through the cobbled courtyard and out a side gate onto a busy street. "I'm not worried. More ... anxious. It's driving me mad not knowing things. You've spoiled me completely in no time at all."

Rylan chuckled as he guided me down the street, stopping at a small cart selling roasted meat on a stick. "I have no regrets about that. The girl I first saw hiding her face from me in the entry hall is quite a long way from the lovely stone kin witchling I have the honor of sharing my bed with."

The casual way he said it made me blush. He was also making it sound much more intimate than it was. I'd been so exhausted by the trials I was being put through that I'd done nothing but sleep once I'd touched the sheets the last few nights.

I glanced around, certain someone had heard him, but nobody was paying us any attention at all. Which in itself felt ... odd. "Rylan?"

He stepped up to the vendor and placed his request, handing over some coins in exchange for two delectable-smelling meat skewers. "Yes, Little Owl?" He handed me mine, and we continued down the road.

"Is it odd that nobody seems to notice us?"

He smiled, using his teeth to pull a chunk off the stick and into his mouth. "Not at all. I always use a misdirection cantrip when I go out. If I don't, I attract quite a bit of unnecessary attention. If I engage directly, they can see me fine, but otherwise I kind of blend in. And you as well, by proximity."

"You attract attention, why? Because you're an archmage?"

He cocked his head to the side and threaded his arm through mine. "I was going to say because I'm so pleasant to look at, but sure. The archmage thing can be a problem sometimes too." The playful wink he gave was exaggerated and kept the statement charming instead of vain.

Surprised at his unusual display of hubris, I laughed. "It's probably all the black. You look very dashing and dangerous." He flashed me a smile that made my pulse pound in my throat. "You're very different here than you are there."

"I could say the same about you, my Little Owl. How so?"

"It's as though coming here makes you younger. You smile quite a lot, and you're much more ... spirited."

"I feel much less burdened here. It's likely why I avoid going back to the manor as often as I should. Which is not a good thing." I hated to have been the cause of his smile turning to a frown. "Finish your snack, if you please. I want to take you into this gown shop."

"Gowns? Why? I have many now, thanks to Serena."

"I know, but none of those were fitted to you, only pulled from the wardrobes of others with a reasonable guess as to your size. I've had the opportunity to see you well fed, and I want you to have things made for your height. Your body."

I would admit there were a variety of issues with the handful of gowns I'd been provided, but they were all serviceable enough. A couple were far too large in the bust, one was so short my shins were always exposed, and another was clearly patched together from pieces left over from full dresses.

"That will be expensive," I complained, handing him my bare skewer. My stomach was pleasantly full, the flavorful meat having settled warmly. "Have you been intentionally feeding me to fatten me up?" I was teasing, but the comment struck a nerve.

He scoffed, eyebrows raised. "Fat? My darling Little Owl, you are the most delectable treat of a creature. I love your long legs, how you fit right into my shoulder when you stand next to me. You are beautiful in every way. I love that you have curves and softness to match your strength. You deserve to feast as often as you please. I will provide anything you desire, everything I can to keep you from going hungry ever again. It is purely of benefit to me to hear the noises you make and the spark in your eyes when you eat something you enjoy."

Speechless, I blushed hot and simply stared at him as I melted into a puddle on the sidewalk.

"Besides, what good would the ostentatious title I carry be if it didn't afford some luxuries? You've seen the ledgers. We do well enough between the manor and the other farms under my watch. I can certainly buy you a gown. Perhaps two, if they have the right fabrics. And some new shoes. And—"

I threw up my hands in exasperation, pushing past him to get into the shop so he'd stop finding new things to purchase for me.

"There's my girl," he said, grazing my cheek with his mouth as he spoke the words low in his throat.

I glared at him, but he only gave a playful smirk, knowing exactly what those words had done to me.

By THE TIME we left the gown shop, I thought the poor seamstress was going to suffer an apoplexy.

While I'd stood on a stool and suffered precisely a million measurements and surprisingly few pin sticks, Rylan had demanded three gowns, each in a slightly different style and fabric. He'd tacked on both a pair of slippers and a pair of boots, plus matching ribbons for my hair. He'd paid half in advance, and she nearly fainted handling the coins.

"It's only me and my apprentice doing the sewing, right now, my lord. We'll need some time to complete your order, but I promise it's top priority."

He smiled at her, and I watched her eyes grow wide with wonder for the dozenth time since we'd arrived. I suspected that she'd been treated badly by other nobles and was bracing for him to lose his temper with her over the inconvenience.

"There's no real rush. Please complete them as soon as you can but not at the detriment to other customers. We're happy to wait our turn in line."

Her mouth dropped open, but she was quick to pull herself together. "Yes, Archmage. Of course. We'll send a messenger to alert you when we're ready for a final fitting."

He thanked her again, and she locked the door behind us as we left, her order queue clearly full for the day. After that, Rylan took me to a candler. He purchased so many tapers they needed a day to make them before they could be delivered. Then we were off to an herbalist, where he picked up some rare items he had run out of. While he had what looked like a very serious, hushed discussion with the wiry old proprietor, I wandered the shop, amazed at the dozens and dozens of jars lining the walls. I skimmed labels with my fingertip, noting with a sense of wonder how many plants and roots could be useful, most in multiple forms.

On the way back to the Whethersly's, we visited another cart to get a fried cake dusted in fluffy white sugar. The tailor was our last stop of the day, where we requested a shirt be made for Magnus.

"These are usually items saved for festivals," Rylan grinned, handing me the paper-wrapped confection. "It seems you have brought us both luck today."

"Me? Why would you assume it's me?"

He took a bite of his cake, the resulting dusting of sugar on his chin and black vest so incongruous to his refined stature it made me laugh. I reached forward to dust it off, and his eyes darkened to red, narrowing in on my mouth.

"You've got a little sugar, right here."

He captured my hand with his, pressing mine flat to his chest with his over the top. "And here I thought you simply wanted to touch me."

"Mm." I couldn't find any words to adequately respond. My heart kicked into a faster rhythm just by moving that little bit closer into his orbit. I looked up, eyes focusing on the sugary patch still resting on his chin. Hands otherwise occupied, I went up onto my tiptoes and used my mouth to remove the sweetness.

Rylan's chest rattled as I did so, my trapped hand suddenly buzzing with energy. "How does it taste, Little Owl?"

I pulled back, running my tongue over my lips. I smiled, enjoying the flash of red my teasing put into his eyes.

He leaned forward, capturing my mouth with his own. It was a sweet kiss at first, light and street polite, but that only lasted for a moment. His hand released mine, tangling in my hair as he cradled the back of my head. Rylan's fingers bent me to the perfect angle as he dove into kissing me thoroughly. His chest rumbled against mine as he tangled his tongue with mine, our breath melding as we vanished into a moment together right there on the street corner.

If I'd thought his misdirection cantrip was at all unnecessary before, that was not the case now. I was perfectly happy to disappear altogether from the passersby on the busy street so that I could remain in that place where my heart beat only for him a while longer.

When he finally pulled away, my lips felt swollen and tingly, and his canine teeth had dropped into sharp points. I reached up to run my fingers along his scalp before the horns retracted again.

Rylan took in a deep breath. "You'll be the death of my reputation, but I don't mind." He smiled broadly.

"Me? Ruin your reputation?"

"You're the first woman to be seen on my arm ... ever." He shrugged, leading me across the street toward the tailor once more. "I'm sure tongues are wagging despite the cantrip. Does that bother you?"

I thought about it. Ego be damned, being seen on his arm felt wonderful. "No. Should it?"

"I suppose not." He grinned, revealing every ounce of the playful devil he was. "Eat your cake, Little Owl."

The way his eyes grazed along every curve of my body made those parts burn. He finished his own treat, then licked the evidence from his fingertips—and mine, with a tantalizing twirl of his tongue—before tossing our trash in a street-side bin.

"Come. We've one more chore to accomplish before I take you back to the apartment, and I'd like to get it done expediently."

I certainly wasn't going to argue with that.

CHAPTER 21
RYLAN

MAGNUS STALKED DOWN the hall in our direction just as we got back to the collegium. A couple of students who were somewhere around the ten-year-old range scuttled out of his way, dipping into an open classroom with wide eyes.

"Did you happen to buy me a shirt during your outing, little archmage?" he teased.

"As a matter of fact, I did. Same color, even," I raised my brows at him as he fell into step with Calla and I. We all moved toward an oval table with stout chairs that Grace had drummed up from somewhere once it was decided he'd be sticking around a while. The long tables were great for the students, but the benches were not built to withstand adult gargoyle use.

"You lot are going to require your very own kitchen staff, I can tell," Grace lamented, appearing as she usually did right at the moment she was needed with her arms full of treats. "Shall I put through my request for help now or later?"

"You know I'm happy to entertain any needs you come to me with," I assured her.

"Yes, I do. But then I'd have to train them to do things the way I prefer, and that's ...." She threw her hands up, as though that explained everything.

"Do you ever rest, Grace?" Calla asked with a smile. I suspected the two of them were on their way to becoming friends and could not have been happier about it, for the both of them.

"Not nearly as much as I deserve," she said firmly, but she softened the words with a wink. "You know better than anyone that I'm more than adequately taken care of for my labors, and I love what I do. Now, is it full dinner you need or just these snacks and drinks?"

"As if you have to ever have to ask me such a question," Magnus groused.

"As if I were even asking *you*. I've had to double my food budget since you arrived." She gave him back as good he dished out to her, and they both loved every minute.

"Well, I never! Treating an honored guest like a burden. Worry not for your blessed budget, I'll only be here a few more days, little kitchen witch. Are you going to sit there and let her speak to me in such a manner, Archmage?" He feigned indignation as he flung an arm wildly her direction. Calla looked as though she weren't sure whether to be amused or horrified.

"*Let* her? I don't allow Grace to do a single thing. This is her domain, she's in charge. Besides, you know exactly how much you eat." I shrugged.

"That's right. And you'll get what I serve and be happy about it, you spoiled, overgrown boulder." She stalked off, throwing a wink over her shoulder at us as she went. "Witch indeed."

Magnus's laugh started as a slow grating rumble in his chest but quickly rolled out as a chandelier-rattling boom. He would likely never stop mourning Ygritte, and Grace had her own messy history with love. Still, they were a good match energy-wise, and it was nice to see them both enjoying such a boisterous friendship.

"Were you successful in your outing today then?" Magnus asked, turning his friendly attention to Calla.

"I'll let you know when the gowns"—she put heavy emphasis on the *s* as she leveled a gaze at me—"are ready for the final fitting."

Magnus smiled, shaking his head. "He does have a tendency to overdo, at times. Take it as the highest of compliments."

"The luxury is new to me. I'm sure of that, even with no memories. In any case, I've given him plenty of trouble over it already. And it wasn't only items for me, his trip to the apothecary and herbalist may have made my jaw drop a little. And his candle order required an extra day for preparation. Though your shirt should be delivered with them, so it worked out nicely."

"Is it a nice linen? The one he ruined was soft as butter."

"He spared no expense."

"You're both horrible gossips," I admonished. My chest felt warm, a happy sensation skating across my skin as my energy responded to the banter. "I'm sitting right here, you know."

"It would be far less fun if you were not." Magnus smiled. "Did the herbalist have anything of interest in today?" he asked me.

Magnus had shared with me that there was someone distributing potions, curses, charms and other magical contraband underground in the city. A few people had ended up injured and worse. The stone kin were working overtime trying to suss out the source of the issue, among other things. I'd offered to use some of my trusted sources to see if I could help.

"Sadly, nothing of interest, though he said he'd start asking around for special orders."

"Mm." Magnus nodded.

Calla watched the exchange with mild curiosity. I disliked keeping her in the dark in such a way, but there was no need to put her in potential danger with such knowledge without reason.

Grace delivered our plates—two for Magnus—and pitchers of ale. We made short work of her poultry pies, my plan to take the plates back to the kitchen myself were thwarted when Grace came back before I could even stand with baskets full of wine, cheese, and fruit.

"For dessert. I know you're headed to the observatory or somewhere else, and you'll be needing a midnight nibble."

"Thank you, Grace." I was grateful as always to have her manning our kitchen.

"What about me?" Magnus asked, tone soft as he pulled a full pout.

"Will you not be with them?"

He stared at her long enough she threw up her hands. "One more basket. But that's all."

As she stomped back to the kitchen, the smile on Magnus's face grew broad. Yes, it was nice to see them both healing in the best way they knew how.

"YGRITTE WAS SO very angry with me," Magnus reminisced. "She just *knew* you weren't like the others. We fought about it more than once, and we never did that. At least not intentionally or where it didn't end in bed, that is."

"And she was right," I reminded him, as always. It was a dance we never skipped steps on.

"So she was." Magnus sighed, a dreamy smile on his face. I suspected he was reliving some of the many impassioned conversations he and his mate had over the subject of demons.

"You feel guilty," Calla assessed, looking at my friend's downcast eyes. "About the lower-level demons."

We'd spent the better part of the evening drinking wine in the upstairs apartment, discussing the past. Calla was a very patient observer as we rehashed memories up to several centuries old.

To my amusement, she even managed to absently log quite a few receipts into ledgers while we were talking.

"Yes," Magnus rumbled low, setting the bottle he'd been drinking on the table in front of the couches. "We were so blind for so many years. Following orders that should have made us pause long before they did. Millions died for no reason."

"Not all of them were good," she argued. It was something he and I had discussed to death, but perhaps her unique perspective would be the one to get through to him.

"But many that were still died nonetheless."

"If they were truly good, even only one in a few thousand, don't you think they'd understand why you were doing what you did? Demons like Rylan left Hell for reasons other than plaguing humanity and are well aware of what some are capable of. What they have intent to do."

"I couldn't say what many of them did or did not understand, but perhaps. And many did cause widespread destruction."

"So you did what was needed. I see no problem in that. And everything was changed because of you, though, right? Because Ygritte stood her ground and took it up the council chain? Is that not worth something?"

"Hear! Hear!" I raised my glass in toast to her sentiments.

"I suppose." Magnus sagged as he let out a breath. The heaviness of the deaths caused by his hand weighed on him. They always had. It's part of what made him a good leader. "You are a very clever woman, Calla. And I thank you for trying to soothe my spirit about my past deeds, whether I deserve it or not.

"In any case, Ygritte saw this detestable creature studying the sky instead of wreaking havoc and decided he was different. No matter how many times I tried to kill him, he simply wouldn't die. I'd get an earful from my wife about trying to end him. Didn't seem worth it to keep trying after so long. It was demoralizing in every sense."

"And look how that turned out," I teased.

"She wasn't wrong about much," he relented, the frown on his mouth cracking the smallest bit.

Calla's brow knit. "When demons are killed, don't they go back to Hell?"

I couldn't help but smile. There was nothing much that got past this woman. It was an excellent question. "They do. But with most things to do with death, there are caveats."

"Meaning?"

"They wouldn't necessarily remember who they were before they were slain. They might be sentenced to inhabit a new area of Hell. Or a new form. Even those like me, who are not here with the sole intent of creating chaos, might end up being tortured after dying. There are many, many punishments in the pit that eliminate all positive thought. That's the point. The whole thing is quite messy. Dead is dead, at least temporarily."

"And permanently, if they are killed with certain weapons imbued with Light," Magnus added, gritting his teeth. He owned a handful of such weapons, though he didn't use any of them unless absolutely necessary.

"Light?"

"Blessed by angels," I clarified. "The ore might be threaded with wing feathers or a tiny drop of their blood or some other heavenly material. There's no coming back from that if you're a demon. Well. Most demons."

"Indeed, there are a select few tough bastards who've managed to survive blades like that." Magnus smirked.

"To be fair, it wasn't at all fun," I reassured him. The searing pain, though centuries old now, was easy enough to conjure a memory of. One of my run-ins with Magnus had left me in much the same shape Cross had left Calla on the floor of her room in.

"I'm sure not. At the time, I was quite sure you deserved it. Have I apologized for that?"

"No, you haven't."

"Mm," he grunted, a smirk lifting the corner of his mouth. No apology had been, or would be forthcoming, I was sure of it. At least not with actual words. He slapped his palms on his thighs and stood. "I'm going up to the observatory. I need ... time. And air. Perhaps Archimedes will be back from his carousing, and I can greet him properly for a change. We've been barely missing one another all week." He bowed to Calla. "Good night, my lady."

"Good night, Magnus."

I stood, walking my friend to the door.

"She's ... spectacular." He shook his head. "But you're in trouble. Mostly because she's exactly like you in many infuriating ways. Though on her, those qualities are much less grating and far more attractive."

I glanced over my shoulder, finding her busily collecting the remains of our snacks to be stored for later. "Truly," I agreed.

He clapped me on the back and took his leave. I worried for him but knew there was no better place he could be than up on the roof with the stars. I hoped he'd decide to take his stone form and rest up there, as he sometimes did.

"Leave it. I'll take it down in the morning."

"Okay." Calla poured the remains of the last bottle into her glass and sat back down.

"Are you tired?"

"Not really. Though the wine is expediting that process."

"Do you have more questions?" I asked, feeling her curiosity as she stared at me, her head tilted slightly to the side.

"Many," she confirmed.

"Any I can answer relatively easily?"

"Do you miss being a soldier? Or a commander, I guess?"

"No. Never. It's a terribly difficult life. Though I'm grateful for the skills I learned doing it and coming up the ranks. I always enjoyed making sure my legions were educated, fed, cared for. I just do that on a smaller scale now."

"Do you like to fight? The act itself, if not with deadly intent."

I sat down, feeling somehow unprepared for her well-thought-out questions. "Yes. I love to battle with swords. It's like dancing—very thoughtful and delicate when done properly. It's one of the many requirements here at the school. Everyone should know how to defend themselves."

"Will you teach me?"

My blood pounded in my ears. Until she'd asked, I'd not thought of doing any such thing. But after hearing her suggesting it, the thought became beyond tempting. "Yes. If you'd like."

Her eyes sparkled. "I think I would like to know how to take care of myself in that way. You would trust me with a sword?"

"We'd start with daggers, but yes, of course I would. The notion is ... very appealing, in fact."

Her smile was slow, but I could feel she agreed with my assessment. "Will you show me your scars?" Her eyes were dark, her pupils enlarged as she watched me. It was unusual that I felt like the prey instead of the predator, but I was certain she would pounce given the opportunity.

My breath stalled. She never failed to surprise me, and always in the most unique and intriguing of ways. "As you wish, Little Owl."

CHAPTER 22
CALLA

THERE WAS SOMETHING wild trapped in my chest, trying to escape through my ribs, I was sure of it. I struggled to breathe in deeply through my nose as Rylan led me into the bathing room by the hand. I'd asked for this, and I definitely wanted it, but the anticipation made my heart pound frantically. Even the wine I'd drunk wasn't helping to slow things down.

He started the water running in the oversized tub.

"Do you have these made special?" I asked, gesturing at the massive basin. "I've never seen the like."

He paused, looking up at me through his loose hair as he tested the water temperature with his fingers.

"No? I do, but I didn't think they were so odd."

I shook my head. "The one we had at the farm was tiny. I could barely fit in it with my knees folded up to my chest—" I stopped mid-sentence, heart thumping for a very different reason than it had been. I pulled in a breath, realizing what I'd said.

"Go on, Little Owl. Tell me more." Rylan came around and sat on the edge of the tub, taking my hands into his as I processed what I'd said and tried desperately to grab onto the memory that floated through my mind. The warm current of his energy soothed me as he rubbed the backs of my hands with his thumbs, gazing up at me encouragingly.

"It was like half the size of this. Round. So shallow there was no way to soak in it at all. The bathroom was always dark because there were no windows, even with oil lamps or candles. The floor was rough wood, so thoroughly walked it never seemed to come all the way clean. Our soap was homemade ..." I scrunched my eyes closed, trying to hold onto the visual with all my might. "Gram made it. From goat's milk. It smelled like lavender."

Rylan let go of my hands and leaned over to turn off the water as I opened my eyes. Tears threatened to spill over, I was so overwhelmed. He pulled me into the vee of his legs, wrapping his arms around my hips and pressing his cheek into my middle.

"You're doing so wonderfully, Calla. Do you remember anything else?" His words were muffled, his breath hot even through the fabric covering my skin.

He started pulling at the laces on the back of my dress as I used my fingers to comb through his thick, long hair. I was oddly empowered by the fact that he'd positioned himself lower than me. I didn't know if it was intentional, but I had a hard time believing that he did anything that wasn't well thought out. Rylan turned his face upward, his golden eyes soft.

"No ... there's nothing else." The image was already fading, though the feeling of the rough wood floor against my feet lingered. "What does it mean?" I asked. "What's working to bring the memories back?" A few tears slipped out as I looked down at him, one landing on the corner of his mouth.

His tongue poked out and he tasted it, smiling as he slowly rose to his feet. He pressed his lips to my cheeks, kissing away my tears. "I don't know." He turned me around and finished untying my laces. "Perhaps you should drink more wine?"

"That feels too easy." I couldn't help but smile at his answer.

"I agree. Perhaps it's the tinctures or the tea. Or the crystals in your pockets." He raised an eyebrow and patted my thighs, the small collection of pretty stones I'd taken to carting around with me rattling at his touch. "You said you were having fewer headaches, and the dreams have been better. It could be all the things combined."

Feeling more drunk on his gentle touches and affection than the wine, I started pulling his shirt from the waistband of his pants. "Maybe it's you," I suggested, voice low.

"The kissing?" He grinned.

"Mm," I agreed, swallowing as I started working on his belt.

His hands fell over mine, his face serious. "You have to be certain, Little Owl. Every step of the way. We've had some deliciously reckless moments, but I want nothing to happen unless you are absolutely sure. Do you understand?"

I nodded. "Yes. I want to see you."

He dipped his head and went still for a moment as he shifted. As awed by the sight now as the first his body grew slightly in size, horns slipped over his scalp, and feathers appeared, I ran my hands up his arms, noting a slight shiver when I skated lightly over his silky feathers. Energy gathered around him; innocuous enough, though it charged the very air with the promise of what came next.

I dropped my hands to his waist, working the shirt up his torso with my palms flat on his firm muscles. Rylan's head fell back, canine teeth pointed, and eyes glowing a heated red as he breathed heavily through his nose. The muscles twitched and rolled under my touch, making me wonder if this powerful, beautiful demon was in fact ticklish. The idea made me snort a tiny laugh.

"Something funny, Little Owl?"

"Just admiring the view."

"Mm."

He helped me pull the shirt over his head and arms, my eyes immediately drawn to the inky black script adorning his skin.

"What does it mean?"

"It's my story in a way. Mostly my rank and standing with the legions of Hell."

I traced my fingers over the curves of the symbols, walking around behind him to look at those too. He shivered again as I walked my fingertips along his shoulder blades, the spot where I thought his wings vanished to.

"Does it hurt when your wings come out?"

"No." He sighed, rolling the muscles as though trying to get them to relax.

"Where do they go?"

"It's complicated, Little Owl. Our physiology is much the same, yet not. They shrink and retract."

I laid my palms flat over his skin, realizing that I felt dozens of raised spots. I leaned close enough to inspect that he flinched under the heat of my breath.

"There're so many. They're everywhere." Tiny nicks to deep gouges, there were scars covering the whole expanse of his back. I'd been this near before but clearly hadn't looked closely enough to notice. There were hardly any large areas of his bronze flesh left unmarred.

Rylan spun, pulling me into his chest. His eyes had faded back to amber when he gazed down at me, though his horns still sat proudly along his black hair. "They don't hurt anymore. Some never did to begin with. And maybe a tenth of them belong to Magnus. Though some of the larger ones are his, like this one." He took my hand into his and used his fingers to guide mine along a strip of knotty scar tissue, right over his heart. "He was sure that was going to be the one that sent me back to Hell." He smirked. "Burned like nothing I've ever felt, but it still wasn't enough."

His chest was as abused as his back, and I took my time exploring the planes and dips. He pressed my hands into his body with his as I reached his waistband. "Calla."

"Rylan," I challenged him.

He removed his hands from mine, red flashes back in his eyes as he watched me undo his belt, then the lashings on his pants. He caught my wrist as the fastenings gave way, pressing my palm to his cheek as he came forward to kiss me. As he licked at my mouth with his tongue, I felt the change in him. He kissed me in earnest, releasing my hand so he could wrap his arm around my body. A slight shift turned us to the side and my eyes opened enough to see his wings expand across the room before they folded around us both, cocooning me in semi-darkness as he devoured me, lips, teeth and tongue.

My fingers slid into the waistband of his pants and teased along the edges of the fabric. My mouth was under siege by his, electricity gathering in the small space between us as I pushed them off his hips and toward the floor.

His mouth pulled away from mine, and I sank to my knees. His cock was hard and proud, jutting up toward his stomach. I'd had it in my hand before but never my mouth. Having come face-to-face with all of him, I realized that's what I wanted to do.

"Calla," he groaned in warning, but I didn't stop. I wrapped my fingers around him near the base and took him into my mouth. His wings drooped for a moment before tightening around us once more.

I tasted iron and salt as I twirled my tongue around his tip while saliva pooled at the back of my throat. I cautiously tightened my fingers around him and pressed forward with my mouth. Rylan groaned. I looked up to find his heated ruby gaze fixed on me. Instead of the embarrassment I expected to feel, I felt powerful. He was at my mercy with the most sensitive part of him literally in my hand, and there was nothing but adoration in his expression.

I pulled back a little, then pushed him deeper into my throat. The noises he made caused an ache between my legs. His fingers sank into my hair, a gentle pressure guiding me as I learned how to stroke him with my tongue and hands simultaneously. I relaxed my throat as he thrust forward, a deep guttural moan rattling through his chest. His fingers tightened against my scalp, and I felt him throb, so I increased the speed at which I was bobbing, and he hissed, trying to pull away from me.

"Calla. You must st—" He moaned as I gripped harder, moving one hand up and down his shaft in time with my mouth and held onto his meaty thigh with the other.

Warmth spilled down my throat as Rylan's whole body locked up and his head fell back, eyes shut. A roar echoed through the room. "Saints," he swore, panting as though he'd just run up the stairs to the observatory. "You make me lose control like I'm an inexperienced youngling." Eyes flashing, he grinned and reached for me, pulling me to my feet before kissing me within an inch of my life. "My turn."

He made short work of removing my dress while I was still inside the warm embrace of his wings, his wild energy swirling around me. When he flared his wings wide, the cool air made my nipples pebble and gooseflesh ripple across my body. His gaze turned feral as he took in my nakedness, which definitely didn't help.

"Bath after," he muttered to himself as he scooped me up and carried me over to the bed. He was in full demon form, fingers blackened at the tips as he ran them down my body on his way to kneel at the edge of the bed. He pulled me right to the edge, warm touch dancing down my thigh as he watched my reaction.

"Are you alright?"

"No."

His hands stilled, his face going serious. "What do you need?"

"I need you to hurry up." I reached between my legs, and my body tensed. "I ache."

The panic softened to amusement, and Rylan chuckled low in his throat, brushing my hand away as he licked his lips. The pulse between my thighs only sped up at the sight.

"I'll take care of it, Little Owl, I promise. I'll always take care of you."

Then he did.

His tongue lashed at my center while his thumb pressed into my clit and rubbed in agonizingly slow circles. "So wet for me," he said, hot breath a tantalizing tease on my sensitive parts. "And here I was worried about you doing something you weren't comfortable with."

His eyes met mine and I arched into his mouth, every nerve crying out for relief. He nipped and played, driving me to the brink of absolute madness before committing to a slow suck with his fingers pressing into my core.

"Good girl," he muttered, moaning himself as he latched onto me again and settled into a rhythm that had my hips moving all on their own. "I can feel you getting close, flower." He was downright cruel then and removed his fingers. I cried out my displeasure and he speared me with his tongue. He took his time plunging in and out of me, rubbing at my clit with his thumb again. The electricity in his touch made me whine. The pressure built in my abdomen to the point I thought I might explode ... and then he stopped. Again.

"Rylan!" I swore, frustrated and thrashing around. I was sweating into the sheets and dying of need. The throb in my center was insistent, bordering on painful.

He chuckled, and it was a dark noise. It spoke to my blood, making me moan in response. "I've got you, Little Owl. I promise. Just be patient a little bit longer."

His fingers pressed inside again, curling up so they rubbed into that soft spot that sent bolts of pleasure through me. He ran the tip of his tongue over the sensitive nub again and again as I became nothing but sensation and desire. I moaned out as hot release finally overtook me. My legs trembled at the sides of his head, and my body pulsed around his fingers.

"There you are, Little Owl. So fucking delicious. The most beautiful creature I've ever seen."

I panted, trying to remember how to breathe as he pulled me into his body. Cradling me against his chest, he carried me over to the tub.

"It'll be cold," I muttered, still hazy around the edges.

"I can fix that." He reached into the water with one hand while still holding me, and within a few moments, plumes of steam rose off the top.

"That's cheating."

"Perhaps." He set me down into the water, then climbed in behind me after retracting his wings. "But very convenient."

I leaned back into his chest, allowing the water to lull me further into relaxation as he helped me wash, my limbs still limp and flesh tender.

It helped that the soap smelled like lavender.

CHAPTER 23
CALLA

"THAT'S NOT A trick, is it? Or you trying to make me feel better?"

Rylan grinned, as wide-eyed as I was, as we stared at the lit candle flame across the room. "I had no part in that. You've done it all by yourself. Now the next step—do it again."

Excitement bloomed hot in my veins at the realization that all my efforts—all the days spent feeling like an utter failure and worrying that perhaps Rylan had been wrong about me having magic after all—had finally resulted in a successful outcome.

"Okay." I turned to the candlestick next to the one I'd managed to light, and repeated the process of gathering the energy, stating my intention, then throwing the energy toward the wick. I exclaimed when the second one lit. Then a third. A fourth.

"Calla, you must be deliberate. Cautious." Rylan's tone was laced with warning as I moved my eyes from one candle to the next.

We were in a small room used specifically for working with powers having to do with energy and fire, so there wasn't much aside from a few marred, stout wooden tables to be careful of.

What all could be made of stone was, and there was very little else in the space.

My hearing grew fuzzy, Rylan's voice distant as I moved from one candle to the next, the task becoming simpler and simpler until I didn't have to think about the process at all anymore. Hot power thrummed through me, leaving my body strangely alight and fully energized. A fierce ache gripped my skull, but I was too excited to pay it much attention.

"Rylan! Do you see? I'm doing it!"

I glanced over at him, confused by the pensive line in his brow. His mouth moved, but I couldn't hear what he was saying. My ears rang, but I assumed it was a side effect of being able to access magic through the memory block.

Frowning, I turned my eyes from him to the dozen or so candles I'd managed to light, a fresh wave of pride surging through me. As the buoyant sensation flowed through my body, I lifted my hands and every potentially flammable item in the room burst into violent light.

I yelped as the vice around my skull warped into a blade that stabbed mercilessly behind my eyes. The previously dead fireplace belched a wall of bright orange, every candle in the room flared, their flames raging a foot taller. Even the chandelier hosted unreasonably high torches.

"What's happen—"

Rylan snatched me back against him as the blaze from the fireplace surged toward me. He banded his arms around my body, pressing mine flat to my sides. That helped dim some of the heat but not much.

I saw a vein in his neck straining as he shouted but couldn't hear anything over the teakettle noise sounding off in my ears. My vision swam as he allowed his inner demon out and released me long enough to run around the room, attempting to put out some of the candles manually with his blackened fingers.

That didn't work, which frustrated him, but the last thing I saw before darkness took over my vision completely was his handsome face contorted into pure panic as he rushed toward me.

THE CONVERSATION WAS hushed as I swam back towards murky consciousness, but Magnus's deep, gravelly voice was impossible to mistake.

My eyelids felt leaden as I struggled to open them. I tried to move my hand and found every part of me was equally heavy and weak, including my tongue. The more I fought, the more frustrated I became. I tried to relax, hovering in that between-sleep-and-awake place while they talked, hopeful that whatever was wrong with me just needed a little more time to resolve.

"Ophelia said she would meet with you both during the dark of the moon, which is in less than a week."

"Thank you, old friend. After today"—Rylan's voice sounded strained—"it feels much more urgent."

"Of course. Your worry is well founded, and Ophelia agreed, obviously. You know how she is about strangers."

"I'm no stranger," Rylan argued. "I think she even likes me. Sometimes."

Magnus snorted. "I'm not sure I would go that far. Ophelia doesn't really like anyone, least of all you or me. I'm fairly certain the intrigue of meeting Calla was simply more than she could refuse."

"Understandable. She's very intriguing. More than we knew even this morning, I'm afraid." The air shifted as he moved toward where I lay to check on me, but he didn't approach the bed directly.

"How long has she been asleep?" Magnus asked, concern laced in his gravelly words.

"Nearly six hours now."

"Is that normal?"

"I don't know. I'm starting to think with Calla there is no normal. She's special. And I don't mean because of how I feel about her."

My heart thumped, and I managed to open my eyes the tiniest sliver. Everything was blurry, but I could tell I was in the apartment bed. I could make out the shadow of Magnus hovering near the door as though he were preparing to leave and Rylan standing behind the sofa.

"How *do* you feel about her, little archmage?" Magnus asked. My pulse raced, and I strained to hear every syllable. "Anyone with eyes can see how smitten you are, but is it more than that? We've no real basis for comparison, not even those of us who've known you eternally."

"If we're fated, does it matter?"

"Of course it does. Do you feel the emotion that should be linked to that bond? You were insistent on marking her the other night so that I, and every other male in the building, would know she was yours, but have you truly claimed her?"

Rylan shifted around on his feet, clearly uncomfortable by the line of questioning. I held my breath, unsure what exactly I hoped his response would be. I'd not examined how I felt about him closely either. Desire was there, certainly, but it was more than that. Simply being in a room with him brought me peace. I couldn't imagine a day without him in it. Was that the fated match and nothing more? Was it real? How would I know? Something dark slithered through my gut, my fingers twitching back to life at the uncomfortable sensation.

"Not that it's any of your business, but no. She's not ready. I don't feel right asking her to give me all of herself until she knows more about who she is. We've already pushed the boundaries quite far. I crave her constantly and immeasurably, but I must be patient."

"What if she never remembers?" Magnus's words were gentle.

"I don't know. I hate to think of the possibility, especially with the progress she's already made. I have a hard time believing the curse wouldn't collapse completely given enough time and effort. It's already cracked. After today ..." The thought went unfinished, but I had the same hope. I had no idea what had gone wrong today, but clearly it was a sign of my true self breaking through.

"You should give *her* the choice, friend. I have no doubt you already know that." There was a moment of silence, and I could make out the sound of Rylan's sigh. "Does she know about Eva?" Magnus's tone was somehow even softer than it had already been.

My blood chilled, jealousy springing up full force at the mention of another woman. Which was surely insane since I held no real claim on this man, not even with the suspicion of us being a fated match. I was merely a woman who had been brought to his house under unfortunate circumstances.

I thought about the heart-call, however, and my negative thoughts wavered. He'd shown me nothing but devotion since the beginning. It felt traitorous to doubt him—he didn't deserve that. I didn't know what to believe anymore, and that, on top of how my body was behaving, left me feeling as though I were floating in space with no anchor to reality.

"I've not told her the whole story, but that I had a woman before, yes."

"Eva died centuries ago, Rylan. Was she your fated mate? Is there a dark place in your soul where she used to live? Do you still mourn her?"

My breath stalled in my throat as I strained to listen. I forced my eyelids to open as far as they could go, but still couldn't see anything but shadows and blurred shapes through the heavy haze.

"I mourn what could have been, Magnus. She should not have died that way."

"You haven't answered my questions."

Rylan slouched on the arm of the sofa. "I felt very strongly for Eva. I loved her. But I did not feel this way."

"Elaborate, Archmage. We may feel things differently—"

"Your stone heart beats more strongly than most, old friend," Rylan interrupted.

"Yes, perhaps, but we are not the same species. There are differences. Still, maybe I can help you compare the two in perspective with what I went through while fated to my Ygritte."

"All-consuming. Those are the best words I can use to describe it. There is nothing before or after Calla. Nothing without her. Every move is motivated by what I think she'd want, need, desire. How to bring her happiness. The thought of her hurt or upset brings my beast to the surface instantly, and I would happily slay anyone who dared touch her wrongly. I already have."

Magnus grunted. "Sounds right. That's love, in my experience, old friend. The fated bond just magnifies it."

Love. The word echoed in my ears. I managed to lift my head the smallest bit and force my eyes open a sliver more.

"I loved Eva," Rylan said, and my heart thudded painfully. "I believe she loved me back. But it was not like this."

"That doesn't mean it wasn't real, my friend. Not allowing yourself to love Calla differently or more is wrong. Perhaps Eva was not a fated match, though she may have been a soul mate. The two are not the same. Do you mourn her still?" Magnus asked again.

My head sank back into the pillow, the energy it required to hold it up more than I could give.

"I would do anything to change her fate, even now," Rylan said. I heard the rasp of his palm against the stubble on his face. "It was not right what happened. I will never stop wondering if I could have stopped it."

"You could not have," Magnus said with authority. "Not even as Great Prince Stolas, commander of legions, with the forces of

Hell behind you and much more blood staining your hands. Her destiny was already set and you know that."

"But if I'd arrived earlier, tried harder, not been so foolish—"

"Then they would have burned you with her, or given it their best effort at doing so. She wanted you to *live*, my friend. She accepted her death and protected you from it. It's what *she* wanted." Magnus's volume rose sharply, but he schooled it, likely trying to keep from disturbing me. "I'll not debate you on that. Not again. Ygritte and I spent decades trying to convince you of your innocence in her death. My opinion has not changed. How I wish my wife were here to set you in your place about it!

"In any case, I see how you are with Calla. The way you move around her. How at ease you are with her nearby. The way you smile. You've long been a man so absorbed in his stars and magic that you forget to look around you, even as the world passes you by. Decades did, in fact. Those of us who know you well have watched in awe, wondering how you seemed to have no carnal needs at all. And for a demon, no less! But with her, you do. So embrace it, my friend. Indulge. Be *happy*, you infernally frustrating devil." Magnus gave a deep sigh, and I heard the meaty sound of his palm landing on Rylan's shoulder.

"I'll do my best."

"I've got patrol this evening but won't be far. There's been more contraband popping up, more deaths. Strange hexes and potions circulating where they should not. The council is becoming quite frustrated."

"I'm always available if you need help destroying or classifying things."

"I know, and appreciate it. I'm hoping we're getting close to figuring out where it's all coming from. Be well, my friend."

"And you, Magnus. We'll see you soon."

The door opened and closed, then Rylan sighed as he crossed the room and sat on the edge of the bed next to me. I struggled to make my eyes open, squeezing his hand back weakly as he clasped mine, the energy that was his signature making my palm tingle.

His deep exhale at the contact told me how worried he'd been. "There you are, Little Owl. Can you speak yet?"

"Heavy," was all I could manage.

"I'm afraid that's partially my fault. Here." He put an arm around me, propping up my limp-rag-doll torso so I could drink another of his bitter potions. "This should help clear off the dampening spell."

"Spell?"

His handsome face was all shadows and bruised hollows. Even the gold of his eyes was muted by exhaustion. Guilt left a sour taste in my mouth. I was the reason he looked like that. The excitement I'd felt at finally succeeding vanished under the weight of my regret.

"Yes. I had to cast a dampening spell to interrupt your magic. Even after you lost consciousness, you had power over the flames. I've never seen anything quite like it."

"What happened?" I finished the drink, and the blur began to fade from the edges of my vision and the mobility returned to my limbs.

"I'm not sure." His mouth drew into a firm line. "But we'll figure it out. Are you hungry?"

"Always." I smiled, and his shoulders relaxed a bit.

He rose and went to the small area where we kept some things to snack on. "We seem to be low on supplies. I'm going to run down to the dining room—"

"Rylan?"

"Yes, flower?"

My heart raced under my ribs, and the rush of adrenaline made my hands shake. The question wouldn't leave my mind, even though I knew the timing to ask him was wrong. "Who's Eva?"

CHAPTER 24
RYLAN

MY HAND STILLED on the doorknob. I needed a moment to consider how to share the story with Calla, but I also didn't want to leave her alone. Clearly, she'd heard some if not all of the conversation I'd had with Magnus.

She sensed my hesitation and swung her legs off the bed. I watched to be sure she remained steady as she stood. "I'm sorry." She shook her head. "I'm fine," she reassured me. "Go to the dining hall. I'll freshen up while you're gone, but I need to know more about what happened today, and I feel like that may lead us back to Eva."

I sucked in a breath through my nose, nodding gently. Calla's gaze upon me was intense but not unkind. "I'll be back as soon as possible."

She headed off toward the bathroom, and I left our apartment, my steps rushed as I dashed down the stairs and through the halls. As I passed the classroom we'd been in earlier, I couldn't help but stop to look. Calla would want to see as well, I was sure, but tomorrow would be soon enough for that. The smell of char still lingered in the air despite all the windows having been opened wide for hours. The stones around the fireplace and the floor were blackened. Dozens of candles were nothing more than melted puddles in silver sticks even though they'd been new when we'd begun her lesson. The chains holding the chandelier in the center of the room were to be tested for damage as a precaution.

She'd been magnificent—a fledgling caster learning to light a candle who'd reveled in her mastery—then it had all gone terrifyingly wrong.

I continued on my way to the dining hall, not surprised to find a few straggling students still hanging about.

"Archmage," a few intoned as I passed, ducking their heads in deference.

"I hope you are all excelling at your studies," I said, forcing a placid smile as I stalked toward the kitchen. I adored all of the students, but did not have the capacity for small talk at the moment.

"Here you finally are," Grace complained as I walked through the doorway into the warm kitchen. "I was about to find one of the third-year students to deliver this to your apartment. Is Calla alright?" She pushed a basket across the counter toward me.

"Yes, I believe so."

"Good. Did she just now wake?" Her face pinched as she consulted the window, finding the sun had nearly set.

"Yes, I didn't want to leave her until she had. Magnus was with me, but he's gone now."

"Frightful, whatever happened." She turned to grab some of the leftover cake that had been served for dessert and added it to the basket. "She'll be needing sugar."

"Thank you, Grace. You take excellent care of us all. I want you to know I appreciate it."

She raised an eyebrow. "Would you look at who's mired down deep in his feelings. You know I love my work, Archmage, and I'd be terribly cross with myself if I didn't do it well."

"I thank you anyway," I said, gathering up the supplies.

"Yes, yes. Get back to herself now. Make sure she eats the cake first, and if you need more, come find me."

I hurried back to the apartment where I found Calla waiting for me in the sitting area. "Grace sends her regards," I said, pulling the cake out first.

"She's incredible," Calla sighed, selecting a slice for herself.

"Most certainly." I doled out the food, but she was already occupied with the sweet. Grace would have been quite pleased.

"I feel like I haven't eaten in days," she complained, stopping to take a deep drink of the chilled fruit juice Grace had packed.

"You used up some reserves you've never tapped into before. The sugar will help."

She gulped the juice again, and I slid my serving to her across the table. "Thank you."

"What do you remember, Calla?"

Her brilliant chestnut eyes met mine as she calculated back through her day. "The first candle lit, then another and another. I got very excited. My ears were ringing, and my head started to hurt, but I figured it was the memory block protesting me figuring out my magic. I could see that you were talking, but I couldn't hear you. Then everything exploded ..." Her brow pinched as she set down her cup. "Why did the flames get so big? I never even asked the fireplace to light. When I raised my arms, it was like I wasn't really controlling things any longer, it was just ... coming through me. Does that make sense? What were you saying? Why couldn't I hear you?" Initial enthusiasm depleted, she sagged.

I pushed the other slice of cake her direction, and she hesitated but eventually accepted it. "Mostly I was shouting for you to pull your magic back. I don't know why it happened or why it didn't stop when you passed out." I hadn't been terrified like that in quite some time. It was as though the blaze in the fireplace had tried to claim her for itself. My gut churned, and I ached to hold her, but could tell she needed some space. I knew she was physically unscathed—I'd checked thoroughly—but watching the flames surround her had left me stuck in an odd place where memory collided with present day.

"And Eva?" she prompted, setting down her second empty dessert plate. "I heard you and Magnus talking for a while before I could move or speak." A blush rose to her cheeks.

"I mentioned that night at the inn that there had been very few others before you."

"Yes, I remember."

"She was the first and last person I'd ever loved. Until you."

Calla blinked, her throat bobbing as she swallowed. That loaded word hung between us, her trepidation at the possible implication that I expected her to return the sentiment clearly left her speechless. I ignored how her silence caused a crushing sensation to compress my chest and continued on. "Eva was a healer in a small village. A talented hedge witch with the ability to tell the future."

"A seer?"

"In a way, yes. She could tell the weather, knew what crops should be planted, and when a sickness was coming. Very useful, especially for that time. Also very dangerous."

"How did you meet?"

I couldn't suppress the smile that always cracked across my face when I thought of that day. "I was not the same then as I am now." Even stating the caveat, I knew there was little chance of me explaining adequately how different someone could be after several hundred years. "I had been making my way across the continent, studying stars and humanity. I was doing all I could to balance this version of me with who I'd been in Hell. When I came across her village, I'd spent the last of my coin and was looking for an easy way to obtain more. I wandered down by the stream to clean up and saw her scrubbing out some laundry on the bank." The memory flashed bright as I closed my eyes to conjure it, the bright sunlight glinting off the water, her golden hair fluttering on the breeze as she turned to face me. I was immediately taken by her simple beauty. "Instead of being wary or questioning me as a stranger, she simply instructed me to haul one of the heavy baskets for her. I was too stunned to disagree."

Calla smiled. "Did she know what you were?"

I nodded, reaching back in the basket for the bottle of wine and cups Grace had packed. "I think she recognized me as something similar to herself, and that was enough. I don't know that she ever said the word *demon*, but she saw me in my other form more than once. She was fascinated by it, like you, though perhaps a bit more fearful. Not *of* me but *for* me. Times were somehow both much more and much less dangerous back then."

"What did she look like?"

"A fairy," I said, and I meant it. "Tiny but mighty. I was always reaching for things from top shelves for her, but I learned quickly it was a terrible mistake to be on the wrong side of her temper. She had gold hair and eyes the color of the sky."

"Perhaps she really was a fairy. Or an angel? Surely those exist here if you do." Calla's gentle understanding warmed my blood.

"I don't think she was an angel, but perhaps. She acted like one, many times." I refilled my wine as the feeling of that afternoon so long ago passed through me like a warm breeze. "I hauled her laundry, and she fed me supper. Archimedes and I slept in her stable with the horses and goats. It was the first time since arriving from Hell that I didn't feel restless."

Calla reached for her glass. I assessed her carefully, searching for any hint of jealousy or insecurity. Instead, I found curiosity and amusement. Her inquisitive nature knew no bounds, even when a splash of envy was present. My heart squeezed. She was the best of people. I could understand completely if she'd felt uneasy at the mention of Eva, but the more I rehashed the memories of what happened to her, the more I realized how different my attachments to them were. There was no comparison at all.

"We became close friends, and then ... more. I became part of the community as a guest of hers, and ended up staying for months and months. There was no real reason to keep traveling. She taught me a great many things."

Eva had been the first woman I'd kissed or lay with Earthside. Our communication was mostly touch and gesture, though we did speak with words too, after some trial and error with a common language. Mostly, we didn't have to speak. She'd had a lovely, musical laugh that she used often. It had been an easy, innate relationship from the very start, so I didn't bother to question it.

"One winter, she saw a sickness coming. She tried to prepare the villagers, because she believed it would be particularly bad for the children. We prepared medicines ahead of time and gave them out when people started getting sick. Unfortunately, when children started dying ..."

"They blamed her." Calla breathed the words, her fingers pressing into her lips.

"Yes." I took a few slow breaths, tamping down the anger that always rose at the memory of those times. "Villagers came to her house with torches. Grieving families looking for someone to hold accountable for their losses. We tried to explain, but it didn't matter. When they tried to attack her in the street one day, I accidentally showed my true form—which only made things worse. She was guilty no matter how selfless she'd been in trying to save them all. They sentenced her to death without stopping to think where they'd be without her help."

"They killed her?" Calla asked, and my heart squeezed.

"Yes, Little Owl. They did."

"I'm so sorry." Her empathy rolled over me in a wave. The sadness in her face tugged at something inside me. This lovely woman mourned the loss of Eva on my behalf because she was a decent soul who recognized a wrong had been done.

"She refused to leave with me. Insisted I go to Magnus or one of my brothers to hide." I chuckled, the notion as amusing now as it had been then. "Hide. Like I was a common lower-level demon with no way to protect myself. She said her time had passed, and she accepted whatever happened to her."

I could almost feel the warmth of her tears as they blended with mine, our cheeks pressed together as we lay in bed that last night. I lifted a hand, finding nothing, but the phantom sensation remained. I closed my eyes, smelling the smoke as though I were still there.

"I was going to spirit her away the morning of her execution, but I made a terrible misjudgment. When I left the house to prepare the horses, they snuck in and took her. She never made a sound." The horror I'd felt when I'd gone back inside caused my heart to pound in my chest as bile rose into my throat. "By the time I realized what had happened, the fire was already lit. She'd already made her choice, and so had they." The last vision I had of her face was of it framed by angry orange flames. "I flew to the town square, but I was too late."

"Oh, Rylan." Calla's voice was choked by tears, and my previously numb heart melted once more for her.

"As Magnus said, I've spent decades beating myself up about how it happened. I should have taken her far away. I never should have left her in the house alone. I should have been smarter. But he's right. She accepted it. The same as I never learned what she was exactly, I have no idea how old she might have been then. We never spoke of it."

Calla came over and sat next to me, curling herself into my side. I wrapped an arm around her, soothed by her nearness. No, the two loves were not the same at all. Eva had been something special, but very, very different than whatever had been gifted to me with Calla.

"I am not proud of what I did, but my grief and rage were overwhelming." I fisted my hand, remembering how out of control I'd felt as the fury took over my body once I'd gotten her off the post they'd tied her to. Calla gazed up at me, tears making her eyes glossy. I suspected she knew what I was going to say before I said it. "I drew energy to myself ... I've never managed the like before or since ... and in moments, I'd razed the entire village. Burned everything to the ground with one blast." It still shocked me what I'd done. I looked at my hand, as though it would someday tell me how I'd done such a thing. "Some families fled, but not many. By the time Magnus arrived, only the children who had been spared by the sickness and a handful of adults—those I was certain had not condemned her—remained."

She exhaled heavily, relieved by my last statement. "Where did the children end up?"

"The remaining townsfolk sought refuge in a nearby village. They took all the children with them, though there were not many. The plague was far worse than Eva had dared prepare for."

"I don't think most people would blame you for reacting that way."

"Eva would've. She'd have been very disappointed in me for doing that. Archimedes certainly didn't approve. He left my side for a very long time afterward." I sagged, remembering how lonely I'd been without my companion, only my guilt keeping me company.

"It seems to me you've punished yourself over it plenty. I doubt she'd pile on."

I chuffed a humorless laugh. "You're unreasonably compassionate, Little Owl. I ended lives. Burned homes. Changed the entire course of life for that village."

"Centuries of regret is ample, Rylan. I'd be far more worried if you didn't have any remorse at all. Would you do it again?"

"Yes, I would. If something like that happened to you, there'd be no end to the Hell I would bring to the perpetrators. I would burn this whole city to the ground."

We were quiet for a few long moments, the story occupying the room around us as if it were a tangible object. I couldn't help but wonder if she was thinking about Cross. I didn't regret any part of what I'd done to him either. I only wished it could have been more.

"Where was the village?" Calla asked, and I tensed, hopeful her understanding nature would extend just a little further.

"Revalia was built on the scars of what remained of that village."

Surprise lit up her face, her mouth forming the letters of my beloved city as she discovered Eva's name hidden within. "Then you've more than made up for what you did, don't you think?" The way her brow scrunched implied that this was obvious.

"What do you mean?"

"You've spent hundreds of years rebuilding what you destroyed. Surely some of those families came back. Some of their children likely had their own families here. You may have had some of them pass through your school, even. You've paid your debt, Rylan."

Stunned, I stared at her. Nobody called me on my nonsense quite the way she did. Magnus tried, and Ygritte, rest her, had had a particular affinity for it, but Calla was in a class by herself. "I don't know that I'll ever feel I have, but I'm happy you think so, Little Owl."

"Besides, if you were responsible for the new name, you know what it means."

"And what is that?"

"Freedom of choice."

I blinked. Her thoughtful expression never wavered as she stared right back at me. "I truly wasn't aware."

"You weren't?"

"No." I swallowed thickly, the size of the name I'd chosen suddenly far more profound than it had been. "It was only a play on *reveal*. I was hoping to make something new. And her name of course."

Calla's mouth ticked, a smile teasing at the corner. "I think Eva may have gotten one final word in about what happened to her."

I smiled then, broad and true. "I think you're right, Little Owl. Thank you."

Calla nodded, then became serious once again. "I saw the panic in your face today. When I was surrounded by flames. I'm sorry for scaring you. I won't do it again if I can help it. It terrified me too."

Guilt ate at me, for asking her, even inadvertently, to carry part of this burden. It was not her fault, but she accepted it gracefully anyway. I found it impossible to believe she wasn't my fated mate. Nothing else made any sense.

She tucked herself even further into my body, and I sank into the cushions, accommodating as much of her as I could. I kissed her on the forehead, feeling wholly unworthy of such selfless devotion and unprepared for the new evolution I was undergoing by having her at my side.

CHAPTER 25
CALLA

"LEAD WITH YOUR left! Arm out straight! Good! Slash, slash, drive! Wonderfully done, Calla, now switch hands."

Rylan called the moves out to me from across an expanse of patchy grass near the stables. He'd woken me bright and early, enthusiasm overflowing, kissed me soundly, then tossed some trousers and a shirt at me. I'd gotten dressed in the strange garments without question, though I'd wondered where they'd come from more than once as I pulled them on. The minute my hair was tied back in a braid, he dragged me downstairs for breakfast. Even Grace had been too caught up in his excitement to question his motives.

It was now close to midday, and I was exhausted. My arms felt like I'd been carrying lead weights around all day when really all I'd done was hold a small wooden dagger. All my practice was being done on a straw dummy hanging from a lamppost.

Rylan was the best kind of teacher—patient, quick with praise—but I was losing patience with the repetition he put me through. I did, however, appreciate the way the trousers he'd provided allowed me to move freely and considered requesting some for everyday use.

"Right foot first, step and jab, step and jab. Slash. Good!"

"I'm about to slash and jab *you*, good sir," I grumbled, tapping the poor straw man with my practice blade.

"Come now, Little Owl, you did ask me to teach you."

I wiped the sweat from my brow with the back of my hand and glanced up to find Archimedes making another slow loop around the yard above us. For an owl, he certainly kept bizarre hours, but nobody seemed bothered by his abnormal ways. Privilege of being the familiar of a demon, I supposed.

"I didn't expect you to attempt to make me a master in a single day."

"Just imagine how adept you'll be when I finally give you a metal blade though."

He smirked as he strode over to me. His cockiness instantly put me on alert while hitting a number of my arousal buttons at the same time. I straightened, holding the wooden dagger like he'd shown me first thing. I was wearing blisters into my palm, but I could deal with that later.

"Show me what you've learned." He took up a defensive position, and I tried to ready myself as though I weren't exhausted. "Where are you aiming your blade?"

I came close enough to touch his body with the dagger. "All the soft, bleedy parts." I tapped his stomach, his chest, his throat. I hesitated, then pointed at his groin and inner thigh, exactly like he'd demonstrated to me when we'd first started. It had the same effect on him it had had on me. He grinned and I blushed, an unexpected pulse thrumming between my legs.

Using my right hand, I went through the motions he'd shown me. I darted forward, blade pointed at his middle, then slashed as though I were going to cut him from shoulder to waist. He artfully moved out of my way, defending against my well-placed moves with ease.

"Excellent." His grin was lustful as he gazed down at me, perpetually dancing a breath out of reach or knocking his metal blade against my wooden one to block my moves.

He allowed me to jab the blade into his stomach, then took advantage of the momentary thrill of me having landed a blow to capture my body with his. He spun me around, my back plastered against his front. He locked my arm above my head with his in one swift move, his other arm across my chest, blade at my throat. "We'll work on strategy another time, shall we?" There was a growl in his voice, his breath hot on my neck as he spoke.

"I still got a jab in. I'm counting it."

"As you should, little flower. I'm actually quite looking forward to the day you've got steel in your hand. You'll be a formidable foe, I'm certain. I'd happily bleed for you."

He spun me again after putting his blade back in the scabbard on his hip, holding me as though we were lovers at a ball. His gaze was heated, adoration flowing from his touch in gentle humming waves.

"It sounds as though you *want* me to stab you," I said, my laugh dying in my throat as I took a good look at his face. His mouth was parted enough I could see his tongue resting right at the corner. His teeth had become the tiniest bit pointed, and his eyes were a lustful red.

He did, without question. It turned him *all* the way on.

I wasn't sure what to do with all that, but I'd reacted in a similar way to his hand and blade at my throat, so we were pretty evenly matched. My hesitation as I studied him left all the opening he needed. He dove in to kiss me, our teeth knocking together in his rush. His arms banded around me, and he walked me backward toward a small cluster of trees without ever breaking the kiss. He dove in time after time to sip at my lips, his tongue darting into my mouth to lick and taste before he'd pull away ... just to do it all over again.

Once we were in the shade of the tree, his wings snapped out wide, a brief dark shadow across his back before wrapping around us. I'd never said a word, but he clearly knew I loved the little cocoon they made for us—safe and warm and private.

I moaned as he bit into my full bottom lip and pressed his body closer to mine. His arousal was very evident against my stomach, and the tang of iron and wine filled my senses.

"I very much like the way you look in those trousers, Little Owl," he growled against my throat, leaving a wet trail of nips and sucks all the way down to my collarbone. One of his hands slid down to my ass and gripped tight through the fabric.

I nearly melted where I stood, vertical only because he held me up. "They're truly quite comfortable. Do you think I could have some made for me? Where did these come from anyway?" I sounded as breathless as I felt. No matter how hard I panted, I couldn't catch a full breath. My chest was too full of heat, too compressed by sensation. When he was this close to me, I felt everything, and nothing else mattered. It was as delicious as it was dangerous.

"You can have anything you want. I raided the stores for the students. It drives me mad to think you're wearing something another man may have worn, if only once." His grip on me tightened, his jealousy clear in the electric current he threw off. "We'll go back to Whethersly's tomorrow if you'd like. A pair made only for you in every color of deer skin leather they have. They'll be so very soft." He groaned as he pressed us up against a tree, his wings protecting me from the rough bark. He ravaged my mouth again. "Pliable." He pressed one of his knees between my legs, and I made a noise deep in my throat as the seam of the pants combined with the pressure of his leg hit just the right spot.

My hands fluttered uselessly for a moment as he pressed his mouth back to mine. I reached up to caress his horns, eliciting a small moan from him as I did so. I locked my hands around his neck, and he began to rock us. The power of his wings combined with the sheer muscle of his body forced me to ride his knee.

"Rylan," I gasped, dropping one of my hands to grope at him through the fabric of his pants.

The charge of his energy became frenetic as he moved, and we melded into a mass of lust and breath. His hand moved from my ass cheek to the tender space between them, his grip forcing me even further onto his leg as he caressed both openings in long, careful swipes. The pressure was exquisite and had me seeing stars as he licked into my mouth.

I gasped, overwhelmed as my climax started low in my middle and spread throughout my body. I moaned into his mouth as he kept the same pace and movements, prolonging the way I shuddered against him.

"There's my girl," he muttered against my mouth, pulling me tightly against his chest. "So gorgeous, Little Owl. Every single time."

My heart pounded against my ribs, and I very nearly passed out right there. I would have, had he not relaxed his wings, reminding me that we were out in the yard of the collegium, in the middle of the day, and there were both staff and students preparing to make their way from all over campus to the dining hall.

"You—"

"I am so pleased by your progress and perfectly satisfied," he interrupted. "You've no idea how fulfilling it is to see you lose control like that, Calla. I could exist on your pleasure alone, never doubt that."

"Doesn't seem fair." My head was losing the fuzzy edges, my sore muscles and hungry belly reminded me of my human needs far too soon.

"I'm sure you'll have your chance to get even." He turned us toward the main building, one arm around my shoulders for stability. "Shall we feed you, then, mighty one?"

"Yes, please. Then a bath."

"I can hardly wait." He linked his fingers with mine as we neared the main hall and students flocked in through the double doors.

I smiled back at him, pleasantly aware that as far as moments go, that one was pretty perfect.

"YOU SHOULD HAVE said something," Rylan groused, examining the blisters on my hands.

"It's fine. They'll heal in no time."

He clucked his tongue at me. "Of course they will. I've got just the thing for this in my medicine case. But you should have spoken up. I would have stopped the training."

"Yes, I know."

He gave me a stern look, so I flicked some water droplets toward his face, which he found far less amusing than I did. "Turn around so I can wash your hair," he said, the low timbre of his voice doing exactly what he intended it to. It was hard to refuse him when he used that tone on me, and he knew it.

We managed to get into the tub together, and while it was more challenging to move around, washing with him had its perks. The water never got cold, for one, and he was extra efficient at helping me wash. In fact, I was sure I'd never been cleaner with how effectively he scrubbed my whole body with his mouth and hands.

I relaxed into him as his strong fingers massaged my scalp and shoulders. "I could return the favor," I offered.

"I'm fine."

"You don't get tense?"

"Not like you do."

"What if I simply want to touch you?"

"Then you are welcome to do whatever you need to do, any time you need to do it. Far be it from me to stop you." I heard the smile in his voice.

For long moments, the only sounds were of the soap in my hair and the water dripping from it into the full tub as he poured pitchers to rinse it out.

Once we were done, we wrapped up in fluffy robes and went to what I'd started thinking of as *our* spots on the sofa. Rylan propped himself into the end cushion and I tucked myself under his arm, curled into the warmth of his side. I was tired but not sleepy yet, though I expected I'd be ready for bed soon. I sampled some of the fruit and cheese we'd brought with us after dinner and sipped at some of the sparkling mead Grace had rounded up. I eyed the ledgers, but numbers felt out of my range at the moment.

The afternoon had proved busier than we'd expected. After Grace fed us a hearty lunch, I'd stopped to look at the practice room I'd destroyed. The char smell was finally gone, but the destruction was still very visible. The chandelier had been taken down, as a few links in the heavy chain had indeed melted and compromised the integrity of the whole thing. It was impressive and embarrassing. I got chills lingering in the doorway. Not knowing how or why it had happened made my stomach twist. The vision of Rylan's panic as he lurched toward me also haunted my thoughts.

As we were headed upstairs, Rylan was called away by a teacher for help in a classroom where they were learning about crafting medicines. I'd felt awkward going to the apartment myself, so I'd gone back to the dining room and helped Grace prepare vegetables and bread dough for dinner.

It had been very peaceful work, moving around the kitchen with Grace, though my already worn muscles protested at times. She was good with small talk, but also seemed to recognize when just being with someone else was enough to fill the void. I grew more and more appreciative of her friendship as the days passed and was reminded of Elizabeth back at the manor.

I hoped things were fine there but could understand how Rylan simply put it out of his mind for such long stretches of time.

After classes were done, Rylan joined me for the evening meal, then we finally had a chance to escape to the apartment. He hadn't forgotten about his promise of a bath even for a moment.

"What are you thinking about?" he asked me, voice rumbly through his chest against my ear. His hand stroked along my hair, lulling me into sleepiness without trying.

"I was wondering how much of a scandal it's going to cause when I start showing up everywhere in a shirt and trousers. I may even cut my hair so it's not such a pain to deal with all the time."

"Hmm." Rylan's amusement came through as warm energy against my skin. "I can't think of anything I'd like more." His tone darkened after a brief pause. "Though I'll certainly have to skin alive any man who dares allow his eyes to linger too long on you."

I wheezed a laugh. "That's a bit much, don't you think?"

"No. I know exactly what you look like in those clothes and precisely how they made me feel. If you add shortened hair I can easily sink my fingers into and grab without a braid in my way?" His smile was warm, a perfect contrast to his threatening words. "Devastating. But tempting to others, the same as me. It would be a fine line between admiration and fantasizing, and I might spend unreasonable amounts of time trying to puzzle out which side they're walking. I don't share, Little Owl."

A shiver ran through me at his proclamation. It was barbaric, certainly, but a primal part of me loved the idea that he would protect what he'd claimed, no matter what. "Perhaps I'd better pass then. I'd hate to be responsible for so many untimely deaths." He was kidding, I was fairly certain, but I knew should anyone touch me in a way he didn't approve of, it would be no joking matter. We'd already been down that particular road.

He grunted, expression going neutral, eyes unfocused as he stared into the low fire he'd started in the fireplace.

"What are you thinking about?" I countered.

"Whether or not I want to stand up again or if we can just pull a blanket over us right here."

I reached for the knitted throw that he kept on the back of the sofa. "Here's fine."

He chuckled, turning so he could slide his arm under my legs. "Let's go to bed, Little Owl. We have much to do tomorrow and the day after that. We need you well rested."

I let him carry me to bed, then pull my body against his once we were between the sheets. It felt too natural not to. I drifted off to sleep with the sensation of his hands possessively holding me to him, and his breath on my back.

CHAPTER 26
CALLA

THE JOURNEY TO the forest on the edge of town where Ophelia kept a small hut was short, but I was so anxious I couldn't help my leg from bouncing. Magnus had opted to find his own way, mostly so he didn't have to cram himself into the conveyance with us, I believed. It would have been beyond a tight fit, so I understood.

"Will Magnus be bringing a separate carriage?" I'd never seen one at d'Arcan, but that meant nothing. I rarely wandered to the stables.

"No, I'd bet he's flying."

"Oh." I felt silly having not considered that, especially since I'd seen his wings. "Do you fly often?" I asked Rylan, the idea of having a way to fly but not using it suddenly made me quite sad.

"Not as much as I should. My muscles are starting to weaken." His smile was gentle. He rotated his shoulders a few times in demonstration. Admittedly, I couldn't tell one way or the other; he was so broadly built.

"What's it like?" I was sure my face betrayed the dreamy way I thought about being able to take flight.

"It's very freeing. But also problematic. Humans are not really prepared to see something my size and shape in the sky. It tends to cause a disturbance."

"How on earth does Magnus get away with it then? Or any of the stone kin for that matter?"

"They fly mostly at night and are excellent at disguising themselves. I used to be better. I'm out of practice." His self-deprecating grin sent a thrill through me.

"Will you show me?" My heart pounded at the thought of seeing those massive wings extended and moving at their full power.

"One day, Little Owl. I could even take you with me, you know. Rides in a carriage"—he rapped his knuckles on the wall—"could be for leisure not necessity if we planned things right."

"I dare not dream about how that would be." The thought made me positively giddy. My stomach did little flips imagining it. The height, the wind against my face, the terror of falling but knowing I was safe in Rylan's grasp. Then a new idea took over, making me sit straight up in my seat. "Do you think I'll get wings?" My hand went to my shoulder blade, my fingertips touching the flat area, reassuring myself I hadn't sprouted any since Magnus informed me I was at least partly stone kin.

"I couldn't say. Not all stone kin have wings. I don't mean to disappoint you, Calla, but I would assume that by now you'd have some physiological signs if you were going to get them."

The wave of near euphoric hope that had spiked crashed just as suddenly. How I'd gone from barely getting through the days washing laundry to hoping I'd be able to shift into a stone creature with wings was an unimaginable leap.

A heavy rustling sound passed by the window, and a gust of air buffeted the carriage, making it rock. Rylan shook his head. "He always did like to show off and make a grand entrance."

"That was Magnus?"

"Yes, the dramatist."

The affection in his words made me smile. I could easily envision the two of them having races through the sky, competitions for style and all sorts of entertaining things. I hoped one day to see it play out.

"Are we that close? We're barely to the edge of the city."

"Yes, it's down this lane." In front of us, a skinny dirt road split off from the main path, heading into a dense copse of trees. "She likes the convenience of being near things but the privacy the woods provide."

"I can understand that," I mumbled, a shiver racing across my skin as we dipped into the dark overgrowth. It felt like a warning.

The carriage stopped abruptly, the horses noisily protesting crossing whatever boundary we'd encountered.

"This is far enough." Rylan rapped against the wall between me and the driver. "Come on, Little Owl. Stay close." He acted like a shield, blocking as much of the doorway as possible as I climbed out of the carriage. Archimedes landed on the roof rail with a heavy *whump*. I wondered how often he was nearby or following us when I didn't see him.

"Is she that dangerous?" I tried to tease, but the crack in my voice gave away my nervousness.

"She's ... unpredictable is all." Magnus gave me a lopsided grin meant to put me at ease. He, too, positioned himself close enough to block me with his body. "Most of the time she's nothing but a temperamental old lady. Other times ..." His mouth pulled into a tight line. "Suffice it to say if she's in a mood, we'll leave quickly."

Despite the sun being high in the sky, very little light penetrated through the trees. Only a small garden patch and a sliver across the front windows of the stone hut were illuminated. The thatched roof and painted window boxes overflowing with flowers and herbs made it appear as though we'd stepped into some kind of fairy tale. The sense of foreboding as we approached the worn wooden door canceled that out in spades, however.

"It's hard to tell what kind of state she'll be in. She was quite spry the other day, however, which is promising. Just follow along, Lady Calla."

"Alright." I'd given up completely on trying to correct anyone who gave me the undeserved title. It didn't do any good.

Magnus flanked me on the left and Rylan on the right. Magnus knocked on the door, a complicated series of taps that was certainly a code for the aged resident.

"Did you bring what I asked for?" a wizened voice rang out from the other side.

"Of course I did."

"Two bags?"

Magnus sighed, affection clear in his face as he reached inside his jacket and pulled out three paper sacks that were so full they were nearly bursting. "Three, Ophelia, I brought an extra. One for each of us since you've so generously offered to meet with us in your home. Could you please relax the wards now? They've done their job as usual. We're all on edge, and you've thoroughly spooked the horses."

The door sprang open to reveal a round squatty woman with pure-white hair. She clapped her wrinkled hands together before reaching out to snatch the bags from Magnus. "Good boy. You always were my favorite."

He laughed. "You say that to whoever brings you candy."

"Of course I do."

"You know, more people would bring you sweets if you weren't quite so difficult to see."

"Yes, well. Maybe I don't want to see more people, did you ever think of that?" She tapped one of her cheeks with her finger. Magnus chuckled low but obliged and put a gentle kiss where she pointed. She looked like his petite grandmother.

"Trust me, it's occurred more than once."

"Humph." She turned her attention to Rylan, though her brilliant blue eyes grazed me on the way. "If it isn't the scholarly devil. You've made quite a name for yourself since I saw you last, Prince Stolas."

"It's Rylan, now, if you please, Ophelia."

"Oh? If you say so." Her gaze landed heavily on me, scanning me up and down. I fought the urge to squirm or turn away from the invasive stare. "You've brought me another sort of gift, haven't you? Come in, come in."

She led us inside her house, the coziness of it a complete turnaround from the urgent sense of wrongness that had pressed on me outside. Near the fireplace was a half-circle of wide, deep-cushioned seats fit for men built like Magnus. Books and papers were stacked haphazardly on any available flat surface, including the floor. Plants in small pots were tucked into the most unlikely of places and the smell of baking bread wafted through the air. It felt like home, and I already wanted to stay as long as possible despite having barely crossed the threshold.

"Sit, sit." She waved us all toward the fire.

After putting her candy away, she collected refreshments from the small but nicely-equipped kitchen. It took three trips, but she provided the bread I'd smelled, fresh whipped butter, honey, and a pitcher of spiced wine. "Now," she tipped herself back into what was clearly her favorite chair by the way it hugged her outline perfectly. "What have you brought me?"

"Ophelia, this is Calla," Rylan said, pouring the hostess some wine and offering her the pewter cup.

"Calla, you say? You're rather interesting, aren't you?" The old woman smiled at me, her teeth few and far between.

"Am I?"

Ophelia scoffed, setting her drink off to the side. I tensed as she placed it on a pile of books but kept quiet, not daring to correct her in her own home. "Most certainly. Could you come closer, dear? Sit next to me, so I can have a better look at you."

Unsure how closely I wanted her looking since she seemed to be able to stare directly through me, I stood to move to the seat on her right.

Rylan also seemed nervous about this, and tension rolled off him in a warm wave. I squeezed his hand to reassure us both before moving, accepting the transfer of his energy as I did so.

"She'll be fine, Archmage," Ophelia muttered, stilling him as he tried to scoot over a seat to follow me. "I mean her no harm, so you can pull back your little zappy-zaps." Rylan blinked, his expression something like that of a scolded toddler, and Magnus covered a choked laugh with a cough. "There we go." She peered into my eyes, then scanned each of my palms in turn. Her warm fingertip grazed the lines there, like she was reading a map. She frowned, going from one hand to the other and back again, as though something didn't add up. "Where did you find her?" she asked Rylan conversationally. I wasn't a fan of being treated like his possession, but I had a feeling there was a purpose to it.

"She was delivered to my manor by wagon, as a matter of fact."

Ophelia's head snapped up. "Pardon? Are you trying to tell me you custom ordered her like a common parcel? Even I know better than *that*, you crafty mage."

Magnus choked again.

"I jest, Ophelia. Of course I don't mean it that way. She was brought to Stolas Manor and the former estate manager hired her in my absence. I was here in Revalia, taking care of some things when she arrived."

"Former?"

"He's dead." Rylan's tone was devoid of any emotion, his eyes betrayed him though, flashing red for the briefest moment.

Ophelia cracked another smile. "I see. But you have a contract with her, yes? I can see the mark of a deal in her palm. I thought you'd moved beyond that kind of thing, devil."

I blinked. Rylan had very briefly mentioned that he used to very commonly make deals with people as a means to trade goods, money, all kinds of things, especially in the early days. He'd assured me that he rarely did so anymore, as they were too easily twisted. He'd benefitted unfairly and didn't want to continue doing so. Gold-hearted demon, indeed.

"I have," he confirmed. "I do still require my employees to sign a contract confirming their pay and position expectations. There are no hidden clauses. She consented to all the terms."

My shoulders relaxed at his explanation. I had indeed signed such a document.

"Yes?" She looked to me.

"Yes, I did. It was a simple form, nothing confusing about it."

"Good, good." She grunted as she got to her feet. "What can you tell me about yourself, Calla?"

I swallowed, suddenly nervous. I had no information to provide to her, and I wasn't sure if that was going to be a problem. "I don't know much, unfortunately."

"Oh?" Her eyebrows pulled together.

"I don't remember anything before arriving at the manor, not even my given name. Rylan suspects some kind of curse."

"A hex? I wonder why someone would do that to a pretty young thing like you."

"It's blocking her memories," Rylan elaborated. "But all of her skills remained intact and we've been successful in putting a few cracks in the veil around her mind, I believe. She's recalled a few things from before."

"That's positive." Ophelia peered at me through squinted eyes, then gestured with her arm. "Come over here."

I followed her to a small alcove at the side of the living area. It sat somewhat behind the kitchen, and had a fireplace on the backside of what was also the oven. There was an altar of sorts set up at the window with candles, stones, and other items I didn't recognize.

"Hold this." She handed me a tightly wrapped bundle of herbs with a red ribbon around it and a small iron bell. The bell was warm from the sunlight as it sat in my palm. "Mm." She mumbled to herself as she opened the window, allowing a gust of cool air to blow through. "Come in, come in," she said, impatiently gesturing to … nothing.

I jumped as Archimedes' heavy wings flapped and he landed on the windowsill.

"There you are, little beast. You're looking hale and hearty!" He allowed Ophelia to stroke the smooth feathers between his eyes, blinking at her softly, a coo purring out of his throat. She continued on, conversational with the animal. "Of course I know it's bothersome, that's entirely the point. But it keeps the riffraff away. You know how I hate strangers cutting through my forest."

I glanced over my shoulder, and Rylan gave me a comforting nod.

Ophelia rearranged some of the rocks and crystals, then put a substance that looked like sand into a small cauldron. After the sand went some herbs she crumbled between her palms, then some coarse salt crystals. She muttered the whole time, moving things around the table as though trying to rearrange the pieces of a puzzle.

"Ah!" she exclaimed, rolling a drop of wine off her finger and into the mix. Once she was satisfied with that, she hung the cauldron on a hook over a low candle flame. "Ring the bell," she instructed.

I juggled the herb bundle so I could do as she asked, and the bell produced a hollow clanking noise.

"No, not quite." She fussed with the table again, then asked me to put the herb bundle down right next to a small pile of crushed amethyst. "Again."

I swayed the bell gently, braced for the same flat noise. Instead, a clear, resonant tone rang out, rattling the windows and all the items on the table.

"Yes, yes. Good." Ophelia smiled again and stepped back as a cat jumped through the open window and perched on the sill beside Archimedes. The two creatures briefly bumped their foreheads together, then the cat rubbed along the bird with her side. It was the oddest interaction, especially considering the overly large size of them both. "Welcome back, old friend." She greeted the feline with a quick head pat and took the bell from my hand. "We've much to talk about indeed, young woman. This is Morticia. She says she's to go with you. For your protection."

CHAPTER 27
CALLA

"PROTECTION?" I ASKED, voice cracking. "From what?"

"That's the question, isn't it? That's the part none of us know until we get there." The ominous words gave me a chill, but the cat seemed unbothered. I tried to pull some confidence from her careless attitude. "Her kind is similar to a familiar," Ophelia explained. "You're very lucky, not many have ever had the honor of such a thing. They generally follow a family line, but not always."

"I didn't realize witches actually had those. Not really. Not outside of stories." I realized how foolish that sounded, especially considering I knew Rylan was a mage who had an owl as a familiar. But I was flustered and had started sweating, desperate not to offend the large black-and-white cat. Meanwhile, the feline was swishing her tail and watching me with relative disinterest in her greenish-gold eyes.

"I was told there's much you don't know. You're here to learn, are you not?"

"Yes," I agreed. I reached out a hand toward the cat, relieved when she ducked forward and rubbed her cheeks on my fingers. "Pleased to meet you." It felt odd to speak to a cat in such a way, but I could tell she was more than *just* a cat.

After performing a very feline stretch that went from her nose to her toes, she plodded across the table with no regard for Ophelia's things or the placement of them. She dropped to the floor and crossed the room with a little prance toward Rylan. She sniffed Rylan's boot but seemed unimpressed. Then, she turned to Magnus and jumped up in his lap.

"Hello, little friend. I've missed you. Been gone many long years to slumber, have you?" Magnus greeted her in much the same way Ophelia had, which made me wonder how ancient the cat might be. His large hand made even the oversized cat seem small, but she gratefully accepted his rubs and scratches after giving a big yawn.

"I need a drop of blood for this next part," Ophelia said, not waiting even a second before snatching my hand and pricking my finger with a needle.

"Hey!" I sucked in a breath as the quick sting from the poke registered, and she squeezed my fingertip over the tiny cauldron.

Rylan was on his feet in a smooth, swift motion, his jaw set and eyes flashing red.

"Sit down, demon." Ophelia sounded exasperated. "I'm already done, and she's no worse for wear."

He ground his teeth together as he looked at me. "You could have asked first."

"Yes, I could have. But I've found over the years this way is much more efficient."

I glanced at Magnus, who seemed nothing more than amused by the whole scene as he stroked the cat, decidedly avoiding the eyes of the rest of us.

"I'm fine," I reassured him, placing the tip of my finger in my mouth to relieve the dull sting.

Rylan settled back into his seat, but every muscle stayed on alert. He no longer sat back against the cushions, instead he was perched right on the edge.

"A little of this, a smidge of that." Ophelia continued to add things into the fist-sized pot until it began to fizz and smoke. "Oh. That's not—" She stopped mid-sentence, backing up a step.

Not at all comforted by that, I stepped back with her, watching as the tiny cauldron started to spark and emit green tendrils of smoke. I was thankful the window was open, but it wasn't helping much.

I felt the press of Morticia's body against my leg, a rub, and then a warm presence as she sat right next to my foot. I looked down, a thrill of surprise running through me when I found she gazed intelligently right back up at me, as uncomfortable as I felt.

Ophelia closed the window after Archimedes fled back outside, muttering something under her breath as the smoke continued to build into a cloud above the table.

I felt Rylan come up behind me, and Magnus towered over Ophelia as he stood behind her. "What does that mean?" he asked, making the tiny woman lean back to peer up at him.

"That means you've brought me the surprise of a lifetime."

The smoke had finally stopped billowing out of the fist-sized pot, forming a green-and-gray haze in a loose circle over the table.

The longer I stared at it, the more shock filtered coldly into my veins. Rylan lifted a hand, settling it on my shoulder. Morticia mewled and moved to stand atop both my feet.

Shifting slightly, the smoke revealed a kind of portrait. There was a woman with sharp features not unlike those on Magnus's face and a man who strongly resembled me. Just as I started to take in the details of their features, the tendrils dispersed.

Ophelia opened the window and blew out the candle under

the cauldron, her pensive features a cross between stunned and shaken. "Well, there's something I never thought I'd see again. Shall I get the whiskey?"

She swept an arm across the tabletop, mixing all the carefully-laid-out items together and even carelessly pushed some onto the floor before stomping off to the kitchen, leaving us all staring after her.

I REGRETTED MY decision to pass on the hard liquor about the time Rylan emptied his second glass.

The amount of information Ophelia had laid out for us once the strange smoke performance ended had my mind spinning. I wasn't sure if it was meant to be comforting or for convenience, but Morticia had curled up next to me and fallen asleep.

"My parents." The words sounded foreign. Wrong.

"Yes. Selene and Kaspar. I'm sure of it. The portrait doesn't lie."

"They've been missing for decades," Magnus said.

"The timing would line up with Calla's birth, if you're correct about her age." Rylan was pensive, rolling his empty glass between his hands.

Ophelia sighed and drained her own tumbler, looking stressed. "He is. I could see in her hands that she's seven and twenty. Her birthday is in the autumn."

"Do you know when?" It was a silly thing to be excited over knowing about myself, but I couldn't help it.

"Of course, dear. You were born on Samhain." Ice trickled down my spine. Of all days of the year, that one felt like a bad omen. She saw my expression and smiled. "Don't fret over it. It's just a day. But it's logical for someone with your powers ... and parentage."

"My parents were warned not to marry?"

"Yes. There were covenants on both sides strictly forbidding it, in fact. But that alone should have told anyone with a brain it was a guarantee they'd end up together." Ophelia rolled her eyes and toddled into the kitchen, returning with one of her prized bags of candy. She offered it around, but I declined after finding nothing but salted black licorice inside. "The line of Morrigan witches alone could have gifted you great power, but to have been birthed by Selene as well?" She heaved a breath. "It's a recipe for uncontrollable power should that magic ever be unlocked."

"But both lines were intentionally dampened ages ago. Permanently. Why would it matter? How would putting the two together be any more a problem than the lines progressing as they had been, with limited strength, on their own?" Magnus asked.

I felt the press of his eyes on me, and while I knew it was friendly curiosity, it still made me squirm.

"Curses can sometimes cancel one another out," Ophelia said, amusement crossing her face. "Or they can compound on one another and then be cancelled out by something else. Something like a secondary curse."

I was starting to understand what she thought had happened. "So my parents—a very powerful witch from a family that had their powers removed or at least dampened, and a powerful stone kin from a line that was thought to be basically extinct for the same reason—somehow found one another and fell in love?"

"Yes. The *how* is a separate mystery, but yes," Ophelia confirmed. "It's been a very long time since either the stone kin or mage councils had to convene to make a decision like that, but it's been done a few times. Selene, Wyrmrose … Morrigan, Eldridge. Those are the ones that I can easily recall, though there were likely more. All permanently dampened due to fears that they would become corrupt. Assumed potentially dangerous because their power had the potential to become too great."

"They got married, or at the very least had me, and then what?"

"Your guess is as good as ours. We've been searching for them a long time." Magnus gave me a gentle grin. There was something else there, a deep pain if I was reading him correctly, but I didn't press.

"I don't think they raised me. Otherwise, I would remember something about them, right? Instead of a woman I called Gram?"

"That's fair to assume," Rylan pondered. "They'd be in hiding since they went against council edicts."

"But I don't do ... stone kin things. I don't shift. Is that odd?"

"Not necessarily. Your grotesque abilities may be more suppressed than the witch ones, or very few might have been passed along. Impossible to say."

"If this new memory curse did in fact nullify the original dampening ones, how do we safely teach her how to use her magic?"

"Is she too much even for you, demon prince?" Ophelia's tone was light, edged with humor as she teased him.

"Yes," he answered plainly. His complete dry honesty and lack of ego in the matter made her face fall. "It took all I had to put her magic down once it took hold. She was only trying to light candles without flame, the very first step in power use, and she nearly burned out a room in the main hall. Even when she lost consciousness, the magic remained at nearly full power. I had to put a secondary dampening spell on her, and she slept for hours afterward. I'd really rather not repeat that every time she uses her magic. I was terrified of hurting her, but there are many other people, including children, that I am responsible for keeping safe also. I was not—*am* not—prepared to manage her repeatedly if she's out of control with that level of power. Not even in my other form and at full strength with the collegium itself and all the staff at my side. I'd thought ... I thought perhaps I'd been sent a witch as my mate, but it's so much more than that, it seems."

Ophelia stared back at him, approval in her gaze. A slither of shame slipped through my gut. I knew it wasn't my fault, but being out of control was still something I regretted.

"Indeed. I hear you, Archmage. Perhaps I can be of some assistance. And Morticia will certainly help." Ophelia got to her feet and shuffled off toward the back of the house.

Hearing her name, the cat raised her head, blinking languidly before giving a wide yawn.

"What ... do I do with her?" I asked, a blush heating my cheeks. I hated the way that question sounded.

Morticia took it upon herself to walk across my lap, bumping my hand with her head.

"Nothing. She will guide you. Be open to having her around when she decides it's time," Ophelia said, returning with a massive book and a collection of vials.

"What's this?" Rylan asked, accepting the items from her with a mild frown.

"Help."

He flipped a few pages with one hand while glancing at the labels. His eyes widened and he looked up at her in shock. I felt trapped in the middle and caught Magnus's empathetic gaze.

"They do this when they get together sometimes," he said with chagrin, giving a shrug.

"This is—" Rylan started.

"Yes, it is, and I know you understand how old and rare it is. I also know you won't waste it."

"See? I told you she liked me," Rylan gibed at Magnus, reverently placing the vials into a pocket on the inside of his vest.

"Don't push your luck, demon." She chuckled, and it was a dry, raspy sound. Her focus returned to me. "You'll try your best to do as he says? He's many questionable things, but he's certainly a good teacher."

"Of course," I agreed.

"You'll come back to me if you need to, but I think between these two and Morty, you're going to be fine. There's something big coming soon. You need to be ready for it."

"Big? Like an event?"

Ophelia shook her head. "I cannot say for certain, I don't know the particulars. But something that will shake your foundations. Both of you." She pointed a gnarled finger between Rylan and I. "Her being a mix of old grotesque royalty and Morrigan blood may be the least of your concerns."

"Thank you," I said, feeling the press of her dismissal.

"Don't thank me, girl. Have Magnus bring you back here if things get desperate. I'm not sure how much help I'll be, but it would be nice to see you again. It's not every day I get to visit with someone who shouldn't exist."

I resisted the urge to bend down and hug the old woman as we made our way to the door of her cottage. I was reluctant to leave the cozy hut but also wondered if that feeling was as false as the sense of danger she'd intentionally created on the outside.

Rylan wrapped his arm around me, and Magnus ducked out of the door first.

"Always lovely to see you, Ophelia."

"And you, Stolas. Stay out of trouble. Care for this one, she's quite special."

"So I keep saying." His lips ticked up into a gentle smile before he pressed a quick kiss to my temple.

Despite the positive energy flowing from him, fear and anxiety skittered down my spine as we walked toward the carriage. Ophelia clearly didn't care to disable her wards, no matter who requested it.

"I'll see you later on?" Magnus asked.

"Yes, we'll be sorting some things out, I imagine," Rylan said.

"Thank you for arranging this, Magnus."

"My pleasure, Calla." Magnus smirked at Rylan as he fiddled with the lacings on his clothes. It took mere moments for him to shift and leap into flight. He seemed preoccupied by what had taken place during our visit, his good spirits a reasonable distraction from his introspection.

"Come, Little Owl. Let's go home."

Morticia bounded ahead of us into the carriage, the door to the hut closed before we even got out of earshot. While I was relieved to have some answers, I spent the whole of the ride back to d'Arcan thinking up new questions. And I was worried that nobody, not even Ophelia, had answers to most of them.

CHAPTER 28
RYLAN

"D O WE NEED a sand box for her?" Calla asked fretting over her new friend as we walked down the hallway toward the apartment.

"I'm not sure. Morticia?" I consulted the cat who was trotting along at Calla's side. The unusually wise eyes turned my way, and I tried to open my mind. It was faint, but I picked up a distinct *no* from her direction. "I think she'll manage. We'll need to leave a window she can access open. Perhaps Archimedes will visit the apartment more often out of jealousy if we do." I smirked at the thought. My companion was stout of mind and only did things he wanted to. We were much alike that way.

Morticia seemed to approve this leap of logic and bumped my leg with her head as we paused to open the door. "We're up quite high, though, and there are no balconies." Morticia mewled as though stating that this was fine. "Oh. Alright then. Food? Water?" Calla looked down at the cat, fingers fidgeting with the end of her braid. She was desperate to do her job as caretaker of the creature properly, which was both amusing and endearing. "Can you eat what we eat?" The cat rubbed along Calla's ankles. "I'll take that as a yes. We should warn Grace." Calla looked at me. "Should I be able to hear her in my mind or something?"

"That's a skill you may have to learn, Little Owl." I patted my vest pocket, trying to decide where best to put the invaluable items Ophelia had sent with me.

"Can we work on that soon?" she asked, walking across the room to open a window. "I'd like to be able to communicate with her more clearly."

"Of course." Morticia hopped up on the coffee table and began grooming herself. "You're an interesting creature," I said. Her eyes landed on me in a decidedly annoyed way, then she turned forward, paws down as though she were posing for a portrait.

Then became stone.

"Oh!" Calla gasped as the cat went from flesh and fur to a statue with bat-like wings sitting on the low table.

I stared at the figure for a moment, then began to laugh. Of course her familiar was a stone kin cat. Nothing could have been more appropriate. "She's resting soundly, Little Owl. This is how they re-energize."

"Did you know—"

"No, I didn't. I'm sure that was purposeful on Ophelia's part."

Calla couldn't take her eyes off the cat, and I couldn't blame her. Not only had she just been told the creature was her familiar, but now it was also stone kin. That was a lot to take in all at once.

I pulled the two vials from my pocket, examining them with care.

"What are those?" Calla asked.

"Insurance," I said. My blood rolled icily in my veins as I thought about the implications of using one or both on her.

She waited for me to elaborate. I walked over to my locking travel case and opened it, making room for the irreplaceable tonics in my hand.

"One is a very potent magic dampening potion. The other is a terrifying agent I thought I'd left behind in Hell when I came Earthside, if I'm being honest. Neither are something I, or any other mage, could recreate without hunting down some extremely rare ingredients. The recipes to make them are likely in the book Ophelia gave me, but I wouldn't be brave enough to attempt it, not even if I could locate all the ingredients. Not without plenty of practice, even at my skill level. They're complicated to say the very least."

She frowned. "I thought the dampening spell you used was effective."

"It was." My chest squeezed as I recalled how I'd had to throw everything I had at Calla to make the flames recede. "But not something I'd like to repeat. It took too much out of both of us to rely on it unless absolutely necessary. A tiny drop of this"—I lifted the glass vial with the glittery violet liquid inside carefully before sliding it back down and closing up the case—"would take away most or all of your magic for perhaps a week or more, I don't really know. It's not a permanent fix, and it's not something I think we should experiment with unless we absolutely have to." The thought that Calla might be injured or worse by them made me feel as though I might crawl out of my own skin.

"We'll be careful then." She nodded.

"Yes, we will." I pulled her to me and breathed in deeply. Her arms wrapped around my center, making me feel more balanced than I had since we'd left for our visit with the crotchety old gargoyle.

Her stomach let out a rumble. "Sorry." She huffed a chuckle against my shirt. "Ophelia's bread was delicious, but I'm starving."

"No apologies, little one. We'll get you fed, then tackle what comes next."

I could only hope that some simple solutions presented themselves fairly quickly.

"ABSOLUTELY NOT." I hated raising my voice to Calla, but she had grown to have no compunction about matching my energy.

If she'd reacted by dissolving into tears—even let out a single sob of despair— I probably would have fallen to my knees and begged her forgiveness. However, much like the way she dug in her heels over seeing Cross punished, she was not giving in. And I was certain the glossy sheen in her eyes was fury, not sadness.

I admired it. It aroused me even, much to my surprise. I took it as further proof that she was absolutely destined to be mine, and my perfect match in every way. But I also hated that she was arguing with me over trying to keep her *safe*.

The conversation had started calmly over dinner, but had escalated once we'd left the round table in the dining room and returned to our apartment.

"It is *my* magic. Shouldn't I get the final say?" She perched her hands on her hips, eyes ablaze.

There was another flash of heat through my blood, and I had to temper the wild flare of energy my body channeled, torn between rage and lust. "You know not what you're asking me!" I saw her flinch at the edge in my voice and lowered my tone. "Calla, please. Try to understand why I'm against it."

She came forward, taking my hands into hers, much like I would do when she needed comfort. I hated that it worked so easily. A full breath filled my lungs, and I felt much calmer than I had moments before. "I do understand, Rylan. Completely, in fact. I need to learn how to use my powers safely. You will not always be at my side to protect me—"

"I will if I can help it," I growled, drawing her frustration in the form of an exasperated eye roll as her head lolled to the side.

"But there will be times, like it or not, when we are not together. And I need to know how to use every weapon at my disposal. Blade, bow, magic. This is what you told me the other day while you tried to make a swordsman out of me."

I got a prickle in my veins at the realization she had turned my own logic against me—and skillfully so. "Yes, but—"

"It only makes sense that I utilize what I have available to ensure I don't destroy myself, others, or any buildings in the process. Please, Rylan. This is important to me. It's part of who I am. One of the only parts I know. Besides, what if this helps break through the veil in my mind? It seems every step we try, we get closer—"

"And every step causes you pain, distress. Destruction!"

"Which only means the sooner I can remember everything, the better, right?" The frustration in her eyes had given way to sadness.

I softened, my shoulders sagging as she gazed at me in that special way she had, like she was looking into my dark soul. Her words were logical, I knew that, but the visceral reaction I had to the thought of her being in danger was riding intensely on every nerve, causing me to be jumpy and irrational.

"And what if even a single drop nullifies your powers completely? What then?"

"You are catastrophizing." Her tone was bland, and I could tell she was building up to rage again as her fingers tightened around mine. "Ophelia wouldn't have given those items to you without express purpose, would she?" She pulled her fingers from around mine. "Though I suppose I could go to her instead. Maybe Magnus could show me what he knows." Her eyes squinted a bit as she grew thoughtful.

The possessiveness I felt for her flared, and though I knew she'd poked that nerve intentionally, I still reacted. I couldn't stop it. "No."

"No?" she scoffed, which only fanned the flames of my irritability. "Why not? If I'm stone kin, I will also need a stone kin teacher, won't I? I clearly inhabit the witch side of my heritage most, but I'll need all the help I can get."

"*Also*. But not as primary. Not when you have me."

"Then *help me*," she pleaded. My heart squeezed, making it feel as though something were lodged in my throat. "Ophelia did tell me to trust you as my teacher. But that means you have to be willing to *teach* me."

"Calla." I sighed, resigned to her sound logic and very stubborn nature, even with everything in my body screaming to shield her from such things.

"I know the candle experiment went very wrong. I'm not suggesting we start with that again, or even use anything fire related any time soon," she argued, passion filling her words with excitement. "You could have me work on tinctures and potions with the first-year students. That's my skill level anyhow, and it doesn't require much magic, right? It's basically cooking. I've already proven I can make salves. This feels like the next natural step. Plus, you said you could help me figure out how to hear Morticia in my head. We could do that, too."

I couldn't help but grin. She was getting what she wanted, and artfully so. I would simply have to make it so I did too. "I think both Grace and Madame Lumell, who leads those classes, would take issue with your comparison, but it isn't far off."

She stared up at me, one hand braced on my chest, and repeated, "I need this, Rylan."

I wrapped my arms around her, the desperation in her voice too much. "I know, Little Owl. I know." After a few deep breaths and feeling her heart thump against my chest while my own tried to match that pace, I relented. "Alright. Potions. I will be there the whole time, just in case anything gets out of hand."

She dipped back, eyes lit up before she went onto her toes and kissed me. "Thank you."

"I will regret this, I'm certain of it."

"Never," she insisted, glancing around. "Have you seen Morticia?"

"Not since we left her resting in stone sleep earlier."

"Maybe she's out getting something to eat." She smiled and took me by the hand. "Come. Show me the stars?"

"Are you trying to make up for forcing my hand?" I teased.

"Maybe a little. But also, I want you to tell me more stories about the constellations. I find the look you get on your face when you're doing so irresistible."

Blood raced to my cock as she winked at me, and I no longer had any will to fight her on anything. If she wanted to spend time with me in the observatory, I wasn't going to argue. In fact, I easily came up with a very mutually pleasing scenario in my head as I took one of the blankets off the back of the sofa and followed her out the door.

CHAPTER 29
CALLA

I T TOOK SOME adjustment for the students to get used to me being followed around by the skulking shadow that was Rylan. Not only was I a new face in classes, but every single student adored him. Some were understandably wary, but all had a tendency to want to show off their new abilities for the headmaster's approval.

Meanwhile, he was caught between falling into playful interaction with them all and getting heavy side-eye from the teachers. The funniest part was that they, too, seemed to struggle in finding balance between the lighthearted joy of learning he carried with him and keeping their classes in order. However, he was very handy to have around, as he could aide for any of the teachers at the drop of a hat, which outweighed the fact that his presence was also a complete distraction.

I'd been unofficially enrolled in three courses that, in my mind at least, were logically complementary. Herbology, Alchemy and Artificery. If I added Astronomy in an official way, Rylan might have exploded with pride, seeing how they were all his specialties.

Though to be fair, we spent plenty of time in the observatory as it was, so I was getting plenty of education about the stars already. The view from the cushions on the floor was spectacular.

The first few days were especially tense as he hovered over my every move through each of my three sessions, but by the second week he was finally relaxing. Even though fire was a problem, but sorting herbs, distilling herbal tinctures, and crafting things out of crystals and metal were all perfectly safe for me ... so far. To be fair, no real magical ability had been required as yet. He also kept me on fighting lessons three days a week, which I had actually started to really enjoy. It was by no means a grueling schedule, but it was quite a change for me and left me starving and exhausted most evenings.

"Are you alright, Little Owl?" Rylan asked with concern as a headache crept behind my eyes.

"I'm fine. I think I'm just tired after a couple of very busy weeks." I focused on sketching the small white flowers of the yarrow plant I'd found near the courtyard gate.

"Come. I can help you with plant identification another time." He took the charcoal stick and sketch book from my hands and helped me stand.

I rubbed the space between my eyes with a finger, trying to relieve the stabbing ache that had formed there.

"Oh no." He chuckled, reaching forward and rubbing at the same spot with his thumb. A smear of charcoal darkened his skin when he pulled it away.

"Is it all over my face?" I looked down at my hands, finding them both messy from my sketching.

"No, that was the only spot, but perhaps we should find you some soap before you decorate yourself again, yes?"

Morticia bounded across the grass behind us, and while we were still working on our communication, I could tell she was disappointed to end her nap in the sun.

She followed me to classes also, her presence just as problematic for keeping the students' focus on the teachers. She'd saunter in behind us, get the attention she wanted, then curl up on a table or other available flat surface and watch me. A few times, she'd gone statue in the middle of class, causing quite a stir when people noticed her in her stone kin form.

Morticia was an interesting addition to our household dynamic. She provided a layer of confidence for Rylan; she was insurance that if something I did went wrong, she'd step in the same as he would. I knew she wasn't a pet, but I'd assumed caring for her would be similar. I learned quickly how very wrong my assumption was. She was gone nearly as much as she was around, and we never had to worry about feeding her or any details like that. All she required was an open window so she could come and go at will.

She and Archimedes were much the same and had a comfortable relationship with one another. Many times, we'd found them snoozing together in the observatory or stalking some kind of rodent prey as a pair on the school grounds. I'd not have paired a cat and an owl together normally and expected harmony, but they clearly had history.

On our way back to the apartment, we detoured by the kitchen. As usual, Rylan managed to talk Grace out of some baskets so we could spend an evening in while I used her sink to take care of my charcoal-covered hands.

"Take extras. I saw your friend lingering about on the roof earlier today."

"Magnus?" I asked, surprised. He'd not returned for a visit since our trip to see Ophelia.

"He seems a little worse for wear. Something we should be aware of, Archmage?"

Rylan frowned, accepting the additional baskets. "I don't know."

"Well, just let me know so I can prepare," Grace said, stress lines bracketing her mouth. "I've readjusted my grocery budget since he stopped coming around but can easily set it back."

We headed straight up to the observatory, cresting the stairs to find Magnus there waiting. He'd taken a seat on one of the many floor cushions Rylan had requested be taken up there for one of his lessons with the students. He had his back against the wall and looked thoroughly exhausted. Morticia was curled up in his lap.

"Are you alright, Magnus?" Rylan asked, setting the baskets on the table but never removing his eyes from his friend.

"I'm fine." Magnus even sounded tired.

"When was the last time you rested?" I asked, approaching the mountain of a man. Morticia gazed up from his lap, her eyes squinted with happiness, a rumbling purr rolling out of her throat.

"I slept a few hours yesterday."

"I mean the other kind of resting."

Magnus chuckled. "I cannot remember, but I'm off for a few days. I thought I might stay right here, if that's alright."

"You know it is." Rylan threw me a concerned look as he approached. We traded places, him squatting down near the gargoyle while I took the contents of our dinner out of the baskets. "What's happening, Magnus? Where've you been?"

"How sweet. Did you miss me, little archmage?"

"I don't know about him, but I have," I interrupted, the stress in the air between them palpable. "I certainly could have used your expertise these last couple of weeks." I smiled, trying to force some joy into the layer of tension.

"I'm sorry, Calla. I had a mission I could not delay. I'm always at your service."

I handed Rylan a plate which he handed to Magnus. I wasn't sure how a couple of weeks had left him so gaunt and thinned out. It worried me.

Morticia hopped off his lap and came toward me, her intent clear in the way she was moving. I offered her a selection of cheese and meat on a small plate. Her purr told me I'd made a good choice.

We ate in silence, even Magnus's normal enthusiasm for Grace's cooking suspiciously absent. "I know I haven't known you that long, but you have me worried for your well-being, Magnus."

His eyes snapped to mine, then drifted to Rylan who nodded in agreement. "A few more of Grace's meals, plus a couple days' worth of stone sleep, and I'll be right as rain. I just pushed myself too hard is all. Though I appreciate the concern." He set his plate aside, and I handed him a pitcher of ale to replace it. "I've been trying to disrupt the black market of magical items that seems to only be increasing in the city. We're getting closer, but ..." He shook his head. "I was also hunting for Selene," he said low, as though sharing a secret.

I stilled. "I thought ... Hasn't she been missing for quite a long time?" I asked, trying to temper the flare of hope that had sparked at the mention of my assumed mother's name.

"She has. They both have. I have been tasked with finding them more than once." He met my eye, empathy in his deep-brown gaze. "I have not yet found either of them, but that doesn't mean I'll stop looking. I have my own reasons, as do the people who've sent me out, yet again, searching for any sign that she's still alive."

My heart sank, but I understood. Rylan pulled over two more cushions and invited me to sit. My headache receded a little thanks to the food, but there was still a dull throb behind my eyes.

"What aren't you saying, old friend?"

Magnus sighed, downing the remains of the pitcher. "You're too observant, demon."

"If it makes you feel better, Grace could also tell something was going on."

Magnus chuckled, nodding as though he might fall asleep any moment while leaned up against the wall. "Selene is one of Ygritte's many cousins. Stone kin genealogy is very complicated. How long most of us live, paired with the fact that we started from only a dozen lines ... In any case, I've been looking for her since she went missing for many reasons."

"She's family."

"Yes, my lady." The easy grin on Magnus's mouth made my chest ache. "She's family *and* one of the few links I have left to my dearly departed wife. I have my children, of course, and fortunately so. But Selene knows things nobody else does. I want to speak with her, if only one more time."

I felt something flutter in my chest, a sensation that was equal parts distressing and exciting. The idea that this lovely man was my actual kin, even if only by a tangled web of marriage relations, was appealing for many reasons. "Does that mean I am also family?"

"I suppose it does." His smile brightened. "You'll have to be introduced to your nieces and nephews ... cousins? I don't know how that works, to be honest, though I consider Rylan a brother, lord help me, so maybe the first. As Selene's daughter ... I'd need to map it out to be sure. In any case, we'll have to introduce you around soon."

"That's—" Whatever Rylan had been about to say was cut short, and his stare became intense on Magnus. A flare of wild energy lashed out as Magnus appeared to nod off, right in the middle of our conversation. "No you don't." Rylan prodded Magnus in the thigh with his hand.

"Hey! Just trying to catch a few winks while I can," Magnus complained.

"You're going to explain thoroughly tomorrow, but for now, I need to know where these came from." Rylan demanded as he flipped Magnus's forearm over, tone low and threatening. The hair on the back of my neck stood up, in response to the unusually cold, abrupt way he was speaking to his friend.

"You know well enough what they are, demon prince." Magnus's words slurred, his exhaustion so great.

The bright purplish-red scratches down the inside of his forearm must have started out as terrible gashes but were somewhere in the middle stages of healing with pinched edges and shiny new skin forming. A few had tendrils of greenish-gray streaks feathering around them, and all looked painful.

"Why do you have wounds as though you single-handedly fended off legions fresh from the pit?"

Magnus grinned, his head lolling as he lost the battle with keeping his eyes open. "Where do you think I've been the last couple of weeks, devil? I was called to manage an infestation. Don't worry, Gaius and I took care of it. Two of my sons and Imogen, the daughter that takes most after my beloved Ygritte, were there also."

Rylan ground his teeth together. "I'm thrilled you got a family reunion. Where is your blade?" Magnus snored in response. "Blasted arrogant statue with marble for brains, *where is your blade?*" Rylan shook Magnus by the lapels, his force frightening me. I'd never seen him quite so urgent before.

"Safe," Magnus sighed. "Safe."

"Turn to stone," Rylan ordered. "You need to heal." When Magnus did not respond, Rylan shifted into his full demon form and grabbed the massive gargoyle under the arms. As he hauled him to his feet, Magnus sputtered, swatting loosely at Rylan. "You need stone sleep, Magnus. Shift. Now." He growled the words, and my skin crawled at the tone. It was the first time I'd felt true fear where he was involved.

Magnus cracked his eyes, registering Rylan for a split second before his chin dropped to his chest in a faint nod. The same shrieking noise I'd heard the first time he showed me his gargoyle form resounded in the room as his stone skin scraped across the marble flooring. This time, however, he turned not only into his stone form, but the statue version. His clothing, sadly, might never recover.

"Something is wrong," Rylan said, frenetic energy pouring from him. On top of his unusual behavior, the unusual attitude made me apprehensive as he approached. Regret flashed in his ruby eyes, and he softened his tone. "I'll be back as soon as I can." He dipped forward and pressed a fiery kiss to my mouth before striding smoothly to one of the glassless windows and launching himself from it.

CHAPTER 30
CALLA

WAS TOO STUNNED to move for a few seconds after Rylan
jumped out the window.

Once I finally got my feet to move and dashed after him, my
rational brain remembered that he did indeed have wings and
would be fine. My heart, however, screamed in abject panic. From
the window, I found him silhouetted against a sunset that bled
orange and red into the horizon. He was a dark shadow against
the sky, his long legs and broad wings difficult to process despite
my up-close knowledge of what that looked like. His arms were
oddly relaxed as his powerful wings carried him thought the sky.

"Well, that's ..." No other words came as I muttered to myself in shock. Once Rylan was out of sight, I blinked to clear
my thoughts, then walked back to where Magnus was frozen
in slumber with Morticia curled up on a cushion near his feet.
"Are you going to stay and keep an eye on him?" I asked her. She
mewled, which I took as a yes. "Alright. I'll leave the two of you
some snacks for later."

I collected the debris from our meal and left everything that wouldn't spoil in two of the baskets for whenever Magnus awoke. He'd certainly be hungry based on how worn-out he'd seemed. I descended the stairs with my arms full and took it into the kitchen where I found Grace toiling over the sink.

"You really do need some helpers for all this, Grace," I chided, rolling up my sleeves so I could do some washing for her.

"I probably should allow the archmage to hire someone, but I've had a few come and go that simply weren't worth the effort, so I'm hesitant."

"Maybe some of the older students could rotate through?"

"We've tried that too. Hit or miss." She sighed and wiped sweat from her brow with her forearm. "I'll admit to being the problem. I'm very particular and end up doing it all myself anyway."

When she turned to get another stack from the counter behind us, I maneuvered my way in front of the sink so I could take over the washing.

"How's Magnus?" she asked, seeing I'd only brought two baskets back.

"He's resting. He ate but was very tired, so I left him some for later."

Grace frowned. "I'll check on him in a bit, shall I?"

I couldn't help but smile. Their contentious friendship was fun to watch. "If you'd like. Morticia stayed with him."

"I like her." Grace grinned, picking up a towel to dry off plates and cups as quickly as I could wash and rinse. "She's very polite when she comes asking for meals, and despite her fondness for chicken and beef, the stables have never been quite so free of mice. Between her and the owl, we'll be pest free before long."

"I'm glad to hear that. I'll admit I'm at a bit of a loss with her. I can't communicate with her easily yet."

"You'll get there," Grace said encouragingly, patting me on the back as she crossed to put some of the clean dishes in a cabinet. "Where's your mage?"

"Oh, uh ..." I wasn't sure exactly how much Grace knew, but I was assuming it was nearly everything. "He wanted to check on something Magnus mentioned."

"Mm," she said, noncommittally.

I finished up washing the dishes, the warm soapy water and repetition having helped with my pounding heart. I couldn't help but worry about Rylan, though it wasn't necessarily for his safety. I knew he wouldn't have left so abruptly without cause, and I'd never seen him act the way he had with Magnus.

"Don't worry, my lady. He'll be fine. He always is."

I pushed a smile onto my lips and accepted the slice of cake she had set aside for me. "Join me?" I asked.

Grace blinked, momentarily shocked by the invitation. I felt a terrible press of guilt then, realizing that while I thought of her as a friend, I hadn't made it a point to treat her as one. She was always taking care of me—of us—but we rarely took the time to include her since we always found ourselves busy with whatever the problem of the moment was. I vowed to change that, in as far as I could.

"Of course! Let me get us some glasses." She collected her own cake plus a bottle of wine and glasses, then we took them to the round table. "How are you getting along with your lessons?"

"Fine, I guess. I haven't set anything else on fire anyway."

"How could you with two nursemaids following you around?" She laughed while pouring our wine. "Don't fret about what happened, Calla. It's not the first time, won't be the last."

I stopped, a bite of cake halfway to my mouth. "Someone else burned out an entire room?"

"Well, to be fair, not quite as dramatically as you did, but yes. Fledgling mages and witches learning how to manage fire and energy and doing spells in general is very messy."

"That makes me feel the tiniest bit better."

Grace laughed. "I'm glad."

We ate our cake and drank our wine, the silence comforting. The dining hall was so very noisy when filled with students, the absolute lack of sound aside from our dinnerware was odd but enjoyable.

"How did you come to run things around here, Grace?"

"Oh my." She chuckled, waving her hand. "That's a very long story. The short version is I used to collect any number of waifs and strays as the daughter of a butcher, long ago. Children that were hungry or those who needed a kind face always managed to find us. My father's generosity knew no bounds and we fed as many as we could. Then along came Rylan, a regular customer from the start, but one with grand schemes for a proper school." She smiled warmly. "When my father retired his knives, we realized how much debt the business was actually in." The smile evaporated, leaving behind a deep sadness that was so incongruent to Grace's personality it made my heart ache. "So we sold off what we could, paid the debt down, and came up with a new plan." She straightened herself and cleared her throat, the emotion clogging it no longer welcome. "My parents have a tidy little apartment near our old neighborhood, and everything is taken care of. And I came here."

"And you?"

"Me?"

"Are you cared for?" I asked, hoping she was truly happy at her post and with her job. It would hurt my heart too much to hear her easy smiles were fake.

"Oh, Lady Calla. I'm so very well cared for here. Who do you think pays for my parents' apartment? Rylan ensures that all under his watch are compensated, and their families are also considered. I'm sure you know that."

I did, though it was nice to have confirmation. "I'm not a lady," I muttered, the title always an uncomfortable thorn despite how often I heard it.

Grace pushed her plate away, the porcelain grating on the table. "This again? Of course you are."

"I mean it, Grace, I'm not. I'm the laundress at Rylan's manor, just a household employee. I don't remember much, but I believe I lived on a farm before that. I'm not nobility. I'm nothing special. Certainly no more worthy of a title than you or anyone else around here."

She clucked her tongue and swallowed a mouthful of wine.

"You are *his* lady. That's all that matters. He made a point to tell everyone that you have the same authority as he does. There is not a word I could come up with to describe how special you are, laundress or not, if only because of how he's changed since he found you." Grace winked at me and I blushed hot, flattered by how easily she turned my self-deprecating thoughts around. "Can you read?"

"Yes, of course."

"Write? Do sums? Stab the straw man in the yard with a wooden sword?"

"Yes, you know I can." I laughed at her, knowing she was making a point, but unsure which one.

"Fantastic, then you're doing better than at least half of the women in this city. Not to mention, you have so much magic in your blood you can accidentally set whole rooms ablaze. Is that not special?"

"Grace, I don't think—"

"And you have an archmage, a full-blooded demon prince at your every beck and call. Hell, I think you'd be *my* lady only for that!"

Her blunt words and raucous laugh stunned me, but then I relented and started laughing with her.

"Thank you, Grace."

"My pleasure, my lady." She winked at me again and collected our plates. "Go on. Go take a long hot bath and read something you've been putting off for when you had leisure time. Hell, take a nap while spread out on the entire bed. He's gone off on one of his missions, but he'll return to you."

I blushed again. "I hope you're right."

"I am," she sang, heading off to the kitchen, brushing off my attempt to join her.

"How much do you know, Grace?" I asked.

"Oh, my friend. There's nothing that happens in this school I don't know the entirety of. Least of all the secrets those men try—and fail miserably—to keep. If you need anything, I'm your gal." She dipped into the kitchen, singing a song as she noisily stacked dishes and ruled over her domain.

I loped up the stairs to the apartment, the prospect of being well and truly alone foreign. I hadn't had such long moments all to myself since I could remember. There had been times at the manor when Rylan had been in his office, but there was always staff around cleaning, cooking, moving things about.

Even though the other apartments on the corridor were occupied, the building was always very quiet. I went inside and took Grace's advice, running the tub as hot as I could stand it.

With a fresh pot of lemon balm tea brewing and my favorite herbal treatment added to the water, I soaked away my stress, or at least tried to, while I wondered where Rylan had gone and what trouble he was getting into.

CHAPTER 31
CALLA

I WOKE UP TO the sound of cursing and the smell of blood.
"Rylan?" My eyes couldn't find anything to focus on the room
was so dark.

"Yes, Little Owl. Sorry, did I wake you? I was trying to stay
quiet, but the feet on this tub have a vendetta against my toes."

I swung my legs off the side of the bed, the chill in the room
telling me that it was sometime in the very wee hours still. "You
can light a lamp if you'd like."

He did almost instantly, the flare illuminating him where he
stood next to the bathtub. As he peeled his shirt off, I knew exactly
where the scent of iron was coming from.

Rushing over, I asked, "How much of that is yours?"

His grin was charged with arrogance and pride. I got a flash of
heat in my lower belly, a liquid metal sensation that burned hot.
"Would you believe me if I said none?"

He ran the cold tap over the shirt and vest, adding his trousers
to the mix, leaving him nude in front of me, nearly every inch of

his skin smeared with blackish fluid. The water swirled dark red, his clothes remarkably saturated.

Rylan turned, shoulder and back muscles bunching as he moved. I held my breath at the sight of him, a feral grin on his lush mouth. I struggled to tear my eyes from his body, shocked by the fact that him covered head to toe in blood wasn't off-putting. In fact, the rugged look caused my pulse to pound in both my throat and the hollow between my thighs. He caught me staring and I sucked in an unsteady breath that echoed through my chest.

"I'll soil your nightgown," he said, lust obvious in the way his eyes flashed.

"This terrible thing?" I plucked at the plain linen that had more frayed edges than smooth hem. It was the original underdress Serena had given me. "It'll wash." Undeterred, I pressed my body against his.

My actions were bold, but I couldn't stop. Everything about him was a beacon to me in that moment. There was something about the primal way his body looked, smeared with the blood of his enemies, that spoke to the parts of me that thrived during the darkness of the midnight hours. With only the single lamp lit, it felt like walking in a dream, partially suspended in the realms between realities. It made me daring, which heightened the emotions between us.

"Calla." He exhaled and brought his hands to my face, gazing down at me as though memorizing every line and feature. Energy hummed through his skin, more than normal. The tingles he elicited traveled down my body, my pleasure zones instantly reacting.

He lowered his mouth to mine, and the intentional softness did nothing to slake my desire as his warm hum of energy transferred through my skin. He sipped slowly, tasting the edges of my lips, then pressed in to feel my whole mouth with his. A nip here, a suckle there. It was death by gentleness, the sweetest torture.

I was certain my heart would pound out of my chest as my need for him to touch me grew. The moment I opened for him, he pulled away.

"There is danger here, Little Owl." He breathed the words against my mouth, and I felt the sharp edge of his fangs against my lip, the points of his claws against my scalp.

Energy pulsed between us and through the room. Instead of being afraid, a whispered moan escaped my lips. And I registered it then, the way he tensed; the incredible amount of restraint he demonstrated as he handled me. He all but vibrated from the effort of keeping his wild energy contained.

"I am not afraid of you," I said softly, meeting his ruby eyes. I lifted a hand and ran my fingertips across the ridges of his exposed curled horn, then over the feathers sprinkled across his broad shoulders. "Never of you, Rylan."

Something rumbled deep in his chest, my skin rippling with gooseflesh at the sound, sending a rush of moisture between my legs. Rylan dipped forward, his mouth hot as it consumed me. It was more than a kiss, it was a melding of him and me, all sharp teeth and wet tongues and rushed breath. The passion in it nearly buckled my knees, and my mind reeled as all the spare oxygen evaporated before it could be useful.

His hands raked across the back and shoulders of my dress, the weak fabric rending under the claws at the end of blackened fingers as he took hold of the linen and pulled it from my body. Exposed, my nipples hardened in the cool air.

Rylan's hands made short work of removing my damp underthings, disposing of the last bits of cloth separating my flesh from his. Energy-charged fingertips coasted lightly up my leg from knee to thigh as he licked into my mouth with his tongue.

With a growl, he lifted me with one arm under my ass and pressed my back against the nearest wall. The sticky, wet slide of the blood coating his chest as he put his whole weight against me sent me further into my most primal self. It was dark, forbidden. It was evidence of violence and death, but only spoke of the passion between us in that moment. The glide it gave, and the iron scent made my skin tingle where we touched. Rylan's wings snapped out wide, a rush of wind buffeting between us. I got a brief chill as he balanced. The rumble in his chest increased to nearly a shout before he hastily pulled his mouth away from mine.

"Calla." He gasped for breath as he broke our kiss, and the energy he put off had risen to a low-level hum throughout the room. "I am not myself after what I just did. I want you more than anything, but I'll not take what you are not freely offering. Do you want this, Little Owl? I need you to be absolutely sure."

I arched into him, my need becoming more urgent by the minute. Slickness coated the inside of my thighs as my core throbbed against the press of his heated skin. I didn't care if it was mouth, fingers, or all of him—I needed *more*.

"I give all of myself freely," I breathed against his lips, trembling as a groan rumbled through his throat. He lowered his mouth to where my neck met my shoulder and sucked. I moaned at the riot of sensations coursing through my body—the sting of the blood rushing to the surface where he lathed my skin with his tongue, the pulse between my legs, the nearly painful tingle of awareness on my flesh. The smell of iron lingered between us, the blackish blood transferring from his flesh to mine.

It should have disgusted me, but there was something about the primal feel of it sliding along our skin as he explored my body with his fingers that made me tremble. I could hardly breathe through the haze of lust while his mouth danced with mine and his hot, hard cock rested against my stomach.

His arms lashed around my back as he spun and walked us to the bed. The feel of his body against mine was delicious, the weight of him atop me upon the mattress simultaneously comforting and arousing. One hand dipped to my leg, pulling my thigh up along his side as he pressed his hardness against my core, the other gripped my wrists above my head. He dove in with his mouth once more, nipping and licking as he devoured me with another kiss that stole my breath.

That fiery mouth traveled down the column of my throat, stopping to suckle along my collarbone on a journey to my breasts.

"The blood—" I panted, glancing down to find myself painted in strokes of maroon, his body having been the brush and mine the canvas.

His blazing eyes met mine as he continued his journey, stopping to lathe the tips with his wet tongue before teasing them with the sharpened points of his teeth, undeterred by the smattering of blood on my skin. Gasping, I made an effort to wriggle away from the mix of pleasure and pain, but he had me pinned both with his weight and his grip. He smiled and continued south, performing the same torture on the sensitive nub at the apex of my thighs.

I cried out as he teased it with the very tip of his hot tongue, then licked along the length of my wet slit. He repeated the process until I was a thrashing, over-sensitized mess on the mattress, begging for dedicated attention that would lead me to release.

"Not yet, Little Owl." Rylan flipped us so I was on top of him, my weight balanced on my knees and his hard length against my center. A breath of intention separated us and nothing more.

"If we do this ... there's no going back. You're mine and only mine. Forever." There was a potency to his voice, a deep resonance that rattled inside my spine like when we'd first met.

"And you'll be mine? Only mine?" The words caused a sudden, sharp pull behind my breastbone, a feeling that bordered on pain it was so intense.

"Always, my beloved. My gorgeous Little Owl."

A wave cascaded through me, warmth traveling from my hair to my toes, as though we'd made some kind of unbreakable vow my body wanted to confirm.

On a deep sigh, I sank down, inviting him into my body, gladly accepting whatever fate I was locking myself into.

CHAPTER 32
RYLAN

LIGHTNING FLASHED BEHIND my eyes as Calla impaled herself fully on my cock. I had a dozen thoughts at once as I allowed the pleasurable sensations her body provided to wash over me. My chest burned and compressed as we joined our bodies as one.

Worry flared to the forefront of my mind, pushing aside the joy our coupling brought for a moment. Doubt that I should have gone elsewhere to clean up set in, somewhere I wouldn't have been tempted by her nearness. The idea that I should have lingered in the observatory, perhaps even to sleep, despite my need for a bath and to see that she was okay once I'd returned. Regret that we hadn't discussed this step in our relationship long before now, how I should have started with touching and kissing and licking and—

The sounds she made brought me out of my spiraling thoughts and fully into my body. My cock throbbed where it was sheathed between her lithe legs. The sight of her atop me, her eyes closed and a hum in her throat as she gently rocked, nearly had me losing all control on my energy. I was already overwhelmed by it; the adrenaline the battle had provided having charged it up, leaving it wild. But this? I was doomed. My control where she was concerned was shamefully low.

"Slow, Little Owl. Yes, good girl, just like that." A dark sound rattled out of my throat as she began to move with purpose. I dipped a thumb between us, gathering a bit of moisture before pressing it into her nub and rubbing with slow, even circles. Something deep in my chest ached, like a door to something ancient and forbidden had opened and sensation rushed in to fill the void all at once.

"Rylan," she gasped, her head falling forward as her motion became intentional, her body having found the spot and rhythm it craved. She rode me in slow, long strokes, my balls tightening as the pleasure settled in deep. I sucked in a breath, trying my damnedest to rein in some control. I didn't want to disappoint my beautiful mate, no matter how good it felt.

My fingers made grooves in her ass as I wrapped my hand around her hip bone. I'd focused enough that my claws were retracted, but my fingers were blackened nearly to where they met my palm. Losing all sense of control as need and sensation took over, I thrust upward, meeting her gentle rocks with a deep plunge. I held her steady, my cock as deep as it would go inside her as she began to flutter around me, her thighs trembling.

"Rylan!" My cock pulsed in response to my name on her lips in that overwhelmed, breathy way. The clench of her body against mine intensified everything further, pain riding the edges of my pleasure as my hips moved in time with hers. Even the air around me seemed to sharpen as I hurtled toward my own release. Her fingers gripped the hand I still had between us, urging me to pull away.

"The energy ... it's too much," she gasped.

"I've got you, Little Owl." I flipped us over again, and the glazed look in her eyes and the flush to her cheeks drove me mad. I lifted one of her legs along my side, pressing her knee slightly outward.

"Ohhh," she moaned, her head falling to the side as I pushed deeper, muscles tightening as I chased the apex I knew was not far.

"Good girl. You're doing so well. It's like you were made for me, Little Owl."

"Yes, yes, yes," she chanted, eyes fluttering closed as her back arched.

Her walls squeezed down on me, and I increased my pace, pressing my thumb back between us, winding her up as I pounded into her with a rhythm that guaranteed I wouldn't last very long. I decided in that moment that I wanted her drunk on me as often as possible, our bodies joined and the fierce lightning of my pleasure blazing down my spine. I felt immeasurably powerful yet delightfully at her mercy. I would have agreed to anything she asked, and happily.

The electricity chased frantically under my skin, and my breath became ragged as the climax built, leaving everything blank for a moment. I bit down on her shoulder, the gasp and sigh she gave pushing me over the edge. The energy I'd been harboring exploded around us as she called out my name again, and I surrendered to the unbearable pleasure only she provided. The smell of lightning hung on the air, the powerful charge crackling as it dissipated.

"Rylan." Her throaty moan echoed around in my skull as I kept myself deep inside her body as my release filled her up.

"You're perfect, Little Owl." I ducked down, balancing on my forearms as I kissed the edges of her mouth gently, then plundered it completely. I licked and tasted as she reached up to smooth my hair out of my face. Her lips curled into a smile as she felt along my horns. Her touch sent new shocks of awareness down my back as she stroked along the black bones on my head.

Guilt surged in as my adrenaline began to wane. "I'm sorry, Calla. That was not—"

"Please don't apologize." Her expressive eyes searched mine, desperate. "Don't regret this. I couldn't bear it."

"No, my love. Don't misunderstand. I should have done things differently, is all. I never intended for that to happen before you got all your memories back."

"Why?"

"Because I wanted to be sure you knew who you were, wholly and entirely, before asking you to commit to such a thing."

She frowned. "I know who I am. Who you are. Who *we* are. And I wanted this, Rylan. As much as you. Maybe more."

"I doubt that very much, Little Owl. I've said it before, and I was not exaggerating. I want you more than I've ever wanted anything in this life." I dipped my head to the hollow between her neck and shoulder, making her shiver as I ran my nose along then sensitive skin there. I pressed an open-mouth kiss to the spot she liked most, tasting her sweet skin as she breathed out a sigh.

"I do love you, Rylan. Even though I've not said it. I do." She leaned up, sealing our joining with a kiss.

I carefully removed myself from her body, rolling away as the words settled into my skin. They were weighty, profound. I would do my best to never take them for granted.

She loved me.

Her soft chuckle shook me out of my reverie.

"We should soak this bedding before the blood sets. My nightgown, I'm afraid, is a lost cause."

I looked over to where the plain linen lay in a tattered heap. "Sorry about that. I'll get you a new one. A dozen, if need be, so I can tear them off you when I like."

Calla sat up, my pulse leaping at the sight of her freshly mussed, smeared in the blood of the demons I'd slain. "I'm wholly unconcerned about my clothing."

I stood and crossed to the bathing room, her eyes trailing me as I wrang the excess water out of my soiled clothes. Tossing them aside for the moment, I rinsed out the basin before running a fresh hot bath, thankful for the intelligent plumbing both the collegium and the manor boasted. Such an advance would never cease to impress me and provoke my gratitude.

"Come, flower. We both need to get cleaned up."

Her fingertips grazed some of the smears of demon blood our melded flesh had left on her skin as she crossed toward me. "Perhaps you can tell me what happened while I scrub the mess out of your hair?"

As the water filled the deep basin, I added some herbs and used a dampened cloth across our chests so the bathwater wouldn't be quite so messy. I held out a hand to steady her as she stepped into the tub, then climbed in myself, sitting down on the opposite end, facing her.

"I'm sorry for leaving that way," I said, reaching for a clean cloth and the cake of soap. "I'm sure it was a shock to see."

"You mean how you leapt out a window at observatory height?" Her tone carried more humor than I expected as she lifted her hand from the water, watching the drops fall back into the tub. Despite my cursory wipe down, the water swirled with pink. "My shock wore off quickly enough. I'm happy to see your wings held you up despite your being out of practice. It was definitely an interesting sight to see your winged figure outlined against the sunset." She swallowed, the column of her throat moving as her eyes dipped below the waterline. "Were you as out of practice as you thought?" Calla gestured vaguely at my upper body.

"Ask me again tomorrow. If I'm sore, we'll both know."

"Where did you go, exactly?"

I used my hands and the cake of soap to lather up her arms, then her chest. She grinned at me, but willingly lifted her hair and scooted forward in an invitation for me to continue on with her back. When that was done, I reached for the pitcher and shampoo. "Turn around. I'll do your hair, then you can do mine."

"I should probably do yours first," she argued. "There's ... bits of things in it." Her nose wrinkled up but she spun in the tub anyway, giving me her back. "Should I have checked on Magnus again? Those injuries looked awful."

"No, I'm sure he's alright by now. I came back in through the observatory, and he was much the same as when I left. Morticia was curled up on a cushion, keeping watch. His injuries might be painful, but he should be healed once he wakes from the stone sleep."

"Where did you go?" She repeated the question he still hadn't answered.

"Not far. I had to be sure that the issue had been handled." I poured water over her dark hair, very aware that she impatiently waited for me to elaborate.

"From the state of you, clearly it wasn't as done as Magnus thought?"

I chuckled darkly, a vision of what the field had looked like when I arrived flashing through my mind. "No, Little Owl. It was not."

"But it is now?"

"Yes. There won't be any more trouble from that area for now."

"For now?"

I poured one final rinse down the length of her hair. "They always return. It could be a week, it could be a decade. But I wouldn't worry over it. Between the gargoyle soldiers and me, there's nothing left of those legions now." I handed off the tools, and she set to work plucking the aforementioned bits out of my hair as she washed it.

"Did you find his blade? You were quite distressed over it."

"Yes. It was his sword that I used to dispatch the demons causing so much trouble. Regrettably, I've left all of mine back at the manor. It was foolish to think I'd have no need of them here. I'll have to remedy that next trip home." I pictured the array of weapons on the wall of my office downstairs.

"The ones in the office?" she guessed smartly.

"Yes, and others."

She stilled, no doubt curious how many I had in total, but not so much so she wanted to ask just then. After she did a final rinse, I sank completely under the suds for a long moment before emerging again.

We finished up in the bath, and I took care to help her dry off before stripping the soiled coverlet from the bed. Thankfully, there were plenty of other blankets to take its place. After laying down, she rolled onto her side, so I curled up behind her, holding her close as I pulled the blankets over us both.

"Do you think ..." She hesitated, and I could almost feel the embarrassment she'd conjured up with her question. "Do you think that was my first time? I mean, at nearly thirty ..." Her hands covered her face. "I shouldn't have said anything." She all but glowed as her skin warmed from the blush.

I choked out a surprised breath. "I'm sure you're better at assessing that than I am, Little Owl. It matters not, though the idea of someone else knowing you in such a way provokes thoughts of violence in my mind." I flashed through visions of dismembering any man who dared touch her, the very recent lower-level demons I'd done just that to providing a visceral example.

She blinked heavily as drowsiness took over. "I don't know. It's strange to finally know how old I am and who my parents are but have no idea if I've ever been in love before. Is that what this feeling is? Or is it the fated bond?"

My own chest squeezed, that hot sensation returning as though the suggestion revived it. "I'm not sure the two can be separated. Can you describe it to me?"

"I have a feeling ... a burning ... like I ate something wrong." She laughed, and the light, airy sound spoke to my soul. "But not. It's distracting but not painful. Along with an anxiety, almost. As though I might die if I ever lost you."

I had to clear my throat. There was no cause for her words to wield such a heavy impact, but I felt them in every part of my soul, because I felt the same.

"I believe it's the bond, but like I said, I'm not sure love can be separated from that." It was a relief to hear that she was experiencing the same symptoms I was. At least we would be in it together, which was all I wanted for the rest of my days. "I feel it too. But you shouldn't worry about such things. I'm not going anywhere." Especially not now. "If you hadn't already gathered, I'm incredibly hard to kill. And you ... you've given me more reasons than I previously had to avoid coming to an untimely end."

"I can't help but worry. When you left, I knew you'd be okay, but I also felt like my chest was collapsing for a moment. Grace distracted me with sweets and wine. Reassured me you'd be okay. But this feeling ... it's frustrating. Comforting. I don't understand it, but I worry I'd also be bereft if it went away."

"I understand and agree completely." I chuckled as I tucked her hair away from her face. "Thank you, Calla." I pressed my mouth to her shoulder, breathing in her scent.

"For what?"

"For understanding me. For finding me."

She didn't respond, but the way she curled her arms around mine, pulling my energy to her was answer enough.

CHAPTER 33
RYLAN

MY EYES DRIFTED open to find Calla sitting upright in the bed, early morning sunlight streaming in the windows giving her a halo. She was gorgeous, lit up by soft light, mouth slightly parted and eyes dewy.

The dreamy image faded, however, as I realized that she was breathing roughly and clutching her chest. "Calla? What's wrong?"

"I remember the earthy smell of horses, and the itch of rye chaff against my skin, trapped between the layers of my clothes during harvest season. The comforting, warm smell of bread baking, and the sound Gram's wooden paddles made as she shaped fresh butter into bricks. The smooth texture of the cloth squares she'd soak in beeswax to wrap food in. I can hear a man's voice telling me stories about the trouble my father used to get into on the farm when he was young. Laughter. The fire crackling as a spinning wheel turned and a rocking chair creaked against the floor. There's so much, but still so little, I ..." Her hands clutched the sides of her head, as though she were trying to keep it from flying apart. A stifled scream grated out of her throat.

I sat up and pulled her to me roughly, every nerve alight as her whole body trembled against mine. "What can I do?" Panic surged through my veins, ice chased by lava making me feel as though I, too, might come apart. I strained to keep my electricity in check, not wanting to harm her further as my hands roved all over her body, searching for the area that needed to be made better.

"Can you check the block? Everything feels wrong. It hurts." The terror in her eyes had me grabbing for her hands.

I sent tendrils of energy through her, finding what she'd predicted. There was a jagged crag across the dark veil in her mind, a space big enough for memories to trickle through. As I probed that area, I received one hell of a shock in return. It was incredible, and I'd never been hurt by my probing before, so it surprised me in addition to causing me pain.

I sucked a breath in through my teeth. The magical shock had caused forced me to shift in defense. My blackened fingers let hers go, and I instead placed them on either side of her face, my thumbs at her jaw and my fingers splayed from her forehead to her temples. I tried to press soothing energy through my touch, but I didn't have a clue how effective it might be.

"Can you let it out?" I asked. "Whatever it is? Can you either fully embrace it or let it go without hurting yourself?"

Calla shook her head, tears welling and spilling down her cheeks. "I don't know what to do."

"Focus on … opening your mind. Allow the memories to come through."

Her face scrunched up as she focused, and I regretted my suggestion as she winced away from however the attempt was hurting her. "I can't do it. I can't. I'm not strong enough to withstand whatever this is—"

"Morticia!" I called over my shoulder, hoping the cat was nearby. I suspected she was still up with Magnus, however. Why she hadn't responded to Calla's distress already was another issue. "You can, Little Owl. You're one of the strongest people I know. You can."

She started to babble and sob, which hit every panic sensor I had. I fought against the reflexive shift my body kept trying to make, calling my horns and fangs back to their resting places. Rage had me roaring at the invisible enemy in her body as I leapt from the bed, pulling on the nearest clothing I could find, then helping her into a robe I could easily wrap around her in a hurry.

When the feline didn't appear, I picked my mate up and hauled her out the door, taking the stairs to the observatory two at a time. If Morticia couldn't help me on her own, perhaps Magnus could perform some kind of stone kin trick to assist.

"Morticia!" I called out again from the stairs as Calla's tears soaked into the linen of my shirt.

I was greeted by an urgent yowl as she hopped down to meet me, then repetitive mewls as I finished climbing the stairs and set Calla down on the cushions.

"I'm okay," Calla sniffled, her face in her hands as she continued to cry.

"Like hell you are," I argued, watching the cat as she walked stressed circles around Calla.

Morticia wiggled her way into Calla's lap, standing on her hind legs and placing her paws over Calla's hands, making a gentle batting motion. She let out a particularly loud yowl, and the sound of Magnus waking drew my attention.

"Ah, little archmage. I should have guessed you'd be anxious to see how I was feel—" His eyes fell to Calla and the cat who was still insistently making yowling noises. "What's happening?"

"I was hoping you could tell me." I was pacing, energy flowing off me in waves. I was thankful the roof was open to the morning air since there was so much of it. "Her memory block has cracked, and it's causing her distress."

Morticia went quiet, her furry forehead pressed to Calla's.

"What can we do?" I asked the cat.

Patience, she sent back, the clarity of her voice in my mind surprising. *Helping.*

Magnus snapped to attention a moment later, however, indicating that her communication had shifted to him. "She wants me to help," he said, eyes grazing mine for approval. "I need to touch her. Calla? May I touch your shoulders?"

"Yes," Calla whispered. "Whatever she's doing is good."

I nodded at him, still pacing in front of them as my concern for her remained at a fever pitch. I walked a short circuit in front of them, my useless hands unable to settle on a resting place. Helplessness suffused me to the bone, which pissed me off. It was not something I was used to feeling and did not care for it at one bit.

Magnus went to his knees on a cushion behind Calla, setting his heavy hands on her shoulders. He jolted as though she'd shocked him. "There's something ..." He shook his head, empathy in his gaze. "We have to lock it down, Rylan. She cannot control it. The crack is allowing things through. It's memories but also magic." His eyebrows drew together and his eyes met mine. "So much magic."

My heart sank. The candle experiment had only been a small sampling of her power, then. I'd foolishly thought if we didn't try to access her magic stores in any significant way, everything would be fine. Instead, they'd needed an outlet, and we'd left them bottled up, ready to explode.

"I have the vial Ophelia gave me—"

"Go get it."

"But we haven't tested it," I complained.

"Get it anyway."

"But it could—"

"Rylan. *Now.*"

I growled in frustration and allowed my wings out partway so I could drift down the stairs instead of walking. Hands shaking, I threw open the door to our apartment and raced to my locked box of potions. With it safely in my grasp, I dashed back upstairs.

Calla was sedate, her breathing level as the two gargoyles held her steady.

"Calla, they think I need to give you the potion. Do you want to do that?"

"Yes. It hurts, Rylan. We'll find another way later. For now, if a drop of that will make this stop, we need to do that. I need to do that." Her big brown eyes opened and pinned me with a piteous stare. My stomach lurched, the hurt in her gaze too much for me to bear. I would gladly kill anyone or anything that made her look that way, but unfortunately, that was not an option here.

Magnus and Morticia watched me intensely, and I felt the pressure to make it all go away keenly. "Alright." I carefully opened the wax seal and pulled the cork from the vial. "She needs only the smallest drop. My fingers are too large."

The feline's greenish-gold eyes opened, and I would have sworn she nodded. Her head tilted to the side, and she used a paw to swipe at her whiskers. A pristine white one fell onto the cushion as she turned her head back to press her forehead to Calla's once again.

"Thank you." I dipped the end of it into the vial, getting the smallest amount of iridescent liquid on the end of it. "Open, beloved." Calla's lips parted, and I placed the tiny drop on her tongue.

Several moments passed, all of us still as we waited to see what would happen. Magnus met my eye, his concern a match for my own.

"It's better." Calla sagged, her eyes clear and much more like herself when they opened again. "I'm okay. Thank you." Gratitude oozed from her shallow smile as she relaxed.

I exhaled, my chest feeling as though a massive weight had been removed. At least until the guilt started to press in.

AFTER SITTING FOR a bit to ensure that she was indeed mostly better, Magnus and I left Calla in Morticia's care in the apartment to round up breakfast.

"What did you see?" I asked my friend. "Inside Calla."

Both of us were pensive, thoughtful. I had more questions than time to ask them.

"I rarely agree with the council's decisions on things, but if what's contained in your little mate is what they foresaw? I understand the mandate they made forbidding Selene and Kaspar to couple."

Ice trickled down my spine. "Is she in immediate danger?"

Magnus shook his head as we rounded the bottom of the stairs and started down the hall. "Not as long as you have that vial. Once the hex starts to crumble in earnest ..." He shrugged, but his mouth pulled tight. "I don't know. It depends on her. There's no telling until it happens."

"Will we be able to help her when it does?"

Magnus took a deep breath, his shoulders sagging when he exhaled. "I hope so."

I did too.

"Thank you," he said, clearing his throat as we entered the dining hall. "For finishing the job."

"My pleasure." I gave him a once-over with my eyes. He looked hale, and his arm had healed, but some injuries could linger. "Are you well?"

"Much better now." He straightened his collar as Grace strode out of the kitchen door with her hands full. "The little surges are getting worse. If I didn't know better, I'd think someone was summoning them on purpose."

"Mm." Paired with the influx of odd magical items we'd been finding in the city, I couldn't help but agree. The two things were linked, no doubt. It was the who and why that remained the most concerning questions of the bunch, though we seemed a modicum closer to the answers.

"I suppose you're here because you're hungry?" Grace asked with a smile, dusting her hands off as she approached. "Good thing I was prepared on my last trip to the market." She eyed Magnus. "Come on."

"Can you throw in some extra cake for Calla?"

"Of course. Did she have another magical blowout?" Her brow furrowed in concern.

"Something like that. We, ah ..." I stopped, realizing I was about to blurt out our private business. "Her memories are trying to break through. She's had a very troublesome morning."

She nodded seriously and started assembling baskets for us. "I hope she feels better."

"Thank you, Grace." I reached for two baskets, and Magnus took the rest.

"Will you be staying long?" she asked him, hand propped on her hip.

"Long enough."

She tossed her hands in the air. "That's clear as mud, thanks. I'll adjust my budget accordingly." Grace shooed us from her kitchen, and we made our way back up the stairs.

I felt the heat of Magnus's stare as we climbed. "Out with it," I sighed.

"Was there something that precipitated Calla's ... event?"

"She was already struggling when I woke this morning."

"So, last night perhaps? After you got back from ..." Magnus stopped mid stair. "Oh."

"Oh?"

"I think I understand." He laughed loudly, the booming roar echoing through the stairwell, then all the way down the hall as we approached the apartment door.

"I'm pleased you're so amused," I groused.

"Ygritte and I used to have some very ... fulfilling evenings after battles, my friend. I understand completely. Did you notice any differences this time to before? Anything that looking back might seem off?" My silence and tight mouth only widened my friend's eyes. "I mean, you had, right? Before last night."

"None of your business, stone man."

"Ah. I see. That's surprising, actually. But explains some things." Electricity swirled under my skin as I glared him down. "Only trying to be helpful," he said, grinning as I opened the door.

"I'm sure you are." I released a bolt of energy at the back of his head as he entered in front of me. His hand flew up to rub the spot, but he was still laughing.

Bastard.

CHAPTER 34
CALLA

RYLAN GROWLED AT the same time I flushed bright red. "What, is it something I said?" Magnus couldn't contain his grin. "I don't mean to embarrass you, Calla. But truly, did you think through what might happen at *all*, Archmage?"

"Of course I did," he snapped.

"Just not that part?" Magnus leaned back into the sofa he was occupying with Morticia at his side.

Grace had provided yet another day's worth of wonderful meals for us. I was sure that two frantic males asking for baskets, one of which freshly awoken from stone sleep and undoubtedly ravenous after healing, had been excellent motivation for her to throw what seemed like the entire kitchen at them. I'd taken leave from all my classes while we tried to figure out the best way to approach the changes in my mental and magical stability.

"Are you saying that us, ah, *consummating* our bond is responsible for whatever is happening to me?"

"I think it's a very likely possibility," Magnus said, much more neutral when speaking to me than he was when he suggested such things to Rylan. Their need to prod at one another knew no bounds. "As an archmage, I expected you to know better."

"You could be a little more grateful that I saved your ass, cleaned up your mess, *and* made sure you healed, you know."

Magnus laughed. "Don't mistake my amusement for lack of gratitude, friend. I'm deeply appreciative for what you did, how you helped me, and the rest you forced me to take. But I'm also surprised you didn't see a link between Calla's memories coming back and your increased ... intimacy."

Rylan sighed. "We've joked about our physical closeness helping, as one layer of potential helpful remedies. I didn't think ..."

"So you admit it." Magnus smiled wide.

"Alright, you two. Points made. We need to be careful, right? We can test my abilities while the effects of the potion are still in my system? No real difference from before."

"In theory, yes." Rylan sighed again, not particularly excited about any of our options.

"Fine. As long as Morticia can be there, and I have you to help me along, it should be alright. I'll let you know as soon as I get even a twinge in my head." It was the same conversation we'd had already, though with much less amusement to go around this time. "We're on an accelerated timeline because we don't know how long the effects will last."

"Or what all they will be, or what happens when we have to re-dose you, or what'll come if the crack increases. I don't like it," Rylan complained.

"Nobody's asking you to. Let us help her."

Rylan's jaw ticked as he mulled over things. "Fine. But if she gets hurt, I'm taking it out of your hide."

"I'd expect no less." Magnus smiled again, as though looking forward to the challenge.

I wondered then, with no small amount of apprehension, what exactly I'd so enthusiastically volunteered myself for.

PAIN. I'D VOLUNTEERED for pain.

Over the next week, I acquired innumerable bruises and bumps, worked myself to exhaustion, received a crash course in stone kin history, and developed a craving for sugar even Grace had a hard time keeping up with.

Rylan's idea had been to find something I could channel my magic slowly into, like a crystal or artifact. After I exploded three increasingly larger geode crystals, we attempted to funnel what we could into a wand.

"Hold it lightly. Treat it as an extension of yourself," Magnus instructed.

"Like a blade?"

"Exactly like that."

"Makes sense," I said, palms sweating as I held the light-colored carved wood between my fingers. "Where did this come from?"

"That's one of those tricky questions you normally reserve for Rylan, so I'm not sure how to answer." Magnus grinned. "Would it serve if I said the source is trusted?"

"I suppose, as I'm sure I don't have another option." I frowned, examining the delicately carved lines and the clear crystal at the tip.

"It's been over a week since you were given the dampening tonic. This should be fairly simple." Rylan paced back and forth, his nerves on display as he instructed me.

"Okay." Nothing up to this point had been simple. I knew he was trying to make me feel better, but it wasn't working.

"It's like lighting the candle. You're going to ground yourself, focus on your magic, then send it into the wand itself."

The comparison to the process with the candle made me nervous, never mind that we'd tried with the crystals to no avail already.

Morticia, who had started spending nearly every moment at my side, bumped my ankle with her head encouragingly. Archimedes was also present, giving a *coo* from his perch in the corner.

I had gotten incrementally better at understanding my companion, which was nice. While I still couldn't hear her in the way Rylan or Magnus could, her body language and nuances had become much more familiar to me. I felt safer with her nearby. She wouldn't allow any harm befall me if she could prevent it.

"Right." I held the wand out as far as my arm would stretch and tried to ground myself as Magnus had been teaching me.

As it turned out—unsurprisingly—since I was stone kin, I was much more sensitive to natural elements. It explained my affinity for plants and herbology if nothing else. But with his help, I'd been able to start listening to the deeper hum of the earth itself.

I reached inside myself, then down through the stones of the floor, into the dirt below. Finding an anchor there, I was able to discover the magic was a distinctly green, airy sensation inside my chest. Then, it was time for the scary part. Moving the magic into the object. Hopefully, it would contain enough of it that what was left wouldn't destroy me when the curse broke altogether.

"You're doing wonderfully, Calla. Just focus on the task. We'll take care of the rest." He said that so confidently, but the last time I'd shattered a crystal, it had taken all three of us, plus Grace, Morticia, Archimedes, *and* some third-year students to clean the mess and care for one another as we recovered from the drain of turning off the flow of magic coming out of me.

"We could go to Ophelia again, maybe?" I suggested, faltering out of fear.

"Perhaps, but that's not what we're doing today." Rylan's voice was as calm as a still lake, and it helped me find my center once again.

Checking my grounding, then resuming my focus, I closed my eyes and sent the tendrils of wispy green through my fingertips into the pretty piece of carved wood. Sweat beaded on my brow as I tried to keep the wisps small and controlled. Right as I was about to celebrate, a surge of hot energy flooded through my chest and down my arm. I grunted, determined to anchor myself and keep it steady, but the wand had other ideas. It promptly burst into green flames, the wood emitting a shrieking sound as it processed the raw magic while it burned.

"Magnus? On three?" Rylan asked, voice tense.

Morticia yowled at my feet. I held fast to the wand, the flames somehow not burning my skin. I looked down at her, finding she was gazing urgently back up at me.

Blade.

I heard the word clearly in my mind.

"My dagger?" I asked, picturing the steel one Rylan had finally upgraded me to. It was up in the apartment though, not at all convenient to retrieve.

Light blade.

I frowned. I didn't have a blade imbued with Light. "Magnus, she said—"

"I heard." He approached me with long strides, holding a dagger with a serpentine blade out to me.

"Where did this come fr—"

"Focus, Calla," Rylan said, an edge to his voice.

Good. Send magic. Morticia's voice came easier to me now that I'd managed to hear it the first time.

Still clutching the wand, which had gone from light ash to blackened with scorch, I accepted the blade with my other hand. Closing my eyes, I asked the magic inside me to change direction, to fill the dagger instead. "I thought this could only be done with artifact-type objects."

"That dagger is an artifact, remember? The steel has angelic properties."

I inhaled, trying to settle the nervous rush of blood inside my body. It felt as though the individual cells were all bouncing around inside my skin, colliding angrily, making me nauseous and giving me a headache.

There was resistance at first, like a magnet pushing back against an identical pole, but then something gave way. As everything successfully began to flow, I focused on the fact that I was actually moving the magic into the blade instead of on the searing pain that streaked across my skull.

Never before had I felt the magic deplete, not even with the last crystal Rylan had seemed so hopeful I was filling up with my wild magic. This time, the dagger accepted all I had to throw at it without issue, soaking it up thirstily. My chest began to feel hollowed out, my breath came easier, and despite the painful throb in my head, a clarity I hadn't realized I'd been lacking returned.

As the magical fuel finally ran out, the end of the dagger dropped toward the floor, suddenly and infinitely heavier than it had been.

Morticia yowled, and I frowned, worried I was missing my ability to hear her again.

Sit. Hurry.

I slid to my knees, the blade clattering to the stones as I all but melted into the floor, sagging forward onto my palms.

Rylan squatted at my side. "Well done, Little Owl. Well done." The pride was palpable in his warm energy as he scooped me up bridal style. Despite the shadowy figure lingering in the corner of my eye, I managed a smile, then floated off within Rylan's grasp as the whole world dropped out from under me.

CHAPTER 35
CALLA

"WHAT DO I do with it?" I asked, pausing between bites of cake.

Grace had sent up a variety of sweet snacks to replenish my energy after my transfer-of-power experiment, for which I was eternally grateful. I'd napped quite hard for a few hours, but overall, the recovery had been much easier than previous attempts.

Rylan kept taking my hand between bites if I set my fork down so he could examine it. Though I hadn't felt any heat from the odd green flames of the wand, three of my fingertips were now blackened like his got when he was embracing his inner demon. He was insistent that I allow him an attempt to correct the situation, and was quite annoyed that he'd had to wait until after my nap to start, especially since one of the main considerations was whether or not I still had sensation and feeling.

"Hold still, Little Owl."

"I'm fine."

"You're *not* fine. Look at these fingers. Is that fine?"

I sighed, exhausted from having the same conversation over and over again. "It doesn't hurt. My fingertips can sense heat, cold, and everything in between. I can hold a quill or a fork." He was not amused by my lighthearted attempts to get him to relax. "They're just a little ... discolored."

"Which is a *concern*," he repeated, turning the flesh this way and that under his closest scrutiny.

"Why do yours change?" I asked, trying to get him to see reason.

"Because I am a demon, and when I channel my dark magic, part of my soul shows."

"I—" My thoughts stuttered. "That's your *soul* showing? How on earth does that work?"

One side of his mouth lifted as he softened the tiniest bit. "I'm a creature of Hell, Calla. When I do things that remind my body of my nature, of my time in the pit, it shows outwardly on my skin. It's probably not literally my soul showing, but it might as well be."

Dark need slithered through my gut at his playfulness. I loved everything about his demon side, and the mention of it never failed to get my blood pumping.

Magnus rolled his eyes dramatically and groaned. "The two of you are impossible, do you know that? But to answer your question, Calla, you use the blade to do ... whatever needs doing."

"But it's not mine." I frowned, the object in question an unavoidable presence on the low table between the sofas.

The forearm-length dagger was objectively quite beautiful, no matter what it symbolized for me now. The hilt was moonstone wrapped in delicate black swirls, the tang the same dark metal. The blade itself was steel polished to a warm satin silver forged into a serpentine shape, except for the three inches or so at the deadly tip.

"It is now." Magnus grinned. "I didn't know at the time why my daughter Imogen gave me that when we met to take care of that legion, but now I do. It was meant to come to you. So take it. You don't really have a choice at this point, anyway. It's full of your magic." He winked at me.

"He's not wrong," Rylan muttered, prodding at my fingers with a metal instrument I didn't recognize. "How many is that one worth?" he asked, turning his attention to Magnus.

"More than most at 276."

"That's what she paid? Can we send her coin for it? I'll find a way to repay you." I blushed, embarrassed I'd so boldly offered to spend his money as though it were my own.

Rylan pulled my hand toward him, kissing my palm. "What's mine is yours, Calla. But no, this currency is not something anyone can repay. Not like that. Perhaps I shouldn't have mentioned it at all."

I didn't understand, but I waited, knowing that between the two of them, they would eventually give some kind of explanation. Neither cared for my staring though.

"Your archmage was asking how many demons were bled to forge the blade."

I stilled. Surely, he didn't mean what it sounded like.

"Bled?"

"Yes. If you collect enough blood, you can extract the metal from it to use for ... other purposes." Magnus glanced between Rylan and me, unbothered by the deep frown he was getting from Rylan.

The idea should have been repulsive. I wondered why I wasn't reacting to the information more viscerally, because by all accounts I should have been. Instead, all I could think of was how dedicated one must be to collect that much blood from their enemies. And how much may have been on the skin between us the other night, never mind in Rylan's clothing.

"Does demon blood have different metals than human blood?"

"Not really. It's denser in us, but our bodies hold less for the most part, especially lower-level demons because of their size." Rylan elaborated as he rubbed a salve into my black fingertips.

"Someone collected the blood of 276 demons for that?" I gestured with my head.

"Yes. Imogen herself, I'd imagine," Magnus confirmed. "She's quite independent, and much like her mother in many ways."

"How? I mean, when you're in the middle of a massive fight in a field, how does that work?"

Magnus chuckled, shaking his head. "You're a marvel, Calla. Every time I think we've asked too much of your patient understanding, out comes a question like that. Wanting logistics instead of an explanation for what kind of barbaric practice we're participating in."

Rylan smiled proudly and kissed my temple. "I told you you had no idea what you were in for with her. I certainly didn't. Still don't, some days."

I couldn't help but blush at the unusual praise, especially because it was followed by his eyes scanning me from top to bottom as though he were picturing me naked.

"To answer," Magnus said, clearing his throat as though to interrupt the surge of lust passing between us like we were misbehaving younglings. "We gather the bodies up once we're done and use whatever we can. As for acquiring Light ... that's a whole process the council manages."

I frowned. "Isn't that confusing, though? Iron from demon blood, forged into steel laced with angelic properties? Doesn't that just ... cancel everything out?"

Rylan chuckled, taking my empty cake plate from my hand and setting it on the table before continuing. "If the blood were from all demons like me, that might be the case. But the lower-level legions are closer to humans in that way. Their magic is very minimal, their Hellish influence nearly nonexistent."

"Huh." I reached for the handle of my new dagger, uncertain how to properly care for such an item. "Please thank her for me," I said, unable to come up with anything else. I was grateful, absolutely, but still perplexed over much of the current situation I found myself in. Long ago and far away were the early days of my residence at the manor, when my main concerns were getting enough to eat and simply surviving long enough to indulge in a hot bath at the end of the day.

"I will," Magnus assured me. "Or you can, perhaps. I do want you to meet my children as soon as we can manage that."

"I'd like that very much. Can you remind me of their names, please?"

"Of course. In order eldest to youngest is Tormund, Imogen, Coltor, and lastly the twins, Lovette and Lionel."

"Lovely names, each of them. Are they all grown?"

"Yes, quite. Tormund and Imogen are both approaching two hundred, Coltor is one-fifty, and the twins are a hundred and twenty-five. Though even hundred-year-old stone kin can behave much like children."

Rylan opened his mouth to crack a joke, but Magnus cut him off. "Yes, yes. As can those of us centuries older, Archmage. Stone kin are no different than any race who lives for so long, eh? Demons are much the same."

"True enough," Rylan conceded with a laugh.

Magnus slapped his thighs with his meaty hands. "I'm off for patrol. Be well, my friends."

"And you, Magnus," we chimed.

Rylan wrapped his arms around me, burying his nose in my hair. "I'm so proud of you, Little Owl." He rumbled the words low against my ear, the heat of them making me shiver.

"Me too," I admitted. "I was terrified, if I'm being honest, but I'm very happy it turned out the way it did."

"Mm. Did you get enough to eat?"

"Yes, I don't think I could manage another bite. Especially not more cake. It's delicious, but once the sugar helps me level out, I start to feel ill."

"The balance is delicate," he confirmed, tracing little circles along my skin with his thumbs.

"Do you think ..." I blushed.

"Do I think what, clever one?"

"I was going to suggest you show me how proud of me you are."

Rylan chuckled, his breath tickling along my neck. "I'd love to. Where shall I start? Here?" He pressed his mouth to my skin, tasting along my shoulder before running the tip of his tongue along the shell of my ear. "Or maybe here?" He dipped to my collarbone, nipping at the skin as he kissed along the sensitive flesh.

"Any of that," I sighed, sensation traveling from his electrified touch to my overly sensitive skin. My breasts tingled, and a familiar ache formed between my legs. "All of it."

"Mm." Rylan teased his fingertips under the neckline of my dress with one hand as he unlaced the back with the other. "I think this is one of the best ideas you've had all day."

"I'm pretty sure it's the only one today I'd claim," I said. He chuckled as he pressed his mouth to the shoulder he'd revealed. A cold shock ran through me as a thought interrupted my dive into pleasure. "Do you think ..."

He raised his head, giving me his full attention at the apprehension in my voice, his eyes that beautiful deep-ruby color. "What is it, Little Owl? What worries you?" His fingertips paused at my back, holding the dress in place.

"Do you think the same thing will happen again? That our ... being together is dangerous?"

His face dropped, seriousness pulling his mouth downward. I'd ruined the moment. The last time we'd lain together, though, I'd woken up feeling as though my brain was on fire, so it seemed an important question to ask.

"I don't know." He toyed with the edges of the fabric, unwilling to stop touching me but now much more cautious. His eyebrows pulled together. "But I'm not sure it's worth the risk. Not until we have a permanent solution."

"And if I think it is?" My chest squeezed painfully at the thought. There was no telling how long that might take or if such a solution existed at all.

He shook his head gently, palm cupping my cheek. His eyes had faded back to their normal golden hue. "Calla. I won't have you risking such things, no matter how much I want to consume you always, body and soul."

My heart thumped behind my ribs. It was all so complicated now. While I didn't want to go back to being a hungry servant who knew nothing about who she was, I also didn't want to be afraid my mind was going to break every time I kissed my ... mate? The word still sounded odd, even though I knew it applied.

The lack of control I had over things in my own body was infuriating. It was as though I were a separate entity from my magic, from my body, my mate bond ... my everything.

"Calla." He said my name with urgency, as though I were physically moving as many miles away as I suddenly felt. His fingers tightened, the pads pressing into my skin as he clutched me closer.

"I'm okay," I said, but the words were unconvincing, even to myself.

"You're not. I'm sorry, flower. We'll figure this out. I promise."

I desperately wanted to believe him.

CHAPTER 36
CALLA

MADAME LAURIER SENT word that all three dresses were ready for a final fitting while we were having breakfast in the dining room a few days later. As the young messenger scurried on his way, hands full of Grace's honeyed breakfast cakes, I sagged in relief. The prospect of leaving behind my training for a day in lieu adventuring out in the city left me positively joyous.

Rylan's face dropped at my reaction. "I've neglected you, Little Owl."

"What?" I scooped up the last of my egg with a piece of toast. "How do you mean?"

"You've spent weeks stuck here, training and learning with no outside entertainment. We went out only the once."

"We also went to visit Ophelia," I argued, but that only intensified his frown.

"I'm sorry, Calla. I brought you here to show you many things, not only the walls of this building."

I adored that he worried so much about such things. I placed my hand over his on the table. His mouth tightened every time he noticed my fingertips, which still hadn't fully returned to their normal color. "To be fair, you brought me with you to be your secretary, and I haven't done much of that either."

Rylan grinned. "You've worked on a few ledgers. In truth, I'm neglecting that part of my job as well. I'm weeks behind on my paperwork. Perhaps my secretary could help me catch up?"

I laughed. "Of course. I just need you to set the stack of journals in front of me and tell me what I'm looking for." Rylan was smiling but still seemed pensive. "It's alright," I reassured him. "We've been very busy. The paperwork will get done, and I haven't missed being out in the world."

"You wouldn't really know, though, would you?" Magnus offered unhelpfully.

"No, I suppose not." My cheeks heated in a blush, though I shouldn't have been embarrassed. It wasn't my fault I hadn't spent time outside of the manor, nor that I couldn't recall if I'd done so before.

The two men exchanged glances, and I sensed a whole conversation took place between them without a word being spoken. Rylan was incensed that Magnus had pointed such a thing out, and Magnus was unrepentant for doing so. They both loved to needle the other over something there was already regret or guilt over equally, and with much enthusiasm. Their bond was indeed very brotherly.

"I do look very forward to seeing how many delicious things we can find while we're out," I said, trying to lighten the tone. "Grace's cooking is always incredible, but that fried cake and meat on a stick were some of the best things I've ever tasted."

"We could all use a day away, I think," Rylan agreed. "Magnus? Care to join us?"

He shook his head and got up from his seat. "No, thank you. I've got contraband hunting to do. Though if you happen to be near that tailor, I can always use an extra shirt."

"What color?" I asked, bringing a smile to his face.

"You choose."

"Red then."

"No!" he barked. "Anything but red or green."

I couldn't help but laugh at his horrified reaction. "Why not those colors?"

"Too bright."

Rylan raised an eyebrow, a smirk on his mouth. "He worries they clash with his skin tone," he said. "Red's more my color, anyhow." He leaned in, fake whispering the words.

"I do not!" Magnus's tone was indignant, but the slight color in his cheeks gave away the truth.

Grace, who had been clearing one of the student tables nearby chuckled as she walked over. "He's half right. Red would wash him out. Green, on the other hand, would bring out his eyes." She winked at Magnus then walked away without waiting for a response.

"What just happened?" I asked, a broad smile on my mouth.

"I have no idea," Rylan agreed. We were both staring at Magnus, who seemed to be frozen. "But I think she broke him."

Magnus huffed and sputtered, but never managed to form another coherent word before stomping off.

Green it was, then.

I FELT NEARLY as out of place doing the final fitting as I had the first. At least this time there were only a few additional measurements involved. The gowns themselves were decadent and lovely, but I worried I'd never wear them for any purpose aside from a fancy dinner or perhaps as part of some kind of court function.

Seeing the glow in Rylan's eyes as he checked them over, however, was the best kind of compliment. I wondered if the flash I caught was him envisioning taking the garments right back off me. The way my own body warmed at the thought, I could imagine him having a similar reaction.

The shoes felt like butter, but they were too dainty. I was sure I'd scuff or stain them nearly immediately, which horrified me. They were clearly meant to be pretty not functional or made for work. Perhaps I'd just wear them around the apartment. The leather boots that'd been made, on the other hand, were supple with a stout sole. I couldn't wait to try them out during our next weapons training lesson.

"And the trousers we discussed?" Rylan asked as the seamstress tucked the gowns into a box.

"I can do the linen, but I'd suggest the tanner on Ashmore for leather versions. He's who makes the boots. I already sent my messenger to him with her measurements."

I blushed again and barely resisted rolling my eyes at Rylan, who was very pleased with this answer. "Thank you, Madame Laurier." I inclined my head, unsure of the appropriate social gesture.

"It's been my absolute pleasure."

"Will you have those sent to d'Arcan for us, please?"

"Of course, Archmage. I'll get my courier to take them shortly."

We left the gown shop, headed for the candler, the same as before. Rylan placed his order, and I picked out a few wide pillars for the holders in the apartment, then he made sure to take me past a host of new food vendors—and I'd never been so excited to be adventurous.

"This is some kind of fowl soaked in a sauce that is both salty and sweet." He pointed to the chunks of glossy meat stacked over a layer of steamed white rice.

I couldn't help but give a little bounce as I tasted it, the flavors indescribably good as they burst on my tongue. "I could eat that every day. Can we tell Grace?"

Rylan laughed. "I'll suggest it, but I'm betting she gets a bit cranky about having to learn a whole new technique."

As we were crossing the street on our way to the library, I saw a wagon that made my head throb. My stomach lurched, leaving the taste of bitter bile in my throat instead of my delicious lunch.

"Are you alright, Calla?" Rylan asked, concern etched in his features as I held my forehead. He patted his vest pockets, searching for the vial he'd begun carrying around while he and Magnus put me through my paces at the collegium.

I knew he'd left it behind, however, as this day wasn't supposed to involve any magic aside from his normal misdirection cantrip. "It's alright." I pointed. "That wagon. There's something familiar about it."

Full attention on the wagon, Rylan pulled me toward where its horses were tied to a post outside the Noble Feather Hattery. I carefully studied the patterns on the outside of the wagon bed, the connections slow to come together in my mind, as though something held them back.

"That's the wagon I traveled in," I said in a shocked whisper. "When I was sold to the manor."

"Is that so?" Rylan's jaw clenched, and he peered in the back as we crossed behind it. There was nothing in the bed except some empty wooden crates.

Rylan dug around in the packing materials, grunting when he came up with what looked like a broken piece of clay. He slipped the item into his pocket. "Shall we wait to see who the owners are?"

Through the glass windows of the shop, I saw four young women all seated on a sofa and an older woman negotiating with the shopkeep. Each of them were dressed in a gown much like the ones I'd just acquired, every girl in her own pastel color.

"Do you recognize them?" Rylan asked, leaning casually against the wagon. His body language was an outright lie. I wasn't sure how he managed it. He was tensed, barely containing his rage but appeared to be the embodiment of calm on the outside. Electricity danced along my skin, a concerning amount of sensation considering we were outside and not within four walls.

"No, but I don't remember any people from that day. I never have. Only that I arrived in a wagon and it departed without me."

As the ladies discussed their hats, Rylan eventually went to see the horses. He stroked their noses and spoke to them in hushed tones. It was a language I didn't recognize, but I felt him asking their permission for something. Encouraging them to remain calm. They seemed unbothered by his presence or touch and happy enough to accept his kind attentions.

I was about to suggest we go back to d'Arcan, as I'd begun to doubt my identification of the wagon when a man approached from around the nearest corner. Awareness tingled in my chest at the sight of him; any doubt I had about this being the right wagon was forgotten. His face was unfamiliar, but my body sent out warnings left and right.

"You there! Step away from my horses."

"These are your horses?"

"Yes, that's what I said, isn't it? Now fuck off away from my wagon."

"No, I don't think I will." Rylan smiled at the man, but there was no humor in it. I swallowed, recognizing that while I mostly got the version of him that was even-tempered, his darkness hovered right under the surface, waiting to be provoked. My pulse started to pound for two very different reasons. "Do you know this woman?"

The man turned his eyes to me for the first time, and I saw the moment recognition hit. "No," he lied. "Never seen her before in my life."

Rylan grinned, the smile all sharp edges. The man seemed to miss every cue that he was in imminent danger. "Are you sure?

Because I have reason to believe you're the one who sold her to my house."

"I mean, maybe. I see a lot of girls, you know? It's a very busy city." He fidgeted with the seam on his vest, looking nervously over his shoulder into the shop.

"A lot of girls, you say?" Rylan asked, venom in his voice. "You sold *this* one to Stolas Manor. I need to know where you got her from."

"Listen, I don't know what you want from me, but I don't know her—" Rylan sent a warning bolt at the man, shocking him in the leg. "Hey! What the gods was that? How did you do that?" He held his hands out, trying to ward off the next blow.

"I'm not partial to liars. What is your name?"

"Okay! Maybe I do know her, but I might remember better with a little coin for my troubles, you know?"

I balked, audibly gasping. I couldn't believe the audacity of the man asking for money when Rylan very clearly had murder in his eyes.

"Of course! How rude of me. Shall we step inside to negotiate?" Rylan's most docile tone was strange coming out of his mouth when he smiled like that. He clapped the man on the back as he led him inside the hat shop. With a glance of ruby eyes over his shoulder, Rylan indicated that I should follow him inside.

Stunned, I watched as Rylan's whole demeanor changed from threatening to accommodating. It was terrifying how completely he shifted, but I found myself unafraid. This man might be a demon, but he was *my* demon.

Unfortunately for the wagon man, he was about to learn just how dangerous the handsome lord of Stolas Manor could truly be.

CHAPTER 37
RYLAN

MY BLOOD ROLLED with a mixture of rage and excitement. The luck of running across the wagon in a city this large and busy was incredible. Calla's memory might be troublesome to access for many things still, but I trusted her recognition of the wagon implicitly. It was where her memory block seemed to end, and considering it had a very distinct pattern along the side, it would be hard to mistake. The curse seal remnant in the crate they were hauling was also a fortuitous find.

"Pardon the intrusion, madam." I bowed graciously to the hatter.

She skimmed my vest, finding my owl insignia. "Sir." She inclined her head respectfully. "Can I help you?" She glanced at the family, who grew nervous at our entrance.

"I'm afraid there's a very serious conversation I need to conduct with your customers. Would it be possible to request you close up? Perhaps you could go find yourself some lunch?" I handed her a coin. One large enough to purchase her meals for a month.

She blanched, one hand rising to her throat. "Oh, my. Yes, of course, Archmage. I'll be happy to leave you in charge here."

There were some fierce whispers in response to her using my title, and the tension in the small shop rose exponentially. I rolled my shoulders back, trying to ensure I could remain calm until the right moment came to lash out.

Calla lingered at my side, obviously uncomfortable but doing her best to hide it. I pressed my palm into her lower back, trying to anchor her nervous energy and calm mine. She stopped fidgeting with her dress but was still flushed, looking from one member of the family to another.

"Have they paid you for your services?" I asked the hatter.

"We'd not yet gotten to that part of our business, but I've taken their requests."

"How dare you!" the woman—his wife, I was guessing—fumed. "It's uncalled for to insult us in such a way. We came in here prepared to pay for what we've purchased or we wouldn't have come in at all."

"Wonderful. You'll finish your business, then, so we can get to ours." I smiled again, and the woman flinched. It clearly hadn't come out as kind as I'd been aiming for.

Hastily, the hatter collected her money from them and locked up the till. "Shall I return in ... an hour?"

"That should do nicely. I appreciate your discretion." I pressed another coin into her hand.

She dipped into a deep nod and went out through the back after turning around her sign and locking us all inside. I went a step further once she was gone and closed the drapes across the windows.

The four girls were all huddled together on the sofa, the two younger ones holding hands. I had a feeling they'd be more helpful than their parents, but I needed to quiet my rage before addressing them.

"I'll start the same way I did with your man." I gestured to the pouting overgrown toddler walking small paces in the corner of the shop. "Do you recognize this woman?"

Each of them glanced at him for direction before looking at Calla. That alone told me everything I needed to know.

"You promised payment," he spat.

"So I did. And I'm a man of my word. But I've gotten no information yet." He sniffed and returned to his pacing. "She recognizes your wagon from when she first became employee of my estate. I'm hoping to find more information about her. What can you tell me?"

There was no noise aside from the rustling of fabric as the girls shifted around in their seats, waiting for their parents to take the lead.

"We picked her up on the road," the woman finally said. "That's all we know."

I tilted my head, not in the least swayed that what she was saying was true. "Where?"

"A distance from your manor."

I clenched a fist. She was bold, I'd give her that. Evasion was a risk with a man like me, and she was giving it her best effort. "Which direction? What road? I fear you're intentionally leaving out details, and I'm growing exceptionally impatient."

Calla took one of my hands into hers, the touch instantly calming my rage.

"Why not ask *her*? Oh, could it be that she doesn't remember?" She grinned, malice dripping from her horrible smile.

Heat burned into my body as I reacted to her provocation. The man snickered under his breath, which only made it worse. Electricity built on the air in the small shop, tingling along the skin of my neck as I focused on holding it in. "Cleverness is not the same thing as intelligence," I said, which earned me a pinched frown. I turned to the oldest girl. "What is your family name?"

She looked from me to her mother, fear pouring off her. They had their daughters dressed up in nice gowns, they were going to buy them fancy hats and send them off to court, but they were not well cared for. Not where it mattered.

"You don't have to be afraid of him," Calla said, stepping forward so that she was slightly closer to the girls than I was. "He won't hurt you. You've done nothing wrong."

The youngest girl, who was perhaps thirteen, began to cry.

"Marchand," the oldest daughter answered.

"Stella! Hush," her mother scolded her, sending another glare my way.

"Thank you, Stella. And do you recognize this woman?"

"Yes."

"Girl, you'll want to shut your mouth!" The man stepped forward, teeth clenched as he shook a fist her direction.

"On the contrary. She's free to speak," I said, raising a hand and sending a paralyzing bolt of power into the man's chest.

"Reggie!" The wife rushed to his side. He'd fallen onto his back and was panting a bit, but was fine otherwise. His eyes were wide as he regarded me again. She was all venom as she protested, "You careless magician! How dare you—"

"Unless you'd like similar treatment, you'll stop."

Her jaw snapped shut, and she plopped herself back down on the sofa, her injured husband forgotten. The girls had watched the altercation with wide eyes, but seemed mostly unmoved by my display.

"I just want to know where my home is. I remember being in the wagon, but not any of you. Can you please help me?" Calla went for sympathy, her eyes glossy as she looked between the girls.

They were too scared of their parents. They knew on the other side of speaking lay punishment, it was clear in the way they huddled together, turning to one another for comfort instead of to the adults who should have been protecting them.

"Calla, would you please take the girls out to the wagon?"

"But—"

I stared into her eyes, wishing for her to understand my motives. "Everyone will be traveling with us back to the collegium."

She nodded despite the confusion pulling her brows together. "Alright. Stella? Girls? Would you come outside with me, please?" She held out a hand.

"Don't you dare! You belong to me," the woman snapped. "We don't know these people!"

"You'll be safe with us. I swear it," I promised.

Stella stood up first, very pointedly ignoring her mother. There was a tremble in her hands, but she walked on steady feet toward Calla, who was unlocking the shop door. Her sisters flocked to her side, provoking quite a lot of shouting from their parents.

"Quiet!" I barked once the door had closed behind them all. I locked it again, allowing the energy flooding under my skin to flow into the room around me. My horns slid out and my teeth sharpened. "We don't have much time. If you tell me what I've asked, I'll consider letting you live."

"You're a devil!" Where I'd hoped for fear, there was only disgust.

"Perhaps only slightly more than you. How many girls have you stolen from their homes for trade?" The very idea made my blood boil, the potent rage burned hot in my chest.

"We are not traffickers!" She was indignant. "We may be opportunists, but we don't trade in lives."

Poor Reggie was finally able to sit up, though speech was probably quite a ways off.

"I'm going to pretend I believe you for now. And you're going to tell me what happened to put Calla into your path."

"Not until we're paid. Reggie said you agreed to pay." She crossed her arms, momentarily having forgotten to fear me.

I pulled a coin from my pocket and showed it to her. "As I said, I'm a man of my word." I folded it between my fingers and released it with a powerful flick. It flashed across the space between us, hitting her between the eyes. She slumped over lifeless, which had poor Reggie groaning incoherently.

Frustrated that this hadn't gone quite as I'd hoped, I shocked the man with enough wild energy he too fell unconscious and prepared to load them both into the wagon like the dead weight they were.

"BLANCHE!" THE WOMAN sputtered as Magnus poured cold water over her face. "My name is Blanche."

"Lovely. Blanche and Reginald Marchand, you are being held on suspicion of kidnapping, at the very least. Nobody will be looking for you, and quite frankly, I could kill you both where you stand ... er ... slump, and never think of it again. My friend here has asked you for information. Between us, we have innumerable ways of extracting it that would be amusing for us and painful for you." Magnus smiled. "I do love to be amused."

Reggie was still having trouble speaking clearly, but given another hour he'd be fine. It was but a matter of him earning that extra hour that was a concern.

Magnus had been waiting for me when we arrived with our unexpected guests back at d'Arcan. It had taken no convincing at all for him to help me escort these two to one of the cells in the basement of the building while Calla took the girls to the dining hall to be fed and hopefully convinced to talk. Whatever he'd wanted to speak to me about had been issued an indefinite pause.

"We picked her up on the road," Blanche repeated through chattering teeth.

"Yes, you've said that. But you're lying," Magnus said drolly, crossing his beefy arms.

"What road?" I asked again, tossing a small ball of flame between my hands.

"The market road. The one that passes all the farms."

"That certainly narrows it down." I glanced at Magnus, indicating my frustration. I released a small fireball at Blanche's chest, the flames hungrily lapping at the lace work on her dress.

She squawked and flailed, trying to put the fire out with her hands. "In Granite Bend, near the pond! Where the cemetery is, the one with all the bird statues on the headstones."

I stilled, as did my friend. I knew the area, though I hadn't visited in quite some time. "Continue."

"We were passing through, headed here. A woman asked if we'd like to take a job. Paid well enough, so we said yes. It seemed simple."

"But it wasn't?"

Reggie had crawled over to his wife's side and attempted to clamp his hand over her mouth. "Dun listn ta her."

She shook him off, sliding across the floor away from him. "It was fine. We were to take a woman from a house, make her drink a potion, and say some words."

My pulse started pounding again. "Then what?"

"We'd leave her here, in Revalia. With the storm, we needed to fix our wagon near your manor, so we decided it was as good an option as any. We left her there instead."

"You were paid twice for kidnapping a woman? How enterprising," I sneered, zapping them both with a bolt of energy in frustration. They squawked but were unhurt. Mostly.

"You're leaving something out," Magnus said, squinting at her.

Anger continued to surge through me, the energy of it crackling off the walls. "Yes, there's quite a lot missing from that story. Who hired you?"

"Goody Kincaid," Blanche said. Reggie hissed at his wife, swatting at her again. "Oh, bollocks to you. Nobody's paid us enough to keep this to ourselves at the cost of death."

"Widow Kincaid asked you to kidnap and curse Calla?"

"Yes."

"For what purpose?"

"She wanted the house. Something about the land being special. I don't really know." Magnus growled in disgust. "I'm only telling you what she said," Blanche groused. "She babbled something about a well, guaranteed crop fertility, magic ... I don't have the first clue what she meant."

"Which house did you take her from?"

"The one nearest the cemetery."

My chest felt like it was going to explode. A debt owed to me that I'd long put out of mind happened to be anchored to that house.

"The Noctua farm?"

"Yes. Whether the girl is a Noctua is anyone's guess. There's never been one."

"I'm aware." I clung desperately to my breath despite the way my throat attempted to close up. "What was the wording of the curse? Was there both an artifact and a potion?"

"Yes, there was a clay seal I had to break after making her drink a spelled vial. She was not to remember anything, not even us. She'd take what happened that night to her grave."

I looked at Magnus, who was deep in thoughtful consideration about the information we'd been given. As much as I itched to dispatch these disgusting humans, it felt wrong to do so before speaking to their daughters.

"Would you mind keeping them company for a while?" I asked Magnus.

"It would be my pleasure. May I?" He gestured broadly, asking permission to toy with them in his own way. "Do you have any more questions you'd like me to ask?"

"Nothing specific, but you're welcome to continue if it makes you happy." I pulled the seal fragment from my pocket and handed it to him. "I found this in the back of the wagon. Seems they do more than occasionally activate a curse on unknowing women."

He grinned, and both of them shrank back from it.

"I've told you what I know! Let us out of here!" Blanche argued as I stalked up the stone stairs.

I turned at the top, a vicious smile on my mouth. She paled as she took me in, my words sinking in as they resonated around the dungeon. "I agreed you'd be paid. There was never any promise of freedom."

CHAPTER 38
CALLA

"THANK YOU, GRACE."

She smiled as she delivered plates full of finger foods to our table. "My pleasure, Lady Calla."

"I'm not—"

Grace waved a hand, dismissing my complaint. "We'll come up with a better title for you soon, but until then, that one will do."

I gave her an appreciative nod and turned back to the girls, who were eagerly dividing up the food amongst themselves. "There's plenty more if that's not enough. No need to worry." Their hands stilled, and I worried for the dozenth time about their treatment. "How about now? Can I know the rest of your names yet?"

Stella, the eldest, looked at each of her sisters in turn before turning back to me. She was clearly used to being in charge. "What's going to happen to us?"

I shrugged. "I don't know. Probably nothing bad. Not unless you deserve it. Rylan is fair, he won't punish you if he doesn't have to."

"You just need to know where you came from?" Stella ate a slice of apple.

"That's the most important thing, yes."

"We picked you up at the Noctua farm," she said.

My chest ached at the sound of that name, but I didn't know what that meant. "Thank you, but I don't know what that is."

"But you can tell him, right? And he will?"

"Perhaps."

"You forgot us. Every time you couldn't see us anymore. You forgot," the youngest girl said quietly, nibbling on a cracker.

"I did? I'm sorry. I have trouble with my memory. I was hoping you could help me understand why."

"Mama did something," the second oldest said. "She made you drink some stuff and broke a coin and said words. It was so you wouldn't remember."

Stella was afraid, but did nothing to stop them from speaking.

"I see. We suspected something like that. Do you know how I can take that away? Where it came from to start with? Or why they'd want to put one on me?" They all shook their heads. "Well. That's unfortunate, but not your fault either."

"I'm Jana," the youngest said.

"Hello, Jana. I'm Calla." I smiled at her, hoping it would encourage her to keep talking.

"Will you send us back with them?" the second oldest asked. "My name is Bridget, by the way. And that's Sara."

"Nice to meet you both. Do you want to go back with them? They're your parents, right?"

She nodded. "They are, but ... I'm tired of doing what they make us do—"

"Shh," Stella admonished.

"Why do you want to keep their secrets?" Bridget scolded her older sister. "They punish you the most."

I didn't like the sound of that. "Are you treated well by them?"

"No," Bridget groused.

"I'm sure I can speak to the archmage about options. This is a school, for example. There may be other places like this in the city you can go. What do they make you do?"

"We steal," little Sara said. "Pick pockets. Smile and distract people while they're shopping."

"Oh." I was surprised by this but tried to keep my face neutral. "I'd bet we can find something else for you to do instead."

"When we don't take enough, we get the switch," Bridget said. "Or we don't get fed."

I swallowed hard, unsure what to say to that and hating that they've endured physical punishment for such a thing.

Grace returned, this time with a plate of sweet cakes for the girls. "Here we are!" she beamed at them. "Aren't you a lovely bunch? I could use girls like you in the kitchen. You seem like you'd be wonderful help." She winked at me as she dashed off again.

Rylan stalked into the dining hall as they started to dig into the sweets. I stood and met him across the room, giving all of us a little bit of privacy.

"Any luck?" he asked.

"Yes. They all gave me their names. They told me I came from something called the Noctua farm?" As the first time, the name made my chest feel funny, but there was no way for me to identify why. "The woman did a curse on me, based on what they described. And they are punished by their parents if they don't grift enough from people in town."

"Well done, Little Owl." He clenched his jaw so tightly I worried for his teeth. "Their parents were similarly forthcoming, though not nearly so willingly. Magnus is going to keep them company for now."

"Grace plied them with food, I just kept asking questions. I think it was her food that did it, if I'm being honest."

Rylan softened, leaning forward to kiss my forehead. "Will they speak with me, do you think?"

"One way to find out."

They all stared, wide-eyed as Rylan approached the table. "Hello, girls. Calla tells me you were quite helpful. We appreciate that very much. Your parents are still being questioned, but I thought it was a good idea to have a moment alone with you. Would that be alright?"

They gave cautious nods.

"Are our parents alive?" Stella asked. She sounded less concerned than I expected.

"Yes," Rylan answered. He didn't elaborate, which left me curious how long they might remain that way. "Where are you staying at present?" he asked.

Stella provided the address of what amounted to a campground on the fringes of the city.

"Where do you keep your belongings?" I asked.

"Everything we own is in the wagon," Bridget added.

There had been a few mostly empty crates in the wagon, some old bedding, and barely enough food for a single meal.

"Do you want to stay with your parents?" There were no verbal answers, and they all did some type of fidgeting instead of responding. "Would you want to live here? Or somewhere like here? Even if that meant you were not with your parents any longer?" I asked.

Bridget was the first to nod, then Sara. Jana followed her sisters' lead, and Stella looked panicked but nodded too.

"We can see about that," Rylan assured them. "Plenty of food, clean clothes. Schooling. Work, too, of course."

"Why would you do that for us? After what we did to her?" Stella asked, suspicious.

"Did you agree to set the curse?"

"No."

"Did you drag her from her house?"

"That was scary," Sara muttered. "It was raining, and Papa was *mad*."

"Yes, I'm sure it was uncomfortable for everyone involved. But you didn't do that, did you?"

"No, but we didn't stop them." Stella sagged. "We held her down like they asked, and just watched it all happen. I was curious, even." She grimaced as though the thought left a sour taste in her mouth.

"That's to be expected when it comes to magic, I expect. As for stopping them ..." His nostrils flared as he took in and released a calming breath. "That was not your responsibility," Rylan assured them gently. "I'm sure that kind of dissent wouldn't have been rewarded." My heart squeezed for the girls. While I couldn't help wishing they'd been brave on my behalf, it wasn't their fault. "It's settled then. We'll get you some rooms set up, and I'll have Grace add you to the meal list. We'll sort out some chores for you to manage and a class schedule. Growing into better people is the justice I'd like to see for your part in the deeds your parents have been asking you to commit."

"Why?" Stella asked again, shock plain on her face, even as the tears started to build. She looked as though she worried that Rylan's offer was some kind of terrible joke. "Why would you do this? Why would you help?"

"Because everyone deserves a chance to thrive," he said softly. "What of your parents? Do you want to see them?"

"Not right now." Little Jana was the first to speak. "Can we keep our dresses?"

"Yes, of course. Why would you not be allowed to keep your dresses?"

The girls exchanged a look. "Because usually once we leave the shops, we have to take them off. They go in a special box. We only get to wear them when Mama wants to seem fancy."

I met his eye, and his nostrils flared again. "I'll bet we can find you some other everyday dresses as well," I assured them. "But for now, your fancy dresses are perfectly serviceable, and you can keep them as long as you'd like."

Rylan went off to speak with Grace, and I quizzed them about their skills. Everyone knew basic home skills like cooking, cleaning, mending, and horse care. They could all read and write, but only the older two could do sums.

"You'll do just fine here," I assured them. "Oh! What are the horses called?"

"Merle and Mabel," Bridget said confidently. "Merle is the one with the white patch on his nose."

"Perfect. Hopefully they'll get to stay in the stables here on the grounds, so you can go visit them."

Grace came back out with Rylan, beaming as she approached the table. "I see I got my wish! Some lovely new helpers!"

They all responded positively to the warm woman, and she hustled them off as soon as they'd collected their dirty dishes.

"That was exceptionally kind," I told him, leaning into his strong body.

"They are not innocent, but they are also not to blame." He sighed, using one hand to cradle the back of my head as he pressed his mouth to my forehead.

"What of the parents?"

Before he even answered I could feel the hot current of his anger pass between us. "Guilty as sin. And they shall be punished."

CHAPTER 39
CALLA

"A BSOLUTELY NOT," RYLAN bit the words off as he flung
the apartment door closed.

"What do you mean? Why not?" I desperately tried to
squelch my temper as emotions bounced around inside me. "If
that's my home, I need to see it for myself. We should be packing
to leave right now!"

Naturally, I'd thought that traveling to the farm the Marchand's
claimed they'd taken me from would be top priority, but Rylan
was against it entirely. Unfortunately for me, Magnus, who had
barely gotten through the door before Rylan slammed it, agreed
with him.

"It is not wise to return there, especially not now," Rylan argued, jaw clenched.

We did not have much history of quarreling with one another,
but recently, it seemed to be something we found more and more
reasons to do. It appeared our honeymoon phase, such as it was,
might be at an end.

"How is it not logical to go there immediately to see if my memories come back? I was kidnapped and cursed to remember nothing. It is completely unfair to ask me to ignore that we now have a probable location for my kidnapping." Tears burned behind my eyes, I was so angry. I didn't want to allow them to fall—I didn't want the men to think I had turned on the waterworks to get my way. That was not at all how I operated, I was just frustrated. It felt as though one of the most important carrots of my life had been dangled out of my reach and then yanked away.

They exchanged a knowing look, which only served to enrage me further. "My lady—" Magnus said, tone delicate.

"I am *not a lady*! I'm a simple girl who was taken from her farm. Somewhere you both clearly know of and yet refuse to let me visit!"

Taken aback by my uncharacteristic shouting, both stood silent and wide-eyed, staring at me as I dragged in breath after ragged breath. "Please sit, Calla." Rylan gestured to the sofa, his tone and demeanor much softer.

"I'd rather stand," I responded, petulant.

Rylan looked to Magnus, who sat first. He took up most of the far sofa himself, and Rylan sat in his normal seat on the one nearest the door. I busied myself with collecting glasses and wine. As a final act of temper, I filled mine nearly to the brim before simply setting the bottle on the table between them.

Magnus's mouth ticked in amusement, but he said nothing as he reached out and poured for both himself and the infuriating man who was the main focus of my ire. "At the risk of losing your favor, I must agree with Rylan, Calla."

I tensed, leaning on the arm of the sofa for support. "I'm going to need some excellent reasoning, Magnus."

"Naturally, my lady. Firstly, we need to further investigate the larger network of people that the Marchand couple was part of. While interrogating them, I learned many things that require further attention."

"If they, as we suspect, are but a tiny cog in a bigger wheel of criminal activity, you returning to that place could alert some of their partners that something is afoot. Their disappearance is likely already raising suspicion," Rylan explained.

I took in a deep breath, schooling my tone into one less biting. My chest wasn't quite so full of rumbling bees trying to fly in all directions, and the hot tears had also retreated. I hated that my emotions had bested me, if only for a short time. "And if they're not part of a larger scheme?"

"They are," Magnus insisted, tone dry. "It's not a question of if but rather how widespread."

"Alright. How long will it take to investigate?"

"Not long, perhaps a few weeks. Likely not more than a few months."

"Months?" I croaked. That felt like an eternity when I knew I could get to wherever this farm was in a matter of days. Hours, if one of the two of them with a set of wings chose to take me by air. That idea gave me the shivers, equal parts terrifying and exhilarating.

They exchanged another look, one that held a full conversation I was not privy to or part of. "What is it you aren't telling me?"

Rylan's mouth flattened. "The locals of the area are not to be trusted. Someone hired that couple to steal you away in their wagon. Someone with access to magic enough to make your curse."

Ice rocketed through my veins. I'd suspected what had occurred wasn't random but hearing that someone specifically set out to have me cursed was still a shock. "You suspect that the source of the contraband is near there?" I concluded. "What you found in the wagon, what was it?"

Rylan sighed. "It was part of a clay seal. Hexes can be made in many ways, but the most common is two parts—a tonic and a clay seal imbued with a charm."

"Was it the one used on me?"

"I'm afraid that's impossible to know, but it may still give a good signature to someone who can see traces. Ophelia may be able to help with that part. I know someone else, but ..."

"But?"

"I'm not sure if my message will reach him. Archimedes will do his best, but the address I have is quite old."

"We also worry that you're forgetting how dangerous—for you—this could be in general, my lady."

I glared at him, and he tipped his head in apology, though the smirk on his mouth negated it. "Everything's been fine since I took the potion. Not even a twinge since, and that was the smallest of drops." I didn't mention how Rylan avoided most physical intimacy since, much to our mutual displeasure.

"It's too dangerous. We have no idea what will happen if or when the crack widens again. I cannot have you in pain like you were before, Calla. I will not." Passion laced his words, and I sagged.

This was not a conspiracy to keep me from learning who I was but only for my own safety. "But the potion—"

"Will only get us so far." Rylan sighed, clearly exhausted from mentally running through hypothetical possibilities I hadn't even begun to think about. "It is not a catchall or a guaranteed fail-safe. We cannot rely on that alone. I'd prefer not to rely on it at all," he grumbled, wiping a hand down his face.

"But we're not only counting on that potion!" I flailed an arm out, sloshing a bit of wine from my glass onto my dress as I crossed in front of Rylan and sank onto the sofa next to him. To prevent further spilling, I set my nearly full glass on the table while Magnus watched with interest, one broad finger pressed to his temple. "We successfully siphoned the overflow of my magic into *that* blade." I gestured at the dagger, which still lay where I'd left it on the table. "I can tell that it's gone! I feel lighter, less weighed down."

"That's not enough—" Rylan protested, but I continued on.

"I've not set anything on fire in weeks. You've taught me to fight well enough. I can defend myself in a tight situation. I can make potions and some helpful cantrips. I have Morticia. I'm not *helpless*." And just like that, the tears were back, burning at my eyes as they tried to escape. I frowned, unsettled that my emotions were so unstable.

"I would never claim you were, Little Owl." Rylan frowned, clearly as frustrated as I was by our disagreement. "But I also cannot agree to going to that farm right now. There's too much we don't know."

I sucked in a breath, blinking fiercely to ward off the tears that were so insistent on falling.

"It's a side effect of the magic." Magnus nodded, sliding a plate of Grace's bite-sized honey cakes across the table. "It can take a while to level out after a purge like that."

I begrudgingly took one, munching on it while I pouted. "We can drop the Marchands off at the stone kin camp, Magnus can introduce me to his children, and then we can go that direct—"

"*Calla*." Rylan injected power into my name, the sound an echoing bass note as it resonated through my spine. The tone and force with which the word was delivered left me shrinking in on myself like a scolded child. I was certain that was his intention, which infuriated me.

"I hear your concerns," I said once I shook the surprise off. "But I do not agree." I bit the words out, teeth clenched tightly as I glared the demon sitting next to me down. "And you will never speak to me in such a way, ever again. I'm not a youngling to be put in her place, controlled by your very voice because you want to enforce your will. This is not your decision to make alone. It is *my* life. *My* memory. Is it that you're afraid I'll learn something you don't want me to? I see no other reason for you to treat me in such a way."

Through the blood rushing in my ears I heard Magnus choke, then stifle a laugh. I turned my eyes his direction and he stopped, waving his hand in apology for the affront. "Nervous habit, my lady. I swear. My deepest apologies. Nothing funny here, I completely agree with your righteous rage."

Wild energy crept over my skin. Rylan gripped the arm of the sofa so hard with one hand I thought the fabric might rip. The other had wound itself in the layers of my skirt that had puddled next to me on the cushion. His jaw was clenched so tightly the muscle rolled under the skin and his fingertips slowly blackened as I watched.

He was angry.

Good.

So was I.

"Well. I've said my piece." Magnus got to his feet, absently clearing his throat as he snatched up the plate of cakes and the bottle of wine for the road. "I agree that caution is best, and this is not the time to go on such a journey. However, I empathize with your very unique situation and understand your sense of urgency, Calla. Perhaps a compromise can be found?" Neither Rylan nor I had moved, our posturing locked in a stalemate. "I've got patrol, but I'll be back in the morning," he added hastily, attention on Rylan as he backed out the door with his snacks, leaving us alone.

Whether that was a wise decision or not on his part remained to be seen. One of us might end up injured or worse without him there to mediate. Tension mounted as we continued to stare one another down, neither of us willing to be the first to break. My breaths came in shorter and shorter bursts as the energy he threw off pressed in on me. It was rage and lust, all mixed up in a heady cocktail.

He finally broke the standoff and turned his body my direction. The ruby of his eyes was crisp, but his features softened as he raised the hand that had been about to break the sofa arm to my cheek.

"You are too valuable, Calla, there's much you don't know. Much I protect you from."

"I thought half the point of all this was so I can protect myself? I am just—"

"It is, of course it is, but you are *just* nothing." He growled the words, fierceness dripping from them as they settled into my skin. I tried to suppress a shiver, but couldn't stop it, my body rippling as it passed through me. "You are the reason the sun rises to brighten the sky and the moon glows to illuminate the night. There is not now, nor has there ever been, anyone quite like you. Do you hear what I'm saying? I will not allow you to risk my whole world so casually. Not now, not ever."

The intense declaration crashed into me like a boulder rolling down a hillside. He was angry because he was *scared*. "Rylan."

Whatever other words I prepared in protest were never formed. I worked to digest the profound statement he'd delivered when my demon leaned in to kiss me. His warm, soft mouth was anything but gentle as he consumed me. The kiss left me breathless, my lips tingling as he pulled away.

"You are mine, Little Owl, and I'll not allow anyone to put you in danger. Not even you."

One clever hand wrapped around the back of my neck, the other maneuvered under my skirts as he hauled me unceremoniously into his lap. He licked into my mouth as he tore away my undergarments, the heat of my body pressing into the firmness in his pants.

I fondly recalled a similar encounter from when we'd first arrived. Need built inside me as his energized fingertips sent tiny thrills all along the planes of my thighs. He roved down one side then up the center, never quite touching where I wanted him to most. The hand around my neck changed angle and tightened around my throat, stalling my breath in a delicious way. My eyes drifted closed as he pressed in on the sides of my neck, and when they opened again, I found those fiery rubies staring back at me, the tip of his tongue resting in the corner of his mouth.

Reaching between us, I grasped at the fastening on his pants, slapping his hand away when he tried to remove mine.

"Calla." He was going to protest, I could tell, but he couldn't bring himself to finish the complaint.

"I need you," I sighed against his mouth, gripping his hard cock in my fist. "Please, Rylan."

"We shouldn't." He argued, at war with himself and me as he dropped his head back in pleasure. "It's too dangerous."

"So you've been saying. We'll be fine. If my head makes a fuss, I'll tell you straightaway. I need this. I. Need. You."

The silky flesh throbbed in my hand as I made slow passes from the root to the tip, using the pad of my thumb to spread around the moisture that had begun to weep from the head. My core clenched as he rumbled a moan deep in his throat and raised his head again, eyes full of lust, all anger forgotten.

Before he could argue again, I guided him to my opening, settling down on my knees as he pressed inside. His Adam's apple bobbed as he swallowed before diving in to nip at my throat with his pointed teeth. One of his arms wound around my back as he sucked at the tender skin of my collarbone, lifting me in rhythm with his thrusts as his need took over.

I experimented with leaning forward, then backward, until I found an angle that had him rubbing a spot inside me that lit stars behind my eyes. He held me right where I wanted to be with one arm, his mouth having traveled as far south on bared flesh as my dress would allow, then simply put his mouth over my breast through the fabric and sucked. The sounds of panting and wet flesh filled the room along with our mingled energy.

"There," I sighed when he moved the tiniest bit and my body zinged with pleasure.

"That's my girl. Tell me what you need." He increased his speed, and I moaned, the new sensation shocking. The coils of my climax tightened in my gut as he stared deep into my eyes. "You feel so good, Little Owl. I understand now the absolute devotion to all things carnal some have. I'd have gotten nothing at all accomplished had you come to me earlier on, I'm sure of it."

Pride heated my blood, adding fuel to the flames he'd lit with his praise. His thumb circled my sensitive clit, the jolts of energy sending me over the edge with a choked shout. The climax was so abrupt and powerful I fell forward into him, pressing both of us into the back cushions as he rode out his own release.

I was a hot, sweaty mess as we sat there breathing, Rylan's hand casually caressing my hair down my back.

"Are you alright?"

"I'm very fine, thank you." I smiled into his shoulder. At his lack of response, I pulled back to look at him. His seriousness took the shine from my afterglow, but I refused to get upset at him for his caution. "I'm fine, Rylan. If I needed the potion, I would say something. Or I'd just get it myself. I promise. You don't have to tiptoe around me. In fact, I'd prefer you not make any decisions for me at all."

I carefully got up and went into the bathing room for a quick cleanup before changing into a nightgown and climbing into our bed. He wisely gave me time to take care of my needs before following behind.

"I do not wish to fight with you, Little Owl." Rylan's tone was weary as he got in bed behind me and pulled me against his chest.

"Nor I you," I admitted, straightening the blankets over us as I sank into the mattress, my body heavy as sleep beckoned.

Wisps of his energy remained, caressing me in a soothing way as he spooned into my back. "I'm only trying to keep you safe, Calla, in all things. There is too much unknown."

"I would argue that going to where my story started is the best way to find out."

He let out a deep breath, then pressed a kiss into the space where my shoulder and neck met but said nothing further. I knew the discussion was far from over, but sleep seemed the wisest course for the time being. There would be plenty of time to argue in the morning.

CHAPTER 40
RYLAN

"RYLAN?" CALLA CALLED from the bed. I dropped another journal to the floor with a soft thump, flipping through the next. I had a whole shelf of books and ledgers stacked next to me but still hadn't found what I was searching for. "Over here, beloved."

"What's this about? How long have you been out here?" She tugged the edges of her robe tighter against the chill of the room. "How can you stand to be out here with no shirt on?"

"I'm rarely cold. I'm searching for something." At her frown, I inhaled and tried to focus on her instead of my mission. "I'm sorry, I have a bad habit of waking you with my sleepless activities."

"That's alright. At least this time you're not covered in blood," she teased. "What are you looking for?" Calla sat next to me, accidentally dislodging Morticia from the back cushion. The cat stretched and yawned, throwing us both a disdainful glare as she moved to the other sofa instead.

"Something that probably isn't here," I admitted, scrubbing a hand down my face. "It's much more likely it's in the formal office at the manor."

"Maybe I can help?" She took one of my hands in hers, the simple contact breaking the frustrated loop I was stuck in.

"Yes, perhaps." I exhaled, taking my hand back so I could move a pile of books back to the shelf. "Calla, I ..." There was no good way to start this conversation, and the anxiety it caused had me frustrated. "I've spoken to you of my deals before."

"Yes." She shifted nervously, her anxiety increasing mine.

"The Noctua farm ... I made a deal there many, many years ago. I suspect it may be connected to the magical contraband infesting the city. To you." It was impossible that she was linked in the way I was beginning to suspect she was, but I wouldn't know for sure until I found the document.

"Oh. So you're trying to find ..." She pulled the robe tighter again, a shiver stealing over her. I suspected it was my words, and not the cold, that had caused it.

"I keep all my contracts, even after they are fulfilled. I was hoping to find my copy."

"What would it look like?"

"I store them in journals, like the one I used when you signed your employment agreement. Which we'll need to destroy the next time we're there."

Calla stilled, reaching for one of the leather-bound journals still on the bookshelf. "Destroy it? Why?"

I blinked up at her, surprised by her wary tone. "Because you don't need a contract, of course. You're no longer my employee."

"You're *firing* me? I know I haven't been the best secretary, but—"

My laugh filled up the room as I tried to figure out the best way to put her at ease. "You're not being fired, Calla."

"No? What do you call it then?"

"I'm not sure *promoted* is the right word, but I'm fairly certain it's uncouth, at the very least, to have one's mate on the payroll when they're your equal."

She opened her mouth, then closed it again. I knew I'd said those words, many times before, but perhaps never quite in that order. "Oh. Am I ...?"

"Are you my mate? Most certainly. I thought we'd agreed?"

"Yes, but ... the other part."

"Equal?" My smile held a hint of fang. "Is that not what a mate should be? I do hope to be far less of an ass than Adam was, but I'd be proud to have you as my Lilith." It was the truth, through and through.

"I'm pretty sure we were made from different clay." Joy returned to her features with the banter. "Besides, there's not much of a garden here, and of the two of us, you're the one with wings. More's the pity."

"Fair enough." I raised up off the seat enough to lean across the table for a quick kiss before reaching down for another handful of books. "You are the queen in my kingdom, Calla. The only one there will ever be. Surely you know that." I hoped she understood my serious tone; that whether or not I'd had doubts before, there was certainly no question now.

She nodded, which was enough for me. Then we flipped pages for several long moments as my thoughts tumbled over one another in a way that left me not trusting my mouth.

"What exactly was the deal?" she asked.

I exhaled a long breath, heart ticking up in speed as I recounted it. "When I came across the young couple who lived there, they were having trouble getting their crops to grow. That land wasn't always fertile, and famine was pretty likely if everyone had another bad winter." I flipped through and discarded books as I spoke as a distraction against the urgency I felt to find and verify the document. "They had a child, a young boy. Despite their desire for more, he would be their only offspring."

She watched me as I scowled into the books I searched, remembering.

"Their success with the farm would in turn benefit me, if only in the long term, as that area functions under the manor's watch. It's quite self-sufficient, so I've not been out there in ages. There was no need to go, and Cross ..." My jaw clenched at the thought of the dead baron. "They had a well that I agreed to enchant. Their crops would prosper as long as their family remained on the land."

"Who were they to me do you think? If that's where I was taken from?"

That was *the* question. She couldn't possibly be tied to it like I feared she was. I'd put measures in place to guarantee such a thing. But at this moment, nothing truly seemed impossible.

"I don't know, Little Owl," I admitted, and it was the truth. "Not for certain. That was perhaps five generations gone now. I was hoping the contract would bring some clarity to that also. I worry ..."

"Worry about what?"

"It's nothing." I couldn't give voice to the fear, it would make it real. I was much happier believing it was an impossibility. "Never mind. I'm probably remembering badly, or overthinking. By the time I visited with them, I was done making only self-serving deals."

"A philanthropic demon?" she teased, admiring me as I stretched out my back, arms high above my head. She smiled as I opened both my arms and wings for her for. Calla walked into the embrace, resting her cheek on my chest as my arms then my wings wrapped her into a hug. "Sounds like you, to be honest."

"Not completely," I objected modestly. "Their success would still be mine. The crops would grow, their family would thrive. Perhaps even some of the nearby land would benefit from the enchanted water. Everyone would have enough to eat to survive the winter, every winter for the rest of their lives. There were no losers in that arrangement." I breathed into her hair, fingertips dancing along her sides.

"It's late. We should get some sleep," she suggested.

"You're probably right. There's much to do tomorrow still." Weariness set in, and I rested my cheek on the top of her head.

I hated to break the embrace, but she pulled away and headed toward the bed. I pulled in my wings and followed, extinguishing the candles I'd been using as light.

"How long were you up working on that?"

"Not terribly long, but a while." Once we were both settled into our pillows again, I reached out to trace her cheek.

"Can someone from the manor check in the office for you?"

I shook my head. "None of them can see the special writing."

"Special writing?"

"Did you see anything in the text that wasn't black ink?"

"There were some that were red, some gold, and a few silver."

I smiled again, her talent never failing to impress me. "Those colors indicate active magic. The staff at the house is mostly human, they cannot see like you and I can. They only see the black."

"Oh." Her eyelids grew heavy as our breathing synced up. I traced my fingertips along her face, a sure way to lull her into sleep.

"We'll all find out soon enough what's going on out in the valley and on that farm." I said, trying to reassure myself as much as her.

CHAPTER 41
CALLA

"I'M FINE," I insisted at a volume loud enough that the students on their way out of the room turned to look. "Honestly, the two of you, it's overwhelming to have both of you mother hen me at the same time. Also, it's completely unnecessary."

As I snatched up my fork, I caught Grace's grin. Then her eyebrows shot up in surprise as she delivered our breakfast plates. "Are these gentlemen bothering you, Calla?" she asked, smile wide as she set down a jug of juice.

"Yes, they absolutely are. Can you please tell them to stop smothering me?"

Grace appraised them with squinted eyes, her hands on her hips. "I may regret this, but what's the problem? Perhaps I can help settle the dispute."

Hope flared. They both trusted Grace and neither cared to argue with her.

"I need you to do me a favor," Rylan said.

"You know I'm always happy to accommodate your requests when I can," Grace replied, head cocked to the side. It seemed she detected something she knew she wouldn't like was about to come out of his mouth.

"Keep Calla company for a day or two while Magnus and I deliver your new staff's parents to the rehabilitation facility."

Grace snorted. "You're taking them to the labor camp then?"

Magnus grinned over his pitcher of ale. "No better place for criminals to learn the error of their ways."

"I agree. It's a rough way to spend one's time, but nobody undeserving ends up there," she nodded. "I'm happy to be of service, as always, Calla."

I appreciated that Grace made a point to address me instead of him. I also noticed that she didn't specifically agree to what he'd asked of her. She was one of the cleverest people I'd ever met, and I was sure that was all intentional.

"Thank you, Grace." Rylan's shoulders dipped in relief and his eyes met mine as he dove into one of the cakes. I barely contained my scowl behind my mug of tea.

"Of course. When are you leaving?"

"After midday," Magnus helpfully supplied. "I need a nap first."

"By all means, we do want to be sure you get your beauty rest," she teased. He pulled a mocking face in response that only made her laugh.

"We'll be taking their wagon, so we'll have plenty of room for supplies," Rylan said.

Grace peered toward the kitchen over her shoulder. "I'll have everything you need ready to go. What about the girls? Will they have a chance to speak to their folks before you take them away?"

Rylan nodded. "They're welcome to see them if they'd like. It will have to be through the bars of the cells in the basement, however. Magnus and I would both be present, of course."

"Naturally. I'll suggest that to them and let you know if any of them take me up on it."

She went back into the kitchen and the table fell into a quiet lull. I picked at my breakfast and drank my tea, still navigating somewhat unstable footing with Rylan, which I despised. The two of us being out of harmony manifested as physical discomfort for me. Churning stomach, increased heart rate—all modes of fight-or-flight activated until our disagreements were resolved.

"It's only a few days," he assured me, misunderstanding my pensive expression. "We'll get them installed in their new home then be back so we can get started on the investigation."

"Mm."

"Calla." Rylan sighed, shifting around in his seat.

"Don't be too cross with him, my lady. He's only trying to keep you safe. I'll be in the observatory sleeping," Magnus said, excusing himself so he wasn't caught in the cross fire yet again.

"I thought we agreed not to argue." Rylan frowned.

"No, we agreed we both had a distaste for arguing with one another. Those are not the same," I replied.

"I don't want to leave with you angry."

"I'm not angry." He raised an eyebrow in disbelief. "I'm not," I insisted. "Not at the moment, anyhow. I still don't agree with you, but I understand your reasoning."

"I'm glad to hear that," he said, hesitation in his tone.

"Go on and get ready. I'll take this mess to Grace."

He leaned in and pressed a kiss to my forehead before leaving the table. For once, I was able to collect the dishes and take them to the kitchen before Grace or one of her new helpers miraculously appeared to clear them.

"So," she said as the kitchen door closed behind me. As I set the dishes in the sink, she leaned against the counter, watching me with no small amount of amusement. She'd intentionally not come back out to get the dishes. She'd been waiting for me. "Care to explain why I've been put on babysitting duty?"

"I think he's worried I'm not going to fare well alone. That, or he's afraid I'm going to take one of the horses and galivant off on my own to investigate where I was taken from."

Grace handed me one of the small pieces of chocolate she kept hidden in a cabinet above the sink. "So?" she prompted, unwrapping the decadent treat. "Which is it?"

I sighed as the rich sweet melted in my mouth.

"Neither."

"I'm not sure if that's a disappointment or a relief. Want a third option?"

"Sure, why not?"

"Take a holiday."

"A holiday?"

"Go see the city. Visit some places you've been meaning to get to. Spend some gold, have some fun! There's no reason for you to hang about the collegium waiting for him to get back. Go adventuring. You've earned that, at the very least."

The idea settled in my chest, a warm buzzy feeling of excitement. I did want to see the library, and perhaps some of the little shops. Grace smiled before grabbing her cloth and washing up our dishes.

"There's lots to see in this corner of the world, you know. I'm sure you would be quite entertained if you went out to find some joy."

"It's not a bad idea." My hesitation was heavy at the prospect of traveling on my own.

"I'll help make you a schedule and a map. Maybe the first day I can go with you, so you get your bearings?" she offered helpfully.

"I'll consider it." I grabbed one of the clean towels and dried the dishes after she rinsed them off. "Thank you, Grace."

"Any time. I think you'll find more than enough trouble to get yourself into once you get the hang of getting around."

Her words were teasing, but a thrill of warning shot through me nonetheless. Trouble seemed to find me, no matter how hard I tried to avoid it.

I STARED AT the pouch of coins Rylan had set in my palm. "What's this?"

"It's a payment against your unforgivably delayed salary." He threw the words out as though it were obvious.

"As we very recently discussed, I haven't been pulling my weight as your secretary, and my contract is ending anyway, so I'm not sure what you using to calculate. How much is in here?" I balanced it, my eyes widening at the weight.

Rylan's jaw twitched. "I also owe you recompense for how Cross behaved. Trust me, that's barely the tip of the iceberg for what you're owed."

"No, you don't." My words were flat. The very mention of the dead man's name put me in a sour mood. I wanted nothing where he was concerned, not ever.

"I disagree. In any case, that money belongs to you." He continued in long strides across the apartment floor, gathering items for his journey. It looked to me as though he might be overpacking, but I had no prior experience, so I kept my mouth shut.

"He's gone. I got what I wanted."

Rylan stopped in front of me, using his hand to fold my fingers over the leather. "Call it whatever you want, but it's your money now. If you need more while I'm away, give the shopkeep this, and I'll pay the debt when I return." He pulled a small metal pin from his vest pocket, carefully fastening it to my collar. It was one of his many owls, this one a dark pewter color with chips of emerald glass for eyes.

"How on earth would I spend this much money and more while you're gone?" I chuckled. "Are you planning to be away more than a day or two?"

He shrugged before wrapping his arms around me, pulling me tight against his body. "No, the plan is to go and return, no dallying. Grace promised to keep you entertained?"

"Yes, she offered some suggestions."

"Lovely. Well, she's quite apt at spending, so I thought it best you be prepared."

"Thank you," I murmured, tucking my head under his chin as he swayed us gently.

"You're truly not angry, then?"

I snorted a laugh into his chest. "No. I said I wasn't."

"I know you did, but I wasn't sure I believed you. I do understand your frustration, Calla. Truly. I promise we'll look into it as soon as we can."

I squeezed my eyes closed, listening to the steady thump of his heartbeat. "I know."

"I'll not be gone long." He pressed a kiss to my forehead, one hand stroking along the back of my head. The two of us just held one another for a long moment, heartbeats and breaths syncing up. Every cell in my body felt *right* when I was this close to Rylan. It was comforting to have such a sense of peace with someone else.

Our quiet moment was interrupted by Magnus knocking on the door. It was time for them to leave.

"Be safe," I said, leaning back so I could look up into his golden eyes.

"And you." He pressed his lush mouth to mine, the kiss sweet and full of longing, and he hadn't even left yet. "I've put the vial—"

"I'll be fine."

"Take no risks, Calla, promise me."

"I promise." I smiled at the demon who was so concerned with my well-being.

"You two take your time," Magnus said from the other side of the door. "I'll be downstairs, Archmage."

"Bring him back in one piece, please," I requested. "And yourself too. Hear me?"

"Of course, my lady. I very much prefer all my parts right where they are." His chuckle faded as he moved down the hall.

"I'll be right here when you get back," I made a second promise. "I've got Morticia and Grace to keep me company."

"It's odd," he said. "I've existed all this time without you, yet now that I've had you at my side, I cannot imagine even a day without you there." His sweet words pressed heavily on my heart. "I'll miss you, Little Owl." He smiled, but it was lopsided. Those incredible amber orbs gazed at me as though the very idea of such a thing were confusing but brought him joy. While I was still melting over the affectionate words, he kissed me again, making sure there was plenty for me to long for while he was away.

"Come back safely to me," I said, feeling my cheeks flush for saying something so cliché out loud.

"Always, my beloved Little Owl." He bowed his head as though swearing an oath.

Then he was gone.

CHAPTER 42
CALLA

THE MAIN HALL of the collegium was a large building full of life all the time, but never felt so quiet as after Rylan and Magnus had made their departure. Grace found me wandering the main hall, peeking into the room I'd set ablaze after breakfast had been cleaned up the following morning.

"They'll be having classes in there again soon," she said, startling me out of the intense scrutiny I was giving the stone walls. "No permanent damage done. You gave it your best shot, though." She winked at me. "Care to come with me to pick up a few things?"

I smiled. "Yes, I'd love that. Where are we going today?" I had the purse Rylan left me safely tucked into the pocket of my gown and my dagger fastened inside a sheath that ran along my leg. I had ideas on how to make getting to it a bit less complicated than hiking up my whole skirt, but they'd have to wait.

"I've got a full schedule planned, since we're taking the day. You can come with me to bargain with all the food merchants, and pay a visit to one of the tailors who is helping keep these constantly growing students in uniforms. Is there anywhere in particular you wanted to go?"

"If there's time, I'd like to go to a bookseller or the library."

Grace smiled, leading me down the hall. "I'm sure we can manage something. Do you need to get anything from your room?"

I shook my head, excitement thrumming through my body. "No, I'm all set."

"Lovely. We'll be on our way then." She strode confidently toward the double doors that opened to the cobbled courtyard, then took me out the side gate much like Rylan had.

"Did you get some rest?" she asked.

"Yes, I think so."

It had been an odd evening, rambling by myself around the empty apartment. It was much like the evening he'd left to put down the lower-level demon horde, with Grace keeping me distracted during dinner with her company and extra treats after. I made a concerted effort at putting a dent in the backlog of paperwork while Morticia pretended I didn't exist from the opposite end of the sofa. Then, I'd soaked in the tub long enough to become a proper raisin before climbing into the large, empty bed. Sleep had been hesitant to come, with the moon keeping me company while I tossed and turned. The only blessing had been that my slumber, while short, had been dreamless. The dark figure that stalked the corners of my mind had been quiet for a while, which was a relief but also seemed suspicious.

I increased my pace to keep up with Grace's brisk trot down the lanes. She wove us in and out of traffic with confident ease, keeping up a gentle stream of chatter as I took in the city at large all around us.

When I'd ventured out with Rylan, I'd been focused on the food and tasks to accomplish. With Grace, I simply kept up while gawking at the bustling life around me. I did notice for the first time that many of the larger buildings hosted stone carvings, and I couldn't help but wonder how many were really only statues.

I watched with a mixture of awe and amusement as Grace bartered with a number of merchants as we traveled through a thriving market. The stalls boasted every kind of food imaginable, the many brightly colored canopies drawing as much attention as the enthusiastic peddlers shouting the prices for their wares.

While Grace negotiated with wide arm gestures and a positively terrifying frown over eggs and fruit, I availed myself of a fresh loaf of bread and some soft cheese. It was odd spending the gold Rylan had left for me. It was strange to think of it as mine. I'd be making record of what was missing from the pouch when we got back to the collegium out of habit, I was sure.

"I swear Magnus is going to single-handedly make me an expert at wildly recalibrating my food budget on no notice," Grace groused, but the tilt to her lips betrayed her. Even if there was never anything between the two of them but playful teasing and friendship, I had a feeling he was stuck with her. She showed her affection through food and sarcasm, and wasn't fooling anyone with her complaints.

After arranging for her purchases to be delivered, we headed off to Spool and Bolt where she browbeat the aged little man into a number of alterations for some of the boys who'd had a growing spurt.

She dusted her hands off, giving me a proud grin after we'd left the poor man to his work. "Now then. Shall we find you some books?" My stomach let out a growl. "I suppose it is close to midday. Let's get some ale to go with your bread, eh?"

"Sounds perfect." Being out with Grace, doing things I assumed friends did together, I suddenly thought of Elizabeth. A pang of sadness shot through me, quickly followed by shame. I hoped the maid was happy. It seemed Rylan wasn't the only one who had a bad habit of forgetting about the manor while away.

Grace led me into a garden walled by hedges and filled with benches and tables.

"This is a beer garden," she said, seeing my confusion. "Go grab that table before someone else does, I'll get our drinks and some sausages."

She went to a window to order our drinks, then joined me. "They'll be right over." Grace shifted her skirts around on the bench, sighing in relief. "That was a morning well managed, I think." She took the loaf of bread I offered and tore off a chunk, munching on it while we waited.

There were fragrant blossoming plants potted in whiskey barrels set between the tables and shade canopies covering as much of the space as possible. Waitresses bustled from the concession window to the full tables in a steady stream, large tankards of ale and sizzling meat on sticks flowing to the raucous patrons. The beer garden was an amusing little ecosystem all to itself in the heart of Revalia, and I was glad she'd brought me to it.

"You doing alright?" Grace asked as I nibbled some bread smeared with cheese from the small wheel I'd bought.

"Yes, I'm fine."

Her eyes flicked to a nearby rooftop and back to me. Eyebrows pulling together, she looked back and smirked. "I had a feeling we were being followed."

I swung my head around to where she'd glanced, heart thumping in my throat. I relaxed when I spotted Morticia perched on the edge of an awning, casually cleaning her face with one white-mittened paw.

"I should have assumed she'd be keeping an eye on me," I muttered, thanking the distracted waitress as she delivered our glasses of ale and two sausages on a platter. "Honestly, I'd have invited her along if she'd been in the apartment this morning. These smell divine." I inhaled the fragrant steam rising from the meat.

Grace grabbed one of the sticks and pressed the sausage into a chunk of bread, making a bun for it before sliding out the wood skewer and taking a bite. "This is my favorite place to stop on my way back to the school. I don't have to cook for myself, it's fast, cheap, and the flowers are always pretty."

"It's a good choice," I confirmed, sampling the ale. It was hoppy and bright on my tongue but left an odd, bitter aftertaste at the back of my throat. "Do you think people recognize this?" I asked Grace quietly, trying to steal a glance at the other tables without being too obvious.

The clientele of the garden was a broad mix of people, but a woman at a table across the aisle was particularly interested in us, glancing over every few seconds. I fiddled with the pin Rylan had given me, placing my fingers over the metal of the owl as I considered taking it off altogether.

"I doubt it. Rylan's never shared his crest with a woman before. Anyone looking probably just sees a pretty piece of jewelry." She glanced from one table to the next, and anyone who had been watching us before avoided her eye. "Don't think twice about it, Calla. You're a lovely woman in a pretty gown. You'd draw some attention regardless."

I gave her a tight smile and tried to relax so I could enjoy my meal. She had returned to her lunch with enthusiasm, so I did the same. I wanted her to be right, but something still felt wrong.

When the waitress left after stopping by our table with a pitcher to refill our tankards, I shifted around in my seat, increasingly uncomfortable. I had a burning in the center of my chest that accompanied a growing sensation of tightness around my ribs. Despite how delicious the food had been, it clearly was not sitting well. The bitter taste at the back of my tongue wouldn't go away no matter how much bread and cheese I ate to disguise it.

Grace listed to one side, a frown on her mouth.

"Are you alright?" The words sounded strange as they rolled off my lips despite how clearly I'd thought them.

"Something's wrong," Grace muttered, the words all running together in a mushy mess.

My heart pounding hard, I turned to see if Morticia was still on the roof nearby. I couldn't find her, and the more my eyes roved the area, the dizzier I got.

"I'm sorry," Grace wheezed, desperation in her eyes as she flung her hand across the table toward mine. "Failed you."

I tried to reach for her, but my limbs were leaden. Each breath I took was more difficult than the previous. I looked over to see the men sitting with the nosy woman had risen from their benches and were on their way to our table. One of them slipped some money to the waitress who had served us. My gut clenched as she pocketed it, stripped off her apron, and promptly left the garden altogether.

Grace slumped across the table, and my attempt to cry out was stifled as a heavy hand landed on my shoulder.

"Must be my lucky day," the woman snarled. Whatever magic she'd used to glamour her face into looking younger slipped away. Her wrinkles appeared as she grinned, revealing several missing teeth.

I was reminded of Cross using those same words before he'd beaten me with his cane. Panic set in, but my body was completely unresponsive to the requests I was making of it. I couldn't even make a fist, never mind raise my legs to try to run.

"I've been looking everywhere for you. You'd be surprised how difficult it is to find the right girl matching your description in a city this large." She turned to the men at her side. "Pick her up."

The men each grabbed an arm, and my head lolled on my shoulders as they carried me between them, thinly disguising that I wasn't walking of my own accord. I tried desperately to access any magic I could, my hand clenching weakly as I tried to grasp for my dagger. I attempted to scream, to wave, to in any way garner attention from the other patrons. I could do none of those things.

It hit me like a ton of bricks: there was some kind of cantrip disguising us. There was no other explanation. This behavior was not normal, yet nobody was interested in the two burly men hauling a clearly intoxicated woman across the grass because she couldn't walk of her own accord. And poor Grace was left passed out at the table. A fresh wash of panic came over me as I thought of her and how she'd be left there alone, vulnerable.

My stomach heaved, and I vomited all over the man to my right.

"Christ. I didn't sign up for this bullshit, Lucinda! Do you see this? Puke all over me." His gaze turned my way. "You disgusting wench, how dare you?" He pulled back a hand.

There was no way for me to apologize or brace for what I saw coming.

"Wait, don't—" the woman warned, but it was no use.

There was a flare of pain down one side of my face, then nothing but darkness as the poison took over.

CHAPTER 43
CALLA

"**S**HE'S WAKING UP," a deep voice grumbled under my ear. My eyes were blurry as I sat up. My skull throbbed as though I'd been hit with a rock, and my heart dropped as I realized the firm chest I was using as a pillow belonged to someone other than Rylan.

"Good morning, sunshine." He grinned as I pulled as far away as possible, which, unfortunately, was only a few inches.

We were in a tiny carriage that bounced and jostled violently while traveling down a rutted path at high speed. Sounds of the horses huffing as trees whipped past floated in through the windows. My stomach twisted, bile burning my throat. My head spun, the same way it had the mornings after we'd drunk too much wine.

"Where's Grace?"

Across from us, the woman snorted, her eyes keen as they watched my every movement. Her face had aged decades beyond what I'd first seen in the beer garden.

"That's sweet, you worrying for your friend. I was sure your first question would be something altogether different, if I'm honest."

Whatever drug they'd used on me released its hold in tiny increments. My vision had slowly become clearer, and I felt like I'd started to get control of my body back, though not completely. I was hungover for certain, dizzy, and my limbs felt heavy. As I stared back at the woman, my heart pounded rapidly behind my ribs.

"Where is she? Did you hurt her?" Frustrated tears sprang into my eyes, but I blinked them away. It would not do to show any kind of weakness to these people. They'd already managed to drug us both in a public venue and spirit me away from what should have been somewhere safe.

The woman sighed as though bored. "She's fine. We put her somewhere out of the way. She'll likely be waking up about now, same as you."

"What did you put in the ale?" I fought against the swimmy sensation in my head by focusing on the tiny window over her shoulder.

She laughed. "That's a trade secret. Maybe once we get a little better acquainted, I'll tell you more."

"Why on earth would I want to be acquainted with you?" My eyes went to the door, which unfortunately was on the other side of the brute sharing my bench.

We hit a rut in the road, and the jolt threw me into the bulky man's side.

"Watch it there, sweetheart." His hands reached out to steady me. I'd expected a firm push, but he'd done nothing more than help me gain my balance.

"I'm definitely not your sweetheart," I groused.

He chuckled. "Fair enough, but you're much better off with me in here than Doyle." He gestured to the front of the carriage. "He's none too pleased your lunch ended up all over him."

Embarrassment that I'd gotten sick all over someone made me flush, but it was only for a moment. I didn't feel bad for doing something their actions caused. I remembered the hit then, a cuffed fist against the side of my face. In response, the area started to ache. My hand prodded gently at my cheek and under my eye, finding it heated and swollen.

"Where are you taking me?" I tried to inject confidence and power into my words like Rylan did. Unfortunately, that talent was not one I shared with him.

"It's a surprise." The woman's smirk chilled my blood. I swallowed over the acid still lingering in my throat. "I think you'll like it, though."

I sat back in the seat, the ache in my head radiating down into my jaw and shoulders. "Can I have some water at least?"

"Of course. We're not animals."

Could have fooled me, I thought as the man pulled a flask out from under the seat.

"Thank you." I sniffed at it once the cap was off, which amused them both.

"She thinks we're going to put her back to sleep, Rupert. What do you think about that? So untrusting."

I took a tentative sip, finding it was indeed just water. Or at least, it tasted like nothing but water. Once the sharp edge of my thirst was relieved, I offered the flask back to the man but he gestured for me to keep it.

"See? Nothing amiss here," she said, which only made me worry.

"And yet I still don't trust you. Funny how that works. Who are you?"

"You'll have to excuse my manners. I'm Lucinda. That's Rupert, and he's—"

"Doyle. I got that. What do you want with me?"

She clucked her tongue as though I were a naughty child asking for another sweet. "All in due time. Relax and enjoy the ride, we'll be there soon enough. Lucky for you, you slept through the Dread Forest."

The old woman reminded me of the evil crone from one of my

favorite fairy tales. She was wrinkled but still spry, as though her body felt the need to outwardly display the ugliness that lingered inside of her.

"Dread Forest?"

She waved her hand as though dismissing my words. "Even the horses don't care to go through a certain part of the woods. It's as though there's some spell there, warning everything away from it. Which is fine. Whatever's there can stay there, but it's the easiest place to cut across to avoid the mountains when traveling where we're headed from the city."

I looked down at the flask, trying to keep my face as neutral as possible as hope flared hot in my chest. I was pretty sure they were talking about the area around Ophelia's cabin, which gave me a vague direction if nothing else. Magnus had called the spells warning people away *wards*. Contrary to my first opinion of the magic that made me feel nothing but fear and despair, I was relieved that they were in place.

"How long until we get ... wherever we're going?"

"Aren't you full of questions?" she teased. Her tone was more mocking than sharp. I had a feeling she spoke to anyone who dared do more than simply go along with her plans the same way.

"Seems a normal response considering," I argued, refusing to back down. My fingertips rubbed at my temple, but the sharpness of the headache was unrelieved.

She gave an airy chuckle, but a chill tingled along my spine in warning. "We're taking a shortcut most won't dare travel. We should be to our destination before first light. Barring any incidents, of course."

"I need to use the toilet," I stated.

Her eyes rolled toward the ceiling. "That's a terribly amateur and pathetic attempt at setting up an opportunity to escape. Did you really think it would be that easy?"

"I wasn't trying to do anything except relieve myself. I drank half a pitcher of ale a while ago, as I'm sure you remember. You were watching the whole time."

Lucinda sighed, studying my face for a hint of deception.

Truth was, I *did* have to relieve my bladder, but I was hoping that getting some distance from her and her goons would allow me to access my dagger if not my magic. I was grateful for the heavy weight of my blade against my thigh, I only needed an opportunity to get it in my hands and the strength to use it.

"We'll stop in a while, when the horses need resting."

"But I need to go now," I protested. The bouncing of the carriage made my need more urgent by the minute and did nothing to help the pounding inside my head.

Lucinda knocked on the tiny window separating us from the man on the bench leading the horses. "When you see a good place to stop for a short rest, take it."

He only grunted in response.

"Thank you," I said, hoping politeness might earn me some grace.

"Mm."

We sat quietly for a number of long minutes, only the heavy beat of the horses' hooves against the rutted road and the thud of my heart kept me distracted. I'd been taken. *Again*. Grace was probably waking up somewhere unfamiliar, confused and maybe hurt. Guilt pressed in, though I knew it wasn't really my fault. I certainly hadn't bribed a barmaid to poison a patron's ale, then dragged them off. I sipped more water, still feverishly thirsty but worried about how long it might be until we stopped.

"You don't look all that special to me," Rupert said before exhaling a breath laced with hops and onions, then settled his arms behind his head. I had to dodge his elbow as he settled in.

"I don't disagree with you," I muttered.

"Hush, the both of you," Lucinda grumbled. "I've already explained why we need her," she chastised him.

"Not to *her*," I complained.

"I told you, in due time." Her tone was sharp, and I sank back against the seat.

I didn't appreciate the way she kept scolding me like I was a child but said nothing.

Thankfully, before I was too desperate, but after I'd started squirming in my seat, the transport began to slow. My head was back to feeling like it might split wide open any moment, and my body still wasn't moving quite right, which was a whole separate worry.

Rupert joined Doyle to take care of the horses, who, despite their exhaustion, were pitching quite a fit. They seemed spooked by something that landed in a tree nearby. It was Lucinda herself who guided me behind a few low bushes that were nothing more than some scrubby herbs crawling low as they tried to stay alive in the stony soil.

"No nonsense, understood?"

"Are you going to stand right there?" I frowned at her.

"If you do more than piss, girlie, those boys over there will knock you out. But this time it'll be the hard way."

"I only meant it would be nice to have a little space," I responded, sidling a few steps away. The bushes afforded very little coverage, but needs must.

I looked closer at the scraggly herbs creeping around the edges of the brush. My good friend lemon balm, along with some rosemary. There were also some little white flowers, which might have been chamomile, fluffy heads of meadowsweet, and a bit of lavender. They all had their purpose, but the meadowsweet would come in handy for pain. The combination of them left me hopeful I could eke out some kind of spell to help myself.

While she averted her eyes and monitored what the men were doing with the horses, I quickly gathered what I could of the herbs and jammed them into one of my pockets. Then, I felt along my thigh for the dagger. I exhaled in relief as my hand wrapped around the hilt, but became frantic as I found that even the magic inside it was muted. Whatever I'd been given had fully dampened my magic, or at least the way I could access it.

It would still be a perfectly good weapon since it was finely sharpened steel, of course, but I lacked strategy for how to take on two large men at once while barely able to stand. Discounting Lucinda would also be a mistake. She clearly held plenty of magic herself, even if she was beyond her best physical years. I'd get rid of Lucinda first, then figure out the men afterward, I decided.

Disguising the sound with my boots scuffing the dirt to cover my latrine, I removed the blade from the sheath as silently as I could. I stood, awkwardly wavering on my feet.

My lack of balance, unfortunately, did not agree with my strategy.

"Clever witch. What exactly do you intend to do with that?" Lucinda asked, seeing the dagger as it tipped forward with my arm as I straightened my back. "Which one of you imbeciles didn't check her for a weapon?" she called out, getting the attention of the two men.

Neither took credit, but I knew my time was short if they were headed this way. The odds of successfully taking on *three* opponents at once while in the state I was in was woefully low. But I couldn't do nothing. I deeply regretted not taking action while in the carriage now that I was attempting it out in the open. Maybe the close proximity would have helped.

I raised the dagger like Rylan had taught me, adrenaline flooding my body. It helped clear my head if only for a few short moments. Taking the opening, with the men still a distance back and Lucinda within range, I struck out with it, a perfectly aimed blow that should have scrambled her insides. Instead, my blade glanced off of an invisible shield, the deflection sparking blue where the steel had made impact. My arms vibrated as they absorbed the rebounded energy I'd put behind the swing, and the dagger nearly fell from my hands.

"I'll give you credit, I didn't think you actually had it in you." Lucinda looked over my shoulder. "Shame I'll have to let them knock you out again."

I cried out, taking another swing, this one far less elegant than the first. It, too, rebounded off her invisible shield but less violently. Which meant there were limits to how strongly it could protect her once it had taken damage.

Putting aside my wooziness, I charged her, hacking with the blade at either side of her neck as she scrambled backward. Rylan would have roundly chastised my form, but I figured considering the circumstances, it was acceptable.

My final blow nicked her skin, a shallow cut just above her collarbone. Lucinda's eyes went wide as she fell onto her back.

"Stop! I command you stop this minute!"

"I don't take orders from you," I panted, raising the blade above my head, the tip pointed straight down at her chest.

"Doyle! Rupert!" She tried to crab walk out from under me.

I plunged the blade down with all my strength, watched in horror as she rolled out of the way. I'd pinned her skirt into the dirt and nothing more. My arms ached from the recoil as the blade slammed into rocky soil.

Hot breath accompanied a grunt at the back of my neck. One meaty hand wrenched the blade out of my hand and another other wrapped around my throat, pinching off my precious air supply as I tumbled to the ground.

"Foolish girl!" Lucinda spat, dusting herself off as Doyle choked the air from my thrashing body.

"You need me," I gasped the words like a fish on land as stars began to burst in my vision. Blackness pressed in as I scratched ineffectively at the hand trying to collapse my windpipe.

There was nothing human about the way Lucinda looked as she knelt over me. I *had* tried to kill her, so I expected no sympathy, but I knew what I'd said was true. She wouldn't have taken care to snatch me alive if she didn't need me to stay that way.

"That may be true, but I'm in control here, child. And once you've fulfilled your purpose, there's no need at all for you to remain on this plane. It's best you remember that. That's a pretty bauble." She snatched the owl pin from my collar, eyes reflecting dollar signs as she pocketed it. "That'll get a nice price at market, I'll bet. Recompense for my troubles, yeah?"

I gasped as air became more and more scant. Doyle leered down at me, glee in his expression, while Rupert stood off to the side, patiently waiting, my blade cautiously held in his hand. There was no expression on his face whatsoever.

While the horses pitched a fit and a strange creature yowled in the distance, blackness swarmed my vision, and my body finally gave up the fight.

CHAPTER 44
CALLA

W HEN I REGAINED consciousness, it was full dark outside, and the wagon rolled at a good clip, though the road had smoothed out considerably. Everything hurt. My head throbbed in time with my heart, and my wrists and ankles ached against the rope they'd been bound with.

The subtle raise of my head tipped off my captors that I was conscious.

"Ah, there's our would-be hero. How are you feeling after that ridiculous display?" Lucinda asked. Her tone indicated she was not genuinely asking, but instead was curious whether I'd learned my lesson.

I glared in response. "Where's my dagger?" My voice sounded as though I'd gargled with broken glass, every syllable a different note of pain.

"Safe," she bit out. "Where does someone like you happen to come across a Light blade, I wonder?"

"It's mine. I want it back."

She made an incredulous noise in her throat, looking away

from me as though the very sight brought her pain. I felt along my skirt, squeezing at the bundle of pilfered herbs still in my pocket. A tiny sliver of hope flared. "Water."

"You'll have *nothing*. You made me waste my very last protection charm and drew blood. Blood!" She pointed dramatically at the tiny cut near her neck.

I was generally not a violent person, but considering I'd been aiming to take her head clean off, I was a little miffed that's all I'd managed to do.

"I need water." I choked on the last word, the dryness and bruising in my throat winning out.

"You'll survive until we get to our destination. All that fuss, and now she's making demands. Honestly. Did you hear that, Rupert?"

"Mm." He refused to make eye contact with me.

I swallowed over the crackly heat in my throat, frustrated that I was so terrible at managing my own survival. The wagon rocked, and I worked to steady myself on the seat, every muscle in my body tired and achy.

"How much farther?" I croaked.

"As I said, we should make it before first light."

"How long is that?"

"Couple hours more," Rupert responded, clearly annoyed by Lucinda's caginess.

"Thank you," I resorted to whispering, which helped the pain in my throat a little. "May I please have the flask back?"

He reached under his seat but stopped as Lucinda raised her voice. "Don't you *dare*. She doesn't deserve a drink yet. She'll be earning it from now on. Trying to pull a stunt like that? Pure foolishness."

All pretense of kindness was gone. I should have been afraid, but I was too uncomfortable to focus my energy on fear.

While they ignored me, I put my hands over the herbs in my pocket, trying to remember the incantation that went along with the heart-call spell. I'd looked at it more than once while in Rylan's office, but I felt addled now as I tried to recall the words. I couldn't reach the herbs to braid them together, nor did I have a proper brazier or candle. It didn't matter. It was something, if only I could find the words.

My fingers clenched at the fabric, crushing them all together as I whispered my best approximation of the spell.

"What's that you're saying, girl? I can't hear you. Has your voice finally gone altogether? I should be so lucky."

"Water," I pled, continuing to mutter the spell as she shouted another denial.

I felt a quiet pulse in my ribs as I repeated the words for a third time, but it wasn't anything like I'd been expecting. I was too weak, with no real preparation, and dampened magic. Whether or not I'd done the spell even partly right was up for question.

I sank into the seat, whispering to myself and clutching my pocket. Perhaps quantity would work over quality, in the end. I had to believe that he'd hear me. That he'd find his way to me if I couldn't get out of this mess on my own.

The closer we got to the destination, the more panic built in my chest in response to the increased pressure in my skull. "Something's wrong," I said more than once.

"You're fine." Lucinda sighed, her tone indicating she was not only unconcerned, but she was bored with my complaints.

I closed my eyes, unsuccessfully ignoring my body's many injuries.

The road changed again, becoming even smoother. The horses' shoes still thudded on dirt, but there was some crunchy gravel mixed in now, and the wheels no longer dipped into gaps and ruts.

All at once, everything changed.

I gasped so hard my chest hurt as my head split wide open. It was like what happened the morning after Rylan and I finally consummated our bond but a thousand times worse. Light exploded behind my eyes and the sound of a million thoughts blared in my ears.

"What's wrong with her?" Rupert asked, looking frantic as I screamed and ineffectively clutched at my head with bound hands.

I sobbed through my screams, shredding my already damaged throat as thousands of thoughts battered me all at once. Scrunching my eyes closed didn't help, but I couldn't open them either. I went through all the motions, trying to relieve the mysterious pain—covering my ears, clenching my jaw, screaming. *Nothing* helped. There was no escape from what seemed like a lifetime worth of memories all arriving at once and destroying my mind on the way in.

A sliver of joy shimmered through the pain, because I had *memories* again. They were still cloudy, terribly jumbled, but they were *mine*. Me with Gram, moments making bread, clothing, and soap. Tending to fields and animals. Laughter and tears. It was all there, but impossible to sort through. It came too quickly to absorb.

I'd wanted to access my magic to fight my captors but was now thankful that whatever they'd given me in addition to Ophelia's potion had muted it. I wasn't sure I would have survived had both been allowed to surge through me uninhibited at the same time.

Lucinda responded to Rupert's question, but I couldn't hear what she said, my head was too loud. Heartbeats and horse hooves struck with painful volume. My body protested more every moment, threatening to explode, melt, shatter ... whatever would protect it from the barrage. There was no stemming the tide, though, not without my stone kin friends and the vial of potion Ophelia had given to Rylan.

"Do something, Lu!" Rupert shouted, clumsily trying to get the flask of water into my hands. I choked, coughing out the first offering but gratefully drank when he managed to get it secured in my grasp.

"There's nothing to be done until we get back," she said, though she was digging through a trunk she'd pulled out from under her seat. "I don't have any of my good supplies with me. I was expecting to have to undo the forgetting curse manually."

Rupert, distressed, clapped his hands over his ears and turned into the corner.

"I remember," I whispered over and over again between sobs. I tucked myself into a ball and rocked, praying for relief that might still be hours away.

DELIRIUM TOOK OVER long before the wagon stopped. I could no longer distinguish between memory and hallucination, nor did I have the energy to try. I was continuously assaulted by images, voices, scents … all piled up and transposed upon one another. Logic and sense did not apply to any of them. It was as though someone had taken them all, chopped them up into bits, and dumped them into my mind. Somehow, I was responsible for puzzling the mountain of pieces back together with no guides.

Just past dawn, as the sun bled orange and red all over the horizon, I was unceremoniously removed from the wagon by Rupert and hauled into a house. He set me down on a narrow mattress in a tiny underground room, then left without a word.

My brain still felt like it was aflame, and everything was sideways when I dared move the tiniest bit. The shadowy figure from my dreams was also walking in the corner of my vision while I was awake, which was disconcerting to say the least.

I felt as though I'd somehow managed to drink an entire vineyard dry of wine in one go, then as punishment for such a poor decision, woken up the next morning to pay penance for my indulgence.

"Drink this," Lucinda shoved a vial at me after untying my hands. Blood flowed back into the skin with a prickle, and I rubbed at the spots where the ropes had burned me.

Despite the pain I was in, I didn't trust her. When I hesitated, she thrust it toward me again, nearly cramming it into my mouth herself. "Do you want to feel better?" she snipped. I nodded, the room tilting at the abrupt movement. A gravelly noise escaped my destroyed throat. "Then drink it. I wouldn't have brought you all this way only to kill you now, would I? Isn't that what you said?"

My fingers trembled as I accepted the thin glass tube from her. Inside was a solution that was nearly black with tiny threads of green-and-gold shimmer. When I took out the cork, the sulfurous smell made me flinch. I wanted to ask what it was, but my mouth wasn't responding to my brain's requests, and my voice was long gone anyhow. Grimacing, took a leap of faith and downed the contents, viscerally gagging on the bitter flavor. I fought to keep it down as my eyes watered and my burned throat tried to eject it the whole way.

"Not so bad, eh?" She smirked, clearly knowing it would hurt all the way down. "Someone will be outside that door at all times, understand? There's no running."

I understood. And there was a less-than-zero chance I'd be doing more than carefully walking anywhere anyway. I slumped onto my side, grateful tears leaking from my eyes as the potion finally kicked in. The noise in my head became muffled as the magic took over.

Blessed silence covered the whole world.

CHAPTER 45
RYLAN

"D ID YOU FEEL that?" I turned to Magnus, one hand rubbing at my chest. Some kind of pulse shot through my body, leaving a residue of panic-laced adrenaline.

He shut the door on the wagon, signaling to the man holding the Marchand's chains that he was finished with both them and the wagon. "Feel what?"

I shook my head, unsure how to even describe it. "Some kind of jolt. Like an earthquake, but only one … quake."

He squinted at me, cocking his head to the side. "I know not what you speak of, demon. Are you feeling alright?"

"Fine, fine."

"Probably indigestion," he joked. "The food here is nothing compared to what you're used to."

Somewhere in there was a compliment for Grace, I was sure. "Perhaps. Though …" I trailed off, focus lacking, as the gargoyle led our prisoners away. My pulse was thick in my throat as my stomach rolled. Something wasn't right.

"You cannot leave us here!" Blanche shrieked, her chains rattling as she tried to pull her hands wider than her waist.

"I assure you, madam, I can," I said, turning my back to the detestable woman. Her refusal to believe their plight continued, and her husband also began to cry out his complaint the farther from us they got.

"But our children! How can you separate a mother from her daughters?"

"When the mother behaves as you have with your children, quite easily, in fact."

The haggard old gargoyle at the lead of their bindings snapped the chains abruptly, silencing them with a growl.

"Many thanks, Tyron."

"My pleasure, Archmage." He turned to Magnus. "Word is there's a horde beyond the edge of the forest. They've not yet called us in, but a messenger arrived not long before you with a warning."

Magnus cursed. "Alright. We'll look into it. Who sent the message?"

"Gaius."

"Damn." My plans to get to the manor so I could find that contract were being frustratingly delayed.

Tyron lifted a hand as he carted the new workers to the small intake building.

The stone kin encampment outside the city had many openings for human help, especially in the rock quarry and mines. The labor was hard, there was no pay, and the food was barely enough to keep bodies functioning. It was a perfect solution for making use of criminals who might otherwise be passed over and allowed to continue doing wrong.

"Perhaps you're missing your mate," Magnus teased, collecting the horses we'd brought.

My mouth twitched at the thought of Calla, my heart giving an odd palpitation. Even my cock stirred, thinking of the smell of her skin, the softness of her flesh ... My fist clenched, and I shook my head, forcing the image of her to retreat. Despite what she'd said, I knew she was less than pleased with me before I left. I knew I was in deep because damned if I didn't look forward to her wrath too.

I'd earned it, if my suspicions were true.

"See?" Magnus chuckled. "Come along then. I'll find someone to deliver these horses back to d'Arcan while we dispatch another crop of demon bastards on our way to your manor."

"Do you keep a stash of swords out here in the middle of nowhere?"

He grinned. "There's always a trove where there's a camp, my friend. Have you forgotten the rules of battle?"

"Never."

I followed him across the yard, trying and failing to ignore the nagging ache in my chest.

"GRACE IS GOING to murder me if I don't stop creating piles of laundry with bloodstains," I grumbled, unbuttoning my spattered shirt and using the end of it to clean my borrowed blade. The sword had been a suitable match for me in the fray, as evidenced by the piles of demon bodies scattered around the field.

I was worn, the hours both by blade and by magic more draining than I'd hoped. Magnus was right behind me in a similar state, dragging along and muttering about needing a dozen good meals. I was setting the piles ablaze as we passed them, the scent of burning demon flesh permeating the small grove they'd erupted into.

This horde had been smaller and less organized than the last we'd put down. Why there were so many coming to the surface in such a small area was a bigger worry. Between the demons and the black-market magic, resources were wearing thinner all the time. Hopefully with the Marchands out of the game, we could stem at least some of the issue.

I sat down on a large stone, rubbing at my chest with my palm. The gnawing ache had progressively gotten worse. I was sure that between swinging a sword a few hundred times and using my magic constantly, whatever the issue was would have resolved. I'd been very wrong.

"Good battle, my friend," Magnus said, grunting as he took a seat on a boulder nearby.

"And you." I offered the sword back by the hilt. "She served me kindly."

He gave a lopsided grin, but waved me off. "Keep it for now. We've been in enough of these skirmishes lately, you need to have something at hand." He shook his head, chuckling. "I can't imagine what the smiths would think if they knew their blade was so well used in the hands of a demon."

"They'd have plenty to say, certainly." I turned my attention to the black sky, the stars masked by the acrid smoke of burning remains and cloud cover.

A familiar screech had my ears perked, and as I watched, Archimedes' large black wings flapped straight for me.

Magnus frowned. "What's your bird doing out here?"

"I have no idea," I said, but the burn in my chest increased as he landed on my arm. "Hello, friend. What tidings? Have you delivered the message I sent you with?"

He paced, pecking lightly at my hair, then my bloody shirt. He was nervous, stepping back and forth across my arm. He took off again, circling the edge of the trees before swooping behind some smoke, screeching as he came back through, causing the cloud to split like a curtain.

"Son of a bitch," Magnus grumbled as a man stepped through

the opening. "You always were dramatic. How'd you get the bird in on it with you?"

"Now, Magnus, that's no way to greet an old friend," he replied, nose wrinkled at the smell the bodies were putting off as they cremated. He straightened his cuffs, looking entirely out of place in his pristine silver vest and white shirt.

"I'll lose credit with my clan if I befriend too many demons. I reserve the title of friend for special circumstances."

"That hurts my feelings, Magnus." His fingertips rose to his chest, feigning offense.

"Apologies, I wasn't aware you *had* feelings, Vassago."

"You wound me, stone man. I'm a cultured, well-rounded specimen."

Magnus snorted. "As you say."

The fair demon stopped in front of us, a smile spreading over his mouth. Magnus tried to keep a straight face, but eventually cracked a grin and started laughing. The booming noise allowed some tension to drain out of my body, as did the way the other demon all but leaped away from the threat of Magnus's blood-soaked embrace.

"Touch me and die, statue," he threatened. "You're covered in filth."

"Fine, fine. I understand completely how attached one can be to a favorite shirt." He glared at me.

"I replaced it for you," I countered, turning my attention to the man in white. "You couldn't have arrived an hour ago, brother?"

He grinned, gesturing widely to the bloody destruction all around us. "What, and rob you of all this fun? It's good to see you, but I have to be honest, I thought you'd left this kind of thing behind a long time ago to pursue your studies."

"It's nice to see you too, Vago. You've arrived at a particularly rough time, I must say."

"Noted. Your owl caught me up on the road. I expected to find you at your school, but he was rather insistent I not arrive there unannounced."

Archimedes screeched in answer, taking off from where he'd perched on a branch and disappearing into the night.

"I see he's still easily offended," he sniffed.

I couldn't help but chuckle. Of my six brothers, Vassago was the one I was closest to. Despite the circumstances, I was very glad to see him.

"Shall we catch up? Have something to eat, drink some wine? That's what families do, is it not?"

"I suppose it is. Though we're not like most families."

"Fair point, and thankfully so." He brushed some imaginary dust from his shoulder. "Either way, I'd appreciate the wine and perhaps a comfortable chair. The seat in my carriage is murder on the back."

"The best I have to offer at this moment is the temporary hospitality of a nearby gargoyle encampment, I'm afraid. If you think we'd be welcome, Magnus? We need only stay for a rest. I'd like to get back to the collegium as soon as possible." I rubbed at my breastbone with the heel of my hand, the ache hot and insistent.

Magnus tilted his head. "No manor?"

"No. We need to get back to Revalia as quickly as we can. Something isn't right. I can't shake this feeling ..." I shook my head, unsure how to describe the panic and dread pressing on my lungs.

"Alright. I'm sure nobody would argue with me bringing guests, no matter their heritage," he teased, a small twitch at the corner of his mouth.

"I've a carriage, just beyond the tree line," he suggested. "Though I don't know that it will fit all three of us."

"I'll fly," Magnus said shortly, standing from his stone.

"A carriage? As I recall, you have quite functional wings that you love to use. Unless that's changed?"

He thoughtfully took in the smoldering piles of remains as I got to my feet.

"My wings are fine, thank you. These days I mostly fly short distances only, unless I'm somewhere with no human civilization. You know what happens when we garner unwanted attention in the sky."

"Indeed, I do."

Vassago had been guilty more than a handful of times for causing uproar and false "angel" sightings. I recalled him being exceptionally cross at least half a dozen times for having to relocate after such an occurrence.

"You're welcome to ride with me, though I don't really want to smell you all the way there," he frowned.

I raised an eyebrow. "It's hours from daylight, and there's no civilization here. We won't be seen."

He nodded. "Fair. I'll let the driver know to continue on without me then. Shall we?"

Magnus grumbled as Vago's white-feathered wings stretched out wide.

"Right this way, Your Highnesses," Magnus mocked.

I hovered between my friend and my brother as Vago dropped down to advise his carriage driver of the situation, then off we all went, into the dark night, a nervous Archimedes on our tail.

CHAPTER 46
RYLAN

A FTER A SHOWER and some fresh clothes—thanks to some old stores Magnus dug out—I was feeling better, though my chest still ached. We'd been put up in a small lounge room with three sofas forming a U shape around a small table and a fireplace. We all settled into seats, piling plates with food as Magnus offered wine around.

The stone kin had been welcoming enough, but as Magnus suspected, perhaps only because we'd arrived with him. Myself being covered in demon blood probably helped our case, but many were young soldiers who knew nothing of demons except the problematic hordes. Their watchful eyes had followed us down halls and into rooms despite our chaperone.

"This situation is ..." He shook his head as he glanced around the room. A smile tugged at the corner of his mouth. "Very ...*you*, Stolas."

"I wish I could disagree." I sifted through the collection of snacks on the low table, wishing I had one of Grace's baskets. "I'm Rylan now."

"Ah. That's fitting."

"I am pleased to see you, Vago, don't misunderstand, but what brings you to this part of the world? I was expecting Archimedes to travel quite far in order to find you."

"Honestly, I might still have been at that monastery searching for relics, but as it turns out, I've been recruited to locate a family heirloom in your city. Some kind of gem. They made an offer I couldn't refuse, so I've been on the road headed this way for a week."

"Interesting that it brought you here, now." I frowned, the coincidence welcome, but still odd. "That sounds very much like a project you'll excel at."

"I thought so," he smiled, pointed canines one of the only signs he wasn't just an overly handsome human. "As I mentioned, I'd also heard there was a collegium there," he started, icy eyes flashing as they met mine. "One that specializes in things arcane and magical." He waved an arm in a flourish. "I came to see if perhaps my services could be useful."

It was not common for those of us who had risen from the pit to congregate in any single area. The balance of energies tended to be thrown off if we lingered in large groups for too long and sometimes even drew an influx of troublemaking lower-level demons. But the idea of having him around did hold a certain appeal, and the demons were already gathering near the city. The thought of having one of my brothers near was oddly welcome.

"Could I stop you from making yourself at home in my city if I wanted to?" I asked as he picked at the bread and cheese we'd been supplied.

"No. Could you ever stop me when I dug my heels in about something?"

"Once," I responded.

Magnus watched our volley silently but with keen interest as he took great bites of his own bread. The only time I'd bested my brother was when I'd taken my leave of Hell. He'd wished to wait a bit longer, to bide our time together before making the journey topside. I'd had enough and was ready to leave. We'd come to blows, and it was the only time in our history that my will had thwarted his. Instead of causing a rift between us, as I'd expected, it had earned me his respect.

I loved reminding him of it, and he tolerated my doing so with a modicum of amusement since it was the only time I'd ever won. "Once." Vassago snorted a laugh, blowing a heavy breath out his nostrils as he refilled his glass of wine. He settled into the sofa as I measured him with my gaze.

He was still every ounce my equal and opposite. We were much the same size, but where I favored the dark in my clothing and features, he was fair. His eyes were the lightest gold and his hair so blond it was nearly white in contrast to my amber and pitch. My skin perpetually held a sun-kissed bronze hue where his reflected his tendency to avoid daylight. Whereas I had once taken the form of a raven or an owl, my brother had been retained the visage of an angel despite his fall.

Such is life.

"Anyway, I was wondering if you would consider putting in a good word for me with the headmaster?" he joked.

"I'll do my best." I chuckled. "I hear he's a rather soft touch about some things, but a right cruel bastard about others."

He nodded, still grinning. "Yes, I believe I've heard that somewhere. Sounds about right, based on what I know of him."

"Really? I've found he's a complete pushover, but at least the kitchen mistress knows what she's doing," Magnus mumbled, eyes closed as he relaxed against the cushions.

"Grace is indeed one of my best assets," I agreed.

If Vago were on staff, I could, perhaps, accomplish a great number of things I'd been putting off. They'd be much more easily done with someone of his strength and knowledge available. His help could likewise be invaluable to helping seek out Selene and Kaspar.

I decided not to show my hand too quickly, however. My brother had an ego to rival any other demon royalty, myself included, and I didn't want his head to swell. Instead, I needled him a bit first. "It would be dreadfully helpful to have someone with your talents around. I cannot tell you how many flasks and books and robes go missing."

Vago choked on the drink of wine he'd taken, and Magnus rumbled a laugh. "You'd waste my talent on classroom supplies?"

I shrugged. "Just thinking out loud."

He narrowed his eyes at me. "You're joking. You must be."

I smothered a laugh and shrugged. "Perhaps."

"Bah," he grunted, pouting into his wine.

Out of habit, we'd left one of the windows open for Archimedes to come in when he was finished hunting. He swooped in on a screech, coming to me instead of his perch, displaying the same nervous behavior as before. He pecked at my hair, my vest.

"It seems he's impatient to get back to the collegium." Magnus frowned. "Is anything the matter?"

I questioned my companion, but his thoughts were too frantic and muddled to get much of a response. His urgency validated my own. I got the distinct impression that he was also experiencing the odd chest discomfort I was somehow.

"We'll go soon, friend." I tried to scratch his head, but he twitched away and fled out the window.

"He's unusually high-strung," Vago observed.

"You're right," I replied, drinking down the last of my glass. "I agree with him, though. I'd like to get back. I'm fortified enough to make that distance, I think. Are you staying here, Magnus?"

"No, I'll come along. I'm very interested in seeing how Calla reacts to being introduced to this one."

I smiled, picturing her inquisitive face as she examined my brother. Jealousy flared hot for a moment, blocking out reason. I threw a glare at him.

"What's that for?" He pulled a face in response. "Who's Calla?" Vago asked, already on his feet.

Magnus grinned, wolfish and wide. "Oh, she's quite something. Passionate brunette. Loves good food, well spoken. Brilliant, among many other things." He layered on the praise like a proud uncle.

"You don't say?" Vago perked, and I barely restrained my desire to punch his pretty face.

Magnus was intentionally goading me while also prodding at my brother. "I do. It so happens she's my kin."

My brother rolled his eyes, tossing up one of his hands in dismissal. "You're trying to pair me up with one of yours already? I've only barely arrived, stone man. Besides, did you not just say we aren't friends?"

Magnus boomed a laugh as he slid his sword into a sheath he had strapped across his broad back. "You wish, demon. Calla is Rylan's mate."

"Mate?" my brother asked, stunned by the word. He turned to me with wide eyes for confirmation.

"It's a long story," I explained, fastening the borrowed sword to my belt.

"I'm fairly certain at this point, brother, there's no other kind."

We thanked the stone kin for their hospitality and departed as quickly as we could, flying as a trio into the threat of dawn.

CHAPTER 47
CALLA

"Get up."

Lucinda prodded me in the side with a bony finger. My eyelids were still heavy, but I managed to pry them open. The idea of being stuck in a tiny, enclosed space with her was wholly unappealing.

I swayed on my feet as I stood, disoriented and exhausted. She handed me a cold, greasy hand pie and glass of water before leading me up the stairs and through the house.

I had no way of knowing how much time had passed thanks to the dark underground room they'd put me in, but it felt like I'd gotten at least a few hours of rest. Everything still ached, but the barrage in my head had subsided to a low background-noise hum thanks to whatever she'd given me the night before. I'd slept, but the nightmare figure lingering in the shadows of every corner would not leave me be. Thankfully, he seemed to have stayed in my dreams for the time being.

It hurt too much to speak, to ask questions I knew would go unanswered. Instead, I took small bites of the pastry, washing each one down carefully with the water.

One of the rooms we passed by was clearly a space for working magic. The walls were lined with shelves, rows of vials and charms arranged neatly by type and size. There was an altar in the center of the room with a large grimoire, plus an array of candles and herbs. I wanted to linger, but Lucinda kept a determined pace

I was allowed a stop in the bathroom on the way through. I paused to splash cold water on my face. I was sure the reflection in the mirror was mine, but it was difficult to find any resemblance to the person I'd been yesterday. The cheek Doyle had struck twice was a swollen, mottled mess. Vessels were broken in both of my eyes, turning most of the whites bloody. The handprint around my throat was a violent purple bruise on the outside, which explained why it felt as bad as it did on the inside.

"Come. You've got work to do." She led me outside and across the yard, where the same small carriage awaited, already hooked up to the horses.

Doyle sat in the bench, ready to lead the horses. It was a small consolation, but he appeared to be as ill-rested as I felt.

"Take us to the well."

"Yes ma'am."

She allowed me to enter the carriage first, slamming the door behind us. Once we were headed down the drive, she pulled a vial from her pocket. "Drink this."

"What is it?" I whispered.

"It should allow you to recharge the well."

I had no idea what that meant, but accepted the small tube. "Well?"

"You'll see. Drink."

There was nothing I wanted to do less than drink another vial of potion this woman had prepared, but I had no choice. If nothing else, I had faith that she wasn't going to kill or incapacitate me before getting whatever it was she wanted out of me.

Our ride was fairly short. When I exited the carriage ahead of Lucinda, I nearly missed the step and fell to my knees in the dirt. As it was, I made a very graceless stumble. She watched dispassionately as my ankle buckled, and I gasped in reaction to slipping on the narrow metal.

When I looked up, none of that mattered. I was breathless for a whole other reason.

I was home.

There was no mistaking the way I knew the small house or the sadly barren fields beyond it. Awed, I approached the split rail fence as tears burned my aching throat. I put my palms onto the rough wood, flinching as the rift in the memory curse gave another rending tear. How there was much of it left at all was beyond me, but the throb behind my eyes indicated it wasn't quite done breaking yet.

Two horses whinnied from a pasture, increasing their speed as they trotted, then galloped my direction. I couldn't help but smile as the animals expressed excitement to see me, even as tears spilled over because I recognized them too.

They nickered and reared up, begging for me to rub their noses once they reached the fence I stood against. Laughter and tears combined as I reached a hand out to each of them, trying to rub the soft hair on their noses but getting affection more along the lines of bumps and nips.

I couldn't speak louder than a harsh whisper but greeting them was worth the discomfort it caused me. "Clementine, you could use a good brushing, sweet girl. And you, Winston! Are you keeping out of trouble? Oh, I've missed you both." Homesickness rushed in, the strange void that had been left inside me while my memories were blocked now full to overflowing.

"What a sweet reunion," Lucinda snarked, walking past me to the house. She rapped on the door, and Rupert answered a short moment later. Anger flared, because he was obviously quite comfortable in what should be *my* home. "Let's go. You've got work to do."

Having joined us, Doyle took me by one arm, then Rupert by the other. The pair led me across the property, Lucinda in the lead. The horses followed as closely as they could, frustrated by the fencing in their way once we left their pasture.

Every step across the soil reverberated through my body. It was like the earth itself was greeting me, welcoming me back. Unfortunately, I was so raw the sensation grated against my nerves instead of soothing them.

When we arrived at the far edge of the property, the men basically flung me toward the stone well.

"Fix it," Lucinda gestured.

"I have no idea what you're talking about," I repeated, much to Lucinda's frustration. Whatever she'd given me in the last potion made me sweat, and every noise was unnaturally loud, every sensation intense. Something bubbled up from the depths of me that had my heart racing and fear skating along my spine. I shook my head, sore throat protesting any further speech. My head throbbed again, and I could have drank the whole well dry of water.

As I stared into the depths of the stone structure, finding nothing but water and my own bruised reflection, Rylan's description of the deal he'd made here raced through my mind. He must have dealt with my ancestors. Great-great-grandparents, give or take a *great*. Something else nagged at me, a piece that was still missing, but I couldn't make the thought form in full.

A few dozen yards away was my family cemetery, which amounted to a handful of simple stones with small carvings of owls on top. Out of the pool of memories overwhelming my brain, one floated up to the top. I remembered as a child my Gram had said that generations before, her family had chosen that spot to put our bones to rest because of the weeping willow trees and wild rosemary. I suddenly had a desperate urge to go visit my grandparents' resting places, but I was surrounded by angry people who wanted me to perform a type of magic I had no clue how to do.

"It's simple. The water," Doyle snarled, "make it work again."

"I don't know how." I shook my head, but placed my hands on the stone rim as though that might do something. "I have no idea what it did before."

"It worked the entire time your grandparents were alive, and their parents before them. Whatever protection spell they cast to hide your existence was good work, I'll give them that. When they both died, you appeared out of nowhere. There'd been rumors for ages about you. We all believed it to be gossipy nonsense, of course. Not only because there's only ever been boys born to Noctua couples, though that's been true forever—there's not been a daughter born to Noctua blood in at least five generations. Your grandparents only ever had a son, and he'd long since run off with that strange woman, so how could there be a girl on the farm?" She flapped a hand as though scolding herself for getting off track. "Once I had you taken away from here, the well stopped working. The healthy crops all withered, and my magic reserves dried up. We'll be without food or money soon if we don't get it working again."

I stared at her. I knew she'd had me taken, but hearing her so casually admit it was infuriating. "Why did you have me taken away?"

She clucked her tongue as though the answer was obvious. "It was never fair they had such a thing all to themselves. You weren't even supposed to exist! I found a way to siphon what I needed, like my mother before me and her mother before her. Both to help my crops grow and to make my magic better. But now it's not working *at all*, and by rights, it should all belong to me! Fix it!" Lucinda snapped.

"They were peaceful people, simple farmers who minded their own business," I muttered, but let the thought drop, perfectly aware she didn't care for my protestations.

A cat walking along the top of the fence surrounding the cemetery caught my attention. At first, I nearly looked away, chalking it up to the fact that there were plenty of barn cats around. Then I realized how large it was and had to focus on containing my relief so nobody else noticed Morticia.

"Maybe her just being back here will make it work," Rupert suggested.

"Perhaps," Lucinda grumbled. "Take shifts watching her. It was your bright idea, so you're up first." She waved a hand at Rupert, and he shifted his weight as though put out by her instruction. "You should be able to handle her now that she's not armed, yes?"

He nodded. "Yes, of course."

"Good. I'm trying to figure out where that family with the wagon has gotten off to, anyway. They owe me for last month's shipment."

"Reggie's usually pretty good about being on time," Doyle agreed, walking off with her.

"The Marchands have never been trouble, though the Williams boy is unpredictable ..." Lucinda's voice faded as they got farther and farther across the field.

I stood frozen, watching what my stone kin friend was doing while processing the conversation. She casually worked her way closer to me, behaving like any other cat as she did so. Once she jumped off the low fence around the cemetery, she rolled in some of the clover grass along the border. She pounced her way closer as though chasing a butterfly. Now that everyone was distracted, she'd made her way to me, quickly, winding around my legs and mewling with urgency.

I closed my eyes, thankful for Morticia's grounding presence. I gathered the pieces of what I knew: This woman was likely the one making all the magical contraband that kept showing up in the city. She hired the Marchands to take me from my home, activate the curse she provided them, and make me disappear so she could have our water. She needed my family's enchanted well to make her magical items. They in turn sold me to the manor on their way to distribute the items in the city, though they initially intended to abandon me once they'd arrived.

It was a small consolation knowing they would never be located by her or anyone else. They had been her mules, but not the only ones. Magnus would surely be interested in all this information. How to get it to him was a problem for later on.

My stomach dropped painfully as Morticia leapt up on the edge of the well and pressed her forehead to mine, sensing my internal distress.

Everything was connected.

Everything.

And all of it all led back to Rylan ... and me.

CHAPTER 48
RYLAN

W E LANDED IN the observatory as the first rays of sunlight crested the horizon.

"That trip is always longer coming back than I remember," Magnus groaned, tightening the lacings on his clothing and stretching. "Do you think Grace has breakfast ready yet?"

Archimedes chittered as he took to his perch, and immediately started grooming himself for sleep. Poor bird had been through more distance in the last couple of days than in the last year or more.

"She's likely to throw a hot pan at your face for demanding to be fed before proper sunrise," I warned.

"That doesn't answer my question."

I shook my head, amused as ever by my friend's appetite. "I'd wager there's bread in the oven, but you may have to fry your own eggs."

"I'm satisfied with that," he grinned. "I can even manage bacon without burning it most of the time."

"I don't fly distances like that anymore," Vago complained, stretching his shoulders after retracting his wings. "By the saints, I'm out of shape."

"I'm still recovering myself," I agreed. "My wings went sadly unused for quite some time, and I paid for it having to make some long-distance sprints a few times. I blame him." I jerked my thumb at Magnus.

"Hey, it's not my fault you're a recluse scholar. If you don't use it, you lose it. And not once have you told me you weren't having a good time when I've called you out."

"That's a lie and you know it. I've said how little fun I've had every single time."

"Pah." Magnus waved a hand and moved toward the stairs. "Perhaps we recall things differently then. Because it always seems as though you're having the time of your life while running lower-level troublemakers through with a blade."

"Maybe there is some enjoyment," I capitulated.

"This is absolutely somewhere I would expect to find you, brother," Vago said, smiling as he looked around the room. "It's only missing some rocks and sticks."

"Crystals you mean." He shrugged, one eyebrow up. *Potato, potahto.* "Come. Let's see if breakfast is ready after all. I'll show you around later." I led us down the stairs, eager to see Calla. My heart felt like it might pound right through my ribs, and I needed to confirm her safety.

"Shall I take your brother to the dining room?" Magnus asked as we approached the third-floor landing. "It's quite early, after all."

"Yes, that's fine. We'll join you shortly." After a beat, I called after them, "Tell Grace I'll make proper introductions when I get there."

"I can introduce myself," Vago argued, an amused lilt to his voice.

"I'll handle it," Magnus grumped. I was sad to miss such an exchange between the two of them and Grace, if I were being honest.

They continued down to the main floor as I charged down the hall toward our apartment. I flung the door open, hands shaking from a surge of adrenaline. My mind shrieked as my chest continued to flame. Everything felt wrong.

"Calla?" I charged through the rooms, finding no evidence of her. The apartment felt as though it had been unused in quite a while.

The ache in my chest nearly made me crumple as a fresh layer of urgency settled in. I left the apartment as quickly as I'd come, taking long strides down the steps and along the main hall. As I was approaching the dining room, Magnus came stomping his way out, murder in his eyes. When he spotted me, he simply turned around.

"We just brought Grace in," he said. "She was in the courtyard."

Panic and rage tumbled over one another as I hurried behind him. "Calla isn't in our apartment. Someone better start explaining," I demanded, rushing toward the table where Grace sat with her back to the door, a cup between her hands. Her hair was a mess, scraps of straw and leaves tangled in it. Her dress was torn and dirty, and I spotted some blood seeping through at the shoulder. "What's happened?"

The four Marchand girls scattered back to the kitchen as my words boomed and they saw the thunder in my expression. I regretted frightening them but panic overrode caution. I reared back, wholly unprepared for what I would find in Grace's face. One of her eyes was blackened, and one whole cheek had deep scrapes from temple to chin. She eyed Vago curiously, but shook her head.

"I'm a fool, is what happened."

"Where's Calla?" I asked, anxiety making my electricity wild. It surged under my skin, requesting somewhere to go as an outlet.

"I don't know," she replied, dropping her eyes in shame.

"You don't ..." I made a noise that bothered Magnus enough he stepped between us, face set in stern lines.

"*Settle*, demon. She is not your enemy." His posture indicated I'd have to go through him if I meant her harm.

"I would never hurt Grace," I assured him, but my tone reflected my overwhelming desire to hurt *someone*.

"Who's done this to you?" Magnus grunted, pacing irritably. His fists clenched, ready to do as much damage as I was.

"I'm alright."

"You're not. There's blood on your dress, and these cuts on your face need tending to," I agreed.

"Shall I go get your kit?" Vago offered.

"Yes, it's the black case with gold trim. Same shape as the one you know but larger. Third floor, last door at the end of the corridor."

He nodded shortly and strode out of the room.

"Who's that?" Grace asked, eyes watery. "His name is Vuh ..."

"Vassago," I supplied. Clearly introductions had been truncated. "My brother," I said, taking a seat next to her.

"I didn't realize you had siblings, Archmage," she hedged.

"I have six brothers, actually. Countless other relations besides, but that's not what we're talking about right now. I need to know where Calla is. Tell me what happened, Grace."

She opened her mouth and choked on a sob. Grace had never cried, not in all the time I'd known her. That alone set my energy on a knife's edge.

"I've failed you both," she sobbed, reaching across the table-top for my hand. I let her take it, making an effort to send back comforting energy and not the frenetic mess that streaked under my flesh. Despite feeling like I was about to crawl out of my own skin, I forced myself to remain calm. Her behavior instilled as much fear in me as Calla's absence.

Vago came striding back in with my case, and I set to caring for her wounds. It gave me something productive to do, if nothing else.

"Magnus, can you get me a warm wet cloth, please?"

He grunted and stopped pacing long enough to lope into the kitchen. I hoped the girls weren't frightened by his glare, but I needed him to move away from me for a moment before we ended up throwing punches.

"Come now. I very much doubt that, Grace. Start at the beginning."

She gulped at the coffee in her mug, and a whiff of whiskey reached my nostrils as she exhaled. Magnus returned with the cloth, and I blotted at the gouges in her face, trying to remove the dirt and debris.

Her gaze flitted to Vago, who took one of the chairs, pulling it away from the table to allow her some extra space before sitting in it. "We went to town. We visited the market, a tailor, nothing unusual. We stopped at the beer garden for a midday meal. Everything was fine, but the ale ... it tasted off. I thought it was perhaps a little extra hoppy, you know? I realize now, there must have been something in it. I'd felt as though someone had been watching us all day but tried to ignore it. I kept telling myself that I was being paranoid. Morticia was following us around, we saw her once we stopped at the beer garden to eat, but now I think ..." She shook her head, tears threatening again. "Who would do that to us? And why? I'm sure all men in power have enemies, but would someone go through us to get to you, Archmage?"

My thoughts spun as I probed her for further injury with my energy before dousing the cloth in an herbal cleansing tonic. "No, not like that. Not that I know of." I relaxed the fist I'd made around the cloth. "This may sting."

She sucked in a sharp breath as I brushed it across her face despite the soothing energy I tried to put behind it. Magnus shifted toward us from where he was wearing a groove in the floor, trading pacing for the seat on her other side. His fist had twitched at her gasp. I wondered if my friend knew how deeply the attachment he'd formed to Grace truly ran.

"She asked about your pin." Grace touched her collar, eyes wide. "She wondered if anyone recognized it. I told her most would think it a pretty decoration."

"Sorry. Just little more. This is healing ointment. Calla's recipe. But you'd be right, Grace. Most don't care about my signet unless they're doing business with me."

The comment made her eyes gloss again. "I don't remember what happened next clearly. We were eating, talking, she was enjoying the new experiences. Then I felt strange ... my words weren't working right when I spoke. I reached for her across the table"—her hand extended in an echo of what had happened, and Magnus brushed her fingertips before she pulled her arm back to her side—"then I woke up stuffed in the back room of a warehouse on the far side of the city. In the dark.

"There were some men there, but they let me leave without further harassment. A bit worse for wear, as you can see. My money had all been taken, so I started walking, not really knowing what direction to go. But the observatory makes a damn fine compass point.

"I hate not knowing." Shame reddened her cheeks. "I don't know what happened to her or where she is. If she's hurt." To cover the sobs welling up again, Grace gulped the rest of the whiskey-heavy coffee down.

"Alright. It's alright. This is not your fault, Grace." *It was mine.* I offered her the soothing words, knowing the part about it being alright was a lie. Electricity charged the room as I gripped the edge of the table. "Keep this," I gritted, sliding her the tin of ointment.

"I'm so sorry, sir. So, so sorry."

"Hush now," Magnus said, covering her hand with his. "We'll figure this out."

The girls rushed out of the kitchen with platters of breakfast, wide-eyed but trying not to look any of us in the face.

"Thank you, ladies." Vago offered a smile as they hustled off behind the doors, causing a new layer of confused discomfort.

Soon enough, students would filter in for their own breakfast before classes, and I was impatient to start searching for my mate. As we quickly ate, more worry settled in. The scant pieces of the situation were not coming together in a way I liked. She'd wanted to go visit the farm. I'd thought we'd come to an agreement as to why that wasn't a good idea, but now I wasn't sure.

"Calla is adept at potions. She could have—"

"Are you mad?" Magnus boomed, pausing with a rasher of bacon halfway to his mouth. "I think you may have shaken something loose in that battle if you're truly suggesting what I think you are, demon."

Vassago watched us both with interest as he sipped at a cup of tea and smeared eggs around with a slice of toast.

"It's a possibility we have to consider," I argued, though even thinking such a thing left a slimy feeling in my gut.

"No, we don't," Grace shook her head firmly. "She would absolutely not have poisoned me. Nor did she have the opportunity, only the barmaids handled the pitcher of ale."

"So, we ask the barmaids," Magnus said, shrugging as though this were simple and obvious.

"It's hours yet until they open." Grace shook her head. "Plus, I wouldn't recognize the one who served us, I'm afraid. They all dress and look much the same on purpose. I go there often and have yet to learn any names."

"Then we'll ask them *all*," I countered.

"I haven't met your Calla, but it sounds out of character for her to decide to leave, does it not? On the way here, you told me much about her. You described the pair of you weathering what I would consider far worse situations together. Her response through all those things was to remain at your side while asking questions, correct? Finding ways to push through, not simply running away.

Does it not seem strange that she would tell you one thing, then vanish to the countryside on foot?"

What he was suggesting rang true, and guilt sank its claws deep, twisting my gut. I was leaping to illogical conclusions in my haste to explain what happened.

I played the way he'd referred to her over in my mind. *My Calla.*

"Yes, that's true." I ran my finger over my lips, conjuring the memory of our last kiss as I tried to imagine where she might be. "The things she's been asked to handle since she was brought here would overwhelm even the most stout of heart."

"But what was her reaction to all of that?" Vago pressed. "From what you've told me, running off would be her least likely response. Is there another option?"

I sat up, threads of urgency pulsing through my body. "Anything is possible."

"She wouldn't run," Magnus agreed. "Not with nothing. And she certainly wouldn't hurt Grace, nor leave her behind on purpose knowing she was unwell. She had to have been taken."

My brother finished his tea, wiped his mouth with the back of his hand, and set his empty cup on the table. "Do you have anything of hers I can use as an anchor to scry with?"

"Yes, there are any number of things in the apartment. Do you think—"

"I think regardless, we'll find something worth investigating, don't you? I can tell you're ready to fly right out of here and search every house in the city if need be. But that will not be productive. Let me help, so we can find your mate faster." The confident grin on his face lit the flare of urgent hope I nurtured into a full-blown blaze. "It's a good thing I decided to visit you when I did, brother."

"Indeed." I knew even the simple compliment would inflate his ego to a devastating level, but I didn't care. I would eat humble pie for the rest of my life where he was concerned if he succeeded in this. And if there was one thing I knew about my brother, it was that he did not fail. None of my brothers did.

We were going to find her.

And when we did, there would be no mercy shown.

CHAPTER 49
CALLA

"DON'T GO FAR," Rupert ordered, settling down in the shade next to the well as I walked toward the cemetery. I'd begged my way into visiting the stones under which my family rested, promising no running or fighting. Truth be told, I wasn't equipped to do either of those things anytime soon, and I think he knew that.

Morticia followed me, bounding over the tall dry grass. As I knelt in front of Gram's stone, she pressed her face to mine again, sniffing at my injuries and mewling with distress.

Hurt.

"I'll be alright. Can you get back to d'Arcan?"

Too far. Protect you.

"I don't think they'll hurt me anymore." My insides swooped at this, worry that they might do even worse something I didn't want to consider.

No, magic hurt. Magic BIG. She bumped the top of her head against my forehead again.

Glancing up to see if Rupert was watching, I brushed some

fallen leaves off of the stone, reverently touching the little stone owl that marked my grandmother's resting place. "I can't feel my magic, but I do have most of my memories back. Kind of. They're messy and don't make much sense yet. Is that what you mean?"

No. Magic free. Unbound.

The sentiment lay heavy as I moved on to my Gramp's stone, clearing it off like I had for Grams'. "I took some of Ophelia's potion ... I don't know when, but more than a week ago. It's been fine. We don't really know how long it lasts, though."

She pawed at my face, making me look at her. *Dangerous. Magic big. Free.*

"I hear you, but I'm not sure what to do about that. I feel fine. Relatively speaking." My throat burned again, so I stopped talking, wishing we were better at simple mind-to-mind communication and that I'd drank from the well before coming over here.

I reached up to sweep some leaves from Gramp's owl sculpture, but something was off. The little creature was turned a little bit to the right when he should have been facing forward. After checking to be sure Rupert was still distracted, I grasped the stone in my hand and tried to turn it back.

There was a grating sound, as stone shifted against stone. I backed up, watching in awe as a drawer opened in the base of the headstone. A beautifully carved wooden box the size of a stack of Rylan's ledgers was inside. After I reached in and took it out, the drawer closed up. As I watched, the owl twisted a quarter turn to the side again.

I moved on to the next grave, clutching the box to my chest. Heart racing, I opened the top while halfheartedly brushing the leaves from Great-Aunt Mathilde's stone. The box was full of documents. I pulled the first tiny journal out, finding a record of Noctua family births and deaths. Adrenaline surged, and I frantically flipped until I found my grandparents' names, and under them was Kaspar.

My heart thumped loudly in my ears as I continued down the tree. Registered next to him, was a wife, Selene. Underneath them, a daughter. Sofie. I blinked, eyes scanning the collection of letters over and over again, willing some kind of connection to form between me and that name. I felt nothing, however.

Frustrated, I moved on, passing up the farm ledgers and diaries for the moment. A yellowed document was nestled in the bottom corner of the box, rolled up like a scroll. It felt important.

Keeping an eye on what Rupert was doing—napping, it appeared—I unrolled the parchment with Morticia at my side. I knew immediately what I was looking at with the silver-and-red script glowing up at me. It was the original contract between Rylan and my three-times great-grandparents.

Blowing out a breath, I made myself slow down and focus on reading what it said. Everything matched up, just like he'd told me—except the clause in tiny letters at the end. I whispered the words aloud, needing the extra step to fully process what was written. Morticia watched, curious and probably well versed in magical documents.

"He offered to enchant the well, for as long as someone in my family lived on the land ... in exchange for the first Noctua daughter." My hands shook as I reviewed it over and over again, the fine print at the bottom drawing my focus. Morticia thumped her forehead into my palm, trying to offer comfort. "He ... he made a deal with my ancestors, and the cost they paid was *me*."

Insides stuck in a cyclone, I nearly missed it when Rupert called out to me. "Hurry up over there," he grumbled.

"Okay, just a minute!" Shouting was out of the question, but the words grated out of my throat in a loud whisper. I sorted through the papers, taking what I could and stuffing them in my pockets and down the bodice of my dress. Hidden at the bottom were a few articles of jewelry I didn't want to risk, so I left them where they were. I hastily opened the drawer again, leaving the box behind.

I tried to make my expression as neutral as possible, and walked cautiously back to the well. I still had no idea what to do, but at the very least needed a drink.

"Can you bring the bucket up?" I asked.

"I suppose." He cranked the handle, and a wooden pail full of water slowly rose to the top. Once it was up, he pulled it off the hook. I used my hands to scoop and drank as much as I could hold. It was the best-tasting water I could ever remember having, and it soothed my aching throat.

"Now what?"

I stepped over into the field of withered rye stalks, worried that it couldn't possibly be so simple, but thinking it was easy enough to try. I gestured around me.

"Want me to pour it out?"

"Worth a try," I said.

Shaking his head, he muttered about foolishness and dumped the contents of the bucket on the parched soil near my feet. Everything was so intensified, I could *hear* the soil absorb the water, felt the way it nourished the roots of the plants that were no more than dry husks. After several long moments, when nothing happened, Rupert seemed as disappointed as I felt. I'd been sure something was going to change if only because I *felt* the process under and through my feet.

Three more times, Rupert filled and dumped the bucket, no more than dampening a small section of the field. The longer we stood there staring at the withered stalks, the sillier it felt. I sat on a dry area, wondering if there were any words I could say, any incantations to be done that would fix things at least long enough for me to get away.

I muttered a few things under my breath that I recalled from my many classes and Rylan's books, but I had no idea if they applied to a whole field of crops. For the dozenth time, I shoved my hand in my pocket, squeezed the bundle of herbs I'd collected, and recited what I remembered as the words for the heart-call, hoping something was getting through to Rylan.

"How long has the irrigation been off?" I asked, seeing that all the piping was blocked.

"When everything started to die, Lu had us kill the water. No use wasting it, she said." I wondered if she understood that continuing to water crops, even when they weren't as healthy as expected, was still necessary to keeping the plants alive. "What's with that cat?" Rupert asked as Morticia climbed into my lap. "Never seen her around before. I'd remember a cat that big running around."

I shrugged. "She must remember me. Maybe she's been living in the woods or something."

"Or something." He squinted a glare at me as he took a seat.

I looked into the cat's eyes as I scratched under her chin, thinking *What do I do?* at her as hard as I could.

Wait, she sent back. *Head okay?*

It was pounding again, but nothing unusual that I could tell. I was growing desperate for some of Rylan's pain remedies, or at the very least, access to some of the right herbs so I could make my own. The way everything was magnified in my eyes, ears, and skin definitely wasn't helping.

I huffed a small breath as she curled up and purred in my lap. Because of course being patient was her recommendation. What else was there to do? Rupert and I sat there long enough my stomach complained in earnest and the sun moved a considerable distance through the sky.

Finally, he got to his feet, huffing in visible frustration. "Come on. Let's go up to the house. I need to eat and clearly Doyle isn't coming to relieve me. Nothing good is happening out here. You're going to behave, right?"

I nodded, thrilled by the prospect of food, a toilet, and being close enough to touch my horses again. The idea of going inside the home that was once mine instilled some fear, however. Would all the memories converge and incapacitate me again? Was I safe from the worst of it because Morticia was near me?

Before leaving the field, I decided to get one more drink from the well. As I enjoyed the way the cool, crisp water soothed my sore throat, Rupert cursed, "I'll be damned." He squatted down near where my feet had been when the first bucket was poured.

Tiny green edges showed at the base of the dried beige stems. I stepped closer to where the plants had been watered and felt the way the plants made happy music in the dirt. Excitement tingled through my veins, and I bent down to sink my fingertips into the soil.

I had no idea what I was doing, but I tried to communicate my appreciation for the efforts they were making to return to health, promising plenty of water if they could continue on.

"Open the—" I stood and turned, finding Rupert two steps ahead of me as he broke down the irrigation restrictions.

Water flowed heavy and fast through the grooves around the field, allowing the trenches between the rows to fill up slowly and the plants to drink deep.

"Lu will be pleased," he muttered, grabbing me loosely by the upper arm as we tromped through the field toward my house. "Maybe you'll get to eat tonight."

I allowed him to tow me along, Morticia on my heels. Despite everything that hurt, I was hopeful that progress would convince the witch of my continued usefulness. Also, I knew there would be a weapon near to hand once we got to the house.

CHAPTER 50
CALLA

RUPERT WAS HESITANT to lead me into the house alone. "No funny business," he repeated. "I promise."

He ducked his head, opening the front door of my grandparents' home, allowing me to enter in front of him. Normally, I would have thought he was demonstrating good manners, but I knew this was something entirely different.

Walking through the doorway was like receiving a familiar hug ... but also like having a bucket of icy water thrown over my head. The dichotomy was disconcerting and left me feeling nauseated.

Everything was mainly as it was, save the influence of Rupert's having lived there while I'd been gone. My chair was right by the fire with one of the blankets Gram had knitted on the back. The dishes were the same ... it all felt familiar but also incredibly detached from my current life. I'd stepped back into my old life right where I'd left it, but it was not my life any longer.

"Bathroom," he ordered, allowing me to relieve myself first, but not trusting me not to run off while he took his turn. He fastened a belt around my wrist, taking the strap behind the door with him. It was ridiculous. At least he undid the contraption once he was finished.

As he put together some food, I did a slow lap around the modest home. I felt like a stranger looking at items I had once known and loved, absorbing the energy of the space I'd grown up in. Blankets, carvings, artwork. Everything was as it had been, and yet was not the same as I had hoped.

I took a seat on the chair in front of the fire, the memory of my last night in the house coming back to me fully fledged. I'd eaten supper after working with the horses and getting the fields prepared before the rain. My favorite cup of tea steeped on the small table to the right of the chair, and my mending basket was exactly where it always sat on the left. I responded to a knock at the door and invited the strangers inside to get them out of the downpour.

Then everything had gone straight to shit.

I sucked in a breath as the memories flooded through me. I was dragged out the door, tossed in the back of the Marchand's wagon. I recalled the girls, the curse, the wheel going out and throwing all of us into one another near the manor.

All of it.

Anger festered in my chest as the recollection of that night washed over me. I'd still been mourning my Gram and trying to figure out how I was going to manage the farm by myself. My first thought was still to be generous, though. Kind. Welcoming.

And then they took me. Made me forget my whole life.

Because Lucinda paid them to. Because she's a greedy, mediocre witch who can only survive by stealing power from people who would have willingly given her what she needed if she'd only asked first.

My mind flipped to the rolled-up scroll I had crammed in my pocket. The original deal. In its whole glory. Where the man I'd believed to be my fated mate actually bargained to own me before I was ever born. Betrayal rode hard on my raw nerves, and I felt magic rise up under my skin. I was sure he'd have an explanation for omitting that detail, for everything. I just wasn't sure whether it would be enough for me to believe him. To trust him ever again.

A burning sensation not unlike that of the mate bond sprang up deep in my chest, leaving an ache behind I wasn't sure I'd ever recover from. Tears filled my eyes and wouldn't quit falling, no matter how much I tried to stop them as a new wave rolled over me, my mushy mind solidifying only the tiniest bits of truth at a time.

I remembered being told from the time I was a tiny girl that I couldn't be seen by the neighbors or by the men at market. The people that Gram saw now and then with injuries and sickness she knew how to heal couldn't know I existed. I was not to be seen by anyone. Not even the good people. I was a secret only meant for my family to know. I was special, and they had to keep me hidden from the whole world.

When we had company, I'd hide in the barn with the horses, or I'd curl into a ball and lay under the house floor in a special room Gramps had carved out near the fireplace. If we went anywhere, one or both of them were with me at all times, and I was never to wander off.

My hands gripped the arms of the cozy chair so hard I tore the fabric, green sparks popping from my fingertips.

"Oh fuck," Rupert swore. Dropping the plate he carried, my food splattered all over the floor.

Then he sprinted out the front door.

"LASH HER TO the post," Lucinda barked as the men struggled to carry my bucking body out of the house. "Quickly!"

"I remember you," I growled, thrashing against their hold. The magic had retreated again, but it would be back. I felt the swirl of energies in my gut, and they were not happy.

"Finally? I'm flattered," she answered, helping tie my hands behind me around one of the wooden porch posts.

"You shouldn't be. You're no more than a common thief."

Lucinda clucked her tongue. "That's unfair. I had an agreement with your grandparents."

"And yet you still decided to sabotage piping and steal from the well at your convenience for your own selfish profit. Just because they never called you out for what you are doesn't mean anything. You flooded fields, killed crops, and left them to struggle with the fallout so you could selfishly collect water for potions you illegally sold to merchants in the city."

"Look who's finally thinking things through! Right enough, I suppose. A girl's got to make a living somehow, and rye makes far less profit than magic."

"You're selling things like curses to people who have no place using them. The council limits practitioners for a reason. It's irresponsible at best. People will get hurt! Some will *die*."

"Your grandparents were shortsighted, lowbrow hedge witches whose own son didn't even stick around to help them in their old age. And that was after he ran off with a stone kin wench and left them to raise his unwanted child in total secret!"

I roared, sparks flying freely around my face. The pressure from screaming tore something in my throat and I tasted blood. My eyes were already sore, but the anger brought a new round of throbbing to my head.

"Sit down, foolish girl. Why were you so protected, I have to wonder. Could it have to do with the demon that used to roam the area now and then?"

My blood cooled at her words. "Demon?" I said, trying to play dumb.

"There were rumors of a girl on this land for years and years. There were only ever sons born to the family all that time. Nobody ever saw you in the flesh until they both died. That's a powerful spell, no matter the witch casting it. And everyone knew the Noctua crops would never fail. Because of their well, you see. The story was that way back, the first Noctua couple to settle here made a deal with a demon to have it enchanted. I would never have let anyone else in on the truth, but gossip spreads far and fast. Country folk do love to tell tales on their neighbors. How many believed it is anyone's guess, but sometimes, the truth is stranger than a tale."

She plucked at some loose strings on her gown, circling in front of me, but at a safe distance.

"I've no further quarrel with you, in any case. In fact, with the crops reviving, I'm plenty satisfied with my decision to bring you back here. It appears you have quite a lot more magic than they ever did, which is an unexpected surprise. Curses do tend to degrade over time. Which is perhaps how you came to be. Things are looking up, I'd say."

I disagreed, but had no choice other than to keep my mouth shut. I'd aggravated my injuries enough I wasn't sure if I'd ever speak the same way again. Doyle had spent his time leering at me, amused by the proceedings. Rupert on the other hand had gone back inside to find himself something to eat. When he came back, he had a flask in his hand.

"She needs to eat and drink. Maybe get some sleep," he said.

"She needs nothing." Lucinda laughed at him.

"If she's weak, she won't be able to ... provide as much magic."

"Fine. Feed her, I guess. But her anger is what really stokes the flames, yes? Perhaps some aggravation to provoke her magic will be in order."

Rupert came close and dripped water into my mouth from a flask, splashing some down my dress. "Sorry," he muttered. He then fed me bites of bread and cheese. It was humiliating, but he was not unkind about it, and I needed the nourishment.

The temperature dropped as the sun set. The trio discussed the best way to transport me back to the other house so I could be thrown into the secure basement room for the night. Doyle volunteered to knock me out again, whereas Rupert argued I should sleep here on the porch.

I focused on getting my hands loose in the rope they'd tied me with, the rough weave harsh on my skin as I twisted in tiny increments and scratched with my nails at the knots.

Morticia kept an eye on the proceedings from a distance. I felt her distress but didn't want her caught in the middle of things. I was unsure if they could hurt an age-old feline gargoyle, but I also didn't want to risk it.

As the moon rose, I got a chill. Every ache I had became pronounced as I sat on the hard wood decking.

My captors had moved inside the house, save Rupert, who was once again on lone guard duty. For a while, he'd busied himself with starting a fire and lighting lamps that hung from the porch eaves, but now he seemed bored. He spun a small knife in a repetitive series of motions, his head leaned against the wall.

I listened to Lucinda spill secrets she shouldn't have been telling out loud while she made tea in Gram's favorite pot. I learned my old hidey-hole in the floor was her new favorite safe, for one. She apparently didn't like leaving things at her own house because anyone who wanted revenge could find it too easily. That was likely where my Light blade was, too. Ledgers, recipes ... lots of things would fit in a space designed to hold a whole person, after all.

I looked up in the sky, the stars Rylan so loved bright, but also ... smeared?

Rupert shifted, watching me intently as my gut roiled and my skin alternated between feeling too tight and detached altogether. "Lou!" he called. "It's time." He offered me another apologetic frown as he got to his feet and stepped away from me, out into the yard near the little fire pit he'd lit.

Anger glowed warm in my chest, a companion to the defeat that squeezed my ribs. He hadn't apologized for spilling the water on me earlier. He'd apologized for what he'd put in it.

CHAPTER 51
RYLAN

THE INTENSE BURN in my chest disappeared the moment we crossed over onto Noctua property. That alone convinced me what I'd been feeling was a side effect of the mate bond.

Three tiny figures dotted the yard in front of a plain, modest house, one more was on the shallow porch. A barn sat a short distance away, and there were fields surrounding the house in three directions.

"This is it?" Magnus asked, nonplussed by the landscape.

"Yes," I answered, slowing the beat of my wings.

Watching the awe settle in on the expressions of the humans as we neared land out of the dark night sky was oddly satisfying. Their openly shocked expressions became clear, as did how woefully unprepared they were for our arrival. Part of me was disappointed, as I was ready for a mighty fight.

There were two men, an old woman, and to my intense and utter joy, Calla. A calm warmth surged through me finding her alive. The relief faded as we got closer and I saw the bruising on her face, very quickly it morphed into incandescent rage.

"Who did this?" I asked, seeing nothing but red mist and my beloved's bruises. I scanned her body, taking stock of every nick and cut—of which there were *many*. I was certain more hid under her clothing, adding fuel to my fury. It was the handprint around her throat and the blood in her eyes that turned off the last bit of control I had. My jaw clenched so hard something in my neck snapped.

Calla's eyes strayed to the slightly taller man as she got to her feet. Her hands were bound around the post, which I wanted to remedy as soon as possible. The well-built man had more courage than sense as he smirked, smug about his handiwork. I did give him some credit for his boldness when he looked down his nose at two fully shifted demons and a gargoyle, then he cockily stepped forward.

"What's it to yo—" He choked and his eyes went wide, hands raising uselessly to the sword now lodged in the center of his body.

"She's *mine*. My whole world. And you've hurt her." I wrenched the blade upward from where it sat in his soft organs, rending a tear in his flesh as I ruptured important vessels all the way up to his sternum. "Did it make you feel big and strong choking the life from a powerful woman? Striking her? Watching her bleed? You are *insignificant*. Less than nothing, and nobody will mourn you after you're dead."

He coughed and gagged, blood pouring from his wounds and his mouth as the sword did its work. I sent a constant current of electricity through it to ensure he felt every bit of my wrath.

When I finally pulled my sword free, dropping the foolish man's steaming carcass to the ground, I noted the other man had stepped back to shield the old woman with his body.

Ignoring them, trusting that Magnus and Vago would make short work of them if they did something like try to escape, I took long strides toward Calla.

"Stop! You must stay away!" she cried. The fear and damage in her voice made my chest feel like it would collapse.

"What? Calla, I cannot—"

"I don't want to hurt you." Her chin wobbled as she choked out the words, forcing me to obey the plea. Her fear was palpable, and I didn't want to cause her further distress. "They gave me something." She shook her head, the motion awkward and disjointed.

"Beloved, it's alright, we're here to take you home. We can get you all sorted out there."

"This is my home." She bit the words out, her voice rough.

My heart squeezed in my chest, unsure what she intended with such a declaration.

Closer inspection showed Morticia, in her stone skin, pacing inconsolably behind Calla. Horses kicked up an intense ruckus in the nearby barn, but there was no helping their distress. Archimedes made a slow loop in the air above us, waiting to see where he was best served.

Morticia came forward and looked into my eyes. *Magic free. Danger.*

"Where is your Light blade, Calla?" Magnus asked calmly as he and Vago slowly herded the witch and the man closer to us.

"Safe from the likes of you," the witch spat.

Calla's head snapped up, a snarl tearing from her throat. Horrified, I watched as wispy tendrils of green seeped from her mouth and nose like smoke. I could taste the wild earth magic coming off of her, felt its intentions. It was no longer content to be contained by its vessel.

She shook her head, like an animal trying to dislodge a bothersome pest. The green dispersed, but only for a moment. "They took it from me. She had a protection charm, but I drew blood."

"Well done, Little Owl." I was frenzied to comfort her, to put my hands on her body and assure myself that she was whole, real. But she needed my steadiness. She was as ready to fall to pieces as I was.

"Is Grace alright?" she asked.

My chest ached. In the state she was in and worried about someone else—this woman surprised me at every turn. "Grace is fine. She's recovering at d'Arcan. Nothing some time and your ointment won't fix. Please, Calla, let me help you."

She groaned, bending in half as the magic surged through her delicate body. "You can't help me."

The old woman peeked around the side of her bodyguard, so I focused on them for a moment. "What's the meaning of this, widow Kincaid?"

She straightened. "How dare you address me so casually, demon. I've no business with you."

"Such bold tongues around here," Vassago grumbled. "My blade is still regrettably clean, brother. How may I be of assistance?" He gave an angelic smile, which in turn had the bodyguard flinching on his feet.

I took a deep breath, relaxing into my human features. "As the lord of the manor your property is served by, you might want to school your tongue."

Wide-eyed, she blinked at the change, her mouth hanging open.

"They're the ones making magic items and sending them to the city." Calla gasped over the words, seemingly in a rush to get things out where she could.

"Shut up, girl," the old woman snarled.

Magnus took a step forward. "Is that so? Profitable endeavor, that. How's distribution lately?"

The man flinched again, which told me enough.

"These baseless accusations will get you nowhere," she argued.

I couldn't help but laugh, the sound unhinged even to my ears. "Do you really think you're going to live through this?" A thrill zipped through my veins as I watched the truth of those words sink in.

"Oh my. They do," Magnus said.

"How unfortunate," Vago added, his smile less angelic and more terrifying by the moment. I wondered how long it'd been since my brother let his darker side out to play.

"Marchand and Williams are two of the couriers she mentioned. They supply out of the neighboring farmhouse, siphoning magic from the well you enchanted for my family."

I inhaled. Her eyes met mine, questions and condemnations both in the brown depths.

"Shut *up*," the old woman snarled.

Calla grated a laugh. "Why should I? What else will you do?"

"Beloved—"

"I saw the deal. It's in my pocket, in fact. *I'm* the agreed upon recompense for you having loaned your magic out to my family." Calla grunted, doubling over as the tendrils increased, swirling around her body.

Frantic energy buzzed inside of me as I lost my grip on everything that made sense in my life, everything that mattered. I knew why she thought that, what the words said, but the text was meaningless. "No, that's not what we agreed, Little Owl, please let me explain—"

Her eyes flashed grass green as the magic took control. Her body suddenly went rod straight, her head thrown back, mouth open in a raw scream as an eruption of green flames surrounded her. The heatless fire licked at the wood of the porch, her clothing, her hair. The ropes binding her hands turned to ashes as I watched.

"No!" I gasped, rushing forward. Magnus caught one arm and my brother the other, my thoughts an incoherent loop of rage and panic as they pulled me back.

The way Calla's frame was silhouetted against the porch post was an eerie echo of how Eva had looked at her last. Her bruised face was terrifyingly calm, fate accepted as the fire crept along her flesh, the heat making her hair rise into a halo of tangled curls around her head. My heart stuttered, every emotion draining away into terror. I couldn't lose Calla like I'd lost Eva. I already almost had, that day in the classroom when she tapped into her magic the first time. I could not watch that again. I would not.

"It's going to tear her apart," Vago said, shifting around on his feet, sword raised in his hand.

We'd done battle together plenty of times before but never against an adversary like this. I wasn't even sure what we were fighting. There was no way to disembowel vapor. And I certainly wasn't going to attack the vessel. Calla was my mate, my everything.

I choked on a breath as her already injured body twisted and contorted around the demands of the magic. "She cannot die. I will not allow it!" I boomed, turning my intention to cutting down the old woman before this could go any further.

"Wait, I was wrong. She's not dying, Stolas!" my brother shouted, his use of my old name capturing my attention.

"Look!" Magnus ordered, stepping forward, his fingers holding my chin still. Anyone else would have lost their entire hand for daring to do such a thing. "*Look* at her, my friend. The flames are not bothering her. They are ... obeying her. One with her. Look at her skin."

I stopped struggling and did what he suggested. My lovely mate was terrifyingly beautiful, bathed in greenish flames as tendrils of black licked up at her from the ground. It was similar to the day she'd channeled into the Light blade but multiplied infinitely.

"She'll be okay," Magnus countered. His eyes were wide, but his jaw set firm. "You have to believe she'll survive, my friend. I do. She's my kin, and I refuse to lose any more members of my diminishing family."

His words battered my already damaged heart, but I nodded my agreement.

"Where is her blade?" Magnus demanded, crowding the man back a step.

"In the house," he offered.

"Where?" Vassago pointed the tip of his sword at the man's throat, encouraging him to be more forthcoming with information.

"The strongbox in the floorboards. Third slat from the edge of the hearth."

"Come, you and I will retrieve them," Magnus grabbed the man up by his collar and dragged him toward the house, giving Calla as wide a berth as he could on his way inside.

"It feels ... calm," she said, her gritty voice dreamy as she examined her hands. The fingertips had all gone black halfway down her fingers, which distressed me.

"Send it somewhere, Calla. Anywhere! You cannot hold onto it."

Her gaze landed on the old woman, who finally seemed to understand that she no longer had the upper hand. She wasn't taking it well, either. I guessed it may have been one of the first times she'd experienced such a thing.

"I'll take what you don't want," she said, still trying to make a bargain. "I'll put it to good use. We can come to an arrangement, I'm sure. Just like the shopkeeps—"

Calla closed her eyes, hands held straight out in front of her. The flames obeyed, dashing from her fingers to the old woman, who looked as though she was being given a gift.

"Thank you! Yes, thank you, girl. I should never have sent you away like that. We could have been partners! How shortsighted of me. I see that now. Perhaps we can come to new terms, yes? With your powers and my craft, we can—" The old woman stopped, her face screwed up. "What's happening? I feel ... younger. Lighter." She beamed.

Calla's mouth lifted on one side, and I watched as she sent a stronger wave into the old woman. "There are no more negotiations to be had here," Calla said, twisting her hands. "You'll hurt nobody else."

The woman began to choke and sputter as she rose into the air. A mighty crack rang out, and her head lolled sideways at a painfully unnatural angle.

Calla lowered her hands, and the woman's lifeless body crashed into the dirt.

Pride in and lust for my mate surged. I would always gladly kill any opposition in her way if I could. Though I did not begrudge her taking the matter into her own hands, I regretted that she'd been forced to commit such an act.

"Oh my. Isn't that a shame." Vago sighed sarcastically.

Magnus and the man emerged from the house but were stunned into watching from where they stood on the porch near Calla.

"Here, my lady." Magnus held out the Light blade to her.

She accepted, and immediately turned, running the other man through with it. Magnus stepped backwards, out of her way. The only indication of his shock at her unusual and abrupt behavior was his wide eyes.

"I'm sorry, Rupert" she said, surprising me by addressing him by name. "You were the least cruel to me." She jerked the blade back out after twisting it, blood and other, heavier matter soaking his shirt.

A smile flickered on the man's face as he sank to his knees. "No apologies. She's had me spelled for years. I'm finally free. I'm so sorry for all I've done." He wheezed the last and slid forward, his face hitting the wood slats of the deck with a meaty sound.

Calla's eyes met mine, and I could see the hurt. The unbridled rage.

Under it all ... regret.

I was gutted by what I found in her soft features. I'd worried about losing her before, when she saw what I truly was. But now ... Now the loss of her would be impossible to recover from.

Unfortunately, the magic wasn't yet finished. It surged through her so bright I had to shield my eyes. She screamed, the sound raw and broken as it tore through her already shredded throat. Her hands lifted as she directed the surge, green flames roaring into the night.

When I was able to see again, she was slumped against the wooden post. Morticia was on her lap, forehead pressed to Calla's.

In the distance, a neighboring farmhouse erupted into black smoke and flames.

CHAPTER 52
RYLAN

I GRABBED UP CALLA and put her in the bed inside while Magnus and Vassago collected the bodies. She slept deeply, fully depleted for the time being. I loosened her dress and found an interesting collection of items hidden in her pockets and down the bodice. I set them all aside to look at later, then tucked her under the blanket, exhaustion weighing my limbs down as I leaned into the mattress. Morticia announced her presence, then curled up in a chair near the bed.

"Thank you, brave little friend. For being with her."

She blinked slowly at me, which I took as acceptance of my gratitude, before going into stone sleep.

As they rested, I found a satchel and collected everything that might be useful from the strongbox Magnus had left open near the fireplace. I didn't necessarily want to linger here, but certainly there were things of value and importance that needed to be sorted through. The manor was a shorter distance away than d'Arcan and had plenty of space for us all. I could request Morticia or Archimedes fly ahead with a note after it was decided.

My heart throbbed sorely in my chest as I recalled Calla declaring that this was her home. I wouldn't stop her if she wanted to stay, and I'd stay with her if she asked it of me, but I wouldn't be able to leave without absolute certainty that's what she wanted.

I shuffled the items out to the porch, finding Magnus and Vago companionably sharing a word over the fire.

"This has always been more your thing, brother," Vago addressed me, gesturing to the smoldering corpses.

"True." I approached the small fire and sent as much energy into the bodies as I could, the flames leaping high as the incineration accelerated under my hand.

"What now?" Magnus asked.

"Calla is resting. I figured we'd stay until she's ready to leave. There are animals in the barn to be dealt with, probably some nosy neighbors once it's discovered that the Kincaid house has burned. We should inspect the grounds for any lingering contraband, also."

"I could use with some rest myself," Magnus sighed. "I'd prefer that to happen after a meal, but I'll take what I can get."

"The house is rather small." I frowned, trying to figure out where we'd all sleep.

"I've had my share of nights in the barn," Vago said, confidently striding toward that building. "Some of them rather memorable, in fact." I twitched a smile at my brother's attempt at levity. "I'll get the horses soothed. They always seem to like me."

"Thank you, Vago."

"Of course. You can give me a proper introduction once we're all feeling a bit better, yes?"

I inclined my head in agreement.

"I suppose the barn will suit," Magnus agreed, following him.

"If she's not ready to leave, you two can go to the manor ahead of us," I told him. "It's closer than the collegium, and Mrs. Brisbane, I'm sure, would be happy to take care of your needs."

"I'll hold you to that, demon." He clapped me on the shoulder before going off to the barn.

I wandered around the house for a little while, touching items and trying to find a connection to Calla in them. I needed her guidance for it to make much of an impact, however.

In the kitchen, I scanned the cupboards for useful herbs, finding quite elaborate stores put back of items that would be hard to find for most, even with resources like I had in the city. I silently applauded Calla's grandmother for her resourcefulness and preparation as I brewed a healing tea and put it into a heavy ceramic pot to keep warm.

Limbs heavy, I slid onto the mattress beside her, soothed by the heavy exhales she made as she dreamed. As I practiced all the explanations I needed to offer Calla in my head, I, too, dropped into dreams.

THE NIGHT WAS deep and quiet when the rustling of sheets and Calla's hands reaching for me brought me out of my slumber. Her icy fingers brushed my face.

"Are you really here?"

"Yes, I'm here."

She exhaled a deep breath, relaxing against the pillow as her hand tangled in my hair. "I broke my promise," she croaked in a harsh whisper.

"Hush now." I helped prop her up enough that she could drink some of the tea I'd brewed comfortably. "This will make you feel better. What promise?"

Her head dropped back against the pillow, her throat working as she swallowed the brew.

"That I'd be right where you left me. In the apartment."

"That's not your fault, Little Owl." I stroked her hair back from her face, pushing comforting energy threads into her skin. "Go back to sleep. We can work this all out after you've gotten some rest. You should save your voice, besides."

"I rarely got to sleep here before," she muttered, words heavy.

"Where, beloved?"

"In the big bed."

"Shhh." I stroked her hair, my whole body crying out to pull her against me, but I resisted. She needed space, rest. Not to have me latched to her side. We were on her terms, now and always.

"I'm angry with you." She breathed the words low.

"I know you are." I blew out a breath. "I know. But I have an explanation for all of it. Get some sleep first. Your body needs to recover."

"Can I have more tea?" she requested.

"Of course."

I lit one of the bedside candles and lifted her upright against the pillows, cradling her hands in mine as she weakly raised the cup to her mouth.

"May I touch your face?" I asked, fingers aching to soothe away some of her discomfort. "I want to help."

Eyes wary, she nodded. The distrust there made me want to howl in despair. I caressed down her cheeks and along the sides of her throat, gritting my teeth against the urge to kill the dead man a second time.

"I've failed you again." I sighed. "Perhaps you should be quite cross with me."

"I don't understand." She snuggled her head into my chest after setting the empty cup down. "I need to feel you, even though I'm angry."

I gratefully wrapped my arms around her body and kissed her hair, heart thumping. As I breathed in, I found the residue of her magic smelled like dark, wet earth.

"It's the bond. And there's never a time I don't want to touch you, Calla. Take what you need."

"Skin," she said, sliding her hands up under my shirt.

The sting of her cold hands left a lingering burn as I dipped down to kiss her mouth. She wasn't satisfied with my gentle peck, however. She opened for me, seeking my taste with her tongue as her busy hands opened the fastenings on my pants.

"Calla." I would not add to her reasons for regret.

"I need you," she whispered. I squeezed my eyes closed, seeking wisdom on how to handle this moment. "Please, Rylan."

There was no way for me to refuse her, even now. She placed her hand on my cheek and slid forward, hiking up the skirt of her dress, throwing her leg over my hip.

I pressed forward, sliding into her warmth on a sigh. We both needed the comfort and connection more than we needed to hash out logic. That was something best left for daylight.

Her hands gripped at my shoulders, my hair, my ribs, touching everywhere they could reach as she angled herself how she wanted. We moved together in a slow, gentle rock, her eyes beseeching mine for the truth as our bodies spoke their secret language.

I bent my head and kissed along her collarbone, still tallying all the hurts I would need to make better. Her heart thumped rapidly under my palm, the warmth of her exhales skating over my scalp as her fingernails dug into the meat of my shoulder blades, right where my wings rested when they were out.

Her body pulsed around me, and I kissed and sucked whatever skin I could get to, hands splayed over her back as I buried myself in her as far as I would go. She leaned her head back, exposing her bruised throat to me. Even her breaths sounded painful as she sucked air across the damaged cords.

I took one hand and wrapped it around her neck like I'd done so many times before. Her flinch drew my anger at her captors back to the surface.

"To make it feel better," I promised, and she relaxed again. I poured warm, soothing energy through my hand, fingers tightening involuntarily in response to the vibrations of her soft moan.

I eased her through her first climax and continued a gentle pace as I chased my own, my skin dotted with sweat, her breath a constant pant.

"Rylan," she moaned, coming around me again as I lost myself in her.

Once I was confident in my ability to stand, I carried her to the small bathing room so we could both have a quick clean up. Words had evaporated again, but the wariness had gone from her eyes.

I got us back in bed after, hopeful because of her satisfied noises and the fact that she snuggled into my arms before falling back asleep.

My heavy eyes closed again, faith restored that we'd be alright in the end. We had to be.

CHAPTER 53
CALLA

HERE WAS NO falling back asleep with the chorus of three frustrated male voices in the other room. Which was unfortunate because the sunlight hurt my eyes, and opening my eyes hurt my everything.

I got out of bed and pulled on one of my old gowns, shocked again at how things were the same as before I'd been taken.

When I entered the main part of the house, six eyes fastened themselves to me, all three men staring with wide eyes and open mouths.

"Good morning, my lady," Magnus greeted me. He grinned widely and even dropped into a bow before taking the several steps between us and pulling me into a very enthusiastic hug.

"Hello, Magnus," I said, my words muffled because my face was plastered into his chest.

"I was worried about you, niece."

"Niece?" I asked, looking up at him as he pulled away.

He shrugged. "Close enough, eh? I made breakfast if you're hungry."

Skeptical, as I'd only ever seen him on the consumption side of food, I glanced into the kitchen. There was a mountain of toast to go with a pan of scrambled eggs.

"Thank you."

Rylan approached, almost shyly, and kissed me on the cheek. "Are you alright, Little Owl?"

I felt no worse than the day before despite my hands being blackened to my wrists. If nothing else, my headache was better and my memories were much more organized. "I'm alright." I sidestepped away from him, which prompted a frown. I was honestly starving, so I went to fill a plate. "What I wouldn't do for some of Grace's honey cake right now," I muttered as I piled Gram's homemade berry preserves onto my toast.

As I took a seat at our small dining table, I realized they were all still watching me, though nobody said a word. It was unsettling.

At my raised eyebrow, Rylan cleared his throat and gestured toward the tall stranger. I could guess he was another nonhuman creature from his exceptionally beautiful features. He had eyes in the lightest of gold and long blond hair that was almost white. How he'd managed to keep his white shirt and silver vest clean was a mystery.

"Calla, I'd like to introduce you to my brother. Vassago, this is my mate, Calla."

"It's my esteemed pleasure to meet you, Calla."

"Hello." I dipped my head politely, then took a bite of toast, rolling around the word *mate* in my head to see how it still felt. "You're free to continue your conversation. I'm not bothered by it."

"We were talking logistics," Rylan supplied.

I recognized the pile of documents stacked on the table in front of me. I'd wondered where all the things I'd stuffed in my dress had gone to. "Logistics?"

"Of getting you, your things. Anything that might contain

valuable information about the Kincaid's magic items trade back ..."
Rylan trailed off.

"Back?"

"I'm not sure how to finish that because I needed to speak with you about where you wanted to go. *If* you wanted to go."

I wasn't used to seeing Rylan's confidence so shaken, but I felt the same instability where the two of us were concerned.

"We're going to inspect the remains of the Kincaid farm," Magnus offered, gesturing for Vassago to go ahead of him out the door.

Silence lay heavy between us when the door closed behind them. I focused on eating another slice of toast, wanting desperately to enjoy my grandmother's jam, but everything tasted like it had been dipped in dirt.

"That'd be the magical residue," Rylan said, and I realized I'd said that part out loud. He went into the kitchen and brewed some more tea. "Your grandmother had a very impressive herbal collection."

I just nodded.

He poured me a cup, then sat in the seat across the table.

More silence battered at my already frayed nerves. This was not who we were.

"You said you could explain?" I asked, wrapping my hands around the warm ceramic.

"And I can." He reached for the rolled-up parchment. "I told you the story of what happened. Your four-times great-grandparents wanted nothing other than a way to make their crops grow successfully. I couldn't speak to the power levels through the generations, though I suspect your Gram was a pretty savvy hedge witch in her own right."

"They both were," I said confidently, my memories nearly completely back . "Gramps was more about the land and the animals. He grew the plants, spoke to the stones and the wind. Gram did the fabricating."

"And you?"

"I did both."

Rylan smiled. "Naturally." He unrolled the document, frowning at it. "I wrote the contract this way knowing full well your ancestors would never have another child. That their son was all they would ever be blessed with. That became a twofold promise, I suppose. Part of my enchantment was that the Noctua line would only continue through male heirs."

"I don't understand."

"I made the deal knowing I'd never claim my due. Provided a fail-safe in the magic so that no girls would ever be born to this house."

"You didn't want payment?"

He shrugged. "I liked making deals but had grown tired of following up on them all the time. I'd already discovered how imbalanced it was to continue doing it the old way. I didn't want to keep participating in that. Taking advantage was the version of myself I was trying to leave behind in the pit. I was trying to be better. So I found a way to skirt the system and still do the fun part while allowing the humans I was bargaining with to come out on top in the end." He exhaled out his nose, the noise amused, but not quite a laugh. "Lucifer would have had me tortured for doing such a thing."

"How awful," I said, picturing him being flogged in the pit for being kind. "A philanthropic demon," I repeated the phrase I'd labeled him with in the apartment.

"Perhaps." He reached across the table and took my hand, toying with my blackened fingers as he continued. "I filed my copy away, like hundreds of others, because it wasn't something I ever needed to see again. I'd never intended to claim a daughter of theirs because there couldn't be one. She wouldn't ever exist, I'd done everything I could to guarantee that. Yet here you are, more than a century after I signed this paper." He cracked a small smile,

his amber gaze burning through me. "Twice now, you have been
the cause for me to believe something impossible has happened."

Silence stretched between us for a long moment. I wasn't
sure how to address that, because I was questioning both of the
impossible things he'd finally come to terms with.

"How do you know when it's time to collect on a deal?" I mused
instead, sipping at the tea to soothe my throat.

"The contract will change color. You saw red, gold, and silver.
The gold are ones I should follow up on sooner or later. That
indicates they've been fulfilled. Sometimes, Archimedes will go
away to investigate, other times that's when he'll reappear after an
absence. He's a bit fickle, so I stopped keeping track by him a long
time ago. Red are in stasis, silver have already been collected on."

There had been quite a few words in gold when we'd been
looking. I wondered what all he had out in the world he was past
due collecting on.

"How did I ...?"

He shook his head. "I don't know for certain, but I suspect perhaps
your mother is the reason. Perhaps her stone kin lineage and power
added into the mix disrupted things. In any case, the contract ink
may have changed, but I wasn't checking on it so I never noticed. I
have to wonder if that's how Kaspar and Selene have gone undetected
all this time. Perhaps their protection has also ended."

I sat up straighter, interested in that as well.

"When did they go missing?"

"I'd have to have Magnus confirm, but I believe shortly after it
was rumored they had paired up. If the council thought the pairing
was dangerous, they would have moved quickly. As I understand
it, they demanded the relationship end immediately, and it was
not long after that Kaspar and Selene disappeared."

"So nobody knew they had a child."

"Not that I'm aware of. And whomever hid you did a truly spectacular job. Only a protection spell from a very powerful caster

could have kept you a secret for nearly three decades. It was tied to your grandparents, though, not you—which is odd. When they died, the spell stopped working, just like when you left the land, the enchantment ended."

"Who would have done that?"

He shook his head. "I don't know. Were either of your grandparents powerful spell casters?"

"No." The answer came immediately. "They were talented, and certainly the enhancements from having the well enchanted helped, but they were simple earth witches."

"Do you wish to stay here?" he asked. "You said yesterday this is your home."

I inhaled a long breath. I had said that. I worried I'd been trying to convince myself as much as I swiping at him with the words, however.

"I don't know. It doesn't feel ..." I shook my head, unsure what I meant to say.

"You don't have to decide right away." He squeezed my fingers in his hand before letting go. "I need to you know, Calla—"

"Sofie," I said.

"Sorry?"

"My birth name is Sofie." I tapped the little notebook of birth records. "It says so in here. I remember being called that now. I didn't at first." My eyebrows drew together, the clash of my identities sending a hot slash of light through my head.

"Do ... do you want me to call you that?" Rylan sat back in the chair. The added distance between us felt more like a ravine than a few inches.

I poured more tea as I considered, unsure why I had blurted that out at all. Sofie had never known Rylan or the manor or the city. She'd had no Grace in her life, no Magnus. Sofie had existed day in, day out for the farm. Her chores, the animals, making green things grow. Sofie bathed in a small, dark room and nursed both of her grandparents through old age and death before getting snatched from her home by people motivated only by money. Sofie had no magic.

Sofie was gone.

Calla was the one who had risen from those ashes.

Rylan's words from that day in the cellar echoed in my head. *I am him and he is me, but we are not the same.*

"No. I'm Calla."

"Good. I need you to know I don't love you because you were promised to me, Calla. I love you because you are mine. You are the only woman in the world I have ever loved in this way, and I will never love another like this again. We are fated—"

"Because of a deal. A contract," I argued. "What if that's not real?" Giving voice to the root of my fear *made* it real, made it grow. My eyes swam with tears as I looked at the beautiful man telling me he loved me. My heart was so sore I gripped my chest.

Rylan's jaw muscles rolled as he ground his teeth. His composure was impeccable as he got to his feet, but I could feel the heated energy pouring off his body. He casually walked to the door and opened it, but I knew he was as disordered on the inside as I was.

"It is, Little Owl. I promise. We'll find a way to prove it."

CHAPTER 54
CALLA

MY HORSES WERE harnessed to the small wagon my grandparents had used to haul grain and supplies back and forth from the market four times a year. The few things I wanted to keep from the house were packed in the back with the remaining chickens.

Magnus and Vassago had both flown on to Stolas Manor with Archimedes, but Morticia had opted to ride with us.

"Are you ready, beloved?"

I gazed out on the land, feeling a stab of guilt that all the green sprouts coming up would just wither and die again.

"Can we save them?" I asked.

"Perhaps. You not being present on the land invalidates the contract, but there may be another way." He tilted his head. "My magic is not of the earth, but yours is. Perhaps another enchantment isn't needed?"

I crossed the grassy pasture toward the rye field. We'd already collected the wooden box from my Gramps's headstone, and I'd said the goodbyes I'd needed to say. The dissonance between the life I'd had here and the one I could see having at Stolas Manor or d'Arcan was too great. This would always be home, but it was not where I wanted to live.

Squatting down, I pressed my fingers into the soil like I had before, seeking the tingling sensations of new life. When I found it, I pushed my magic out, requesting that the plants grow strong and healthy rather than giving up once I was gone. With a green pulse, energy shot across the field in a wave, and I got back some signing agreement from the dirt. A contract, though one without paper and ink to bind it.

When I got back to Rylan, he was grinning, wide and proud. It made my heart thump.

"What?" I asked, dusting my hands on my skirt as I climbed up onto the buckboard.

"You're magnificent."

Then we were off, making the trip from my family home to the manor for the second time in months, though the journeys couldn't have been more different.

THE WELCOME HOME from the staff was warm and reminded me how much I loved the way the house itself felt. It was stout, constant, but full of life and love.

During the journey, we'd discussed the possibility of sending one of the hands to live on my property so the farm could continue to be cared for. Incorporating the Kincaid land was also a possibility if no kin stepped forward to claim it. I liked the idea of a new family there, so I was keeping it in mind.

"Welcome home!" Mrs. Brisbane enthused as we came through the main hall. She gasped at my appearance, but our repeated assurance that my injuries were being cared for put her at ease.

The staff had not lined up for inspection this time around, as it was both late and we hadn't announced our arrival.

"Eleanor. How have things been in my absence? Everything alright?"

"Wonderful, sir. Truly. Seems the house is a finely tuned machine after all."

"That's lovely to hear. Apologies for the surprise arrival."

She waved a hand as she led us through the house toward the kitchen. "It's *your* house, sir. You come and go as you please. Let's get you some supper. What shall I feed the cat?"

"No need to trouble yourself, I'm sure we can find something. She only needs a bit of meat or cheese. She can hunt for herself."

"No trouble at all, I've got the perfect thing for all of you."

She served us up bowls of hearty stew, fresh bread, and whipped butter. Morticia was spoiled with a plate of chicken innards. I was positive Mrs. Brisbane and Grace would get along swimmingly and decided the two should meet as soon as possible.

While we ate, she gave Rylan a thorough rundown of everything we'd missed and an accounting of how the house finances stood.

"It would appear we already had an excellent manager in place all this time," he complimented her.

She played it off, though she blushed as she said, "Just doing what I've always done."

After supper, Rylan muscled his way to the sink to do our dishes, the sweet cook complaining the whole time. He sent her off to bed with dry hands and a smile on her face.

Despite how weary I was, there was business we needed to attend to before lying down for the night. And *where* I ended up lying down might be another issue altogether. I led the way to the downstairs office once we left the kitchen, Rylan right behind me in silent agreement.

Approaching the shelves behind his desk, the old black ledger was the one that called my attention. Rylan stood to the side and allowed me to sift through the pages until I found what I was looking for. I pulled the copy my grandparents had out of my pocket, comparing the two.

Their copy remained black ink, but Rylan's glowed gold.

My heart beat for this man. I loved him, craved his touch. But at the moment, I didn't trust that those feelings were real. I wasn't sure they were mine. It was impossible to feel confident about a relationship when those things were true. But I also believed what he'd said, that he never thought I'd exist.

"Shall we destroy them?" he asked quietly, moving deliberately and speaking in low tones as though he might spook me.

"What will that do?"

"If they don't exist, the conditions no longer apply. If there's no deal, then we should be able to tell whether or not the mate bond is valid."

Terror chilled me. I was torn. If he destroyed the contracts and the bond went away, I would be devastated. But if he destroyed the contracts and it remained, I still wasn't sure I would trust it. There was no easy way out of the conundrum tearing me apart inside.

"Yes. Do it," I said hastily, nodding my head.

Rylan bowed his head and muttered an incantation over the documents, one hand on each of them. The parchment glowed solid gold for a moment, then they both smoldered into ash under his touch. He then pulled out my employment contract and destroyed it as well. I wondered if a visit to Ophelia would show the absence of a deal mark in my palm.

"What happens now?"

"Now we go to bed."

"That's it?"

He took one of my hands between his, pressing a kiss to my knuckles. "That's it. Let's get you a bath and some rest."

Numb, unsure what direction to send my emotions, and unable to think of a logical protest, I followed him to his rooms. He drew me a bath, washed my hair for me as I soaked, then got me towels and a gown to put on. His overwhelming care and empathy was frustrating. I felt like I was holding in a lifetime's worth of screams, yet he was being sweet.

I was driven to accomplish something, but I couldn't identify the source of my motivation. My heart constantly beat too fast as I worried my way through every possibility.

We sat on his plush green sofa with only a few candles lit. Morticia was already asleep in one of the end cushions. I tried to summon the natural comfort the room had brought me before. Even the air felt heavy as he ran a wide comb through the tangles in my hair.

"Do you know what Noctua means, beloved?"

"Night bird," I said. Gramps had loved to tell me stories about our ancestors flying around in their avian forms. I couldn't help but wonder if perhaps some of my relatives had been more stone kin than we were, and had wings of their own.

"Owl," he confirmed. "So many signs pointed to who you were ... I'm sorry for missing them. Perhaps unintentionally ignoring them. I knew you were mine from the moment I saw you in the hall, but I didn't understand how that was possible."

I didn't know what to say to that. A confession bubbled up inside me, the fact that I was facing away from him helping me get the words out. "I remember my grandparents warning me about you," I said. His hand stilled. "They told me from the time I was small to be wary. You were our own personal boogeyman, I suppose. The story had been passed along so many times, it was exaggerated maybe, but not quite a joke. You were to be feared even though you weren't cruel or conniving. I think it was a layer to the protection spell."

"Mm." He made the noise in his throat and continued combing out the knots.

"In any case, they tried to instill fear in me for the one who'd vowed to claim me. Instead, what the warnings fostered in me was ... a fantasy. The picture they painted wasn't scary, after all. An incredibly handsome devil would come to take me out of my mundane life one day. His natural form would probably be terrifying. There might be horns and claws, perhaps fangs. A forked, clever tongue designed to tell elaborate lies. But he'd be unerringly devoted to only me. Wise and powerful. Wealthy. I'd never want for anything ever again, and I'd know an all-consuming love that came with no conditions. Whether I wanted it or not."

Rylan's hand twitched, the comb going sideways and snarling in my hair. He freed it, then set it down on the table. I turned to face him, his hands gripping his thighs as though barely restrained from reaching out for me. "I am truly sorry, Calla. I had no intention to deceive you. I did promise no deception ... not if it could be avoided. It was that caveat that left me a tiny sliver of room to rationalize keeping that detail to myself because I didn't believe it could be true. I wanted to verify first. I planned to come here, to get the contract right after delivering the Marchand's to the camp. Then I almost lost you."

I understood why he'd done what he had, even if I wished it had been different. "The thing is ... they weren't wrong. That describes you perfectly and is exactly how falling in love with you has always felt. Too right. All-consuming. As natural as breathing."

His amber eyes searched mine, hopeful. He said nothing, just patiently waited for me to finish my explanation.

"Magic was used to keep us apart, and it was magic that brought us together. The way I felt like I knew you immediately, the heart-call working ... all of it made perfect sense when I saw the contract. I was so angry when I started to remember what I'd been warned of. It felt like ... like someone had shown me a mirror and told me that everything I thought was real was a lie.

This isn't a lie, is it, Rylan? That's where I'm struggling right now. I have too much going on in here to know the difference." I tapped my temple with a finger, the noise in my head quieter than it had been but never silent.

"No." He breathed the word out heavily, as though it had been held prisoner behind his lips. "No, this is not a lie. This"—he touched the space right above my heart—"is the most real thing I've ever known. It was all real, Little Owl. Every second."

"How can I convince myself to believe it?" I teared up again, and I hated it. Despite being in full control of my magic, knowing who I was and all the parts of my life coming together, I was utterly lost.

"The contract is destroyed. Do you still feel the bond?"

"Yes. I think so. But I don't know if I trust it."

"Have I done anything that would make you not trust me? Told you lies? Acted in a way that was anything other than honest?"

I considered, and other than his one omission … no. There was nothing. I knew the moment I met him that this man was not a liar.

He continued, "You have made me better in every way since you came into my life. I'd like to think I've done the same for you."

"You have," I rushed to say. "I'm so much more than I would have been had I never met you."

"Can you trust *me* then? Put your faith in me to know the difference in how things would feel if the bond was false?"

I stared at him, finding as many mixed emotions in his face as I was feeling in my chest. I watched as the sadness in his eyes turned to anger. I understood it. I wished I could get to that angry place because it might help me believe, but I wasn't there yet. There was too much other noise in the way.

"You know you can trust me, Calla. So do that. Trust me. This is real. I would run down any man who dared touch you in an untoward way. I already have, and I'd do it again, though I might ask if you wanted a chance to do it first. There's still blood in your eyes, and a handprint of death around your throat." His volume steadily rose, tendrils of electricity curled off his body, teasing along my skin. "There is absolutely *nothing* I wouldn't do for you. No lengths I wouldn't go to find you if you were lost to me. Please believe in that."

I considered how he'd dealt with Cross. How he'd flown in like an avenging angel and ended Doyle with declarations that should have made me melt into a puddle at his feet. We were never grounded in control. I was the Lilith in our scenario, and he a much better man than Adam. Still, doubt gnawed. Because if I discovered one day that this was all somehow false or contrived, I would be utterly destroyed.

"How *did* you find me?" I asked, distracted by that detail.

"Vassago can scry, among other things. He used your hairbrush."

That was quite handy, actually.

Warnings, hesitancy, true adoration all mixed together in a heady cocktail that made it hard for me to breathe. My thoughts pulled in all directions again, memories overlapping and blurring. Instances of Rylan being everything I could ever want or need pushed forward but only frustrated me.

My fingers were still black, though my palms had mostly gone back to their normal color. As I started to get worked up, sparks flew from my fingertips, and he exhaled firmly through his nose, calming himself.

"It's all right," he soothed. "I don't want to fight with you, but I will fight *for* you, beloved, always. Even if my enemy *is* you."

"I don't want you to be my enemy," I sobbed.

"No more than I want to be yours. What will help you? What can I do?"

"I ... I just need some time to think." I sucked in some breath, my body as disorganized as my mind. "I should go to my room. Perhaps if we have some space ..." I couldn't even finish the thought out loud, but I forced myself to my feet. Then I insisted my feet move me across the room toward the door.

"Anything you need, beloved." He gritted the words out, but I felt him pleading with me to stay. He looked as though the thought of me going only as far as down the hall made him want to pull his beating heart from his chest. But I knew he would let me go. "If you want to go, that's fine. I'll be right here."

I found myself nodding, turning my head away like a coward before dissolving into quiet sobs as I walked out his door and down the hall. Before I even got to the door to my suite, I'd crumpled and slid down the wall to my knees as I cried, my emotions a confused mess.

Rylan pulled me to my feet, wrapping himself around my body. He stretched his wings out and curled them around me as well, enveloping me in the cocoon I always loved so much. I lashed my arms around him, everything in me screaming that whatever decision I made, I was wrong.

Rylan lifted me up and walked us through the door of my rooms and over to the bed.

"Lie down with me," he said. He pressed soft kisses to my cheeks, my mouth, my forehead. The love he sent through the energy in his touch registered loud and clear. "I am yours, Little Owl. Always. And you are mine." He wasn't going to give up without a fight, but he'd made his fight gentle. For me. "Go to sleep, now. Everything will feel better with some rest."

That was a lie, though. Perhaps the first he'd ever told me.

I fell into a dreamless sleep in the foreign bed, but when I woke up, he'd done what I asked.

He'd given me space, and nothing was better.

CHAPTER 55
RYLAN

I'D FLOWN A broad circuit around the house in the dark, numb to the cold night air buffeting against my skin. Numb to it all, if I was being honest.

Everything looked orderly and serene under the moonlight as I focused on breathing around the searing ache in my chest. By the time I'd tripped up the hidden stairs and collapsed on the sofa in my tower office, I was no longer capable of processing a coherent thought.

Magnus woke me the next day for supper, making an inconsiderate amount of noise coming up the stairs, banging on the doorframe until I lifted my head in response to his presence.

"Archmage! There you are. It's quite inconvenient finding this room, my friend. Have you been sleeping all this time? Calla is up and about but here you lie. I was sure we'd see you last night or this morning at the very least. Why are you not in your bed?"

"How did you find the entrance to my secret office, Magnus? It's hard to find for a reason. And I went for a late-night flight to survey the grounds."

"Oh? Alone?" His face fell, but he didn't answer how he'd come to find the hidden staircase. He let himself into the room, carrying armfuls of food. Vago, who must have been lingering in the stairwell, followed closely behind. Even though he didn't say the words, I heard his question. *Why were you flying around all night and not in bed with your mate?* "Mrs. Brisbane worried you'd be hungry." He unloaded everything onto the low table as I pulled myself into a seated position. "I like her." He grinned.

"What was so important on the grounds that you left your mate unattended?" Vassago asked as he plunked himself down on the sofa, groaning his approval for the deliciously comfortable cushions.

"She was safe in her rooms," I groused. They both blinked at me. "Calla asked for some space. She needs to think." My mouth pulled into a frown so hard I felt it in my jaw.

Magnus paused mid wine pour. "Oh? I suppose that's ... not unexpected."

"It's not?" I asked, taking the full glass from his hand.

"Hey, that was mine," Vago complained.

I gulped at it while giving him a foul hand gesture, and they both shook their heads.

"Alright. Start at the beginning then." Magnus grunted as he dropped into a seat and started filling a plate. To my surprise, he handed the overflowing dish to me when he was done.

"The good news is she's got full control of her magic and seems to be healing quickly."

"Well done, her." Magnus nodded, slapping my brother's hand away from the platter of meat.

"That's quite rude," Vago complained. "First he takes my wine, now I'm not allowed to eat?"

"I'll be done in a second, demon. Wait your turn. Go on, Rylan."

"Her memories are all back also. She's far stronger than any of us could have guessed."

"Speak for yourself," Magnus mumbled over a mouthful of cheese. "I saw what was inside her, you recall. I'm impressed that she's already mastered such an intense gift."

"As am I. But the memories returning, knowing that there was a deal in place has all left her ... conflicted."

"Conflicted?" Vago asked, finally managing to assemble a plate for himself.

"She worries our mate bond isn't real. That it's only a by-product of a contract I had with her ancestors. I can understand her hesitation, though I'd do anything to prove it's real. I may have lost her trust forever, and it's my own doing."

"Why?" Magnus looked scandalized. "What could you possibly have done to cause such a thing?"

"The universe delivered her quite literally to my door, and I denied the possibility that she was meant for me, that she could be who she is. Not intentionally, not the whole time ... but the result is the same."

"That's all?" Vago asked.

"It's important." I explained the deal I'd made with the Noctua family over a century ago, how everything was connected back to that farm.

"Why didn't you call upon me? You know I could have helped locate her. It's kind of what I do, you know." His nose crinkled as though he were offended I'd left him out of such things.

"Even if I'd known where to find *you* for certain, the problem wasn't that she was lost. She simply wasn't supposed to exist. I wasn't looking for her. The contract was shelved with many others. I never intended to collect the debt. The magic should have ensured only male heirs forever. But it seems fate had other plans once Kaspar and Selene found one another."

"Mm. But what if the deal hadn't existed? She may not have ever ended up at the manor, right?" Magnus suggested. "This is one of those ouroboros situations, no beginning and no ending, only possibilities. There's no way to know for sure what would have happened otherwise. She might still have landed there since you're fated. Or perhaps you might have stumbled upon her in the city one day. But that's not how it went. There was a deal, and magic in play beyond that, so it happened how it did, and now there are consequences to be managed."

It felt like my head might explode. I finished my wine and ate several bites of a sandwich I made from all the things on my plate.

"I don't know. When do you meet with the duke?" I asked, reminded of his other reason for coming to the city.

"Next week. He's seeking some kind of priceless gem. The description was actually quite similar to the necklace Calla found in her family's safe. The duke's got two daughters." His eyebrows went up. "Should be interesting."

I scrubbed my face in my hands, the unrelenting ache in my chest making me crazy. "This is maddening. I underestimated her and fate at every turn, even after I knew better."

"She does seem quite formidable," Vago nodded.

"I told you," Magnus piped up proudly.

"I don't know her well, but I like her," my brother added. I made a noise in my throat and he tsked at me. "Not like that. She's lovely, but she's definitely all yours. I'll be perfectly satisfied with her as my sister-in-law. You and she are an excellent match."

"Would you mind telling her that?"

"Christ you're morose," he scolded me. "I've missed much hiding out in monasteries between stints crossing the globe in order to hunt down relics, but I remember this mood you get in. I never liked it, not even when there were six of us around to poke fun at you to cheer you up. I think we may need more wine, at the very least, if this is going to continue." My brother's shoulders dipped, the thoughtful line of his mouth sinking into a frown. "Shall we go fight? Get your blood up? I'm not sure I know what to do with sulky, heartbroken Stolas."

"Maybe later."

Grief had cut deep furrows into my heart. Even Mrs. Brisbane's stomach-filling offerings were wasted on me. Nothing tasted right, everything hurt. I'd slept less than a couple of hours after my flight, restless and plagued by nightmares when I did finally drop into dreams. My immortal body was decidedly not dealing with the emotional distance of my mate in a healthy way.

"You get today to pine, little mage," Magnus said, relaxing back into the sofa. "But that's all. Tomorrow, the three of us are sparring before you help me make a list of all the shops that have been distributing that dead witch's magic. We can make a quick day trip into the city perhaps, work our way through them?"

"That'll be a very good distraction from your self-pity," my brother agreed. "Besides, she's still here. She was out collecting weeds in the chicken coop this morning. Been in your office downstairs, too. Looked as though she might be trying to catch up on some paperwork."

Of course she was. It was a good distraction; one I'd used myself plenty of times.

Magnus began listing supplies he wanted to collect before returning to the city for his justice and torture methods he considered using for the occasion. Vago, of course, wanted to debate him at every turn, which eventually resulted in Magnus threatening to disinvite him from the hunt altogether.

"Do either of you care to explain how you found your way up here?" They looked at me, then back to one another, but said nothing.

I cracked the smallest of smiles as they carried on loudly around me, grateful to be in good hands and hopeful Calla would come to some kind of enlightenment sooner rather than later.

IT TURNED OUT, untangling the web of shop owners who'd partnered with Lucinda Kincaid was a very effective way to pass the time. One of the journals she'd hidden in the strongbox detailed all her business dealings, which was exceptionally helpful to our mission.

All told, there were dozens of intrepid shop owners beyond what we'd already discovered on our own who had aligned with her to distribute illegal magical contraband. It took several dedicated hours of work, but we went down the list in her book and prepared to displace them all.

Magnus would handle the paperwork with our mutual councils, much to my relief. Dealing with them was always one of my least favorite tasks.

"We need to take care of them. And soon," Magnus said as they helped me replace a few broken roof tiles. "I know you don't want to leave, even for a day, but we need to take them out before they get wind of what's happening and disappear."

"I know." I glanced over my shoulder to where Calla was helping Elizabeth distribute midday meals to the field hands. "We'll have to move swiftly or they'll get word something's happening."

"Yes, we need to deal with them all within a few hours or the gossip will have them on the run," Vago confirmed, nailing a tile down with precision.

I nodded. "Tomorrow, then. If we leave before dawn, we can be back by sundown."

Later that evening, Calla emerged from her room just as I was heading to mine. My heart tugged as I realized she'd washed her hair without my assistance.

My expression betrayed me.

"Are you alright?" she asked, coming closer.

"Of course, beloved. You?"

"Yes. I'm fine." Her bruises turned a fainter purple by the day, and she was less hesitant to approach me than she had been.

I reached out, eager to touch her. She accepted my hand, linking her fingers in mine. "We're going into the city before first light. Only for the day, if all goes smoothly."

"The merchants?" she asked, nodding in understanding.

"Yes."

She closed her eyes as she leaned her cheek into my hand. "Be safe."

I leaned down and pressed a kiss to her forehead, reveling in the way she leaned her body into mine. I could have stood there in the hallway all night.

Perhaps we were not lost after all.

THE THREE OF us descended on Revalia just as the sun appeared over the horizon.

We'd plotted a route that moved us in a circle through the city, tightening from the fringes in as we went.

In the end, Vassago was not only allowed to come along, but his sword, which went sadly unused at the farm, got a fantastic workout. Magnus in particular seemed to delight in watching the fear settle in on the merchants' faces when they realized not only would that income stream dry up, but there were quite severe consequences to their actions.

With the Marchand couple already out of the picture, we only had to track down the Williams boy for distribution. He turned out to be a desperate kid who had muled her wares once or twice in an effort to keep his family in food and shelter. Magnus hired him to work for the stone kin instead, which would be a much healthier and more profitable endeavor in the long term.

The fire Calla had started on the Kinkaid property had destroyed nearly everything, so there was no risk of continued supply showing up in the streets. Anything the fire hadn't reduced to ash, Vago had taken care of himself.

Classes had wrapped up for a couple of weeks, so the students were away on break. Since there was less demand on her time and four additional sets of hands to help her get tasks accomplished, Grace had arranged for two of the empty apartments to be outfitted so that Magnus and Vago could both have somewhere to go when they were in town. Over a hasty midday meal, once we'd finished checking criminals off the list, she delivered the keys to our table.

"Here we are," she said handing one set to each of them. "The green ribbon is for the moving mountain and the silver for the distinguished gentleman."

Magnus grumbled about her designations, but did eventually eke out some gratitude.

"Thank you, Grace," I asked. "Are you feeling alright?"

"Perfectly well, Archmage, thank you." Her tone was clipped, and her answer always the same when I asked.

She'd yet to come back fully to her normal self, but her wounds were healing up fine. Any attempts to minimize the scarring on her face came with a rebuke. She wanted there to be marks so she'd never forget the mistake. No amount of arguing with her, either from me or from Magnus, swayed her. I hoped Calla might be able to talk some sense into her when she returned. I thought perhaps getting the opportunity to apologize in person would allow her to return to her normal, more jovial self.

While my brother and Magnus explored their new apartments and cleaned up, I went to our apartment to bathe, anxious to get back. The mate bond was more displeased than ever with our separation, and I wanted to waste no time getting back to the manor.

I sat on the bed to finish dressing. The sheets still smelled like Calla's floral soap, and if I closed my eyes just right, I could imagine her lying next to me.

I was positively miserable. Lovesick like a youngling. I'd promised to give her time and space, but I got closer to breaking that promise every moment that passed.

A knock on the door broke my reverie. "Time to get on the wind, Archmage," Magnus said from the other side of my door. "I know you can't wait to get back."

I opened the door and found him dressed but not for travel. "Aren't you coming?"

He shook his head. "No, I have to report to the council, and Vago—"

"Can speak for himself," my brother said, appearing behind the gargoyle. "I'm to meet with the duke. We'll be here, in any case. But you need to go home. To her. No more distractions."

I glanced between them and nodded sharply, stopping only for a quick moment to grab them each into a one-armed hug, thumping their backs with my fist.

Then I ran up to the observatory and leapt into the sky.

CHAPTER 56
CALLA

MRS. BRISBANE CATERED to my every need as I rattled around aimlessly. I was fed, supplied a constant flow of tea, and was accepted as the lady of the house despite my protestations.

I spent the first couple of days walking around in a haze, wandering room to room, not purposely avoiding my mate, but finding any reason not to go down the hall that led to our bedchambers unless absolutely necessary. Lucky for me, there were quite a few hallways to explore.

Elizabeth had found me straightaway and was as good as the lovely Mrs. Brisbane about making sure I ate, drank, and functioned like a normal person without asking me too many pressing questions about the tension between Rylan and me. She also got me up-to-date on all the happenings with all the staff.

Elizabeth herself was being courted by Jacob, one of the field hands. It sounded pretty serious, and I couldn't help but smile when she turned bright red recounting how he'd brought her a bouquet of my lilies one day. I thought perhaps they'd be a good choice to send off to the Noctua farm, if they wanted it.

In an effort to stay busy, I'd jumped into working in the office downstairs. I made a project of going through the contract ledgers and sorting them out so there would be no surprises in the future. I made a list of outstanding debts, plus ones that were already closed that needed collecting on. If he started soon, he'd only be gone for a few months going from place to place. My secretary duties had never been done quite so thoroughly.

Morticia followed me room to room, sending peaceful thoughts, though they weren't actually words. I was frustrated that we still hadn't nailed down good, consistent communication, but we kept working on it. I appreciated her more than she knew, and tried to show it through special treats and extra scratches when I could.

I found myself deeply anchored, energetically speaking, on the manor's land. I felt connected to the stones of the house, the soil underneath, and all the creatures that lived there. It was still an odd sensation, having my magic available at all times. It sat as a cool knot in my gut until I called upon it, then became a heavy prickle of energy in my hands and through my head. I practiced a little bit a few times a day, mostly to be sure I was still in control. I lit candles and fires, mixed up ointments and potions. I even tried some of the more complicated spells in one of Rylan's grimoires. Those were hit or miss, but I liked the practice. It made all the noise in my head fade into the background for a while.

My thoughts, much to my dismay, were never truly quiet. Between the ledgers, I started to journal my memories from as early as I could recall, writing down anything and everything that felt important.

"Mistress, you need a warmer for those hands," Mrs. Brisbane chided me as she delivered lunch one day. "The weather here is mild, but you do so much writing! You'll get the palsy once you reach my age."

"I have some ointment. Seems to do the trick."

"You come tell me if you need anything, alright?"

"Thank you."

She nodded and swept away one set of dishes while leaving another.

I'd reached the point in my story where Rylan was one of the main characters. I found myself blushing, aching for his touch as I recounted some of our encounters. I missed him, and he wasn't even really gone.

He, Magnus, and his brother were all over the manor. Repairs were getting done, grain measured and prepared for sale, sparring in the yard—much to the entertainment of the staff.

I'd caught him more than once smiling as he watched me as I did some mundane chore. The more I wrote, the more convinced I became that I'd been wrong to ever doubt the truth of what was between us. Every day I busied myself with avoiding him, my chest hurt, and every night I got less sleep. When I dreamt, he was always there. Smiling at me, encouraging me to do something new. Wrapping me up in his wings and showing me how much he wanted me.

The contracts were gone, and yet I needed him just as much as I always had. Shame fueled my efforts at practicing magic. I realized I'd been a fool to doubt any of it in the first place.

I watched them fly away toward Revalia, the three of them silhouetted against the dawn as their broad wings swept them along.

Rylan had been a constant presence but never pushed. I knew this was my chance to prove to us both the truth of our bond.

Like a shadow, I went up to his tower office and made my preparations.

AS I WAS going through one of the big leather volumes, my head popped up, every sense on alert. I put the book aside and got to my feet.

Rylan had returned maybe an hour before but had set to wandering the grounds again, distracting himself the same as I'd been. He'd greeted me with a kiss to the cheek, then gone out the kitchen door. Heart pounding, I'd taken that opportunity to finish what I'd started before the sun rose, still unsure it would work but hopeful all the same.

I left the office and took a handful of steps down the hall toward the front doors. The pressure in the atmosphere dropped, a heavy press against my skin as I stared at the stout wood, willing someone to be waiting on the other side.

I jumped as the wood burst open, revealing Rylan's full demon form, silhouetted by the dim twilight. He'd not even touched down with his feet yet, wings fully extended and urgency scrawled over his tense features. The wings I loved so much snapped closed as his heels hit the ground. His long strides ate up the distance between us as I tried to remember how to take a proper breath. My lungs felt compressed, like there was no oxygen to be had in the hallway at all. Raw strength, the hum of his energy, and the smell of iron and wine filled my senses.

"It worked," I gasped. "You came."

He didn't stop until he was right in front of me, eyes wild as he gathered me into his arms. "How could I not, beloved? You called."

I dissolved into laughter and tears at the same time as his heart beat frantically under my ear. Apologies fell from my lips, but he shushed me. The pace of his pulse slowed until it matched mine, and I took a calming deep breath. I raised my head so I could look at his face. I pressed a hand to his cheek, my thumb tracing over his full bottom lip.

"I'm so sorry, Rylan. I was a fool."

"Never, my love. You simply needed time, as you said. That's something I always have to give. Besides, I needed some of my own in the beginning, yes?"

He bundled us into his room so we could have some privacy.

Then his mouth fused to mine, heat and longing pouring out of him as he wrapped himself around me.

"I missed you terribly, Little Owl. And I apologize again for the stress the heart-call caused you. That felt positively dreadful, and I only had to come from as far as the yard. These are for you, by the way," he said, offering me some half-crushed purple lilies. I smiled against his mouth and set them on the side table.

We sank down on the couch, his arms around me as I straddled his lap. I tucked my face into his neck, breathing him in. "I'm sorry, Rylan. I did not trust you when you'd given me no reason to be doubtful."

He tightened his hold on me. "No, Calla. I'm the one who's sorry. I should have been forthcoming the moment I realized you were the woman I'd never believed I'd meet. I should have told you every detail of the contract, especially the most important one. It was too much to keep from you, especially knowing your preference for full honesty, even when painful. It's one of the things I love most about you. I allowed my disbelief to keep it from you."

He rocked me gently, my soul knitting back together as I held on tightly, my arms around his waist. My heart thumped sorely in my chest but breathing in his citrus and iron soothed my frayed nerves.

"Will you forgive me?" I asked, lifting my head to peer into his eyes.

"There is nothing to forgive, but as you wish. I told you before, I am yours always. You need only ask, and I'll never leave your side again."

That sounded perfect to me. I kissed him again, long and slow. He dissolved into me the same as I did into him, our breaths aligning as his energy and my magic slowly swirled around us.

When I pulled away, intent on divesting myself of some clothing, I saw that the two had merged. Ribbons of green and gold tangled together, languidly drifting through the air around us.

"Look," I said, pulling his attention from where it rested on my face to the room around us.

"There's some proof, if I ever saw it," he mused, wide-eyed. "I've never seen the like before. Sounds about right where you're concerned, Little Owl." He slowly ran his fingers up and down my legs, his arousal obvious against my center as I straddled his lap. He did nothing else until I met his eye again.

"What's wrong?" I asked.

"Nothing." His mouth quirked into a half smile, his eyes glowing with the love I felt coursing through my skin everywhere he touched me. "Nothing is wrong."

His arms gripped me tight, and he stood, carrying me over to the bed. Rylan proved his patience and did nothing without intention as we reacquainted ourselves.

Slow, blazing fingertips traced the edges of my dress, then down to where the lacings kept my aching skin bound inside. He ran his mouth along my flesh wherever he could find it, drawing the fabric down my body with a painful slowness.

I focused on breathing as sensation mounted on sensation and I watched our magic increase speed as it spun on the air. The cool night air tightened my nipples into firm points as he removed his shirt and then his pants. His proud cock bobbed at his stomach. He gripped it in one hand and stroked, dropping his head back before sinking to his knees.

With a firm grip on my ankles, he pulled me to the edge of the bed and began to feast. Despite his enthusiasm, he wasn't in any hurry. Every nip and suckle was languid, like he was memorizing the taste of me. His clever tongue dipped and swirled, my body twitching and bucking as he teased me. A hand reached up to caress my breast as he lapped at my center, a climax building so quickly I felt it in my toes.

"Rylan." I gasped his name, clenching my stomach muscles and reaching for his hair, as the warm knot tightened low in my gut.

Then he stopped.

I cried out in protest, sitting halfway up to glare at him. He grinned back at me from between my thighs, mouth slick. His tongue slid along his lower lip as he crawled up my body.

"Not yet, beloved. When you come, I want to be inside you."

He lifted one of my legs so my foot was flat on the bed, then crashed into me at the same time he lowered his mouth to mine. He drank my moan as his tongue tangled with mine, his thrusts punishing as they sent me barreling right back toward orgasm.

Gripping his shoulders, my nails dug in as he caged me in with his arms. With a roar, he increased his pace, wings snapping out and horns appearing as he claimed me fully as his for the first time.

My body responded to the change with enthusiasm, clamping down on his cock as I moaned into his mouth.

"Mine," he growled, thrusting deeply one final time as he found his release.

"Yours," I sighed, panting from the pleasure as the magic danced all around us. The ache in my chest expanded, and I placed my hand over his heart, and drew his over mine. "Do you feel it?" I asked and he nodded, staring down at me.

"The bond," he said.

We inhaled at the same time, his wings snapping back out as the bubble that had been building inside us both burst. The magic around us exploded into green and gold sparks as tingles shot down my limbs, and a gentle warmth filled my body.

"Fate," he said, gathering me into his arms and smothering me with more kisses.

There was no arguing with any of that.

EPILOGUE
CALLA

WATCHING GRACE AND Mrs. Brisbane work together in concert was quite a thing to behold.

"No, no. You take the glasses and plates over there," Grace barked at the terrified third-year student. He changed direction, and she threw up her hands in exasperation.

"No, the cake goes on the *round* table," Mrs. Brisbane explained, her tone as impatient as Grace's. "The long benches are for the entrees."

"How are things going?" I asked with a laugh.

They both spun, eyes wide.

"Calla! What on earth are you doing down here! You should be getting ready," Grace admonished.

"I was tired of sitting in the apartment by myself," I shrugged. "And I could use a snack. May I?" I gestured toward the kitchen.

"I'll get her something," Mrs. Brisbane offered.

"Thank you, Eleanor. I'll get the china dealt with. You!" Grace shouted, hustling off for another student who had gone against the plans.

"Just a little something to tide me over, I can manage it. I know you're busy, and I appreciate how hard you're working." I couldn't help but blush, embarrassed that such a fuss was being caused over me.

"No bother, my lady," she said, piling some fruit and cheese on a plate.

"Not you too," I groaned.

Mrs. Brisbane laughed, shooing me off with my plate. "Best get used to it, dear."

I returned to the apartment with my snack, surprised to find it was not as empty as I'd left it. Magic tickled along my arms, ready to strike if I needed it. I inhaled deeply, sending it back to rest. These were not enemies, after all.

Two stone kin women occupied my sofas, and Elizabeth busily adjusted my gown where it hung near the bath.

"Hello," I greeted them.

"Calla?" the smaller one asked. She had yellow hair cut into a bob and kind blue eyes.

"Yes?"

"I'm Lovette," she said enthusiastically, thrusting her hand out in greeting.

"Hello, Lovette. It's so nice to finally meet you." As I shook her hand, the other woman got to her feet. She was tall, like Magnus. "You're Imogen?"

She beamed. "Yes. Pleasure to meet you. Father has had much to say about you."

"Likewise." I returned her gentle smile, shocked that this quiet-voiced woman was the same warrior I'd heard stories of. "Thank you for the blade," I blurted, glancing over to where I'd fastened it on the wall.

"Oh." She looked over and her smile grew wider. "That was *my* pleasure, absolutely."

"Cheese?" I offered the plate, unsure where we should go with niceties from here.

"No, thank you. We thought ... we thought you might like some company while you get ready?"

"Weddings and other big events are usually a time family prepares together," Lovette said.

Her simple words carried a profound punch as they landed in my chest. As they settled, a warmth trickled through my entire body.

Family.

"Yes, thank you. I'd like that very much." I got the words out, but barely, before my throat closed up with emotion.

Between the three of them, I was dressed and made-up head to toe without lifting a single finger. Their friendly chatter filled the room around me as I floated from one task to the next, being cared for and loved without being stifled.

When I was all dressed, they stood back and admired their handiwork.

"It's so perfect," Elizabeth sighed. "I hope I'm this beautiful at my wedding."

"Which is soon," I reminded her. "I can't wait. You and Jacob are going to make the perfect couple."

"Rylan's going to faint," Lovette teased. "Look at that hair. It's magical."

"Wouldn't that be something? Big bad demon just tipping over and hitting the grass?" Imogen laughed, and it was loud and booming like her father's. He could only find his wife in her, but all I saw was him.

"This necklace is so unique," Lovette said, straightening the oval moonstone pendant around my neck. The gem itself was the size of a quail's egg, and the setting had antiqued to nearly black with age.

"Thank you. It has stayed with the women in my family for many generations. I'm the first to wear it in quite a long time."

"How incredible that Rylan matched your ring to it!" Elizabeth gasped.

"It was a lucky thing, for sure. The necklace was still safely hidden away when he got my ring."

Imogen squinted, a playful grin on her mouth as she gestured at my blade, the one she'd made with the same stone as the handle. "Luck was only part of it, I'm guessing. Moonstone is your gem, after all. It follows you."

As I pondered that, there was a knock at the door, and Grace peeked her head in.

"Oh! Look at you!" she gushed. "It's time."

I took a deep breath, slid my feet into a new pair of ridiculously fancy slippers from the seamstress who'd made this gown like my others before it, and followed them down the stairs.

THE WOMEN ALL left me standing on my own at the back of the yard and went to their seats. Nerves set in, but I wasn't anxious. I was excited.

All the students were seated in neat rows, along with the entire staff of both the manor and the collegium. Magnus's family had their own row near the back, which was good since they were all quite large, though he himself stood near a tree so he could walk me down the aisle and both Lovette and Imogen were posted up front as my bridesmaids.

Even Ophelia had left her cottage for the event, a bag of candy in her hand and a bright-red ribbon around the bun of her hair.

Archimedes had his own special perch near the altar, and Morticia sat under it on a cushion.

Rylan was as dashing as ever in his all-black attire, hair loose around his face, and a smile on his mouth. All six of his brothers had turned up, which neither of us had been expecting. Five of them stood at his side, which was a true sight to behold. I'd wager the gathering of them in one small space would have made the guests more nervous, but they were all quite beautiful at the moment instead of fearsome.

It had taken Archimedes more than a week trying to deliver the news to them all. We didn't anticipate they'd stay long, but it was nice to meet them all, if only briefly. Each was so very different, I was curious about how they interacted with one another. At least two of them were not permanent residents this side of Hell, and I had a million questions about how that worked to say the least.

As I took in the amount of people celebrating our union, I nearly missed my cue when everyone stood and turned my way. Flustered, my magic flared up in my anxiousness, giving my bouquet a little burst of fireworks as Magnus linked his arm in mine.

"You look lovely."

"Thank you, Magnus."

"I trust my daughters were well met?"

"Yes, thank you for sending them to me."

His chest puffed and we continued our slow march between the guests, my heart fluttering behind my ribs as I took in all their smiling faces.

"Friends and family, please be seated," Vassago said as we approached the altar. Magnus relinquished me, standing on my side with his daughters.

Vago had offered to officiate, and took great joy in his role. He started through a speech, but I was lost in Rylan's smile. It wasn't until Rylan started repeating the things Vago was saying that I snapped to attention and did the same.

"Always," I said, staring into my demon's eyes.

"Always," he repeated, then, at Vassago's instruction, leaned down for a kiss.

The vow echoed through my chest, and I released a tiny burst of magic to seal it. The pronouncement was made, and to raucous applause, we made our way back down the aisle, hand in hand.

"Shall we slip off, Little Owl?" He leaned close, whispering in my ear, "They can continue the party without us."

"We should at least dance," I argued, blood pumping at his words, nevertheless.

"A quick visit to the stable then?"

We'd walked far enough away that nobody would follow, though if anyone searched, they'd find us. "We'd stir up the horses, it would draw attention."

He groaned. "But I have a mighty need to consecrate this deal I've made to make you my wife."

The word made me shiver, and he backed me up against a tree to put his face a breath from mine as he tangled his fist in my hair. "Deal? My beloved demon, what have you talked me into this time?"

"Marriage is a contract," he breathed, pausing to mesh his mouth with mine. "You signed your name already. Sealed the document with your blood and magic. Do you not recall? You agreed to share your life with me, eternally."

"I do remember that, of course. And you? What did you trade for my hand, sir?" I teased, knowing full well what the terms were.

"Everything." He smirked as he snapped his wings out and surrounded us both, and the young tree to boot. "I want nothing without you, my beloved Little Owl. You are my whole world."

His hands lifted my legs, and I locked them around his waist as he dove in, kissing me so hungrily I was sure all the careful cosmetics Lovette had applied were doomed.

"Here's fine," I gasped, already throbbing with need.

His nimble fingers shifted our underclothes with impressive speed. "I'll be quick then," he said as he sank into me.

He muffled my moans with his mouth as he lifted and sank my body to his liking with his hands gripping my ass. Magic flowed between us, enhancing the sensations and making me feel like I was ready to tip over the edge far too quickly.

He groaned, leaning his head back as he powered through my climax and right into his. Rylan pressed his forehead to mine as we both panted like we'd sprinted across the field.

"That's my girl," he grinned, kissing me once again. "Now, shall we go celebrate?"

As though he hadn't just debauched me against a tree, my demon helped me settle my dress into some kind of order, took me by the hand, and led me back to our friends and family.

Not ready to say goodbye to Rylan and Calla?
Get a bonus scene by visiting:

https://BookHip.com/RWCHJTZ

Want to be the first to hear breaking news and
other info from L.? Sign up for her newsletter!

http://bit.ly/ALANewsletter

You can also join her reader group to chat
with her and other readers!

https://bit.ly/LilysReaderLounge

Did you like The Demon's Deal? Leave a review
on Amazon, Goodreads or Bookbub to share
your thoughts with other readers!

WHAT'S NEXT?

Magnus and Grace have met their match in one another. Will they finally give into the tension boiling over between them?

Get The Gargoyle's Grace to find out!

Vassago is hunting a missing necklace for a client, but one of the duke's daughters proves much more interesting than any gem.

Grab Book 2 of The Demon Princes Series,
The Demon's Discovery!

ACKNOWLEDGEMENTS

You GUYS. Thank you so much for taking a shot on me and this book! This is a series I've had in my heart for years and getting to finally put it out into the world is so amazing! That you picked it up and read it out of all the incredible books out there means everything to me.

As always, this book wouldn't have happened without Shain Rose and Danielle Keil pushing me to listen to my heart and holding my hand the entire way. If you're not reading them already, you should be!

My husband deserves all the credit for being my perpetual idea sounding board, first editor and often, my hero inspiration.

Huge thanks to my editor Krista, who spiffed up, de-repetitioned and completely prettified this story. I appreciate you so very much! Jessica, you made me the most gorgeous cover! Sitting on it for five months nearly killed me. Stephanie as always, thank you for always being sure I put the prettiest pages out there! <3

Meri, you get a special ENORMOUS THANKS because as a first reader, idea bouncer-offer, lore expert and the provider of gorgeous fiber goodies... well you're the bee's knees. I hope you know how much of an impact you've had on my life as a writer. XOXO

Beta & ARC readers! Do you even know how vital you are to authors like me? I hope you do. You're the cat's freaking pajamas and I cannot express how grateful I am to those of you who allowed me to slide into your DM's and shoot my shot. Seeing any post with my stuff on it is a humbling, thrilling experience. I couldn't do this without you. <3

I can't wait for you all to see what's coming next! Magnus and Vassago and more demons oh my! This world is planned to be seven books, one for each brother. I hope you stick with us!

For sneak peeks, discussion and other fun tidbits, make sure you're signed up for my newsletter, & join my reader group.

ABOUT THE AUTHOR

L. Alexander writes Paranormal and Fantasy romance with sweet & spicy cinnamon roll heroes, fated mates, monsters, magic and more. She guarantees a happily ever after no matter what and has a soft spot for broody anime characters.

www.authorlilyalexander.com

@lilyalexanderwrites on Instagram

Lily Alexander on Facebook, TikTok,
BookBub and Goodreads

L. also writes Contemporary Romance
under the name Lily Alexander.

Made in the USA
Las Vegas, NV
02 April 2025